"The MacKenzies saga continues and readers will be thrilled. . . . I can't wait for the next book."
—Romantic Times

A VIEW OF PARADISE

His arms and shoulder muscles burned as he climbed toward the hot air balloon. Pausing, he glanced down and gulped—the ground was a good forty or fifty feet below. There was no place to go but up!

Suddenly a heavy coil of rope hit him in the head, and his legs and one of his arms slipped off the line. Glancing up, he saw Cynthia leaning over the railing twenty feet above him.

"Oh, Dave, I'm so sorry," she cried out.

He was too breathless to shout at her, but his anger gave him a much-needed burst of energy. When he reached the gondola, Cynthia's outstretched arms pulled him over the top.

Dave opened his eyes and looked up into the sapphire eyes that just a short time ago had given him a glimpse of Eden—and knew with certainty that God had just given him the boot out of Paradise.

It had been a short but sweet stay. He started to laugh.

Other *Leisure* and *Love Spell* books by Ana Leigh:
THE MacKENZIES: CLEVE
THE MacKENZIES: FLINT
THE MacKENZIES: LUKE
THE GOLDEN SPIKE
ANGEL HUNTER
PROUD PILLARS RISING
THESE HALLOWED HILLS
SWEET ENEMY MINE
A KINDLED FLAME

The MacKenzies:

Ana Leigh

LOVE SPELL

NEW YORK CITY

LOVE SPELL®

May 2004

Published by

Dorchester Publishing Co., Inc.
200 Madison Avenue
New York, NY 10016

ISBN 0-505-52563-1

Printed in the United States of America.

Visit us on the web at www.dorchesterpub.com.

Prologue

1879, The Atlantic Ocean

He's the handsomest man I've ever seen, Cynthia thought. Seated at the captain's table, she watched the movements of an attractive couple on the dance floor as the mellow strains of a Strauss waltz floated above the low murmurs and occasional laughter of the other passengers dining in the ship's ornate salon.

"Would you like to waltz, Miss MacKenzie?"

Glancing at the distinguished gray-haired speaker seated at her right, Cynthia shook her head. "If you don't mind, Sir Haynes, I prefer not to."

"Of course," he said.

The English diplomat then spoke to his wife and the two rose, moving to the dance floor.

Cynthia found herself alone at the table and once again her blue-eyed gaze sought the dancing couple. From the time the ship had left England yesterday, she had noticed the handsome pair—it would have been difficult not to. Tall and broad-shouldered, the man appeared to be in his late thirties or early forties. His black hair was neatly clipped to the back of his neck and a dark mustache added to the masculinity of his bronzed face. Moving with a patrician grace and confidence, his partner was exquisite-looking, with the olive complexion and dark hair of either a Spaniard or a Mexican. Having spent the last two years in Europe, Cynthia instantly recognized that the woman's elegant gown could only have come from the renowned House of Worth in Paris.

The couple was so obviously in love, Cynthia couldn't help feeling a sense of envy. Would that be the answer to her restlessness and unhappiness—finding contentment in the arms of a man? She had tried with Roberto—but the attempt had failed miserably. Eventually Roberto's charm had worn thin, and she came to see him as a shallow man, content to live a worthless life in pursuit of pleasure. For two years she had roamed the Continent with him: the bistros of Paris, the snow-capped peaks of the Austrian Alps, the marble palazzi of the Italian riviera, and the sea-kissed shores of the Greek Isles—flitting from one group to another in a relentless and futile search for an alternative to boredom. But now she was going home.

Cynthia felt a stabbing pain in her breast. Right now, she faced a much more serious crisis than mere boredom.

Oh, Daddy, she thought woefully.

Tears trickled down her cheeks. Swiping them away, Cynthia jumped to her feet, and in her haste she crashed into the handsome man, who had just seated his wife.

"I'm so sorry," she murmured, and sped from the room.

Discovering that the deck was empty, Cynthia walked over and leaned on the railing, where she gave in and let the tears flow. From the moment she had received Beth's cable informing her that their father was dying, Cynthia had lived with the fear that she would be too late to say good-bye to him—

to admit her mistake and apologize for how she had hurt him.

Oh, Daddy, I love you so much. I'm so sorry I was such a disappointment to you.

"Do you have any idea how heart-wrenching it is to see a beautiful woman standing alone at the railing of a ship sobbing?"

Startled, she turned to see that the handsome man had followed her. Quickly brushing away her tears, she said with embarrassment, "I thought I was alone."

"Here, will this help?"

Smiling sheepishly, she accepted the folded handkerchief he offered. "Thank you."

"Forgive me for prying, but my wife and I were concerned about you. She insisted I follow you to make certain you're okay. Is there anything we can do?"

Cynthia smiled. "You have a very lovely wife, sir. And a very compassionate one. Most women would not encourage their husbands to follow another woman."

He grinned. "Especially one as attractive as you."

"I envy her; it must be comforting to feel that secure about the man you love."

"Adriana is a remarkable woman."

"Adriana. What a beautiful name."

"Yes it is, Miss . . . ?"

"MacKenzie. Cynthia MacKenzie."

He chuckled warmly. "What a coincidence." He lightly tipped his head in a salute. "A pleasure to meet you, Miss MacKenzie. And my name is *Cleve* MacKenzie."

"Oh, really?" she said, surprised, then smiled with pleasure. "Well, I guess that explains your kindness, doesn't it, Cleve MacKenzie? All of us MacKenzies just naturally have an empathy for one another, wouldn't you say?"

"I've always found that to be true. Where are you from, Miss Cynthia MacKenzie?" She liked the way his grin carried to his eyes.

"From Denver, but I've been touring England and Europe for the past two years. And where is your home, Mr. Cleve MacKenzie?"

"Texas. My brothers and I have a ranch in northwest Texas near the Red River."

"Texas!" she exclaimed.

He looked at her quizzically. "Is that some sort of omen, Miss MacKenzie?"

"Oh my, no. It's just that I remember my father telling me he had a brother who died at the Alamo. That has—" She stopped abruptly upon seeing the startled look on his face. "What is it, Mr. MacKenzie?"

"My father died at the Alamo. His name was Andrew. My mother once told me that he had a younger brother named Matthew."

"My father's name is Matthew MacKenzie," she half whispered with astonishment.

"No, it can't be! Is it possible we're kin, Cynthia?" He grasped her by the shoulders and turned her toward the light to study her face. "You sure have the MacKenzie eyes and dark hair, all right." His smile broadened into a wide grin. "A cousin! Wow! Wait until I tell my brothers."

"Actually, you have *three* cousins. I have two sisters: Elizabeth and Angeleen."

"And I have two brothers: Luke and Flint. Now, I want to hear all about those other cousins. Why don't we go inside and flesh out this situation a bit more, Cousin Cynthia."

Grabbing her by the hand, Cleve MacKenzie led her back into the salon.

Chapter 1

Colorado

After six frustrating days of endless delays and changes, the train finally chugged to a stop at MacKenzie Junction. Worrying if she'd reach home in time to find her father still alive, Cynthia stood up and pinned on her bonnet. From the time she had said good-bye to Cleve and Adriana in New York, her stomach had been tied in knots.

Bending down, she peered out of the window, expecting to see her sisters or Pete Gifford, the foreman of the MacKenzie ranch, the Roundhouse. She hoped they'd received the wires she had sent from New York and Omaha.

"Thank you, Jacob," she said to the black man who assisted her off the train. He had been the porter on the first railroad line her father had ever built, and now trunks of the Rocky Mountain Central stretched out from Denver to the Union Pacific Railroad, farther north.

"Ah sure hate to hear the Chief's been ailin', Miz Cynthia. Fine gentlemin that he is. You be sure to give 'im my regards, ma'am."

"I certainly will, Jacob."

"You got someone comin' to meet you, Miz Cynthia?" he asked worriedly. "Place sure do look a mite wantin'."

"Yes, I wired ahead. I'm sure someone will show up soon."

"I'll get your luggage, ma'am."

Cynthia took a long look around her. Nothing appeared to have changed since the day she had left over two years before. Built for the private use of her family and located five miles north of Denver, the station was nothing more than a wooden platform, a log station house, and a small roundhouse for the storage of her father's private railroad car.

Cynthia lifted her gaze. Golden spires of aspen lined the hillside, and in the distance wispy patches of morning haze spiraled upward toward a bright blue firmament shimmering brilliantly above distant snow-capped peaks. Truly the landscape of an artist, she reflected with an unusual feeling of nostalgia. How often had she awakened to that sight?

Tucking her hands into a fur muff to ward off the chill of the fall day, Cynthia closed her eyes and drew a deep breath of the crisp, mountain air.

The brief moment was interrupted by the arrival of a buckboard. She waited as the driver climbed down and approached her, but she did not recognize him.

The man was tall, and the hip-length jacket he wore did little to disguise his long, muscular legs, clad in faded jeans. The collar of the sheepskin-lined coat was pulled up around his neck, and his face and eyes were cast in shadow by the Stetson set squarely on his head.

"Miss MacKenzie?"

Under other circumstances the deep voice would have raised a provocative curiosity in Cynthia, but concern for her father kept her from giving it further consideration.

"Yes. Are you from the Roundhouse?" When he

nodded, she asked quickly, "How is my father?"

"He's had a restful day . . . so far."

Had she imagined the sarcasm at the end? She grabbed for her bonnet as a burst of wind threatened to swoop it off her head.

"You'd be better off inside the station, Miss MacKenzie. I'll get your luggage."

"Thank you . . . ah, I don't believe I know your name."

"Dave Kincaid," he replied in a clipped voice.

"Thank you, Dave."

He had already walked away, leaving her staring after him. Now she was certain she hadn't imagined his hostility toward her. What was the reason behind it? Surely it couldn't be because she hadn't known his name; she knew she'd never met him before. If any of the ranch hands had looked like him, she wouldn't have forgotten.

Another gust of wind tugged at her bonnet and whipped her mantle around her ankles. Braced against the wind's force, she hurried into the station house.

Through the window of the one-room building, she watched Dave Kincaid and Jacob unload her luggage, exchange a few words, and wave good-bye when the porter climbed back on board as the train puffed noisily away.

Cynthia waited impatiently for the ranch hand to finish loading her numerous trunks onto the buckboard, then she went out and joined him. In silence, he took her arm and helped her to climb up. Once seated, she tucked her hands again into the muff and waited as he walked around the buckboard and hopped up beside her.

Although he made no attempt at conversation on the ride to the house, Cynthia was very conscious of the man beside her. Silent or not, he had a very commanding presence. She had always held the upper hand with men, but there was something about this Dave Kincaid that made her feel she had lost that edge where he was concerned. It was undoubtedly because she was distracted about her father.

"Where are you from, Dave?"

"Cambridge."

Astounded, she glanced at him. "Massachusetts?"

He turned his head and looked at her. At this closer proximity, she saw that his eyes were a deep brown.

His mouth curled into a grimace. "Right smart of you, Miss MacKenzie."

Cynthia ignored his attitude. "A little far from home, aren't you?"

"Oh, I'm a big boy, Miss MacKenzie." The irksome smirk appeared again.

"I'm sure you are, Mr. Kincaid. And how long have you worked for my father?"

"About four years."

"Strange . . . I don't remember meeting you before. What's your job on the ranch?"

"I don't work on the ranch."

"You told me you were from the Roundhouse."

"That's where I came from when I picked you up. I work for the Rocky Mountain Central."

"Oh, I see! So you're 'a steel-drivin' man.' "

"I've done my share of it."

"Knowing Daddy, I imagine he's told you about his crazy dream of building a direct line between Denver and Dallas."

"I don't consider it crazy, Miss MacKenzie. When a man believes in something that much, it should not be a subject of ridicule."

"Perhaps, but absurd dreams should not be encouraged either." She sighed. "Even so, it's a pity Daddy probably won't ever see his dream fulfilled."

"Well, at least he lived long enough to see it begun."

She jerked her head toward him in surprise. "What do you mean?"

With a withering look of contempt, he said, "Pity you didn't bother to keep in touch with your father, Miss MacKenzie. We've already laid over two hundred miles of that track."

Too astounded to reply, Cynthia decided not to attempt any further conversation. She had too much on her mind to worry about Dave Kincaid's obvious antagonism toward her.

As the buckboard passed under the threshold gate of the Roundhouse, Cynthia caught a glimpse of the ranch's main house, standing tall and stately amidst the aspen and pine that surrounded it, and her heart leapt to her throat.

"Please stop for a moment, Dave."

He reined in. "Is something wrong, Miss MacKenzie?"

"Guess I didn't expect that seeing the place again would affect me the way it does."

Kincaid relaxed and leaned back. "Yeah, it's quite a sight. First time I saw it, I couldn't believe the size of it. Must have cost a small fortune."

"It did. After striking it rich in the California gold fields, Daddy came here and started building the house in 1850. It took two years, and by that time he had met and fallen in love with my mother, the daughter of the local preacher." She smiled to herself. "My mother's name was Elizabeth MacGregor, but Daddy always called her Betsy."

"And named his first engine after her," Dave said.

She glanced at him in surprise. "Yes, how did you know?"

"The Chief spoke of it often," he said. His tone had softened.

She sighed deeply, then continued. "As soon as

the house was finished, Daddy and Mama married and settled down to a life of ranching."

"He's never mentioned how he happened to get into building railroads."

"When the transcontinental railroad was completed in '69, Daddy saw the potential of a railroad here; that's when he formed the Rocky Mountain Central and started laying track to link Colorado to the Union Pacific in Wyoming and Nebraska."

"I helped lay some of that track."

"It was after Mama died—"

"When was that, Miss MacKenzie?"

"Ten years ago. She fell from a horse and broke her neck, and Daddy was lost without her. Once he got interested in the railroad, he started devoting all his time and attention to it."

"And you resented him for it."

She jerked around in indignation at the reprimand in his voice. "No, I didn't resent it! I was happy he found something to get interested in again. You may drive on now, Dave."

As they pulled up to the house, the door opened and her sisters came hurrying out.

"Beth! Angie!" Not waiting for Kincaid's assistance, Cynthia bounded off the wagon and rushed into their outstretched arms.

Hugging, they huddled together in a circle.

Finally, breaking apart, Beth said, "Oh, Thia, it's so good to see you. We've missed you so much."

"I've missed you all, too," Cynthia said. She hadn't realized how much until this very moment—her heart felt tied in a knot. While growing up, she and her auburn-haired sister, who was only one year older, had been inseparable companions. Smiling into Beth's sapphire eyes, now glistening with tears, Cynthia said, "And you're as lovely as ever, Beth."

"You should talk! I didn't think it was possible,

but you're even prettier than I remembered," Beth replied.

Cynthia stepped back to take a long look at Angeleen next. Two years had brought a big change in her younger sister, who hadn't quite turned eighteen when Cynthia left. "And look at you, Angie! You've grown into a beautiful woman."

"What did you expect? I'm twenty years old now," Angeleen said with a giggle, brushing aside a thick dark curl off her cheek.

Cynthia shook her head. "I guess we're all getting older."

"Cynthia MacKenzie, I'm only twenty-four and you're twenty-three," Beth declared. "I don't think we're ready for rocking chairs yet." Beth hugged her again, then her smile faded. "Oh, Thia, I'm so glad you're home." An undertone of desperation had slipped into her voice.

"How is Daddy?" Cynthia asked solemnly.

"As comfortable as we can make him. He'll be so glad to see you."

"What does the doctor say?"

Beth's eyes welled with tears. "Daddy's lungs are congested, and he's been coughing up blood. He's so weak, Thia; he could go anytime. I think Daddy's just willed himself to stay alive until you got home." Tucking an arm in Cynthia's, she added, "It's chilly out here. Let's get inside."

Once inside the huge foyer, Cynthia paused to glance around. Nothing appeared changed: the marble floor tiles that her father had imported from Italy glistened like glass; the dark mahogany balustrades and oaken steps of the wide, curved stairway still gleamed with polished luster.

"Let me take your coat and hat, Thia," Angie said. As Cynthia shed her outer garments, the young woman's eyes glowed with admiration. "Oh, this hat is so chic, isn't it, Beth?" Angie tried on the bonnet. "Wherever did you get it, Thia?"

"In Paris, Pumpkin."

"Imagine, a genuine Paris bonnet. It sure looks stunning on you." Turning her head from side to side, Angeleen studied her image intently in the ornate foyer mirror. Then, sighing, she removed the hat. "But it's just not me."

"You're worse than a man," Cynthia teased, fluffing Angeleen's head of thick curls. "You're just not comfortable in any hat but a Stetson."

"Excuse me, ladies." Dave Kincaid stood in the doorway carrying one of Cynthia's trunks.

"Oh, sorry, Dave," Beth said.

The women stepped away from the entrance to allow him to pass.

"I assume you want this in your room, Miss MacKenzie," he said to Cynthia. He climbed the stairway without waiting for her to reply.

"Lord, what an unpleasant person!" Cynthia exclaimed.

"Thia, that's rude," Beth whispered. "Dave's just serious and hardworking. And he's very smart. Did he tell you he's the engineer in charge of the railroad expansion?"

"No, he didn't," Cynthia replied, with a disgruntled look up the stairway. "He just said he works on the railroad." She swallowed and took a deep breath. "I'm going up to see Daddy now."

"We'll wait for you in the parlor," Beth said.

Cynthia hurried up the stairway and quietly opened the door to her father's room. She nodded to the nurse, who stood up when she entered.

"I'm Cynthia MacKenzie," she whispered. "How is my father doing?"

"He's resting comfortably, ma'am. He'll be so happy to see you. I'll be right outside, if you need me." She slipped out the door and closed it softly behind her.

Moving to the bedside, Cynthia had the shock of her life. Grateful that her father's eyes were closed, she took time to adjust to the change in his appearance.

Her father looked thin and bony, ravished by consumption, the flesh white and loose on the once-muscular body. His face was lined and drawn, the accustomed tan replaced by pallor, and his thick, wavy hair, once streaked handsomely with silver, was now as white as the pillow it lay against.

She gently picked up one of his frail hands, resting on the counterpane.

At her touch, her father slowly opened his eyes. "Betsy?" He blinked several times. "Betsy, is that you, beloved?"

Tears glistened in her eyes, and she raised his hand to her cheek. "No, Daddy, it's me—Cynthia."

"Thia!" A warm glow replaced his dazed look. "I'd forgotten how much you resemble your mother. You're the spitting image of her, my dear. So, my prodigal daughter has returned," he said affectionately. "A shame an old man must die to lure his daughter home again." He began coughing, bringing a handkerchief to his mouth. She released his hand and sat down on the bedside. "I've missed you, honey," he said when the spasm ended.

"I missed you, too, Daddy. No one's scolded me in two whole years," she teased lightly.

"Was I that hard on you, Thia?" he asked, regret in his voice.

"It doesn't matter now, Daddy. I just want you to get well."

"I was so afraid I'd lose you, like I did your mother. You're so like her, honey, in so many ways: that same reckless streak that she had. There wasn't a thing either one of you wouldn't try on a dare. I've been so foolish, Thia, for in trying to protect you, I drove you away . . . and lost you, too."

"You never lost me, Daddy. Don't you know that bad pennies always show up again?"

He raised a hand and cupped her cheek. "You're not bad, honey."

Cynthia's voice trembled. "I always thought you believed I was—that you didn't love me as much as you did Beth and Angie. Oh, Daddy, I love you so much. I'm so ashamed for all the grief I've caused you."

He looked up into her anguished eyes. "How could you ever believe I didn't love you, Thia? My beautiful Thia . . . so much like my beloved Betsy."

He reached out to her and Cynthia clasped his hand. "Tell me about Mama, Daddy. I was still so young when we lost her. There's so much I no longer remember."

"She had such a passion for life, Thia. I can still see her racing across the hills on her chestnut mare—leaping fences, brooks, or anything in her path." His voice drifted lower as he gazed pensively into space. "And you know, honey, there are times that I can even hear the lilt of her laughter, just as it sounded when we'd walk hand in hand on a summer evening."

"Oh, Daddy, how wonderful that she knew such love and devotion in such a short lifetime. Think of all the women who grow old and never know such happiness. I'm sure I never will."

"Of course you will, my dear. When you least expect it, true love will seek you out as it did me . . . as it will your sisters."

Slipping back into reverie, he smiled with contentment. "And soon I'll be with my love again. My end is near."

"Don't talk nonsense, Daddy. You still have a long future ahead of you."

"No, Thia. I'm ready to go. Your mother's waiting for me—I can feel her near me."

Suddenly, he was gripped with another spasm of wracking coughs, and Cynthia reached for him, propping up his frail body to ease the strain.

He lay back when the coughing subsided. "I must rest now. I'm glad you've come back to us, Thia. We'll talk again, honey," he said feebly. Closing his eyes, he dropped back into slumber.

Cynthia stood up, her eyes clouded with tears. "Yes, Daddy. We'll talk again." Leaning over, she kissed his cheek.

She walked pensively down the stairway. For years, she had lived with the belief that her father was deeply disappointed with her. The pain and heartache of her mother's death had driven her to recklessness, which had led to what she'd felt were unjust restrictions and domination by her father. If only they had opened their hearts sooner to one another.

Elizabeth and Angeleen were waiting in front of a warm fire blazing in the fireplace. Cynthia slumped down on a camelback sofa and buried her head in her hands.

"How could Daddy deteriorate so rapidly? I wish I'd come sooner to spend more time with him."

"Thia, I tried to notify you as soon as he took to his bed," Beth said. "You traveled around so much, it was hard to locate you."

Cynthia got up and walked over to Beth, pressing a kiss to the top of her sister's head. "I'm not blaming you, Beth; it's my fault. I was so utterly bored that I just kept flitting from country to country, while you and Angie were here bearing all the responsibility."

"How could you be bored?" Angeleen asked. "Especially engaged to that Count Cellini? He sounded divine."

"Oh, he's very handsome and charming, but in truth, my dear sisters, poor Roberto is really quite vapid. I think he was one of the reasons I grew bored with Europe. I thought I loved him, but actually I had nothing in common with him. Thank goodness I realized it before I made the mistake of marrying him."

"Well, I still want to hear more about this count and everything else you've been up to these past two years," Beth declared.

Cynthia's eyes flashed saucily. "Oh, my! Are you certain you want to hear *all* else? I'm sure it will make our little sister's ears turn pink."

"Oh, I can't wait," Angeleen exclaimed excitedly. "You must tell us everything, Thia."

"Let's have Middy bring us some tea, and we'll hear everything," Beth suggested.

"How is the old darling doing?" Cynthia asked.

"Middy will never change," Angeleen said. "She still insists on supervising the household staff and fighting with the cook. We must have had a dozen different cooks since you've been gone."

"I'll go and get the tea since I want to say hello to her anyway," Cynthia said. "Maybe afterward Daddy will be awake again."

Cynthia hurried to the kitchen and stopped in the doorway when she saw the old woman in the pantry. Absorbed in the task at hand, the housekeeper was unaware of Cynthia's presence.

On tiptoes, Cynthia snuck up behind her, clamping her hands over the woman's eyes. "Guess who?"

The startled woman dropped the bag of dried peaches she had in her hand. "Thia MacKenzie!" she exclaimed.

Laughing, Cynthia spun her around and hugged her. "How are you, Middy dear?"

Matilda McNamara had been forty years old and widowed for four years when she became Matthew MacKenzie's housekeeper. After his wife's death,

Middy had become the self-appointed mother to the three girls. Now age had slowed her step, whitened her hair, and wrinkled her face, but her blue eyes still shone with a youthful gleam.

Dabbing at her tears with the hem of her apron, Middy gazed up affectionately at Cynthia. "So, you've finally come home, have you," she scolded. "And I can see you're just as troublesome as ever. Give your Middy a proper kiss."

"I missed you, darling," Cynthia said, hugging and kissing her.

"Yes, and it's a sad circumstance that's brought you back, but I'm glad you're home, child."

"I wish I'd come back sooner, Middy. I should have been here."

Reaching up a hand, Middy patted Cynthia's cheek. "You're here now, honey; that's all that matters."

In an effort to hide her tears, Cynthia turned away. "Beth and Angie are in the parlor, Middy. Will you please tell the cook to brew us a pot of tea?"

"I'll do it myself. That wretched woman who called herself a cook up and left us not more than thirty minutes ago. A blessing it was, too. She was impossible—thinking she could order me out of the kitchen, just because I decided to bake you something for your homecoming."

Smiling, Cynthia spun around. "Peach cobbler!"

With a sly wink, Middy said, "Still your favorite, isn't it?"

"I haven't had a decent piece of peach cobbler since I left here."

"Then get out from under my feet, gal, and let me get these peaches to soaking," Middy declared, rendering a light smack to Cynthia's rear. Laughing, Cynthia hurried from the room.

Dave Kincaid was just departing as Cynthia

crossed the foyer. He paused in the doorway. "Your luggage is all in your room now, Miss MacKenzie."

"Thank you, Dave."

"From the amount of it, you must have needed a ship of your own to float it across the Atlantic."

"Not at all, Kincaid. The captain was very enterprising; he just threw a net around it and keel-hauled it across."

He grinned, despite an effort not to. "*Touché,* Miss MacKenzie."

"We don't stand on formality around the Roundhouse, Dave. My family calls me Thia, and most of my friends call me Cyn."

"Spelled S-i-n, no doubt."

"Ouch!" Cynthia exclaimed, raising a delicately curved eyebrow.

The man was a challenge all right. Pity she hadn't met him at a more favorable time. She'd enjoy making him eat those words. Her mouth curved into a suggestive smile. "Hope you didn't have any problem finding my bedroom."

"Not at all."

"This is a large house. Sure you had the right room?"

"Yeah, I'm sure."

"And how did you happen to know which room was mine?"

"I've stayed in the house before."

"I doubt in my bed," she said archly.

"That's right, Miss MacKenzie. I don't like crowds." He tipped his hat and stepped outside.

"Damn you, Kincaid!" she muttered, and slammed the door.

Chapter 2

After tea, Cynthia excused herself and went up to her room to unpack. It wasn't long before Elizabeth and Angeleen traipsed into her room to join her.

"Oh, my, that gown is gorgeous!" Beth exclaimed when Cynthia unpacked a dark blue velvet gown with a grosgrain red-and-green plaid bodice and overskirt.

"Look at this!" Angie exclaimed. She held up a black silk nightgown and peignoir. "Why, Thia, it's positively wicked. It's almost transparent, there's no sleeves, and look at the low décolletage. It must have cost a fortune."

"I wouldn't know; Roberto bought it for me."

Angeleen's mouth gaped open and her eyes rounded in shock. "Roberto! But it's so . . . daring. Besides, it's improper for a gentleman to give a lady such a gift."

Cynthia winked at Beth, who shifted her gaze to the ceiling. "Honey, I never said Roberto was a gentleman, and I never claimed to be a lady."

"Of course he's a gentleman; he'd have to be—he's a count."

"If you say so, Pumpkin."

"And you are too a lady, Thia," Angie declared adamantly. "You always try to make us think you're improper. But that's not true and you know it."

"Ah, my dear, sweet, innocent Angeleen. Whatever you do, don't ever change," Cynthia said, giving her younger sister a hug.

Angie looked puzzled, and then said hesitantly, "Are you implying that you and the count *were* . . . intimate?"

"Good Lord, Angie, how naive can you be?" Cynthia asked. "Explain it to her, Beth. You've really been negligent in this girl's education."

"Why do I always have to be the one to play mother?" Beth asked. "You're the one with all the experience." She patted the bed. "Come over here and sit down, Angie."

Tossing the revealing negligee aside, Cynthia joined them, too. With their legs tucked under them, the three women sat in a circle on the bed.

Beth cleared her throat. "Now, if Mama were alive, Angie, she would be the one to explain this to you properly."

"I certainly understand what it means for a man and a woman to be intimate, if that's what you're going to say," Angie said indignantly.

"Don't go getting all puckered up, little one. Your big sister just wants to explain the facts of life to you," Cynthia interjected.

"Angie, I've never asked you," Beth said, "but you've been kissed before, I'm sure."

Angie's blush spread to the roots of her hair. "Of course."

"Have you ever gone beyond a kiss?" Cynthia asked.

"What do you mean by 'beyond'?" Angie asked suspiciously.

"You know—petting and the like," Beth said.

"Well, one time when Jamie Skinner took me

sleigh-riding, he fondled me under the buffalo robe."

"Tsk! Tsk! Tsk!" Cynthia clucked. "I always suspected that James Skinner was a little sneak."

"Thia MacKenzie, will you be still," Beth said, trying not to laugh. "You're not making this any easier. And I declare, if you don't stop grinning like that Cheshire cat in Lewis Carroll's book, I'm going to let you do this yourself. Now, where did Jamie fondle you, Angie?"

"I told you—under the buffalo robe."

"I mean, what did he fondle?" Beth said patiently.

"My breasts."

"He didn't! That cad!" Cynthia exclaimed. "And did you let him?"

"Of course not," Angie declared. "That wouldn't have been proper."

"Oh, hang the *proper* part of it," Cynthia said. "Did you like it enough to want him to continue?"

"I don't know." Angie looked totally confused. "I stopped him so quickly, I didn't have time to know if I liked it or not."

"Well, it's like food, honey. You don't know if you like it until you try a taste of it," Cynthia explained.

"Don't listen to her, Angie, she's just talking smart again," Beth said, struggling to remain serious. "You were absolutely right in stopping him. But men are different from boys—"

"*Vive la différence!*" Cynthia exclaimed.

Beth frowned and continued. "Sometimes a kiss can . . . arouse a man more than it does a woman. Even a little weasel like Jamie Skinner might have a problem trying to control himself. Isn't that right, Thia?"

"That Jamie Skinner is a little weasel? Absolutely."

"Thia," Beth groaned.

"All right, I'll be serious. Yes, you're right. And if the woman is in love with the man, Angie, she may lose control, too."

"Is that what happened with you and Count Cellini, Thia?" Angie asked solemnly.

"That's right, Angie. I was in love with Roberto. We were going to wed. Oh, I've teased the opposite sex from the time I understood the difference between a man and a woman, but Roberto is the only man I've ever been intimate with."

"Oh, Thia, how tragic," Angie said sadly. "To think that now you've fallen out of love with him."

"I guess that happens sometimes. It makes you wiser and more wary, I'll tell you that! But it's the risk you take when you give your heart to a man."

"Then I shall never take that risk," Angie declared. "I shall hold on to my heart—and virginity—forever!"

Cynthia started to laugh. "Heavens, no! You wouldn't want to die wondering, would you?" She picked up a pillow and tossed it at Angie.

Angie caught it and threw it back, but Cynthia ducked and the pillow hit Beth.

In the flick of an eye, the tension they'd been under for the past weeks erupted in an unexpected release as, scrambling and giggling, the women engaged in a full-scale pillow fight until they fell back on the bed exhausted.

Later, before sitting down to dinner, they were able to spend a half hour with their father before he tired. Cynthia hung back after Elizabeth and Angeleen departed. For a long moment, her gaze lingered on his face. Tenderly, she reached out and gently stroked his cheek.

"I love you, Daddy," she whispered, then tiptoed out of the room.

The others had been waiting for her outside and

they all descended to the dining room together. Elizabeth sat at the head of the table, with Charles Rayburn, the MacKenzie lawyer, to her right; Dave Kincaid took the chair to her left. Angeleen was seated next to Charles Rayburn, and Pete Gifford had the seat at the other end of the table. Cynthia had no choice but to accept the chair to the left of Dave Kincaid.

"You're looking good, Giff," she said to the ranch foreman. It was the first chance she'd had to see him since her return. "I bet you've got every young girl's heart palpitating in a fifty-mile radius."

His grin grooved laugh lines at the corners of his eyes. "Still worrying about my love life, huh? It's good to have you back home again, Thia."

Giff was seven years older than Cynthia, and the source of many of the warm memories she treasured whenever she thought of home. His father had also been the ranch foreman, and Giff had been a pal to her and her sisters as they were growing up. When their mother died, it was Giff's understanding and care that helped them through the heartache. When Cynthia was fourteen, she had developed a girlhood crush on him but had outgrown it; as the years passed, Giff had become her confidant and brother. He staunchly defended Cynthia's streak of wildness to her critics, and through the years had beat the hell out of any boy or man who attempted to dishonor her or her sisters.

Now, at thirty, Cynthia observed, Pete Gifford's handsomeness lay in his ruggedness: a granitelike face and jaw tanned by sun and wind, clear blue eyes, sun-bleached blond hair, and a tall, lithe body that had been conditioned by over fifteen years as a working cowboy.

When Buck Gifford had died two years ago, his son—well-liked by the men, as well as being a skilled rancher—had moved easily into his father's job. Giff knew every inch of the Roundhouse, and the men often joked that a calf couldn't mewl or a snake slither across the ranch without Giff knowing it. As his reputation had spread, he had received several offers from larger ranches, but his steadfast loyalty to Matthew MacKenzie was legendary.

Throughout the meal, while Elizabeth and Charles Rayburn talked business, Cynthia flirted outrageously with the foreman. Although Giff was unaffected by it, Cynthia took great pleasure in how much it appeared to annoy Dave Kincaid.

After dinner Giff left to check on a mare having a difficult delivery; Angeleen followed to offer assistance. Elizabeth and Rayburn went into the library, and Dave Kincaid simply disappeared.

Bored, Cynthia stepped outside. Sighing, she leaned back against a column of the portico and gazed up at the sky. How could it look so tranquil when so much heartache prevailed below? The stars looked close enough to touch—to make a wish upon. She and her sisters had often done so while they were growing up. Then afterward, they'd compare their wishes to see which one of them had made the best wish.

Well, there was no doubt what each of them would wish tonight. Closing her eyes, she murmured, "Star light, star bright, first star I see tonight; wish I may, wish I might, have the wish I wish tonight." Closing her eyes, she said a silent prayer for her father.

Turning to go back inside, Cynthia stopped with a start when she saw the nearby glow of a cigarette. "Who is that?"

Dave Kincaid stepped out of the shadows. "Sorry if I startled you, Miss MacKenzie."

"Not at all. I just thought I was alone." She walked over to him. "I thought we agreed to drop the formality, Dave."

"I don't recall agreeing to anything, Miss MacKenzie."

She laughed to cover her annoyance. "You know, Dave, you really have a big chip on your shoulder. What's the matter—some woman do you wrong? Or is it just me you don't like?" She moved nearer. "I could use a smoke myself."

"You're out of luck, lady. I borrowed the makings for this one from Giff." The timbre of his voice curled around her spine with the same lazy caress as the thin wisp of cigarette smoke swirling around his dark head.

Cynthia took another step closer to him and looked boldly into his eyes. In the dim light they appeared chocolate, mysterious, and inscrutable. She was so near she could smell the musky scent of his shaving soap and feel the exciting vitality he generated.

"Then we'll just have to share, Kincaid." Taking the cigarette out of his mouth, Cynthia drew a deep drag from it, then replaced it between his lips.

"Most of the *ladies* I know don't smoke, Miss MacKenzie."

"They sound dull."

"Well, then, you can save yourself some effort here—you'll find me just as dull."

"I can't believe that, Dave. You must have some vices."

"Vices are luxuries I don't have time for, Miz S-i-n. I rarely smoke, drink, or . . ." He paused and took a deep drag on the cigarette.

"Or what, Kincaid?"

"Or play parlor games, Miss MacKenzie," he said, exhaling a stream of smoke.

"I didn't have the parlor in mind, Dave," she replied in a throaty whisper.

He shook his head in a gesture of contempt. "Men are just fish in a pond to you, aren't they, lady? You think all you have to do is toss in your line and we'll all bite."

"That's been my experience. Although on occasion I have pulled up a toad, Kincaid," she taunted.

"Well, the bait would have to be a damn sight more inviting than what I see dangling in front of me right now." He casually removed the cigarette from his mouth and slipped it between her lips just as she had done to him.

"Enjoy the smoke, Miz Sin." He walked back inside.

Cynthia's mouth curved into a cunning smile. "Oh, Kincaid, if only this were a different time and a different place." She took a final deep draw from the cigarette, flicked it into the air with a finger, and entered the house.

Awakened by the urgent rapping on her door very early in the morning, Cynthia bolted up in bed and began to tremble as a wave of apprehension coursed through her.

"Hurry, Miss Cynthia, it's your father," the nurse cried out.

"I'm coming." Cynthia jumped out of bed and pulled on her robe. The silk peignoir was too revealing, so Cynthia hastily rummaged through the drawers until she found a long-fringed Spanish shawl that hung to her knees. She hastily wrapped it around herself to cover the flimsy robe.

Elizabeth and Angeleen were at their father's bedside when Cynthia rushed into the room. Pete Gifford stood solemnly against a back wall with an arm around Middy. Then Dave Kincaid arrived, pulling on a shirt as he entered the room.

Angeleen was sobbing quietly and Cynthia slipped an arm around her sisters' shoulders. They stood together, gazing helplessly at the still figure in the bed. A few minutes later, Matthew Mac-

Kenzie opened his eyes. At the sight of his daughters at his bedside, a tranquil smile crossed his face; then he closed his eyes again.

The doctor moved past them, and after a brief examination turned to the girls. "I'm sorry. He's gone."

Angeleen broke into loud sobs, and Pete Gifford came over to place a hand on her shoulder. She turned into his arms and he embraced the broken-hearted girl. His saddened gaze met Cynthia's. "There's nothing we can do here. Let's go downstairs."

She nodded and he led Angeleen away, stopping to pull the crying Middy into his arms as well.

"I can't believe he's gone, Thia," Beth said blankly.

Cynthia squeezed her hand hard. "Think about how happy he is now that he's with Mama, Beth."

Hand in hand, Cynthia and Beth moved slowly to the door, pausing when Dave Kincaid stepped up to them.

"I can't tell you how sorry I am," he said.

Beth grasped his hand. "Thank you, Dave, and we're grateful you're here supporting us."

"I loved him, too," he said.

"He felt the same toward you," Beth replied. "Daddy considered you and Giff the sons he never had."

Cynthia had no idea her father and Dave Kincaid had been so close. She wondered if her sister was just saying the customary words of one in mourning, or if there actually had been a deep relationship between her father and this antagonistic man.

As if he had read her thoughts, Dave's gaze locked with hers for a long moment. She felt herself flush under the intensity of his stare before continuing out of the room.

The rest of the day was spent in making the preparations for the following day's funeral and wake. Beth, Pete, and Charles Rayburn handled the arrangements. Cynthia spent the day comforting Angeleen and Middy, both of whom broke into tears every time Matthew MacKenzie's name was mentioned.

That evening before retiring, Cynthia slipped into Angeleen's room. "How are you doing, Pumpkin?"

"I don't think I'll ever be able to stop crying," Angie said. "You and Beth are so strong, and I'm just a dripping dishcloth."

"There's no shame in shedding tears over someone you love, honey." Cynthia climbed into the bed and gathered Angie in her arms. "Besides, that's your privilege—you're the baby of the family."

"I'm twenty years old, Thia; I'm not a baby anymore."

"You are to me, Pumpkin, until I have one of my own. Of course, with the luck I've been having, that prospect is very slim. So like it or not, Little Sister, you're stuck with the role." Cynthia kissed her on the forehead.

Sighing, Angie cuddled closer. "I'm glad you're back, Thia." Angie's voice began to drift off. "No matter how gloomy things are, you always make everything seem brighter . . . and happier. Now that you're home again, if only Daddy were . . ." She slipped into exhausted slumber before she could finish.

Cynthia eased herself out of the bed, tucked the quilt snugly around the sleeping girl, and tiptoed out of the room.

Once in the privacy of her own room, Cynthia crawled gratefully into bed. She knew sleep was most likely an impossibility, but she was grateful to finally be alone and have an opportunity to mourn privately—to shed the tears she had stoically fought throughout the day.

The first rays of a rising sun were creeping across the floor of her room by the time she had cried herself to sleep.

"Wow, who is that? He looks gorgeous from here!" Cynthia exclaimed the following morning, glancing out the window at the tall man who had just stepped out of a carriage.

"I swear, Thia, you're more outrageous than one of those rowdy soaplocks down at the waterfront," Beth said, walking to the window. Her smile disappeared instantly, and she returned to her dressing.

Cynthia watched as the tall, dark-haired stranger shook hands with another arrival before entering the house. "Well, who is he? He looks good enough to eat."

"His name is Michael Carrington," Beth said, closing the row of buttons on the long, fitted basque front of her gown. "He's one of Daddy's business acquaintances. Owns a railroad in Texas."

Cynthia winked at Angeleen. "Hmmm, sounds like you've been holding out on us, doesn't it, Angie? Keeping him to your yourself, are you?"

"You're welcome to him," Beth said bitterly. "Let's finish Angie's hair. The guests are arriving and we should be downstairs."

"You go ahead," Cynthia said. "I'm almost through with Angie." She gathered up a thick lock of Angeleen's hair and wound it around the curling iron.

"Oh, I look terrible," Beth said, stealing a final peek in the mirror.

"You look stunning, Beth," Cynthia replied, studying her older sister.

Elizabeth wore a black cashmere basque over a pleated faille skirt, the only adornment a grosgrain cravat at the neckline. Her auburn hair was pulled off her face and wound into a bun on the top of her head, a style which, rather than detracting, tended to emphasize her high cheeks and wide blue eyes.

"As a matter of fact, you look lovely," Cynthia added.

"My hair's burning!" Angie cried out.

"Oops, sorry!" Concentrating on Beth, Cynthia had forgotten about the hot curling iron. She hastily removed it as the pungent odor of scorched hair tweaked her nostrils.

"Don't dally too long; I need the two of you. Lord, I didn't think I had any more tears left to shed," Beth said, dabbing at her eyes as she hurried from the room.

"What am I going to do now? My hair is ruined!" Angie wailed.

"It is not," Cynthia said calmly, tucking under the burnt ends. She wove a velvet ribbon through the cluster of tight mahogany curls pinned to the back of Angie's head, and stepped away to admire the result.

"There, no one's the wiser."

"They will be, if they've got a nose," Angie declared.

Putting finger to chin, Cynthia studied her sister critically. Angeleen's black faille gown was embossed with velvet and had a long, graceful velvet drape in the rear. "But you need something," she said.

"Yeah, a new head of hair," her sister grumbled.

"I know exactly what it is. Wait here." Cynthia dashed to her room and returned quickly with a string of pearls. After draping them around Angeleen's neck, she smiled with approval. "There, that's the touch it needed."

Angie gingerly fingered the pearls. "But, Thia, these are so expensive."

"Then they're meant to be worn, not lie in a box."

"I've never worn anything so elegant," Angie breathed. Her eyes welled with tears. "If only Daddy could see me."

Cynthia felt the rise of her own tears. "He can, Pumpkin." She put her arms around Angie, and for a moment they stood drawing much-needed strength from each other.

"Now off with you," she said, with a pat to Angie's rear. "I'll be down in a moment."

As she watched Angie leave, Cynthia drew a deep, shuddering breath to compose herself. The despair she felt was overpowering. Despite having made her peace with her father before he died, she still felt guilty for the heartache she had caused him.

She walked over to the mirror to give herself a final inspection. Earlier, she had gathered her hair into a rolled upsweep on the top of her head, leaving only a dangling ringlet at each temple. Now she desolately wound a narrow fillet of black satin around her upswept hair. She supposed many of the old biddies in attendance would disapprove of her gown, but it was the only black dress she owned. Embroidered with black jet beads, the form-fitting satin gown had a deep flounce of shirred satin side panels, a low square neckline, and long transparent lisse sleeves gathered at the wrists. A corsage of variegated pink lisse roses adorned one of the narrow shoulder straps.

As her confidence wavered, she thought of the words that the famous French impressionist Monet had once said to her as they were admiring some fashion plates.

"Who can say what is fashionable, my darling Cyn? What one wears is of no consequence; the panache with which one wears it is the dictate."

Squaring her shoulders, she lifted her chin, "Well, dear Claude, here goes. Let's hope I don't botch the panache."

Chapter 3

Pausing at the top of the stairway, Cynthia surveyed the floor below. The crowd of mourners had overflowed into the foyer. She observed Dave Kincaid at the bottom of the stairs in deep conversation with another man. Dave glanced up, and when he saw Cynthia, he stopped in midsentence. The man with him turned his head to see what had caught Dave's attention, and Cynthia realized the man was Michael Carrington. Now, with a clear view of his face, she saw that the wealthy Texan was younger and even more handsome than he had appeared from her window.

The two men continued to stare boldly as she came down the stairs. *Bet I could float down on the strength of their stares*, she thought, amused.

Smiling graciously, she offered her hand to Carrington. "How do you do? I'm Cynthia MacKenzie."

"Michael Carrington," he said. "May I express my sympathy, Miss MacKenzie. I respected and admired your father greatly."

"Thank you, Mr. Carrington. Had you known my father long?"

"For the past two years."

"I see. Are you one of the local ranchers, Mr. Carrington?" she asked, feigning innocence.

"No, I live in Texas. I came to Denver on business and heard the unfortunate news about your father."

"Well, we appreciate your sympathy, Mr. Carrington. It's a pleasure meeting you."

"I only regret it couldn't have been under more felicitous circumstances, Miss MacKenzie."

"Perhaps someday it will be." She nodded at Michael Carrington, then strolled casually away—not permitting herself even a glance in the direction of Mr. David Kincaid.

Clutching together the opening of her short opera cape, Cynthia listened to the drone of the minister's voice eulogizing Matthew MacKenzie. To keep from crying, she tried not to associate the clergyman's words with her father—to pretend this was the body of a stranger he was committing to an eternal rest.

She glanced at Pete Gifford. Throughout the ceremony, Giff had stood silent and unwavering, but his suffering was clearly etched on his face.

Suddenly, she felt the draw of an intense stare. Shifting her eyes, she met those of Dave Kincaid. Unlike Giff, his expression was inscrutable, and she wondered what he was thinking. Perhaps, like her, he was trying to shut out his pain by concentrating on something else—like his dislike of her.

They continued to stare at each other until the people started to stir around them when the ceremony ended.

Of all the mornings to oversleep, Cynthia fretted, pinning a few loose hairs in place as she sped down the stairway. Emotionally drained and exhausted from yesterday's funeral, as well as the restless nights prior to her father's death, she had fallen back to sleep after Middy awakened her that morning.

All eyes turned to her when she rushed into the library.

"Good morning, Cynthia," Charles Rayburn said, his impatience evident as he put on his glasses.

"I'm sorry I'm late; I rarely oversleep." She glanced apologetically at her sisters; Beth offered a sympathetic smile, but Angie looked solemn. *The poor little darling looks like she'll never smile again,* Cynthia thought with a tender smile for the younger girl.

Pete Gifford grinned and winked at her as she sat down in the chair between him and Middy. Cynthia was surprised to see that Dave Kincaid was also present. She looked at him long enough to receive his usual glare of disapproval.

"I believe we can now proceed with the terms of the will," Charles Rayburn said. He settled down in the chair behind Matthew MacKenzie's desk. "Rather than read the will in its entirety, I had my office make copies of it for each of the main beneficiaries to read at their leisure. The document is rudimentary and written in the direct manner intrinsic to Matthew MacKenzie. Basically, it was Matt's wish that all of his assets are to be divided equally among his three daughters with the following exceptions: each servant and ranch hand is to be given one hundred dollars in cash; and Matilda McNamara is to receive a sum of five thousand dollars, plus a permanent home at the Roundhouse as long as the ranch remains in the hands of the MacKenzies."

"God bless the dear man's soul. A saint, he is," Middy mumbled, bringing a handkerchief to her eyes. Cynthia slipped an arm around the shoulders of the sobbing housekeeper.

"In appreciation to Peter Gifford for his long years of loyalty to the MacKenzies, Matt bequeathed all of the ranch north of Willow River, plus twenty heifers and a young bull to start his own herd."

Giff looked astounded. "Willow Range! That's some of the best grazing land on the ranch."

The lawyer handed the foreman a folded document. "Here is a survey map specifying the exact coordinates, but I'm sure you are well acquainted with the area."

Giff appeared dumbfounded as he took the map from Rayburn. Smiling, Cynthia leaned over and patted his knee. "I'm happy for you, Giff."

"Dave," Rayburn said, turning to Kincaid, "Matt hoped that you would continue on in your position with the railroad, and if so, upon completion you are to be awarded a five percent interest in the line. In the event you choose not to continue, he bequeaths to you the sum of a thousand dollars. If a decision is made to sell or discontinue the line by the stockholders before it is completed, you are to be given the sum of five thousand dollars."

Astonished, Cynthia looked at Dave Kincaid. He was staring at the floor. Why would her father offer him such a benevolent gift? Surely the unpleasant man wasn't as irreplaceable as the bequest would imply.

Rayburn cleared his throat. "Matt also made two stipulations in the will. First, no land can be sold to any outsider. Therefore, Giff, in the event you decide to sell your property, as long as the MacKenzies own the Roundhouse, you will have to sell it back to the estate. Also, the only way the Roundhouse can be sold is if you three ladies all agree to sell out together."

"And the other stipulation, Mr. Rayburn?" Elizabeth asked.

"No owner of the preferred stock of the Rocky Mountain Central can sell it or sign it over to another, except by mutual agreement of all stockholders." He glanced up at them. "In other words, ladies and gentlemen, it was Matt's dying wish that all of the Roundhouse and Rocky Mountain Central remain in the hands of the people in this room."

"Aren't there any outside investors in the railroad now?" Cynthia asked, surprised.

"No. Daddy's been buying them out for the past two years, and he retired the shares of common stock issued," Beth said. "I found that out when I started to do the ledgers for him. He sold off all his other investments to do it."

"His mining interest, too?" Cynthia asked, appalled.

Rayburn handed her a sheet of paper. "Here is a list of the existing assets, Cynthia."

Cynthia quickly perused the top sheet, glanced up in displeasure at Rayburn, then flipped over to the next page. "It appears most of Father's capital is tied up in this damn railroad venture," Cynthia said.

"Not most—all," Rayburn replied. "With the exception of this ranch, of course."

"According to this statement, the railroad's been operating at a loss for the past two years. Were you aware of this, Beth?" Cynthia asked.

"Of course; after all, we're expanding."

"And if we don't finish it, the Rocky Mountain Central will go under."

"Sounds like you don't have much confidence in my ability, Miss MacKenzie." The challenging remark came from Dave Kincaid.

Cynthia glared at him. "Nothing personal, Kincaid. In times of crisis, I only have confidence in my own ability. From what I can tell, at the rate we're losing money, we'll run out of cash long before the railroad is completed."

"There are always government grants and loans, Miss MacKenzie," he replied, disgusted.

"And of course, you can't lose, Mr. Kincaid. Either way, you get a percentage of the railroad or five thousand dollars."

"You don't get it at all, do you, lady? This isn't about me. The railroad is your father's dream."

Pete cleared his throat. "This is also a working ranch, Thia. If the railroad should belly up, you can still live comfortably off the proceeds of the Roundhouse."

"Apparently we might have to! Am I the only one in the room who can read a financial statement? Don't any of you see a problem with this?" Frustrated, Cynthia handed the report back to Rayburn, sat back, and folded her arms across her chest.

"Well, you can always sell the railroad, ladies, before that happens," Rayburn said. "As a matter of fact, since the subject has arisen, we do have someone interested in purchasing the Rocky Mountain Central."

"Hallelujah!" Cynthia exclaimed. "How good is the offer?"

"It's a very generous offer from the Lone Star Railroad."

"The Lone Star!" Beth exclaimed. "That's owned by the Carringtons, isn't it?"

"Yes, it is. As a matter of fact, that was the very reason Michael Carrington happened to be in Denver when your father died."

"Well, you can tell Mr. Carrington that the Rocky Mountain Central is not for sale," Beth said with an emphatic toss of her head. "Now, if you are through, Mr. Rayburn, I'm sure breakfast is ready."

"There's just one more thing." Rayburn extracted three packages from a bag on the floor. "Your father asked me to give these to you girls." He handed each of them a wrapped box and a sealed envelope. "His instructions were that the boxes can be opened whenever you wish, but he requested that none of you open the letter until you reach a time in your life when you miss or need him the most."

"I miss him right now," Angie said. "Maybe I should open my letter now."

"Each of you must make that decision herself," Rayburn said. "So, if there are no more questions, I believe we are through here."

"We're through, all right," Cynthia grumbled, rising to her feet. "Let's eat."

What Cynthia had anticipated would be a quiet, restful day turned out to be just the opposite. Matthew MacKenzie had been well thought of by rich and poor alike, and throughout the day, those in the community who were unable to attend the funeral came to pay their respects. In the afternoon, more than a dozen telegrams with expressions of sympathy were delivered.

Consequently, having agreed to open their gifts together, it was almost the dinner hour by the time the three women found themselves alone in the parlor.

"You're the eldest, Beth," Angie said. "You go first."

Beth weighed the package in her hands. "This is very heavy. What do you suppose it could be?"

"Let's hope it's a gold brick," Cynthia joked. "Mine's very light. Probably filled with feathers."

"You mustn't tease, Thia," Angie said. "You know Daddy wouldn't do that."

"Well, he did have a sense of humor, Pumpkin."

Angie's expression was solemn. "I just have a feeling that these gifts are very special. Hurry up and open yours, Beth."

"All right."

Angie and Cynthia waited anxiously as Beth slowly untied the string and removed the paper on the package. She started to lift the lid of the box, then hastily slammed it shut. "I think we should wait until after dinner," she teased.

"Oh, fiddlesticks, Beth!" Angie groaned.

"Get on with it, Beth, before I do it for you," Cynthia complained.

Giggling, Beth lifted off the box lid and took out a small train engine. Her eyes suddenly lit with pleasure. "Why, it's a miniature replica of the Betsy, Daddy's first engine."

"I don't understand why he just didn't give you the larger one he has on his desk," Cynthia said.

"It's exactly like I said," Angie declared. "Daddy had this made just for you, Beth, because he's sending a message."

"I think you're right, Angie. If he'd given me the one he had, I wouldn't have questioned what it meant. He *is* saying something, and I know what it is. He wants me to continue on with the work he began."

"You don't know that," Cynthia declared. "Lord, Beth, I realize how much you're involved with the railroad. Neither Angie nor I have ever felt the way you do about it. But let's be practical—it's a losing cause. Why keep on throwing good money after bad? It'll take another year or longer to finish laying that track. We'll be ruined financially by then."

"Daddy believed we could do it," Beth insisted.

"Mr. Rayburn said that this other line made a generous offer. I think we should consider it and cut our losses immediately."

"We can't do that," Beth said. "That railroad is Daddy's dream. We can't abandon it."

"Beth, we can't afford not to," Cynthia argued. "We could lose everything—even the Roundhouse."

"That's a chance we have to take." Beth came over and sat down on the floor at Cynthia's feet. Grasping her hands, she pleaded with her sister.

"Thia, this was Daddy's vision. He told me that once it was completed, the railroad would be like the Mississippi River—linking the South to the North, bringing Texas cotton to Denver, and Colorado wood or Nebraska corn to Texas. That's why he linked the railroad to the Union Pacific line. We can't sell out that vision of his. That's what Michael Carrington sees too, or he wouldn't be so willing to buy us out."

"He's got the money and people to do it. Lord, Beth," Cynthia said gently, "we're just three women with limited funds who know nothing about building a railroad."

"We don't know—but Dave Kincaid *does*. Daddy had a lot of trust in him. It's clear you don't like Dave, Thia, but he's a brilliant engineer and knows what he's doing."

"I never said I don't like him; it's just the opposite: Dave Kincaid doesn't like me. And just what would we do if he left and went to work for the competition?"

"Dave's too loyal to do that. Furthermore, he has a lot to gain by remaining with us." Beth's eyes were pleading. "Oh, Thia, I know you're fond of fine clothes and a more glamorous life than we have here in Denver, but Daddy dreamed of this—we can't forsake his dream."

"How do you feel about it, Angie?" Cynthia asked, turning to their younger sister.

"Beth's right about Daddy's dream, and you're right that we don't know anything about building a railroad, but . . . I guess I believe we should do everything in our power to fulfil Daddy's dream." She knelt beside Beth, slipping an arm around her shoulders. "So I don't think we should sell the railroad either."

"Oh, thank you, Angie," Beth said, hugging her. Tears glistened in Beth's eyes as she looked up hopefully at Cynthia. "What about you, Thia? We must all agree to this. I don't want us to have any bad feelings over it."

Cynthia shook her head. "And you're supposed to be the businesswoman in the family. Why, you're just a sentimental darling without one smidgen of practical business sense."

Slipping off the chair, Cynthia joined the other two on the floor. "But I love the both of you too much to quarrel, so I agree: we don't sell the railroad."

Elizabeth and Angeleen squealed with delight as the three hugged and kissed, laughing through their tears of joy.

When they pulled apart, Cynthia drew back and shook a finger at them. "Just remember, when we're all old, gray-haired, and living in poverty because no man with a drop of blue blood in his veins would have one of us, I intend to spend my old age reminding the two of you that I told you so."

"Well, now that we've settled that, let's get on with opening the gifts. You're next, Thia."

Smiling at Beth, Cynthia opened her gift to discover a painted, acorn-shaped case containing a silver thimble.

She slipped the thimble on her finger. "Not quite the finger adornments I'm used to; I really prefer rings. What message do you think Daddy's sending me?"

Beth shrugged. "A stitch in time?"

"A stitch on what?" Angie asked, confused. "This is a real puzzler."

"Maybe Daddy's suggesting I should *mend* my ways." After all, her father must have picked out the gift before they had had their talk.

"Well, open your gift, Angie. Dinner will soon be ready," Beth said.

Angeleen's gift was a round music box in a Morocco leather case, about three inches in diameter. When she wound it up, a tutu-garbed equestrian standing on the back of a black stallion circled the lid as the music played.

"Oh, listen, the tune is 'Londonderry Aire,' " Angie exclaimed. "That was Daddy's favorite song."

"Remember how Mama used to play the tune and sing to him, Thia?" Beth said.

"I can see him sitting in the chair by the fireplace, smiling as we sang the words Mama taught us," Angie added, smiling wistfully.

She got up and sat down on the piano stool, then wound up the music box. As she accompanied the melody on the piano, she began to sing in her lilting soprano.

I know a place, no other place is quite so dear.
It's filled with love, and happiness and cheer.
And in that place, I thank the Lord content to be.
For it is home; the home God gave to me.

Elizabeth and Cynthia walked over to join her, their voices blending harmoniously.

Attracted by the music, Dave Kincaid and Pete Gifford slipped into the room. With hat in hand and still in his overcoat, Michael Carrington suddenly appeared in the parlor doorway.

The women continued to sing the words of the haunting melody as the three men stood listening with rapt attention.

When they finished, Cynthia turned away from the piano and drew up in surprise. Seeing Michael Carrington holding his hat, she said, "Mercy, you must forgive us, Mr. Carrington, we had no idea you were here. Have you been waiting long?"

"Not long enough, I'm afraid. I would have enjoyed hearing more," he said.

"Why, thank you," Cynthia replied, aware that

Dave Kincaid was following the exchange. "Let me take your hat and coat. We're about to have dinner; I hope you will join us."

Beth spoke up sharply. "I'm sure Mr. Carrington has other plans, Thia."

"Not at all, Miss MacKenzie," he said to Beth. "If you're certain I'm not intruding, I'd be honored to join you."

"I assume Mr. Rayburn has told you that we're not interested in your offer. The Rocky Mountain Central is not for sale, Mr. Carrington."

"Yes, he told me," Carrington said. "I came here tonight hoping I could persuade you to change your mind."

"Then you've made a trip for nothing," Beth replied curtly.

He smiled at her. "At least it wasn't a complete loss, Miss MacKenzie. Hearing your lovely voices was well worth the trip."

The tension between Beth and Michael Carrington was thicker than London fog, Cynthia observed. Fortunately, Middy chose that moment to announce dinner. Carrington smiled and offered Beth his arm.

"We have an added guest for dinner, Middy," Beth said. Ignoring his proffered arm, she walked past him.

Amused, Cynthia stepped forward and slipped her arm through his. "While I, on the other hand, never refuse a gentleman's offer to take me to dinner," she said lightly, handing Middy his coat and hat as they followed into the dining room.

After Carrington left, the household quickly settled down for the night. Giff returned to the small house he occupied on the ranch, and since Dave Kincaid was leaving for "end of track" in New Mexico early the next morning, he retired for the night. Yawning, Angeleen excused herself and went to bed. A short time later, Cynthia and Elizabeth decided to do the same. Once upstairs, Beth paused at her bedroom door.

"Thanks, Thia, for agreeing not to sell the railroad. It means so much to me. I know everything will work out in the end."

"Of course it will," Cynthia said, with more enthusiasm than she felt. "Good night, Beth." She gave her a hug and continued down the hallway.

Once in her room, still plagued with the feeling they were making a mistake by not selling to Carrington, Cynthia paced the floor until she finally gave up and went to bed.

She spent a restless night, tossing and turning as a multitude of questions swirled in her mind: the railroad, Dave Kincaid, the mysterious Michael Carrington.

Where did she go from here? The thought of remaining in Denver held little appeal to her, and she certainly didn't want to return to Europe. Besides, she'd have to start tightening her belt; she no longer could afford her former style of living. Unless, of course, she went back to Roberto.

And she'd never be that desperate!

Carmine streaks of dawn were just piercing the gray sky when Cynthia rose and dressed. The household was still asleep as she quietly pulled on her cloak and went outside. With the morning mist curling around her ankles like a chilly steam, she headed for her father's grave.

Nearing the small cemetery, she was surprised to see Dave Kincaid at the grave site. "Good morning."

Clearly she had surprised him, and he appeared embarrassed as well.

"You're up early, Miss MacKenzie. Or are you just getting home?"

After the troubled night she had just spent, Cynthia was in no mood for his sarcastic remarks. "Just what is your problem, Kincaid?" she lashed out. "You've been rude and insulting from the time we met."

"If I have, I apologize. A man I cared deeply about was ill and dying."

"I cared about him, too."

"Actions speak louder than words, lady."

"What is that supposed to mean?" she snapped in confusion.

"I'm referring to the way your conduct hurt him these last few years, and the Lord only knows how much before that."

"You don't know what you're talking about, Kincaid."

"Maybe not, but I saw his face when he opened a letter and read the news clipping about his daughter cavorting drunk and naked in some fountain in Rome. I saw pain, lady."

"So that's what this is all about—that damn Italian newspaper story," she said with disgust. "Well, for your information, Kincaid, that article was grossly exaggerated and inaccurate. I wasn't drunk, and the naked woman wasn't me."

"Of course not," he said scornfully, turning to leave. She grabbed his arm.

"Damn you, Kincaid, I don't care whether you believe me or not."

"Good, because I don't believe you. Lying is just another one of your vices, Miz Sin."

Cynthia's anger turned to rage. Before she even realized what she was doing, she slapped him in the face.

He paled, his lips thinning with anger. Pulling her into his arms, he lowered his head, his mouth capturing hers in a hard punishing kiss, savage in its intensity.

Forcing her lips open with his tongue, he ravished her mouth until it felt burned and bruised under the fiery possession. Blood pounded in her temples and ears as she struggled to free herself. Then the struggle evolved into one with herself when his kiss became less punishing, and more urgent and exploratory. Shivers of desire started to race through her, and she returned his kiss, surrendering freely to the rising passion that was consuming her.

When he drew away, she stared at him, her emotions racing with a confusing mixture of hope and resentment.

Then his mouth curled into a sardonic smirk. "I guess that kiss has been on both our minds from the time we met."

She felt a flush of humiliation and anger as she watched him walk away.

Chapter 4

Cynthia left her room and paused at the top of the stairway. On impulse, she sat down on the balustrade and rode it to the floor below, just as she had often done when she was younger.

After being back home for two weeks, she understood why her sisters hadn't married. Other than Giff, who was more like a brother, there wasn't one interesting bachelor in all of Denver. Apparently the eligible men were either away at college or off with the army in the Dakota Territory chasing Sioux and Cheyenne Indians.

Too bad Dave Kincaid had left Denver, Cynthia reflected. He certainly could keep her from being bored. The memory of his kiss played on her mind constantly. Despite his attempt to humiliate her, the kiss had been exciting—and arousing. And she was experienced enough to know he had felt it, too.

Seated behind their father's desk, Beth glanced up at Cynthia when she entered the library.

"Beth, I need something to keep me occupied. Unlike our beloved younger sister, I am not interested in riding the range checking fence with Giff and the other hands, nor do I care to drive smelly cattle from one spot to another. Unless you have something for me to do, I swear I shall perish from boredom."

Laughing, Beth leaned back in the chair. "I wish I had your problems. I'm so busy, I don't know where to begin."

"Well, you could start by agreeing to sell the railroad. That would free up plenty of your time to relax, and I could be ransomed from captivity."

"Do you want to go back to Europe, Thia? I still have my share of the inheritance that Grandfather MacGregor left us. If you're really that bored, I'll be glad to give it to you."

Cynthia plopped down in a chair and flung her legs over the arm. "I wouldn't think of taking your money, Beth. And furthermore, I have no desire to go back to Europe. France and Prussia are always squabbling, and there's forever some ruckus between Spain and her neighbors."

"What about your Count Cellini? Maybe you aren't over him as much as you think you are."

"Oh, I'm over him, Beth. I have been for some time." She shook her head. "It's hard to believe that at one time I loved Roberto enough to surrender my virginity to him."

"Don't be so hard on yourself. You aren't the first woman who's made that mistake."

Seeing the downward shift of her sister's eyes, Cynthia asked, "Are you speaking from experience, Beth?"

Beth shot forward in her seat and began to rustle through the papers on the desk. "I've got to get back to work."

"I'm right, aren't I?" Cynthia exclaimed, sitting up. "You're hiding something. Who was he, Beth?"

"I swear, Thia, don't you ever listen? I'm truly busy. There's a supply train leaving for end of track in an hour." Glancing at a pile of rolled-up charts in the corner, she added, "Dave's waiting for those diagrams and some financial figures he asked for. I need to get on with it."

"Give me the information. I'll deliver it in person."

Beth laughed lightly. "You really are bored if you're willing to ride a supply train two hundred miles."

"I think I'd like that."

"You *are* serious!" Beth said, astonished.

"I certainly am. Matter of fact, the more I think of it, the more appealing it becomes. Just tell me what you want him to know; I'll do the rest. And don't be surprised if I stick around down there for a while."

"Cynthia MacKenzie, you're sweet on Dave Kincaid, aren't you? And here I thought you didn't like him."

"I don't know what I feel for him. That's why I think I should pursue it."

"You're wasting your time, Thia. Dave's a wonderful guy, but he's not your type. He's serious and hardworking; you'd find him boring."

"Maybe I will by the time I return. Right now, I find Mr. Kincaid anything but boring."

"Right out of the frying pan into the fire, hey? You won't find any fancy hotels or palazzi at end of track, Thia—it's primitive, noisy, and dusty, and everyone lives in tents."

"Well, while I'm there I'm not living in any tent. I'll take Daddy's private car." She clasped her hands together. "Now, what is it you want me to tell that beautiful physical specimen?"

Beth came over and pulled Cynthia to her feet. "Train's due here soon. If you're serious about going, you better get moving." Slipping an arm around Cynthia's waist, she said, "I'll fill you in while you're packing."

As the train inched slowly into camp, Dave hopped up into the cab.

"Boy, am I'm glad to see you. We're almost out of rail," he said to the grizzled engineer and the young fireman beside him. "How was the trip down?"

"Ah, she ran like greased lightnin', Davey me boy," Patrick O'Hara said. "You lay a good track, lad."

"What was your speed, Paddy?"

"I opened her up to thirty-five on the straight track and cut back to twenty on the sharp curves." He winked at Dave. "I'm thinkin', though, we mighta been goin' a mite faster on some of them grades."

"A damn mite faster," Dan Harrington said, his teeth flashing whitely against his soot-covered face.

Unruffled, O'Hara patted the train's panel. "Ole Clementine here hugged 'em curves as tight as a tick on a mule's arse."

"That's good to hear," Dave said, entering the information on the chart he held. "I see the Chief's private car is attached. Did Miss MacKenzie come with you?"

"That she did, lad," O'Hara said, raising a bushy brow.

"Well, I better go see what she wants."

"From the looks of her, it ain't hard to guess," O'Hara said, poking Harrington in the ribs. "But if you ain't up to the task, lad, Patrick Michael O'Hara is offerin' his services."

"Let's cut that kind of talk, Paddy. She's a lady, and the boss to boot," Dave said, jumping off the train. "Just get the train set to unload, and be sure and see me before you fellows head back to Denver."

O'Hara stuck his head out of the cab window and waved to an older man walking past. "Hey, Sean Rafferty, you'll be buyin' the drinks tonight. Made it in six hours, I did."

"Is that true, Harrington?" Rafferty yelled to the fireman.

"The big pile of bluster cud never ha'e done it without me help," Harrington said.

"Stop your palaverin', Danny Boy, and get that car unhooked."

"I'll do it," Dave yelled.

Bisected by the main track, a circle of temporary track formed a turnaround for the supply trains. Parked on one half of the circular turnaround were the work engine and several uncoupled railroad cars.

After Dave threw a switch on the turnaround track, O'Hara gave a long tug on the train whistle and slowly eased the locomotive forward onto the side track. After making a sweep around the semicircle, the locomotive was back on the main track pointed toward Denver.

Dave waited as the tender and a half dozen flatcars inched past him. "Hold up," he yelled when the private car on the end of the train reached him. Crossing the main track, he threw a switch on the opposite side, and the experienced train engineer backed the private car onto that track. Dave quickly uncoupled it.

"All clear, Paddy," he shouted.

Accompanied by the sound of squealing air brakes and puffs of black smoke from the stack, the engineer inched forward, and Dave returned the switches to their proper settings.

Curious about why Elizabeth had made the trip, Dave tapped on the door of the detached car. He had the shock of his life when it was opened by Cynthia MacKenzie, dressed in a white robe.

"What in hell are you doing here?" he blurted out.

"A pleasure to see you too, Kincaid," she replied. "Do come in."

As he entered and passed her, the faint fragrance of what had to be an expensive French perfume started his nerve ends hopping.

Dave never ceased to gawk in wonderment every time he stepped into the car. What the compartment lacked in width, it made up for in length. Matthew MacKenzie had spared no expense or luxury when he had this traveling home built. It included a sleeping compartment, a water closet with marble tub and accoutrements, and a fully stocked kitchen with its own refrigerated compartment.

The windows were draped in red velvet and the floor was covered in a mosaic pattern of red, gold, blue, violet, and black Brussels carpeting. Four crystal chandeliers were suspended from a ceiling of hand-carved inlaid walnut panels. The paneled walls of the car were adorned with crystal wall sconces, several mirrors framed in gilded walnut, a gun rack, and additional rich wall hangings.

"Make yourself comfortable, Mr. Kincaid."

Shoving his hat to the top of his forehead, Dave sat down on one of the many plush chairs fringed with ivory satin. He swung his booted right foot across his left knee.

"This place sure doesn't lack anything, does it?" he said.

"Nothing . . . except the right man," Cynthia said, draping herself on a huge circular sofa built around a velvet-covered column that formed the back and the headrest. "Is there anything I can get you?"

"No, thank you."

Her gaze remained fixed on his face as she lounged on the red velvet sofa, looking like a white, furry kitten eyeing a bowl of cream.

"Do you have any idea how much longer Elizabeth will be? I'm on a pretty tight schedule."

"Elizabeth isn't here."

"What?" David bolted to his feet.

"She sent me."

Frowning, he stared at her. "Why in holy hell would she send you?"

"Someone had to come, so I volunteered. My sister said you were waiting for some drawings."

"She could have just sent them; you didn't have to deliver them personally."

"It was the least I could do for you—but I'm sure I can do even more . . ."

His gaze shifted to her mouth as she ran her tongue across her lips. The sensuous gesture was a provocative reminder of how sweet those lips had tasted . . . how sweet they would taste again.

He was hungry enough to accept the invitation, all right, and she sure as hell was willing. Or was she hoping he'd be sucker enough to try so she could laugh in his face?

"Just give me the drawings, lady, and I'll get out of here. I've got work to do."

"That's why I'm here, Kincaid. We thought you needed someone to help take some of the load off those broad shoulders of yours."

His mouth curved sardonically. "You don't mean *you!*"

She got up and walked over to him with her languorous catlike stride. "Yes, doesn't the thought just thrill you?"

"Not a snowball's chance in hell, lady."

"You don't have much to say about it, Kincaid. Orders from the powers that be. I'm just the messenger. The drawings are on that table over there."

"I don't need any help—especially the kind you're offering."

"What kind is that, Kincaid?" she asked with that feigned wide-eyed, innocent look that infuriated him.

"Just stay out of my way, lady."

Dave strode over to the table, snatched up the

drawings, and slammed out the door, the sound of her light laughter ringing in his ears.

Sean Rafferty approached Dave as soon as he got outside. "I've got a problem."

"Dammit, when don't you?" Dave snapped. Then, slapping the rail boss on the back, Dave said, "I'm sorry, Sean, I just had some bad news."

Sean Rafferty was a hard worker and a good foreman. Four years earlier, Dave had been a member of Sean's rail gang when they were laying track in northern Colorado, and he respected the foreman's fairness and integrity. Dave's trust in the older man was irrevocable, and he'd put his life or reputation on the line for Sean anytime.

A widower for ten years, the fifty-year-old foreman had been left with a six-year-old granddaughter to raise after a premature blast had caught his son, who had been Dave's best friend, in a rock slide the previous year.

"So what's the problem, Sean?"

"There ain't enough rail on the shipment that just came in to keep me crew workin' for more'n a couple days. And we're short of spikes, too. Can't lay rail wit'out spikes."

"How the hell could that happen?" Dave groaned. "According to my figures, we should have plenty of rail and spikes. What are you guys doing, eating them?"

"Yeah, been chokin' 'em down with the dust we've been swallowin'."

"Dammit, we'll never get this railroad built with these kinds of delays. I'll see what I can do to get some more here as quickly as I can, but if not, your crew's gonna have to man picks and shovels or go help the trestle crew."

"They ain't gonna like that, Dave. They're spikers and gaugers, nae bridge monkeys."

"I'm counting on you to convince them otherwise, Sean."

The foreman grinned. "I'll see what I can do."

Dave entered his office and sat down at a battered desk strewn with papers. Unlike the lavish private car he had just left, the caboose that served as his office and quarters contained only a desk, a table piled high with drawings, a battered safe in the corner, and a potbellied stove. The sleeping quarters were even more spartan, consisting of a bunk and a bedside table. His clothes were kept in a trunk at the foot of the bunk and hung from a pole in the corner. A curtain separated the two sections.

For the next hour Dave riffled through papers, studying bills of lading and rechecking his calculations. The rail shortage made no sense to him. Finally, disgusted, he tossed aside the pencil and cradled his head in his hands.

"Things can't be that bad, Kincaid."

He jerked his head up, then sucked in a breath that slammed into his gut like a fist. Looking like a painting by Titian, Cynthia MacKenzie stood in the doorway twirling a lacy parasol over her shoulder. For an instant he thought the beautiful vision in crimson was a figment of his imagination, belonging in a marbled ballroom, not the doorway of a run-down caboose.

"What do you want, Miss MacKenzie?"

"I came to offer my assistance."

"I thought I made myself clear. I don't need your help—unless, of course, you can tell me why I'm short of rail." He shoved his chair back and stood up. "You'll have to excuse me. I have to ride out to check on the trestle we're building."

After strapping on his gun belt he tried to brush past her, but she didn't budge. For a moment he thought he'd have to pick her up bodily. "You're in my way."

"I was hoping you'd show me around the camp."

"I figure you can find your way around anyplace. I suggest, though, that you change into something more practical. You look ridiculous strutting around in that fancy gown and lacy parasol, and you'll most likely twist an ankle in those shoes you're wearing. In case you haven't noticed, this isn't Trafalgar Square or the Champs-Elysées, Miz Sin."

"I don't have to guess your choice of spelling, do I, Kincaid?"

"I'm still confused, I reckon. Spelling always was my weakness."

"Oh, you have others." Smiling, she reached up a gloved finger to trace the circle of his lips. "But you know what, Kincaid? Before I go back to Denver, I'm going to put a smile on this mouth of yours."

He snatched her wrist away. "You can do that now by promising to be gone by the time I get back." Tipping his hat, he nodded. "Have a pleasant day. Oh, and don't forget to dress for the daily concert—the coyotes start howling about sunset."

Chapter 5

Upon leaving the caboose, Cynthia decided to tour the tent town. Leisurely twirling the open parasol resting on her shoulder, she strolled among the tents and makeshift huts that were broken down and moved each time another forty or fifty miles of track were completed.

Signs such as GENERAL STORE, INFIRMARY, and SALOON were pinned to the fronts of those tents to identify them; but the majority were the dwellings of the men who were building the railroad and their families.

The ground beneath the small community had been stripped down to a flat surface of dirt and pebbles, broken only by trees rising like an oasis amidst a canvas desert. Swirling dust clung to the tents, clotheslines, hammocks—and people. An occasional potted plant strived vainly to give a homey look of permanency to the rudimentary homes.

The improvised town was all that Beth had claimed it to be—primitive, grimy, and overcrowded. Yet, as Cynthia walked among the women and listened to them calling out or chatting with one another as they did their laundry, hung up clothing, and cooked over their open fires, she sensed that the small community throbbed with an energy that paralleled any city lined with paved streets, picket fences, and multistoried brick buildings.

Wherever Cynthia walked, she drew attention. The women would stop whatever they were doing to stare blatantly before offering a greeting or nod. Whispered comments of "Who is she?" or "Look at the elegant gown, will ya" carried to her ears.

After thirty minutes, Cynthia admitted to herself that she should have taken Dave Kincaid's advice: her crimson gown was now coated with dust, and she was certain a blister had formed on her heel from walking among the rubble footpaths in high-heeled pumps.

Pride be damned! Ignoring the curious stares that followed her every move, Cynthia pulled off the shoes and limped back to her car.

Casting aside the shoes and parasol the moment she entered, she plopped down in one of the plush chairs. Clearly, she would have to do something about her inappropriate clothing and shoes.

Just as she had suspected, there was a bloodstain on the heel of her white hose. Grimacing, she slowly eased the stocking off her foot and examined the painful blister. She limped across the floor to the water closet but couldn't find medication or a bandage. Replacing the hose, she went into the bedroom and found a pair of soft kid slippers. After she slid her feet into them, she tested them and decided they would do well enough to get her to the general store. She glanced in the mirror and laughed: she was still wearing the expensive French chapeau, trimmed with ostrich feathers especially dyed in crimson and white to match her gown—another fashion dictate that was unnecessary in this community. Removing the large, wide-brimmed hat, she tossed it aside and limped outside, headed for the store.

* * *

Darkness had already descended by the time Dave returned to camp. After unsaddling his horse he headed for his quarters, too exhausted to even stop to see if he could dredge up something to eat from the dining car.

Attracted by shouts and hoots, he saw that a circle of men were squatted around a barrel. From their remarks, he knew they were shooting craps. He didn't encourage gambling around the camp, but Lord knew there was little diversion for the men—especially the single men. Once a month, a gambling tent and prostitutes moved in for a weekend.

Dave stopped in his tracks when he heard a voice yell, "Roll 'em dice, Miz MacKenzie."

"Oh, no," he groaned. "What the devil is that woman up to now?"

Hurrying over to the spot, Dave figured Cynthia MacKenzie couldn't shock him more than she had done already, but he had underestimated her. Shaking the dice, she was leaning forward over the barrel, a pair of Levi's hugging her long legs, slim hips—and very feminine derriere. She always looked sexier fully clothed than some of the women he'd known had managed to do naked.

"Miss MacKenzie," he snapped gruffly.

About to release the dice, she paused with her upraised arm in midair and, along with the men, glanced in his direction.

"I'd like to see you in my office please."

"Sure, as soon as I'm done here," she replied.

"Now, Miss MacKenzie." He spun on his heel and strode away.

"Sorry, boys," he heard her say. "Maybe I can join you tomorrow night."

"Like hell you will," Dave grumbled to himself.

Entering his office, he lit a lamp, then hung up his hat and gun belt. He was seated behind his desk by the time she sauntered into his quarters.

"Close the door," he ordered.

She complied silently, but with a smile of amusement that fueled his anger even more.

"Just what the hell are you trying to do, lady?"

"I don't know what you mean," she replied, not cowering under his scathing glare.

"What with accidents, short supplies, and shorter tempers, I've got enough problems around this camp. I don't need you adding to them by riling up the men."

"What are you talking about now, Kincaid? I get along well with the men."

"I bet you do—too well! By next week, they'll be at one another's throats fighting over you. I'm not going to let you interfere with finishing this job, lady. Like it or not, you're headed back to Denver on the next train."

"All I was doing was shooting craps with them."

"Dressed like a little . . . tease."

"You told me to wear something different. What's wrong with what I've got on?"

He raised a brow. "Aside from the impropriety, you look vulgar."

"Vulgar! I'm completely covered from my neck to my feet."

"Those pants leave little to the imagination, Miz Sin."

She leaned over his desk, glaring right back at him. "Maybe to *your* filthy imagination, Mr. Kin—*c-a-d*," she spelled out, and walked to the door. "Furthermore, I'm one of the owners of this railroad, and whether *you* like or not, I'm staying."

"Owner or not, lady, I give the orders around here. Everyone pulls their load or we don't have room for them. You'd better find something to do other than causing trouble!" he shouted at the door she had just slammed.

* * *

Cynthia lay awake going over the argument with Dave Kincaid. The man infuriated her as much as he fascinated her. He had really gotten a rise out of her that night, but she vowed that in the future she would not let it happen again.

As she thought of her past encounters with him, one fact began to materialize: Dave Kincaid had an Achilles' heel—and she was it. He was as fascinated with her as she was with him. All she had to do was get him to break down and admit it. Then, after she made him apologize for all the nasty things he'd said to her . . . well, then, maybe they could pick up where they'd left off with that kiss.

But first she had to break him down, she reflected, beginning to doze off. It wouldn't be easy.

Cynthia awoke the next morning feeling well rested and prepared to do battle. Springing out of bed, she contemplated what would be the first thing she could do to please him.

To her dismay, as soon as she went outside she discovered that the working day had begun much earlier; the crew and Dave Kincaid had already left for end of track.

Refusing to be thwarted so easily, she went to the corral where the workhorses were kept, saddled a mount, and rode out of the tent town. It was a longer ride than she anticipated, but by following the course of the track she reached her destination with no mishap. Reining in, she surveyed the scene.

End of track was a beehive of activity and noise: the ring of hammers on steel, the shouts of men, the clatter of horse-drawn wagons carrying ties to the railers or hauling dirt and gravel away from the grading area—and all played out under an ever-present cloud of dust.

Looking troubled, Dave Kincaid walked over to her. "Is there a problem, Miss MacKenzie?"

"A good day to you, too, Mr. Kincaid."

His expression changed to exasperation. "There are few social graces around a job site, Miss MacKenzie. What are you doing here?"

"I thought I would ride out and see how the railroad was progressing."

"Why?" he asked with restrained impatience.

"Actually, Kincaid, I'm crazy about the sight of sweaty male bodies."

"Miss MacKenzie, there is a standing rule that women and children stay away from the job site."

"Why?" she asked.

"There's a lot of equipment moving around, we're often blasting, and they can be a distraction. For that reason, I prefer them to remain in camp."

"Well, this woman usually does what *she* prefers, Kincaid."

"No doubt. However, I'm responsible for every person and piece of material connected to this project. Therefore, while you're here, you remain in camp. Have I made myself clear, Miss MacKenzie?"

"I can take care of myself. And I don't take orders from anyone, Kincaid."

He ignored the challenge. "On your return, I recommend you stay close to the track. It's very easy to get lost out here."

"I always know where I'm headed, Kincaid."

"I assume you're referring to a sense of direction, Miss MacKenzie."

"You really have a strong dislike of me, don't you?"

"Does that bother you, Miss MacKenzie?"

"My curiosity more than anything else."

"That killed a cat, lady. Remember?" He strode away.

Wheeling her horse, she rode off. Oh, how the

man infuriated her. And he certainly had the upper hand this time; she had made a fool of herself riding out uninvited. But she was no novice in this battle of the sexes—she would find a way to beat him at his own game.

The next morning the camp had just begun stirring when she left her car, walked over to Dave's, and tapped on the door.

"Come in," he shouted.

Cynthia stepped into the car, then drew back in surprise. Shirtless, barefoot, and wearing only his faded Levi's, Dave stood shaving in front of a mirror hanging on the wall. "Oh, it's you," he grumbled.

Only partially clothed, he appeared even taller, his shoulders broader and more powerful, his hips slimmer. Her blatant stare followed the patch of dark hair on his muscular chest to where it tapered into a narrow trail that disappeared beneath the open waistband of his jeans.

"Good morning, boss." She managed to sound cheerful despite the lump that had suddenly swelled in her throat.

"You've got that right, lady." He dabbed a razor into the basin of water and resumed shaving. "What do you want, Miss MacKenzie?"

"I'm here to make myself useful."

"Such as?"

"I could help you finish dressing."

He stopped shaving long enough to throw her a contemptuous look. "Figured your specialty would be *undressing* a man." He returned to scraping the soap and whiskers off his chin.

"Oh, I have all kinds of talents," she teased. "For instance, I could even finish shaving you. I'm pretty good at that, too. I often shaved Ro— . . . my ex-fiancé."

"Ex-fiancé? What happened; he wise up?"

"No, actually, I did."

"Spare me the details. I've got an empty stomach."

She laughed lightly. "You're not going to get me angry, Kincaid, no matter how much you try. So let's declare a truce."

"I guess I could tolerate one until tomorrow." He toweled the rest of the soap off his face. "A supply train's due in then, and you'll be out of here."

"We'll see about that," she said confidently. Moving to his desk, she sat down in the chair behind it.

"I see you're limping. Sprain an ankle, Miz MacKenzie?" The smugness on his face was infuriating.

"No, I did not sprain an ankle, Mr. Kincaid."

After brushing his teeth, he tossed the water in the basin out the window. "Now that we've reached an agreement, why don't you get out of here so I can finish getting dressed?"

"What's the sense of my getting out? I've already missed the interesting part."

"Lady, you're shameless!" He sat down on the edge of his bunk.

God, he's beautiful! she thought, fascinated by the flow of rippling muscle across his shoulders and down his arms as he pulled on his stockings and boots.

Dave looked up and caught her staring at him. "What?" he asked.

"Nothing," she said nervously. "I, ah . . . after you left yesterday, I went over some of the bills of lading and I may have figured out the reason for some of that rail shortage you're concerned about."

"Sure you did." He tucked his shirttails into his pants, then buckled his belt.

"Hey, Kincaid, I'm very good with figures."

"Yeah, especially when they concern money. I noticed that at the reading of your father's will."

She gave him a wounded glance. "I thought we agreed to a truce."

"So what's your theory about the missing rail?"

Picking up paper and pencil, she began to write figures on the sheet. "Well, there's fifty-two hundred and eighty feet to a running mile, right? And the rails are twenty-six feet long, so it takes four hundred and six rails to a mile of track."

"That's right," he said, walking behind the desk and bending his head down beside hers. The provocative scent of bay rum accompanied his move.

"But you come up two feet short for every mile—"

"That's right. Therefore, every thirteen miles of track we lay takes another two rails—or approximately fourteen rails every hundred miles."

"Oh, so you already thought of that," she said, disappointed.

"Of course," he said, straightening up.

"Well, what about the turnaround?" she asked hopefully.

"Twenty-eight rails on each side, which makes fifty-six altogether. But we dismantle it all when we move on, so that rail is accounted for. Nice try, Miss MacKenzie, but I've gone over all those angles already. Besides, we've laid over two hundred miles of track, and it's only since we've hit this stretch that we started coming up short."

"Then that means either the shipments are being shorted or the rail is coming through shorter than it's supposed to be."

"Yesterday I ordered the new shipment counted. I hadn't thought about skimping on the length of the rail. Seems unlikely though; after all, the rails are cast. It would take different molds and machines to change the length. That would be a pretty costly expense. Besides, we've been getting our rail from the same company for years; they're an honest operation."

He plopped his hat on. "I'm going to breakfast. You coming?"

Her spirits soared at the invitation. She pushed back the chair and stood up. "Yes, I'm coming."

"Have you ever eaten in a dining car before?" Dave asked as they walked to breakfast.

"Of course, many times in Europe and back east."

"I'm not talking about one of those fancy trains. I mean in the dining car that feeds the railroad crew."

"No, I haven't."

"It should be quite an experience for you. I'm sure you'll be able to amuse your friends with vivid descriptions of what it's like."

The moment Cynthia stepped into the car, she understood what he meant. Nailed to the floor was a long table with benches, stretching from one end of the car to the other.

When they entered, Dave grabbed a knife and fork for each of them from a table piled high with the utensils. Then they moved down to several wooden buckets.

"What do you want: bread or corn bread?" he asked.

"Bread."

Dave reached into one of the buckets and extracted two pieces of bread. "Here, hold these," he said, handing her the utensils and the bread. Cynthia managed to juggle them and keep them from falling while he picked up a couple of tin cups and dipped them into another bucket filled with coffee.

"Let's sit over there," he said, nodding toward a couple of empty seats near the end of the table.

Most of the men were already eating. As soon as any of them left, young boys rushed over to swab off the tin plates that were nailed to the tables.

"How efficient," Cynthia remarked drolly, less than thrilled with the crude method of sanitation.

"You got a better way to feed a hundred men a day?"

"Do you have much of a problem with sickness among the men, Kincaid?"

"No, these guys are healthier and more robust than any you'll ever meet."

"That's good to hear," she said, eyeing the plate in front of her. "So where's the bill of fare?"

"Don't need one. Food's the same every morning. Bacon?" he asked, reaching for a nearby wooden bucket. She noticed there were similar ones about every yard along the table.

"Just a slice," she said.

He reached into the bucket and put a piece of bacon on her plate and several on his own. "Fried potatoes?" he asked, reaching for another bucket.

"No, thank you. The bread and bacon are plenty. I have to watch my weight, you know."

"Why bother? Considering those tight pants you're wearing, all these guys will do it for you." He spooned some potatoes onto his plate.

"I noticed they aren't as tight as those you're wearing, Kincaid. Did you say you eat this same breakfast every morning?" she asked, nibbling on the piece of bacon. When he nodded, she quickly said, "What would you say if I fixed you breakfast in my car tomorrow morning?"

"Don't bother. I like eating with the crew."

Just then a couple of men walked by and nodded. "Morning, Cyn. Dave."

Cynthia recognized them from the previous night's craps game. "Good morning, fellas," she greeted pleasantly. "That's *C-Y-N*," she murmured to Dave, "since you're still confused about the spelling."

As soon as he finished eating, Dave stood up. "As

pleasant as this has been, Miss MacKenzie, I have work to do."

He dashed off, leaving her sitting with the other men in the room staring at her. She slowly sipped her coffee until only the young boys who were swabbing the plates clean remained in the room. Then Cynthia got up and headed for the privacy of her own car.

A short time later, after making herself a pitcher of lemonade, Cynthia went out and sat on the observation platform to enjoy it. The blister on her heel was still painful, so she removed her shoe and stocking to allow air to get at it. Since she had failed the day before in finding a bandage at the general store, and since the camp doctor was not due back for several days, Cynthia figured she would either have to walk around barefoot or keep irritating the blister by wearing shoes.

While fretting over the decision, Cynthia became aware that she was being watched by a young girl standing a short distance away. The child looked like a waif: her long blond hair was tangled, one of her stockings had slipped down and bunched at the ankle, and her plain homespun gown was in sad need of laundering.

"Hello," Cynthia called out.

"Ma'am."

"What's your name, honey?"

"Maggie Rafferty." The girl stepped closer, and Cynthia saw that she couldn't be much more than six or seven.

"How do you do, Maggie. I'm Cynthia. Why don't you come up here and join me?"

"Grandpa says I'm not to bother people while he's gone."

"You're not bothering me, Maggie. Besides, I'm lonely. Would you like a glass of lemonade?"

"Never had one, so can't say if I like it or not.

Had some chocolate milk once. That sure was good. You got any of that?"

"No, I'm sorry, Maggie." Funny, Cynthia thought, she hadn't drunk chocolate milk since she was a child, but she remembered how much she had liked it, too.

Maggie came up and sat down on the floor of the platform. "What's wrong with your foot?"

"I've got a blister on my heel. It doesn't seem to want to heal."

"Yep, blisters sure hurt. Had me one on my finger. Grandpa called it a blood blister and popped it with a needle." Her mouth curled into a grimace. "Then it bleeded and went away."

"I'm afraid this one isn't going away so quickly. Let's go inside; I bet I can find some sugar cookies to eat with the lemonade."

As soon as they entered the car Maggie gasped with awe, her blue eyes brimming in amazement. "I ain't never seen anything so beautiful."

"Would you like to see the rest of the car?"

"You mean it?" Maggie asked, thrilled.

"Of course, dear."

Maggie ran her hand across the cushioned sofa. "Is this where you sleep?"

"No, there's a bedroom compartment."

"Boy, you must be the richest person alive to live in this."

"No, not really. This car belonged to my father. He died a few weeks ago."

Maggie continued her inspection of the room, touching the ornate lamps and porcelain figurines on the tables. "My daddy's dead, too."

"I'm sorry to hear that, Maggie. Tell you what, you go into the bathroom and wash your hands, while I get the lemonade and cookies." Cynthia opened the bathroom door for her.

"Wow! This sure is a fancy privy!" Maggie exclaimed. With mouth agape, she stared at the claw-foot bathtub attached to a water heater. "What is this?"

"The bathtub."

Cynthia's heart lurched in her throat as the child looked up, her clear blue eyes round with amazement. "Me and Grandpa just use an old wooden tub."

"Do you and your mother live with your grandfather?"

"No, just me." Maggie picked up a bar of soap. Sniffing it, she grinned. "Sure smells good."

"What happened to your mother, Maggie?"

"She's gone. There's only Grandpa and me. Boy, I bet it's fun to take a bath in that big white tub."

"If you want to take a bath, you may, Maggie."

"You mean it?" Maggie started to kick off her shoes.

"But first the water has to be heated. Let's sit down and you have your cookies and lemonade, then we'll go over to the general store and get you a change of clothing."

"What's wrong with what I got on?" Maggie asked.

"Honey, it doesn't make sense to get all cleaned up underneath, then cover it up with soiled clothing. I'll even let you use some of my perfumed soap."

"You me—"

"Yes, I mean it!" Cynthia laughed, finding the child's enthusiasm infectious.

Cynthia lit the water heater and then joined Maggie at the table. "How did you like the lemonade?" she asked when Maggie had emptied the glass.

"It was very good, Miz Cynthia," Maggie said politely. "But I think I like chocolate milk better."

"You didn't like it, did you?"

Maggie giggled. "No."

"I could tell, you little minx," Cynthia said, tousling the child's hair even more than it already was. "Let's get to the store. The water will be hot by the time we get back."

Forsaking her hard leather boots, Cynthia slipped into the soft kid slippers she'd been wearing the past two days.

Chapter 6

Cynthia had a great time selecting clothing for Maggie. She had hoped to find a fancy gown with ruffles and a big satin sash for the young girl; however, the only dresses available were similar to the one Maggie had on.

"This all go on your grandfather's bill, Maggie?" the storekeeper asked after totaling up the purchases.

"No, I'll pay for them," Cynthia said, adding a brush and comb to the pile.

Bewildered, the woman raised a brow. "Just as you say, Miss MacKenzie."

When they returned Cynthia filled the tub, and soon Maggie was splashing amidst a soapy lather of perfumed bubbles in the warm water.

Cynthia delighted in the young girl's pleasure as much as Maggie did. She shampooed the girl's hair, and when the youngster squealed as Cynthia dumped pitchers of water over her head to rinse out the lather, Cynthia couldn't help smiling, reminded of the many times she and her sisters had done the same thing to one another when they were younger.

Later, after Maggie was dressed in her new clothing, Cynthia brushed out the girl's long hair and tied it back with a ribbon. Taking Maggie by the hand, she led her over to a cheval glass mirror.

"There, my little beauty, see for yourself. Aren't you the pretty one!"

Maggie beamed at her image. "Wait until Grandpa sees me. He's really gonna be surprised."

"You love your grandfather very much, don't you, honey?"

"Oh, yes," Maggie enthused. "I love him more than anyone in the whole world."

"Won't he be upset that you weren't in school today?"

"I don't have to go to school."

"You don't!" Cynthia exclaimed. "How old are you, Maggie?"

"Seven."

"I would think that's old enough."

"The school's too crowded, so only the boys have to go to school."

Cynthia was shocked. "You mean not any of the girls in camp attend school?"

"Miz O'Leary says only the boys can go."

"Is Miss O'Leary the teacher, Maggie?"

"Yeah, and she says she's got her hands full with just them."

"I think that's terribly unfair to the girls."

"Oh, I don't care 'bout school anyway. Grandpa says I'm a smart little girl even without proper schoolin'."

"Can you read and write, Maggie?"

"Grandpa tries to teach me when he has the time, but that ain't often."

Stroking the young girl's head, Cynthia smiled sadly. "Your grandpa was right, honey; you're a real smart little girl. Now, let's get your dirty clothes washed before the water cools off too much."

They washed Maggie's clothes in the bathwater before emptying the tub, then Maggie hurried back to her tent to hang them out to dry.

Cynthia had a serious issue to take up with Dave Kincaid—that of the girls not going to school. She hurried over to his office, tapped on the door, and entered without waiting to be invited. The car was empty and the curtains to his sleeping quarters were open. She was about to leave when she noticed a framed picture on the nightstand next to his bunk. She was certain it hadn't been there earlier and must have arrived with the mail that came in with the supply train.

Curious, Cynthia walked over and picked it up. The young woman in the photograph was lovely. Cynthia felt a surge of envy. The woman must mean a lot to Dave, for him to set her picture by his bedside.

"What the hell are you doing snooping in my quarters?"

At the sharp allegation, Cynthia almost dropped the picture. Dave Kincaid strode over and snatched the frame from her hands.

"I wasn't snooping, Dave," she denied. "I was curious. She's very lovely. Who is she?"

"If I thought it was any of your business, I'd tell you." He set the frame back on the bed stand. "Now I'd appreciate your getting the hell out of here." He pulled the curtains shut, then sat down behind his desk.

"There's something I wish to discuss with you."

"I'm not interested unless it directly concerns the railroad, Miss MacKenzie. Furthermore, my mind's made up: you're on the next train back to Denver, and I'm too busy to listen to any more reasons why you think you should remain." He picked up a sheaf of papers and began looking through them.

"I understand the girls in this camp are not permitted to attend school."

He glanced up momentarily. "That's right." Then he returned to perusing the papers in his hand.

"Isn't the company paying for the services of a teacher?"

"That's right." This time he didn't bother to look up.

"When my father provided for the children's education, I'm sure he didn't intend for the girls to be excluded from the classroom. Were you the one who made that decision?"

Exasperated, he put down the papers. "No, I was not, Miss MacKenzie. There were too many children for Miss O'Leary to handle, so the crew decided it was more important that the boys get educated. As it is, the school is still overcrowded."

"By 'crew,' you are referring to the men in this camp, no doubt."

"No, Miss MacKenzie, the crew of the Union Pacific," he said sarcastically.

"I can't believe my father would sanction such a decision. Especially since he had three daughters of his own."

"I never discussed it with the Chief."

"Well, if this Miss O'Leary couldn't handle the number of children by herself, the logical thing to do would have been to hire an additional teacher."

He stood up. "Look, lady, I've got my hands full as it is, trying to get a railroad built. I don't have time to be a social director. If a man brings his family along on the job, he has to be prepared to make some sacrifices."

"It doesn't sound like *he* is making the sacrifice at all—his daughter is the one being denied an education. Good Lord, Kincaid, this is 1879—not the Dark Ages."

Dave Kincaid leaned over the desk, his dark eyes glaring. "My problem is to build a railroad."

"I still don't like this at all, and I intend to do something about it."

"This is none of your concern. My advice—"

"I'm not interested in taking your advice, Kincaid, any more than you do mine."

She spun on her heel and slammed out the door. Departing thusly was beginning to become a habit, Cynthia realized—and it rather spoiled the dramatic effect by having to limp away when she did.

As soon as the last boy left the railroad car that served as a schoolroom, Cynthia went in to speak to Lydia O'Leary. From the number of boys she had seen leaping out of the boxcar, Cynthia could tell the teacher had not exaggerated the abundance of students. Nevertheless, there had to be some kind of solution; denying the girls an education was unacceptable to her.

The schoolroom smelled of chalk, paste, and stale air. Seven rows of six desks each practically filled the boxcar, and maps and blackboards were nailed to the walls.

Seeing a woman seated behind a small desk at the far end of the car, Cynthia walked over to her.

"Miss O'Leary?"

The woman looked up. Obviously surprised to see Cynthia, she rose hastily. "Oh, you must be Miss MacKenzie. I heard you were here. I'm so glad you stopped by."

The spinster was easily in her late thirties, if not her forties, with plain features that bordered on homeliness: a long angular face, a pointed nose, and blue eyes as lusterless as the brown hair pinned in a bun at the nape of her neck. A sweet, shy smile softened the lines of her face, but Cynthia doubted that facing a room full of boys every day in the stuffy room gave the teacher much cause for smiling.

The gray dress she was wearing, with a high collar that buttoned under her chin, did nothing to enhance her looks; instead, it made her complexion look sallow.

"Miss O'Leary, I want to speak to you about the education of the crew's children. I was very disturbed to hear that all the girls are banished from the schoolroom."

"Yes, tragic, isn't it?" Lydia O'Leary said. "But as you can see, Miss MacKenzie, there is no room for any more students."

"Surely, Miss O'Leary, you don't believe that it's not necessary for girls to get an education."

"Of course not. Heavens, I'm a teacher. It's as disturbing to me as it is to you, Miss MacKenzie, but the parents of the children feel an education is more critical to the boys since they must become the wage earners."

"Whereas a girl *merely* has to get married, stay home, and have their babies," Cynthia said, disgusted.

"Which cannot be said for all of us."

"I would guess not."

"I can assure you, were it humanly possible, I would include the girls in my classroom."

In the face of the teacher's pleasantness, Cynthia lost any zeal to take the teacher to task for the abominable situation. It was a miracle to Cynthia that the poor woman managed to handle the number of students she did each day. Hiring an additional teacher was the only intelligent approach.

"I'm sure you would, Lydia. I hope you aren't offended by my informality."

"Not at all, Miss—"

"Cynthia. Please call me Cynthia, Lydia."

Lydia smiled, and once again Cynthia saw the pleasing effect the smile brought to the teacher's face.

"Well, I intend to do whatever I can to bring in an additional teacher. From what I've observed, there must be at least seventy-five children in this camp."

"We think of this as a town, Cynthia—Tent Town."

"Really." Cynthia laughed lightly. "I suppose that makes Dave Kincaid the mayor of Tent Town."

"No, I think he's more like the town's sheriff. Sean Rafferty is the people's chosen leader."

"Lydia, I'm so glad we had this talk, and I'm going to do everything I can to get you some help. I know we'll be great friends, so please come and visit me whenever you're lonely."

Because like it or not, Dave Kincaid, I'm not going anywhere tomorrow, Cynthia thought as she returned to her car.

Having survived the experience of eating breakfast with the crew, Cynthia decided against tempting the gods again, settling instead for cheese, an orange, and a glass of wine for lunch. Then she sat down and worked out the costs of hiring an additional schoolteacher. By the time she finished and walked over to discuss it with Dave, evening had descended and the camp had begun to settle down for the night.

He was seated behind his desk when she rapped on the door and entered.

"What is it this time, Miss MacKenzie?" he asked with a long-suffering glance.

"I worked up some figures on the cost of hiring an additional teacher. As long as the Rocky Mountain Central intends to pursue the construction of this railroad, I think it's imperative for the children's sake that we hire an additional teacher."

"You do," he said, not even looking up at her.

"Dammit, Kincaid, the children are important. You could show some interest."

He put down the pencil he was using and leaned back. "Okay, let me see it."

As Cynthia waited for him to read the figures, she couldn't help noticing how especially virile he looked that evening. His shirtsleeves were rolled up to the elbows of his tanned, muscular arms, his chin was shadowed with a dark stubble of whiskers, and his hair was rumpled enough to make her yearn to go over and run her fingers through its thickness. When he finished, he handed the sheet back to her.

"Well, what do you think?" she asked anxiously when he resumed his paperwork.

"Very impressive; you're right on the mark. Hope you didn't spend too much of your valuable time working up those figures, though, because I could have told you what a teacher costs us a year."

"Then we both agree that the cost is a minor expense for the value received from it."

"No question about it."

"Does that mean you're willing to hire another teacher?"

He tossed aside the pencil and leaned back again. "Miss MacKenzie, *hiring* another teacher was never an issue—finding one willing to travel along with a railroad under construction *is*. It's not a pleasant existence. Miss O'Leary is very unique because she is willing to endure the inconvenience. However, most teachers prefer to settle down in a town or city."

"Did you try finding one in Denver?"

"Yes, we did," he said, folding his arms across his chest and looking smug.

"Did you advertise for one in the eastern newspapers?"

"Certainly. That's how we got Miss O'Leary."

"What about the California papers?"

"We did."

"Dallas? New Orleans? St. Louis?"

"Miss MacKenzie, if you'll excuse me, I have work to do."

"Does this mean you do not intend to pursue hiring another teacher?"

"Did you miss the point? I already pursued it—to no avail."

"Do you have an objection if I pursue it?"

He looked up at her. "Miss MacKenzie, once you return to Denver, I don't much care who or what you *pursue*." His tone and cold-eyed stare left no doubt of his meaning.

"Why, Kincaid?" she demanded, exasperated by his imperiousness. "Why the attitude? I'm concerned about the welfare of the girls in this camp . . . ah, town. Why do you find fault with that?"

He exploded, tossing down his pencil and bolting to his feet. Before she could react, he was around the desk and grasping her by the shoulders.

"It's a pity you couldn't have bestowed some of this compassion and concern you feel for others on your own father while he lay sick and dying."

Her shock yielded to fury. "So we're back to that, are we? No matter what I say or do, you won't believe me."

"Not for a minute, lady. Any scheme you've got floating around in that head of yours is to benefit you and nobody else. You'll stoop to anything to serve your own purpose—including selling out your father's dream. Thank God your sisters aren't that mercenary. Well, since I'm not swallowing your act, Miz Sin, get the hell out of here."

"I will, if you release me," she declared.

For several seconds they stood glaring at each other, his head bent over hers, their mouths so close that her heart was hammering and her breath was coming in breathless gasps. She had no idea what might have followed, because he dropped his hands from her shoulders and walked over to open the door in answer to a persistent rapping.

"Come on in, Sean."

The railroad foreman entered, glancing at Cynthia. "'Tis sorry I am for disturbin' ya at this late hour."

"You aren't. Miss MacKenzie is just leaving."

"Wud ya be waitin' up, mum?" Turning to Dave, Rafferty said, "I'd be grateful, lad, if yud be givin' me an advance on me wages."

"Of course, Sean. How much do you need?"

"Seven dollars and twenty-two cents."

Recognizing the figure at once, Cynthia tensed against the wave of apprehension that swept through her.

Dave went to a corner safe and returned with the money. As soon as he gave it to Sean, the foreman handed it to Cynthia.

"I don't want your money, Sean," she said, trying to return it to him.

"It's thankin' ya I am fer yur kindness, mum, but I'll not be takin' charity," he said firmly.

"What the hell's going on here?" Dave asked, his expression grim.

"It wasn't charity, Sean. I wanted to do something for Maggie—she's so sweet and adorable."

"Aye, that she is; ye're nae tellin' me nothin' I don't know, mum. The child's me heart and soul. But I take care of me own, so yer nae to be doin' it again."

He nodded to Dave and departed.

"What did you do now, Miss MacKenzie?"

Staring numbly at the money in her palm, Cynthia managed to relate the incidents of her afternoon spent with Maggie.

Dave was disturbed when she finished. "Dammit, you had no right to interfere in the lives of these people."

"I just wanted to bring some pleasure into a little girl's life. What's wrong in buying her a few pieces of cheap clothing?"

"Sean Rafferty is a proud man; you've embarrassed him."

"That was not my intention."

"Intention or not, that's what happened," he lashed out. "Dammit, stop meddling in people's lives."

"Meddling! How can you accuse me of meddling? You're as narrow-minded as he, if you can't see my motive behind it."

"And you're just as guilty if you can't see how you've insulted his pride. He sees your actions as an indication that he can't take proper care of his granddaughter."

"Oh, for heaven's sake, that's childish. But as long as you've mentioned it, Maggie *did* look neglected; she was untidy and her clothes were worn. If this Sean Rafferty is as great as you claim, why does he leave a seven-year-old on her own all day, knowing he's one of the people responsible for her not even being admitted into a schoolroom?"

For the first time since the discussion began, Dave did not raise his voice. Calm and sincere, he spoke from the heart. "Sean Rafferty is a fine and decent man; his word is his bond. He's worked for the Rocky Mountain Central from the time your father formed the company. Don't besmirch his character just because he approaches life with a different attitude than yours."

"I'm not trying to."

"Furthermore, his life hasn't been easy: he lost two infant sons to influenza, a wife in an Indian attack, and shortly after his daughter-in-law ran off with a whiskey drummer, Sean witnessed his son being blown to smithereens while we were blasting a passage through the mountains. Now he's the only one left to raise his granddaughter, and Maggie is the dearest thing in his life. Any child loved that much is not neglected just because of a worn dress and dirty face."

"You plead a good case, counselor. You've missed your calling: you should have been a lawyer."

He flashed a rare grin. "I'm happy with what I'm doing."

"Well, despite what you've said, I still think it's wrong for a seven-year-old to be on her own all day."

"These people look after one another. If you understood them, you'd know that. And if you want to get along with them, don't interfere in their lives."

She looked at him, her indignation drained. "I never meant to interfere. Whether you believe it or not, I only intended to bring some pleasure to a little girl. I think I did that."

"Maybe you did, but a mixture of the wrong ingredients can cause good intentions to backfire, Cynthia."

As she lay in bed that night, Cynthia sifted through the events and conversations of the day. It suddenly occurred to her that somewhere in one of those conversations Dave Kincaid had addressed her by her given name: not a *Miss MacKenzie* said in sarcasm, *lady* muttered in anger, or *Miz Sin* spoken in contempt—David Kincaid had called her *Cynthia*.

The man had begun to mellow. Cynthia stretched and smiled. She was beginning to break him down.

Chapter 7

The next morning when she awoke, Cynthia lay for a while pondering the mysteries of mankind. There were times in one's life, she reflected, when one felt warm and serene; when the mind wasn't cluttered with anger, guilt, or regret; and the heart was full of charity toward one's fellow man—usually attributable to self-satisfaction; and at such times one could often have a moment of unadulterated inspiration. Cynthia knew she was experiencing such a phenomenon. Sitting up, she exclaimed, "I'll do it!"

She leaped out of bed. Why hadn't she thought of it immediately? After dressing, making certain to wear her plainest gown and not the Levi's that annoyed Dave so, Cynthia sat down and penned a letter to Elizabeth, enclosing a well-thought-out list. Then she wrote several notices and hurried outside to nail them to the trees in Tent Town.

Returning to her car, she pinned up her hair in its most becoming fashion, then sat down and waited. The wait wasn't long.

"Come in," she called out sweetly in reply to the pounding on the door. Dave Kincaid came through the door looking primed for bear. "Good morning, Dave."

"What's this all about?" he demanded, waving one of the notices she had written.

"It says there's a school for girls starting today. Would you like a cup of coffee?"

"Funny, that's what I thought it says too," Dave said. "Now who do you suppose would post such a notice, Miss MacKenzie? Surely it wouldn't be someone who's going to be putting her little butt on a train and heading out of here today."

"Coffee?" she repeated calmly.

"No, I don't want any damn coffee. I want an explanation for these notices you posted all over town."

"I thought I made it clear to you that I intend to see a school established for the young girls. Matter of fact, you gave me your approval to pursue it."

"To pursue hiring a teacher."

"That's exactly what I did—and for much less than we anticipated. Would you like that cup of coffee now?"

"Oh," he said, suddenly cooled by abashment, "so you found a teacher. That surprises me; I had already checked among the married women before I even hired Miss O'Leary."

"It's not one of the married women." She got up and walked into the kitchen. Dave followed her.

"Who is it then?"

"Me."

"What!" he bellowed. "Not a prayer, lady! You're out of here today." He spun on his heel to leave, but she grabbed his arm.

"I'm staying whether you like it or not. This camp needs a teacher, and I'm remaining until you replace me with one."

He glowered with anger. "Or until the novelty wears off. There's no limit to the lengths you'll go to get what you want, is there? And you don't much care whom you trample in the process: your father, probably that poor sucker you were engaged to in Europe, now even these innocent children here."

"I'm not thinking about myself. I care about these little girls."

"Sure you do," he scoffed. "And as soon as you get bored with the game, you'll take off and to hell with 'these little girls.' "

"That's not true, Dave. I want to help them."

"Like you helped Maggie Rafferty yesterday—interfering in their lives by teasing them with a side of life most of them will never experience. You aren't fooling me for a minute, Miz Sin. We both know what you want—that you came down here for *this*. Maybe I should have done it sooner to get rid of you."

She was caught by surprise when he pulled her roughly to him, his mouth covering hers possessively in a hard kiss. Whimpering under the assault of his punishing mouth and probing tongue, she twisted in his arms, struggling to get free. The opportunity came when he slid his hand down, securing it against her spine to press her tighter against him. She wedged her released arm between them and shoved him away enough to free her mouth.

"Let me go," she cried out breathlessly.

His hold on her only tightened, and she leaned back, trying to avoid the kisses he trailed to her ear.

"This is what you've been waiting for, isn't it?"

His hot breath at her ear tantalized her senses. "No, not like this." Despite her fear, his hand felt warm and provocative as he slid it up the column of her back and firmly cupped the nape of her neck.

Panic pounded at her temples when his mouth closed over hers again in forceful domination. Her knees weakened, along with her resistance. She felt her passion rising as his own grew stronger, his body aggressively pressing her against the wall.

Groping for her skirt, he began to pull it up. "You

want it here, Miz Sin, or on the floor?"

The vulgar innuendo was worse than a slap in the face, and the heat of her passion froze at his cold contempt. She turned her head aside. "Let me go, Kincaid."

He released her and stepped back. "Don't try to pretend this isn't what you've been waiting for."

"I don't have to pretend. Despite what you think, Kincaid, I am not a whore, and I don't appreciate being treated like one. Don't ever touch me again unless I invite you to."

"You have my assurance of that, lady." He walked to the door, then paused and turned to her, his expression scornful. "You're still not fooling me. We both know what you came here for, so why the phony act? You liked it."

"Apparently not as much as you did, Mr. Kincad. The next time you kiss me, it will be on my terms, not yours."

"What makes you think there'll be a next time?"

She smiled, then replied just as mockingly, "Now who's trying to fool whom?"

Shirtless, his arms and chest coated with perspiration, Dave drove the long spike into the rail. It felt good to be working with his hands again, and the hard labor helped to work off some of his tension.

Concentration came hard for him; no matter what he did, his thoughts slipped back to the morning's encounter with Cynthia. God, he really had lost it! Sure he was angry at her for interfering in these people's lives, but he hadn't meant to go as far as he did. He'd intended only to give her back some of what she was pulling on him—play the same game. After all, his eyes were open; he knew he was just her latest diversion to keep from being bored. Once she got him where she wanted him, she'd move on to some other poor fool. Chase and conquer was her game. But why in hell had she chosen him? He had his hands full trying to finish the railroad, without becoming a plaything for a spoiled rich girl out for a good time. And as sure as God made little apples, the seductive little tease would have her way. He wanted her all right. At the moment, he felt hornier than hell, and Lord only knew how much longer he could hold out. He had to ship her back to Denver, or she'd have him right where she wanted him.

He walked over to the water barrel and dumped a ladle of water over his head, allowing the cooling liquid to slide down his face and onto his shoulders and chest. Then he grinned, wishing he could dump some down his pants as well.

Knowing the paperwork waiting to be done, he plopped his hat back on his head, grabbed his shirt, and headed back to Tent Town.

As he neared the outskirts, he saw Cynthia in the trees a short distance away, a small circle of girls clustered around her. Dave dismounted, leaned a shoulder against a tree, and folded his arms across his chest. She had changed her clothes; her hips and long, slim legs were outlined in those damn tight Levi's again. He felt the draw at his loins.

"Hi."

Dave straightened up, looking around for the speaker.

"I'm up here, Uncle Dave."

Dave glanced up and saw Maggie Rafferty sitting on a limb high in the tree. "Maggie, what are you doing up there? You could hurt yourself."

"I'm just lookin' around."

"I thought school was starting today. You skipping school already, Maggie?"

"No, Uncle Dave. Miz Cynthia said 'til she gets the supplies she needs, we'll be doin' outside lessons."

"So why aren't you over there with her and the other girls?"

" 'Cause I'm testin' my wings."

"Well, I guess a tree's the best place to do that, but if you try to fly, you might be in for a big surprise." He chuckled. "Now, what's the real reason you're not with the others, honey? It's not like you to fib."

"I'm not fibbin', Uncle Dave. I'm testin' my wings. Miz Cynthia told us to climb a tree. Then she said to pretend we're a bird and try to see the earth as a bird does flyin' above it. 'Ceptin' a bird can see farther if it's a mind to."

"But you don't have wings, Maggie. If you climb too high, you might fall and hurt yourself."

"Oh, Uncle Dave, I know I can't really fly. Miz Cynthia said it's just a an— . . . ah, an—"

"Analogy."

"Yeah, that's it. She said that's how we learn our limitations while 'spandin' our horyzons."

"I think you mean expanding your horizons, honey," Dave corrected.

"Yeah. You knowed 'bout that too, huh? She said we ain't to climb no higher than we're ready to, 'cause the 'portant thing in testin' our wings is not how far we fly but knowin' that we're free to fly. But if we climb too high, then we'll get scared, and if we're scared, then we ain't thinkin' of nothin' 'cept how to get back down. And if we ain't gonna pay no mind to what we see, there ain't no purpose to climbin' the tree to test our wings."

Dave grasped Cynthia's philosophy, but he couldn't believe the young girls did. "So how's your flight, little bird? What can you see up there?"

"Well, I saw you comin'. And way up the track I kin see the supply train headin' this way, puffin' black smoke in the air. When I look down the track I kin see the dust risin' from where the crew's workin'.

I kin see the bridge they're buildin' and the river that's flowin' under it. And I kin see how the land—all pretty and peaceful like—just seems to go on and on like there's no end to it." Her little face creased in a serious frown of concentration. "And you know somein', Uncle Dave?"

"What's that, honey?"

"Afore I climbed this tree, all I cud see was Tent Town."

As he thought about Maggie's words, he stared at the jeans-clad figure in the distance. One of the girls climbed down from a tree and ran to her. He watched as Cynthia hugged her, then walked over to another tree, reached up, and swung Catherine Mary Dennehy to the ground. Funny, why did he know she'd be smiling down at the youngster? he thought with a whimsical smile.

Shoving the thought aside, he said to Maggie, "I've got to go, honey. Sure you don't need any help getting down?"

" 'Course not, Uncle Dave. I know my limi . . . tations," she said proudly.

He cast a quick glance again at the slim figure standing in the circle of the little girls. "I wish I knew mine," he murmured, and swung himself into the saddle.

While waiting for her supplies to arrive, Cynthia had no choice but to continue her school sessions in the outdoors. Sitting in a shady copse, she had been reading to them for about forty-five minutes when one of the listening girls interrupted with a question about the story.

"Miz Cynthia, why'd the women have to leave just 'cause the men were gonna light up cigars?"

"Yeah, me and my mama don't leave when my papa smokes a cigar," nine-year-old Shannon O'Neill said.

"Well, dear, it's usually done in respect to the ladies. The smell of a cigar and the heavy smoke can be very offensive to some women."

"Well, if them men mean to be so respectful, why don't they go somewhere else to smoke? Why do the women have to go?" The challenging remark came from Peggy Callahan. Her twin sister Polly, sitting beside her, nodded in agreement.

"My mama says she likes the smell of my papa's cigars," Katie McGuire said softly. The eight-year-old little redhead had a freckled face that always wore a smile, which now broadened into a wide grin. "One time Mama even helped Papa smoke one." The revelation caused a wave of murmurs and giggles among the girls.

"Did your mother say she liked it?" Cynthia closed the book, recognizing that the girls' minds had shifted to a new topic.

"I think so," Katie said. "Mama and Papa laughed real much, so I laughed too."

"Miz Cynthia, why can't women smoke cigars or chew tobacco same as men do?" Maggie Rafferty asked.

"My dear, as you grow older you will discover there are many things in society that are frowned upon as improper conduct for a woman—smoking cigars and chewing tobacco among them."

"Don't see why women can't do it," Maggie said. "'Pears like it ain't hard. Don't have to be strong or big like a man, 'cause all you do is sit there and spit out the juice or blow out smoke."

"Yeah, that's what I say," Katie said, her classmates nodding in agreement. "I bet I could smoke a cigar."

Catherine Mary Dennehy scrunched up her nose. The five-year-old was the youngest girl in the class. "I couldn't. They're too stinky. And Papa's breath always smells stinky after he does. I don't want mine to smell stinky like that."

"Catherine Mary has made a very good point, ladies," Cynthia said. "There's a very unbecoming odor that lingers afterwards."

"Well, there'd be never no mind to it if everybody was doin' it," Maggie said. "A pig don't stink to another pig, does it?"

"Yeah, but it does to us," Peggy said.

"That's 'cause we ain't pigs," Maggie declared. "Bet we stink to them, too."

"Each species has its own scent, ladies. Some animals with strong smelling abilities, like dogs, can track another animal or human by following a scent."

Catherine Mary stroked the head of the large mongrel dog sleeping stretched across her lap. "Snoozer can sniff out anything. Mama says a varmint don't dare come near our tent without Snoozer sniffin' him out."

"Well, I don't care how I'd smell," Katie declared. "I still think I could smoke a cigar just like my papa does. I think women oughta smoke cigars just like men do."

Delighted with the young girls' exchange of opinions and viewpoints, and seeing the girls nodding in response to Katie's declaration, Cynthia made a decision.

"Then that is what you should do. The greatest way to satisfy your doubts is through experience. Would you like to try it?"

"Yes! Yes!" came the chorus of replies.

Cynthia hadn't spoken to him since their quarrel a couple of days before. In truth, she appeared to be deliberately avoiding him—a fact which bothered Dave, for some perplexing reason.

He'd see her moving around the camp, looking

like the Pied Piper, her devoted flock of a dozen girls trooping behind her. Yesterday he'd noticed that three dogs had also joined the parade. But at night, she disappeared behind the door of her private car and did not come out until the following morning.

Whether he liked it or not, Dave knew he would have to seek her out if she didn't approach him soon. Cynthia MacKenzie was not one to be left unconstrained for any length of time—without it leading to trouble.

He straightened up with interest when he saw the subject of his musings heading for the general store, followed by her entourage. The children and dogs waited in an orderly fashion outside the store while Cynthia went inside. Within minutes she reappeared carrying a small bundle, and the children crowded around her excitedly to observe the purchase.

What in hell is she up to now? he wondered. At least she didn't have them up in trees today. As soon as they were out of sight, his curiosity prevailed and he strode over to the general store.

After a minute or two of glancing at the shelves, he grabbed a cigar and plunked down five cents.

"You oughta hold off with this cheap cigar, Dave," the shopkeeper said, leering over the top of her glasses. "Miz MacKenzie was just in here and bought a whole box of 'em dollar Cuban ones. Figured she'd be sure to be offerin' you one next time you pay her a visit."

"I don't *visit* with Miss MacKenzie, Mrs. Collins, so I'll buy my own cigars."

"She bought a plug of tobacco, too. Must have found herself a boyfriend. Sure wonder who it can be."

"I don't chew tobacco either, Mrs. Collins, so I can't tell you."

Dave grabbed the cigar and strode back to his office. No wonder he hadn't seen her for the last couple of nights—she was entertaining some fellow behind the closed doors of that fancy car of hers. Well, that was that poor sucker's problem, not his. At least she was out of his hair. He tossed the cigar onto his desk and left, heading for end of track.

Only a few miles now separated the track and the trestle, and the trestle was completed except for the reinforcement of the center span. Once they laid track across the bridge, they'd have crossed the Canadian River and be pointed toward Texas. In a couple of days, they could move Tent Town to the other side of the river.

Things were going better than he expected, and he could only hope they'd remain that way. The thought of trouble immediately brought the image of Cynthia to mind again. Who was she entertaining at night? Dammit, it better not be one of the married men. That would stir up a hornets' nest among the crew—like the one he already had inside of him.

He prodded his horse to a gallop when he saw a cloud of smoke rising from the area where Cynthia had been holding her school sessions. Racing to the spot, he reined up in shock at the horrifying sight he beheld.

Doubled over, moaning, most of the girls lay strewn on the ground, their little faces mottled or so pale they looked ghostly. Cynthia was walking calmly among them, offering sympathy, comfort, and collecting the cigars from the few who still sat in a cloud of smoke.

"What the—?" he asked, shocked and speechless.

"The girls decided they wanted to experiment with tobacco," she said. "Oops, careful there."

Her warning came too late. He slipped on a wad of regurgitated chewing tobacco and for several seconds struggled to stay afoot before he finally caught his balance. Enraged and appalled, he stared at her.

"Good God, woman, have you no conscience! How could you do this? They're just children."

"Do you think for a moment I'd have let anyone get seriously ill? They're sick from watching each other get sick. It was a chain reaction from the time Maggie swallowed her chewing tobacco and threw up."

"Maggie! Where is she?"

"Over there by the tree."

"You better hope that child's okay. Sean Rafferty is very protective of his granddaughter."

"So I've been told," she said, unperturbed. She bent down and extinguished the last cigar.

Dave rushed over to where Maggie lay doubled over. "Honey, are you feeling better?"

"Hi, Uncle Dave," Maggie said pitifully.

"Is there anything I can do for you? You look a little green around the gills, honey."

"I'm beginning to feel better." She sat up, and he was relieved to see color returning to her face and a familiar warmth to her blue eyes. "But I'll not be tryin' to chew tobacco again, Uncle Dave. *It tastes terrible!*"

"Good for you, Maggie."

"Same for me," Katie McGuire said. "Sure don't know why my papa likes cigars."

"I told you they was stinky," Catherine Mary spoke up.

Dave looked up at Cynthia, horrified. "Not the little one, too?"

"I didn't smoke a cigar, Mr. Kincaid," the child said. "I was too smart."

"Looks like you're the only one in the crowd who was, Catherine Mary." He tousled her dark hair and stood up.

"I think we're all smarter now, Mr. Kincaid," Peggy Callahan said to him.

"Yeah," her sister, Polly, agreed. "The dumb boys can smoke 'em. I never want to again. If we do *everything* that they do, we'll be as dumb as they are."

"Exactly," Cynthia said smugly.

Her self-satisfied grin rankled as she handed him the remaining plug of tobacco. "Chaw, Kincaid?"

Chapter 8

Bright and early the next morning, Sean Rafferty was at Dave's door. "Gotta talk to you, Dave."

"Hope we still aren't coming up short on the rail."

"Naw, ain't got nothin' to do with the rail. It's 'bout that Miz MacKenzie. Folks ain't likin' what she's doin' with our girls. The womenfolk are threatenin' not to send the gals back to her."

"Sean, I know what happened yesterday and I don't approve of it either, but I think I understand why she did it."

"Then you best be explainin' it to me," Sean thundered, " 'cause I sure as hell don't."

"How old were you, Sean, when you tried your first chaw of tobacco?"

Shrugging, Sean said, "Reckon 'bout six or—"

"Seven. Same as Maggie. So she was just as curious as you were, wasn't she?"

"Yeah, but Maggie's a girl. That's a lot different."

"Why?"

"Dammit, you know why, Dave, same as I do. It ain't proper for a gal to be spittin' tobacco or chompin' on a cigar. That teacher had no call to be puttin' them kind of ideas into them young gals' heads."

"I don't think that was her purpose. Just the opposite, Sean. By letting them test their curiosity, she showed the girls how to make the decision for themselves. It's no longer necessary to forbid them—they *choose* not to."

"Yeah, but who knows what ideas she'll put in their heads next? She'll have 'em demandin' that the men don't use tobacco either—and a chaw or lightin' up a cigar is comfortin' to a man."

"But not to every man. He is able to make that choice for himself—a woman never could. Despite a few unpleasant moments for the girls, Miss MacKenzie let them find out for themselves that it's not necessary to do everything a boy does."

"Makes sense, I guess," Sean said, relenting. "I'll see what I can do 'bout settlin' the men down. The only one that saw the humor to it was Tim McGuire. Said he was sorry to have missed it."

"Thanks, Sean. I appreciate your help." Dave grabbed the cigar from the top of his desk. Slapping the foreman on the shoulder, he handed Sean the cigar. "Here, how about a smoke?"

"Thanks. Think I'll *choose* to have it later," the foreman said, with his wide Irish grin.

As he watched Sean walk back to join the crew, Dave exhaled a deep breath. That probably ended the cigar incident. If he was going to allow Cynthia to remain—and it looked like the matter was out of his hands now that she'd started her damn school—they would have to sit down and have a long talk. Grudgingly, he could see she was a good teacher, and it was obvious the girls adored her; but it appeared that some of her methods and ideas were just too unconventional for these simple folks to accept. If he was going to maintain a modicum of peace in the camp, he and Cynthia MacKenzie would have to reach an understanding on that subject.

* * *

Later that day, the supply train arrived with more rails and ties, along with the items Cynthia had ordered. As Dave checked in the delivery, he was amazed that Elizabeth had been able to assemble it all so quickly. There was even a tent among the dozen large crates that had been shipped.

Dave wasted no time seeing that the tent was erected, choosing a vacant area near Cynthia's private car. As he carried a large carton marked "Racquets and Shuttlecocks" into the tent, he put it down, pausing to speak to Cynthia.

"You have more supplies here than Miss O'Leary does."

"Yes, isn't Beth amazing?" Cynthia replied with a beaming smile.

"Just what do you need racquets and shuttlecocks for?"

"I intend to teach the girls how to play badminton. A young lady must have a well-rounded education."

"I hope this badminton is more fitting for a young lady than climbing trees or chewing tobacco, Miss MacKenzie."

"Oh, the girls will love it. Haven't you ever played badminton, Dave?"

"Can't say I have."

"I was introduced to the game in Gloucestershire when I visited Badminton Hall—that's the ducal residence of the Beauforts. Dear Henry, he's the eighth duke of Beaufort; invented the game, you know."

"Heaven forgive me, but I didn't know that about dear Henry."

"Hence the game is called badminton."

"Who would have made the connection?"

"Well, surely you must have heard of the Badminton Hunt. Henry's father established it."

"No doubt the seventh duke of Beaufort."

"That's right. Scoff if you will, Kincaid, but the Badminton Hunt is world famous."

"Let me guess—you ride to the hounds in pursuit of shuttlecocks."

Cynthia grinned. "You know, Kincaid, I bet you aren't as serious and stodgy as you'd like people to believe. From time to time, a hint of humor slips out from under that grave manner of yours. I think if you'd let yourself, you could enjoy life much more."

"I'm happy just the way I am, Miss MacKenzie. Now that you have the classroom you wanted, I think the girls have *tested their wings* enough for a while. I expect you to concentrate on teaching them the ABC's."

"I intend to do just that, Mr. Kincaid, as soon as we get these supplies unpacked." She laid a thick art book down on her makeshift desk. "There's so much for them to learn."

As he departed, he glanced back at her. Cynthia and her twelve assistants and three sniffing dogs were delving into the contents of several of the cartons. Despite her quick capitulation to his demand, Dave was suspicious as to just what she'd meant by her last sentence.

He devoted the next few hours to checking inventory sheets and calculating the next week's supplies, and managed to hurry out and give O'Hara the list before he headed back. As Dave watched the train pull out, he realized there had been no further talk about Cynthia's returning to Denver. The clever little minx had dug in, and there wasn't too much he could do about it for the present.

With the trestle across the Canadian near completion, Dave spent the next two days across the river rechecking surveyor markings as the graders prepared the railroad bed for laying track. Within fifteen minutes of his return to Tent Town, he saw an angry mob of women approaching his quarters, their hands moving as furiously as their mouths. From what he could see, the only thing missing was someone carrying a noose to string him up with.

What in hell did that woman do now!

Dreading the ordeal ahead, he stepped outside to confront them.

"Please, one at a time," he shouted when they all began yelling. "Mrs. Dennehy, why don't you explain exactly what this is all about."

"Why, 'tis the things that woman is teachin' our children, Mr. Kincaid."

"I've ne'r seen the likes of it," Mary Callahan declared, folding her arms across her large bosom.

"It's shameful, it is," Margaret O'Neill said, adding her objection to the others'. "Showing my Shannon a book with pictures of naked men."

"What?" he exclaimed. Whatever he thought of Cynthia, he couldn't visualize her showing pornography to the girls.

Mary Callahan snorted derisively. "Called it art, she did."

"Oh, now I understand. There are many famous and priceless works of art that involve nudity, ladies."

"Well, she's fillin' their heads with highfalutin ideas 'bout testin' their wings and bein' independent."

"It's not good for the girls, Mr. Kincaid," Patty Dennehy said. "We thought the woman would be teachin' the girls how to read and write just like Miz O'Leary does to our lads."

"Miss MacKenzie simply has a different approach to teaching than Miss O'Leary does," Dave said in defense of Cynthia. "She looks at life with more of a free and independent attitude."

"Free, indeed!" Mary Callahan exclaimed.

"I've observed some of Miss MacKenzie's teaching technique, and I think it's very effective. And I believe she genuinely has your daughters' interests at heart. I will, however, relate your concerns to her."

"Well, if she don't change her ways, I'll not be sendin' my Katie back to her classroom," Rosie McGuire announced.

"I'll look into the situation at once, ladies, but I must warn you: if I see nothing wrong in what Miss MacKenzie is doing, I will not interfere in her methods."

As soon as they marched away, Dave headed for the school tent. He paused before entering when he heard Cynthia speaking to the class.

"The gowns are always very colorful and ruffled. The dancers hold up the front of the skirts because of the high kicks and splits they do."

What in hell was she talking about?

"What are splits, Miz Cynthia?" Shannon asked.

"A split is when you lower yourself to the floor by extending one leg straight in front of you and the other to the back of you."

"Wow, I bet that sure hurts," Catherine Mary said.

"Not if you do it right, dear. It's a movement very common in ballet also. The difference is that a cancan dancer jumps quite high in the air and comes down hard, whereas a *danseuse* usually glides quite gracefully into a split."

"What's a *dan*— . . . ?"

"*Danseuse,* Maggie. Marvelous!" Cynthia exclaimed. "That will be our *D* lesson for tomorrow."

"Will you show us the cancan, Miz Cynthia?" Maggie asked. Shouts of "Yeah" followed the request.

"All right, ladies, but I'm really not properly dressed for it. As I mentioned, the gown and petticoats are ruffled, and normally the dancer . . ." Cynthia hesitated when she realized what she was about to say might be too improper for the young ladies' ears.

"What about the dancer, Miz Cynthia?" Maggie pressed.

Well, if she was going to educate them there was no sense in dodging the facts, though it would probably get her into more trouble with Dave. "Normally the dancers don't wear unmentionables."

Giggling, the girls put their hands to their mouths. "You mean you're taking off your drawers, Miz Cynthia?" one asked.

"Definitely not—mine stay on."

Dave couldn't help grinning when the remark caused an outbreak of girlish laughter.

"Now, all of you clap your hands like this," Cynthia said, setting the tempo by clapping her hands and loudly singing the syllable *la* to each beat of the rapid melody. "As you can tell, the music has to be very fast, and, I should add, very loud. So clap as hard as you can. As the women dance, they yell or shout above the sound of it."

Dave figured he had to stop her—until she lifted up the front of her skirt. The sight of her long, shapely legs caused him to forget his purpose for being there. As spellbound as the girls, he watched Cynthia kick higher and higher, then couldn't believe it when she ended the dance by leaping into the air and landing in a split on the floor.

Lord knows where she learned to do that!

Her audience applauded with delight and eagerly shouted to be allowed to try it, too. They formed a circle, and Dave watched them hopping and kicking, trying to balance themselves. Ultimately most of them landed on the floor laughing—Cynthia among them.

It was as good a time as any to interrupt; so, wiping the smile off his face, he entered the tent. "What's going on here, Miss MacKenzie? I thought you were conducting school."

"I am," Cynthia said, standing up and brushing herself off.

"Miz Cynthia is showing us the cancan, Uncle Dave," Maggie said.

"What has the cancan to do with teaching them how to read and write?"

Little Catherine Mary came up and tugged at his hand. "I know, I know, Mr. Kincaid, 'cause C is for cancan."

Responding to his look of confusion, Cynthia said, "My method of teaching them the alphabet."

"Whatever happened to C is for cat?"

"Oh, how blasé. Ladies, who wants to show Mr. Kincaid what you've learned?" Cynthia said.

"Me first," Maggie said. "*A* is for Adam's apple—a pro— . . ."

"Protrusion," Cynthia prompted.

"A protrusion right here in your neck." Pointing to her own slim neck, Maggie added, " 'Cept yours is bigger than mine, Uncle Dave."

"A little lesson in anatomy on the side," Cynthia explained quietly to him.

Peggy Callahan stepped forward. Making certain to enunciate every word properly, she said, "*B* is for *Blue Boy*, a famous painting by the English artist Thomas Gainsborough."

Cynthia poked him lightly with her elbow. Putting a hand over her mouth, she whispered, "I could have used belly button, but I'd already had an anatomy lesson, so I decided they'd benefit more from an example from art."

"C is for cancan," Polly recited, taking the same care as her twin sister. "A lively dance performed primarily by women in France."

"And they don't wear underdrawers," Catherine Mary interjected, hands on hips.

"I don't get it," Dave mumbled.

"Merely a simple introduction to the mores and cultures of other countries, Kincaid."

"I mean, I don't get why you make it so hard."

"It's not hard for the girls; their minds aren't cluttered. In addition to learning the alphabet, they're also learning something new. *A* is for apple, *B* is for boy, *C* is for cat. Ridiculous, Kincaid! They all know what apples, boys, and cats are, so why waste time with those examples? Education should be an introduction to new knowledge." She leaned forward and murmured softly, "Don't tell me you're one of those men who think a well-rounded figure is more beneficial to a female than a well-rounded mind, Kin-cad?"

Maggie came up and showed him the sheet of paper she'd been working on. "Look, Uncle Dave, I can write them, too," she said proudly. "This is printing and this is cursing."

"Cursive, Maggie," Cynthia corrected.

Maggie had written the first three alphabet letters in neat rows of print and script.

"This is great, honey," Dave praised.

"Wait 'til Grandpa sees it; he's gonna be so proud of me!" She took the sheet from him and ran back to join her classmates.

"Don't you think it's too much for them to learn the alphabet, printing, and cursive at the same time?"

"They didn't seem to have any problems with it. Did you ever play bridge, Dave?" He shook his head. "That surprises me, because Daddy loved the game. He taught it to me and my sisters at the same time. Angie learned it the fastest, even though she was only twelve, while Beth and I were fifteen and sixteen at the time. And you know why?"

"She's probably a smarter card player."

"Possibly, but she also had an advantage over us. Beth and I knew other card games; Angie didn't. Our minds were cluttered with other rules for other games; Angie's wasn't. See how much quicker you can learn with an open mind? You should try it sometime, Kincaid."

"I'm not much for card playing, Miss MacKenzie."

"I'm talking about keeping an open mind."

He started to sputter, and she turned back to the class. "School's out, girls. See you all in the morning."

"Bye, Miz Cynthia. Bye, Uncle Dave," Maggie yelled out, skipping away with her friends.

"This is the textbook you're using?" Dave asked, flipping through the pages of the thick art book.

"Yes. The girls loved the picture of *Blue Boy*. They think he looks like Jimmy Donovan, whoever that is."

Dave suddenly froze, stopping at a picture of Michelangelo's famous statue of a nude David. "Good God, lady, no wonder I had a delegation of indignant mothers at my door. Do you actually believe these little girls are ready for this?"

"Art is art, Kincaid, whatever form it may be. A child's mind is open to accept that. It's their parents who have closed ones, along with a certain railroad engineer I know." She cast another sidelong glance at the picture. "Hmmm, maybe I should change tomorrow's *D* lesson from 'Dainty *Danseuse*' to 'Dangling David.' " As she grinned, he glared in disgust. " 'Daring David'?"

Dave slammed the book shut. "You know, you invite trouble, lady. And since I'm the one who must contend with the irate parents, forget the art lessons. Jump right ahead to the *R*'s and concentrate on reading, 'riting, and 'rithmetic—or you're through playing schoolteacher, Miss MacKenzie."

He left before she could offer any further argument.

He saw her later that day, showing her class how to bat a shuttlecock over a net.

That doesn't look like the ABC's to me, he thought. But he'd give her the benefit of the doubt that she was also teaching them academics as promised.

The badminton game appeared to attract the attention of others as well. A group of spectators had assembled to watch, among them several mothers of the girls in Cynthia's class and some hooting and jeering boys, who were on recess from their own classroom.

When a couple of the boys asked to try it, Cynthia cleared the court to referee a match between the Callahan twins and the two boys. Neither side was too successful at serving or returning the shuttlecock. The few times one of the boys or girls did manage to hit it back to an opponent, the dogs ran among the players, snatching the feathered object from the ground or out of the air. More time was spent scrambling after the dogs to retrieve the shuttlecock than learning how to become skillful at the game.

The clang of Lydia O'Leary's school bell ended the fracas. Grumbling, the boys returned reluctantly to their schoolroom, Cynthia's girls traipsed back into their tent, the dogs laid down to nap, and the crowd dispersed.

David Kincaid sat back down at his desk. It hadn't appeared to be one of Cynthia's more successful teaching attempts, but it sure had been humorous to watch.

Maybe some of his criticism toward her was unwarranted, he thought, still smiling.

* * *

There they go again; you could set a clock by them. Dave paused in his shaving when he saw Cynthia and her entourage headed for the river. *Why did they always look like an army marching off to do battle?* Each girl carried a neatly folded bundle consisting of an extra shift, drawers, and a towel.

Shocked to have discovered that only the Callahan twins were able to swim, and then only minimally, Cynthia had shifted from teaching her fledglings how to fly to teaching them how to swim. For the past four days, she had started off the morning with a swimming lesson.

At least the days had passed without any further complaints about Cynthia's teaching. Perhaps she was changing her ways, Dave thought as he finished shaving.

"Yeah, right, Kincaid," he scoffed, tossing his shaving water out the window. *Leopards don't change their spots!*

He had just returned to his office after eating breakfast when someone knocked at the door. Suspecting it was Cynthia, he braced himself for the worst.

"Come in."

Astonished to see Lydia O'Leary enter, Dave shot to his feet. The only time she had stepped foot in his office had been the day of her arrival in Tent Town, over two years before. Dave suspected that the incredibly shy woman had been embarrassed because of the proximity of his office to his sleeping quarters. In deference to her maidenly modesty, he had made it a point to go to her classroom whenever he found it necessary to speak to her.

He liked Lydia O'Leary. She rarely complained or made demands despite the many hardships of living in a railroad camp; and despite her lack of physical attractiveness, he found her shyness feminine and appealing. It was clear to everyone that she worshipped Sean Rafferty, but the foreman appeared oblivious to the fact.

"Mr. Kincaid, I apologize for disturbing you."

"It's no problem, Miss O'Leary. Please sit down," he said, drawing up a chair for her, then waiting for her to broach the subject.

"Mr. Kincaid, a serious discipline problem has developed in my classroom."

"I'm sure if you speak to the boy's parents, they will intercede in your behalf, Miss O'Leary."

"It's not that simple, sir. You see, it involves not just one student but all of them. The boys have been observing the good times the young ladies are having and . . . and they . . ."

"They what, Miss O'Leary?"

To Dave's horror, she began to dab at her eyes. He bolted to his feet and went around the desk to comfort her. "May I get you a glass of water?"

"That's most kind of you, Mr. Kincaid, but it won't be necessary." She sat with downcast eyes. "I apologize for my unprofessional behavior."

"I'm sorry to see you so distressed, Miss O'Leary. What exactly are you trying to say?"

"I've tried to do my best, Mr. Kincaid, but obviously I've failed. I think I should resign."

"I won't hear of it. Of course you haven't failed—I've never heard a complaint against you. You're a wonderful teacher, Miss O'Leary."

"The boys insist on joining Miss MacKenzie's class."

"That's normal for boys. They all get restless at a certain age."

She raised her head up enough to peer at him. "Mr. Kincaid, the boys' ages vary."

"Well, that, too," he said hastily. "Have you spoken to Miss MacKenzie about this problem?"

"Oh, I don't want to. She's such a pleasant woman—and so dedicated."

"I don't think we're talking about the same woman. I'm referring to Miss Cynthia MacKenzie, not her sister, Miss O'Leary."

She looked perplexed. "Well of course, sir. So am I."

"I'm sure Miss MacKenzie's stay here is only temporary. I suspect she will soon grow weary of teaching and return to Denver."

"Oh, I hope not," Lydia said with sincerity. "She is such a fine instructor. How I envy her verve. Her methods may be unconventional, but they're so effective." She stood. "Well, I must get back to my classroom."

"And I don't want to hear any more talk about resigning. I'll speak to Miss MacKenzie and see what she suggests; I'm sure this matter can be resolved quickly."

Dave sat back down and cradled his head in his hands. What in hell was he to do? On top of the problems of trying to get a railroad built, he had to contend with tobacco-chewing little girls, disgruntled parents, an unhappy schoolteacher, and now, a bunch of mutinous schoolboys. And what was the common demonimator? Cynthia MacKenzie!

Chapter 9

The one thing Dave didn't need to add to his troubles struck during the night—a torrential downpour. Rain came down faster than the ground could absorb it, running off the rocks and trees in small waterfalls with a force that could sweep a man off his feet. Work came to a standstill, driving everyone into the shelter of their tents. By midday, Tent Town had become a quagmire.

The following morning, with no sign of the rain diminishing, Dave was faced with a greater problem: the riverbanks were near to overflowing, endangering the unfinished trestle.

"Pull out all the rope we have in camp, and we'll angle some lines on the end sections," he ordered.

The supply of rope was nowhere near what was needed, but for the next few hours, under Dave's watchful instructions, the men angled several taut lines off each end of the trestle and tied the ropes to trees.

By evening, water washing down from the granite crests of the distant Rockies began to reach them—a rushing wall of water driving everything in its path ahead of it. Uprooted trees and limbs, drowned cattle and coyotes, and tons of sludge slammed against the trestle, and the unfinished section swayed under the steady force pounding at its infrastructure.

"We've got to reinforce the middle section," Dave said as he and Sean huddled against the fury of the storm, viewing the site. "The whole trestle could break apart if we don't."

"If this damn rain would have held off for one more day, the section would have been finished. But those bridge monkeys can't work in this storm, Dave. Footing's too treacherous," Sean warned. "If they fall, that current'll sweep 'em away."

"I know. I'd never ask them to, but the middle of that trestle needs some more weight. I figure the section could withstand the water pressure if it had more weight on top. If we could lay track across that span, I could weigh it down with an engine."

"But then if ya lose the trestle, you'll lose the engine, too, lad! What good will the engine do?"

"Statics mechanics. Statics is the field that deals with bodies at rest, or in motion with a constant velocity. In our case, by adding greater weight to the vertical *stationary* body at rest—the trestle—it will take a greater energy force by the lateral *moving* body—the river—to dislodge that section."

"And who wud ya be thinkin' is crazy enough to drive an engine out there?" Sean asked.

"I am," Dave said. "But I need another two hundred feet of track to do it, Sean."

For a long moment the older man stared at Dave. "You'll nay let me talk you out of it?"

"Sean, it took us months to build that bridge—we can't afford the time and money to rebuild it."

Sean nodded. "Ya got yur track, boss."

"Good man!" Dave exclaimed, slapping his foreman on the shoulder. "Only volunteers, Sean—and no married men."

Word spread quickly around the camp, and many of the men and women ventured from the shelter of their tents and rode in wagons to the site to watch. They waited in hushed circles, Cynthia among them.

The previous night, Sean had given Maggie permission to spend the night with Cynthia. Now she hugged the stricken little girl as Maggie clutched at her legs, fearing for the safety of her grandfather. A grim and distraught Lydia O'Leary stood beside them.

They watched Sean lead a ten-man crew onto the trestle. Each man, carrying an eight-foot-long railroad tie, moved cautiously onto the swaying structure where a mere slip of his foot could send him plunging to a sure death in the raging water below.

Once the ties were lined up, two five-man crews each carried a heavy rail onto the trestle and placed them on the ties.

While the men returned for more ties and rail, four gaugers moved out on the trestle and began to carefully measure the distance between the two rails before they could be spiked. It was critical that the width between the rails be exactly four feet, eight and one-half inches. Even an eighth of an inch variance could cause a derailment and send the engine plunging off the bridge.

When the gaugers finished, four other men spiked the rails in place, then the ends of the new rails were coupled to those of the previous laid rail. Due to the slippery and swaying trestle, Sean cut back on the usual number of crewmen, and to the people watching, the work seemed to move at a snail's pace. The eight sections of track that Dave had ordered took over thirty minutes to lay—a job that normally would not have exceeded ten or fifteen minutes for the experienced crew.

Finally the locomotive was fired up, with a tender and two flatcars still coupled to it. Cynthia was startled when Dave climbed down from the cab of the work engine and spoke to Sean.

"What are they doing now, Lydia?"

"Sean told me that Mr. Kincaid intends to drive the engine to the middle section of the trestle."

"You mean drive it himself?"

"That's my understanding, Cynthia."

"But if that trestle doesn't hold, he could be killed!"

"I'm sure he's aware of that, but you know Mr. Kincaid; he would never expect a man to do something he's not willing to do himself."

"No, I didn't know that," Cynthia replied pensively. "I didn't know that at all." She thought for a moment, then suddenly said, "Please look after Maggie, Lydia."

"Of course," Lydia said.

Having finished his instructions to Sean, Dave was just climbing back into the cab when Cynthia hurried up to him.

"Dave, I must speak to you."

"Not now. I haven't time."

"I don't want you to do this, Dave. It's too dangerous."

"Don't think I'm looking forward to it, but we can't afford to lose this trestle."

Rain pelted her face and ran down her cheeks as she looked up at him. "We can't afford to lose you, either. Your life is worth more than any damn train trestle."

"Never thought I'd ever hear that from you, Miz Sin."

"Please, Dave, this is no time for joking."

"You're right; time is running out. See you when I get back." He shifted the throttle lever and the locomotive inched forward.

Beth had spoken of Dave's dedication to completing the railroad, but Cynthia hadn't realized he'd be willing to risk his life to do so. As the tender car started to pass her, she made a decision. Hopping on the car, she scrambled forward into the cab.

"Dammit, get out of here," Dave shouted, bringing the locomotive to a screeching halt.

"I've got as much right to be here as you have."

"I haven't time for any of your crazy whims, lady—there's too much at stake here, so get the hell off this train and go find your excitement somewhere else."

"It's not a whim, Dave; it's something I *must* do, too."

"What's that supposed to mean?"

"I guess I have more railroad in me than I thought," she shouted, trying to be heard above the fury of the storm and the noisy idling engine. "Since I returned from Europe, you, Beth, and Angie have reminded me that building this railroad was my father's dream. Yet you seem to think fulfilling that dream is your exclusive responsibility. Well, it's not. No matter what you think, I loved my father; so I share the responsibility of seeing his dream achieved. I hadn't realized that until a couple of minutes ago. We'll take this ride together, David Kincaid. If you're willing to die for Daddy's dream, then so am I."

A violent shifting of the trestle caused her to cry out as she was flung against him, and his arm encircled her waist protectively. Cynthia held her breath, expecting the trestle to break apart at any moment. She was scared, and found it impossible to pretend she wasn't.

"Well, you may be short on brains, but you're long on nerve, lady," he said. "I'll give you credit for that." He eased the throttle lever forward.

The nearer they got to the center, the greater the trestle swayed. Suddenly the locomotive rocked violently, pitching her to the other side of the cab.

David grabbed her arm as she was almost tossed out the door.

"Grab my arm!" he shouted.

She clenched her lower lip between her teeth to keep from screaming, groping until she managed to get a firm grasp on his arm. Fighting gravity, he slowly pulled her over to him and she clamped her arms around his waist.

"Hang on," he said.

The squeal of the brakes could be heard above the sound of the storm as David brought the train to a stop. "Okay, this is far enough. Time to test your wings, teacher."

"What do you mean?"

"Unless you can fly, we have to climb out of here. We've got to get to the rear of this train. Let's go."

Dave took her hand and they climbed over the coal in the tender. Cynthia felt ill as the smell of coal dust, fear, and the swaying motion of the structure combined in an assault on her senses.

Dave leaped from the tender to a flatcar. The gap between the two cars looked too wide to her. She froze. "I can't!" she shouted, swept by a wave of dizziness.

"Yes, you can. Come on, Cynthia, jump. I'll catch you."

"I can't make it."

"This whole structure could collapse any moment. You've got to jump. Just trust me."

Drawing on the remnants of her shattered nerve, she closed her eyes and leaped over. His arms closed around her like a vise, preventing her from toppling off the car.

"Good girl!"

Dave took her hand, and they scampered together over the piled-up rails. Her body felt numb, responding by instinct instead of conscious thought. A flatcar of ties remained to hurdle. This time, she didn't hesitate when he ordered her to jump. Once again, his waiting arms were there to support her.

When had her legs become numb? she wondered when they no longer seemed able to support her body. Still she managed to stay on her feet as they continued their flight.

By the time they reached the end of the train, her mind and body did not seem to function in tandem. Was the trestle swaying more violently—or had she just become dizzier?

Dave climbed off the train, then reached up and swung her down. They had about another hundred feet of trestle to cross. She wanted to get down and crawl, but he held her hand and led her down the middle of the track. Several times she tripped or slipped off the ties, but his firm grasp on her hand kept her from falling.

Cynthia wasn't aware when her feet touched firm ground. Suddenly, they were surrounded by a circle of people laughing and congratulating them.

"We made it, Cyn! We made it!" Hugging her, he swung her in a circle. Then, as the rain continued to pour down on them, he tipped up her chin and grinned at her. "The Chief would be proud of you, Cyn."

"Like hell he would. He'd be furious with me!"

Dave broke into laughter.

She forgot the crowd, the water running into her eyes. She forgot how uncomfortable she felt, soaked to the skin. She forgot that only seconds before, she'd been overwhelmed with fear. Their past quarrels, his dislike of her, his unkind jibes—all disappeared, obliterated by the sound of his laughter and the warmest pair of brown eyes she had ever seen.

He hugged her again, and she wanted to sink into the sanctuary of his arms. "I think we better get back and get you out of those wet clothes, Cyn."

Reviving a saucy smile, she glanced up at him.

"Hmmm, that has some intriguing prospects. You're beginning to talk my kind of language, Kincaid. By the way, is that an *S* as in sin or *C* as in cancan?"

"More like a *C* as in cheeky Cynthia, lady." Taking her hand, he led her over to a wagon.

A bright glow on the eastern horizon seemed to promise the dawning of a rain-free day. A misty hush hung over the tall structure as Dave walked the wooden planks of the trestle.

The bridge had weathered the storm. He knew that one day the wooden structure would be replaced by cement and steel; but last night, for a few moments on its timbered rafters, twenty men and a spunky woman had played out a drama that he would remember the rest of his life.

We'll take this ride together.

Cynthia's words echoed again and again in his head.

Hands in his pockets, he stood gazing into the swollen but peaceful-flowing waters below. Already there were signs that the river had begun to recede. Since it had crested last night, he knew that within days it would be back to its normal depth.

And the trestle had held!

A plethora of emotions churned within him: pride, the satisfaction of accomplishment, gratitude to his crew, and the realization that Cynthia MacKenzie had begun to mean something to him, though he had tried to fight it from the moment he looked into her mesmerizing sapphire eyes.

He turned away. Patting the side of the old workhorse locomotive, he climbed into the cab and fired up the engine. Within minutes, he'd slowly backed it off the trestle.

When Dave climbed out of the cab, the crews,

standing in silence, were waiting. Dave looked at Sean Rafferty and grinned.

The foreman nodded in understanding. Then, turning to the waiting men, he shouted, "Let's be movin', lads. We've a railroad to build."

The crew bounded to action: the bridge monkeys swarming over the crosspieces, the railers and spikers toting sections of heavy rails, and the gaugers following behind with their measuring tools. Dave smiled.

By the following Saturday they were approaching the town of Childs. The trestle lay behind them, and Tent Town had been moved across it. Everyone's spirits were high. The courage Cynthia had shown the night on the trestle had even redeemed her in the eyes of the crew and their wives.

In appreciation for their hard work Dave had given the crew the weekend off, and the men and their families headed to town, where a traveling carnival, stranded earlier by the storm, had set up its operation.

A kaleidoscope of color, the carnival grounds blazed with brightly painted wagons, pennants, and flags of all hues flapping in the breeze.

Cynthia, Lydia O'Leary, and a goggle-eyed Maggie moved from booth to booth, not wishing to miss one exhibit when they stopped to listen to a smooth-talking pitchman hawking the virtues of a nostrum he was selling as the ultimate remedy for every ailment, Dave and Sean came up behind them.

Tongue-in-cheek, Dave said, "Wouldn't you say this sales pitch is a *P* as in poppycock panacea, Miz MacKenzie?"

"Oh, no, Uncle Dave, that's not right," Maggie corrected immediately. "*P* is for prosaic Philistine," Maggie recited. "An inhabitant of ancient Philistia guided by material values instead of intellectual ones." She managed to get through it without catching her breath or mispronouncing one word.

Smiling smugly at Dave, Cynthia patted Maggie on the head. "Well done, dear."

Giggling, Lydia put a hand over her mouth, but Sean threw his hands in the air, clearly exasperated. "What the dev'l are yer talkin' about?"

"Just a word game Cynthia likes to play," Dave spoke up in explanation.

"I'm thinkin' there's more game playin' than learnin' in yer class, Miz MacKenzie."

"Not at all, Mr. Rafferty," Cynthia replied, fending off the accusation with a smile. "Whoever said learning has to be dull?"

They moved on and joined a crowd gathered at the base of a stage, on which stood a woman holding a snake twined around her neck, a scantily clad woman whose body was covered with tatoos, and a markedly heavy "fat lady."

Turning away in disgust, Sean grumbled, "This is not for the likes of me." Spying some of the crew, he and Dave headed over to join them.

For fifty cents a try, the men were competing in a game of strength, the object of which was to thrust, by a single blow of a sledgehammer, a spring-driven disk up a post to strike the bell at the top.

"I don't believe it," one of the fellows complained. "Been drivin' steel for two years and I can't ring the bell."

"What's the prize for winnin'?" Sean asked.

"Double your money back," the barker said.

"Give me that sledge," Sean said confidently, rolling up his sleeves.

Sean Rafferty had been a steel-driving man from the time he came to America fifteen years before. But after two attempts, even he had failed to win.

"Who's next?" the barker asked. "How about you, my friend?" he said to Dave.

Dave shook his head. "If they can't do it, I'm sure I can't."

"Ah, give it a try, boss," Tim McGuire said. "I missed it by just two inches. Bet you can't beat that."

"I'm not even gonna try. You fellows are wasting your money. The machine's rigged so you can't win."

"You're wrong. It's an honest game," the barker denied.

"These men drive spikes through steel rails all day, and you're trying to tell me they aren't strong enough to beat this game?" Dave shook his head. "It's crooked."

"Tell you what, my good man," the barker said. "I'll give you a free try. Unless you're afraid this stout fellow here will show you up?"

"I think he's right, boys. The boss don't want to be showed up," McGuire said with a grin.

"The day hasn't dawned that I can't beat you driving spikes, McGuire," Dave said good-naturedly. "I'm willing to put it to the test on the rails where it will do some good."

"Forget the railroad. Prove it now, Mr. Boss Man," Cynthia said. She and Maggie and Lydia had walked up and were listening. "What have you got to lose?"

"I don't like anyone trying to make a sucker out of me."

The barker handed him the sledgehammer. "I'll even sweeten the pot, neighbor. You ring that bell and I'll give *all* these fellows their money back."

This met with hoots and hollers of approval from the rest of the men. "Have a go at it, boss," Sean said. "It won't cost you anything."

"You can't refuse that offer, no matter what you think," Cynthia taunted.

"You can do it, Uncle Dave," Maggie assured him.

David turned to Lydia for support. "Miss O'Leary, you're the only one in this group with some common sense. Explain to these naive fools that there's no way I can ring that bell."

Lydia smiled shyly. "Well, you really aren't risking anything either, Mr. Kincaid."

"Other than that Tim might have a stronger swing than you do," Cynthia goaded.

"Yeah, so quit stalling, boss. Let's see you swing that hammer," McGuire said.

Shaking his head, Dave removed his jacket and handed it to Cynthia. "Okay, we'll just see who has the stronger swing. Two inches, you say," Dave said, rolling up his sleeves.

"Two inches is the best of this lot," McGuire replied.

Picking up the sledgehammer, Dave swung it a few times like a baseball player testing a bat.

Sean joined the teasing. "I think yer to be hittin' the bell, boss, not swattin' the air."

"I'm just testing the weight of this sledge," Dave replied.

"Always the engineer. Right, Kincaid?" Cynthia teased. "I'll buy everyone a drink if he rings that bell."

Dave stepped over to the machine, swung the sledge to his shoulder, then slammed it down. With the speed of lightning, the disk shot up the post and hit the bell.

The men went wild, clapping and hollering. McGuire and the others slapped Dave on his back, good sports all.

Cynthia was awestruck. The more she discovered about David Kincaid, the more remarkable he seemed. She had never met a man who raised her interest and curiosity the way he did. Granted, when they had first met she had found his animosity titillating, but since that time she had discovered that her interest in him went far deeper than just a physical attraction. Although, she admitted to herself, at the moment her heart was pounding just from being near him.

She watched him intently as he rolled down his sleeves and put on his jacket, sensing he was embarrassed by the crew's congratulations. He didn't like to be the object of attention. And he simply did not know how to have a good time, to laugh at himself or with others. What really gave him pleasure? she wondered. Recalling his smile that stormy night on the trestle, she realized that she had seen a side to him that he rarely revealed to anyone. A side that had set her heart to hammering and her pulses pounding. That armor he hid behind was beginning to slip.

And that was the side of him she was determined to reach.

At that moment, a group of horsemen rode in and dismounted. Their leader was big and broad, with bronzed, rugged features. He appeared to be in his late forties. As they passed, he paused and sneered. "Railroad." Then he spat and moved on.

"*Who* was that?" Cynthia asked.

"Will Bonner, lady," the barker said. "Owns the Lazy B—and practically everything else around here. Sure wouldn't cross him if I was you."

Cynthia insisted on buying them a beer to honor her bet, so the adults walked over to the nearby beer garden. Maggie chased off with some of the other children to watch the launching of a hot air balloon.

The place was jammed, but Sean and Dave managed to get them a table. After Cynthia paid for everyone's drinks, she and Lydia sat down with

Dave and Sean. She noticed that Bonner and his men were down at the end of the bar.

As they were enjoying the cool drinks, two men entered the beer garden. The younger man, who appeared to be around twenty, pounded on the bar, demanding a whiskey with a beer chaser. Turning, he leaned back arrogantly, his elbows resting on the bar, and surveyed the crowd.

"My name's John L. Sullivan," he announced in a booming voice. "I can lick any son of a bitch in the house."

His companion picked up on the challenge. "Fifty dollars to anyone who can last three rounds with him."

"Will ya be watchin' your language, lad. There be ladies present," Sean declared.

Sullivan swaggered over to their table and doffed his derby, his florid face breaking into a smile. "My apologies to these charmin' ladies. Did I hear a touch of Erin in your speech, old man?"

"You did, indeed, me lad," Sean replied.

"My own father came from Tralee in County Kerry."

"I know the place well," Sean said.

Sullivan's gaze swept past Lydia and settled on Cynthia. "The next drink's on me, lovely lady."

"Thank you, but I'm not interested in another drink. One is my limit."

"Now, darlin', you wouldn't be refusin' to drink with John L. Sullivan, would you?"

Sullivan clearly fashioned himself to be a ladies' man, but Cynthia found the young braggart obnoxious.

"I think the lady made that quite plain," Dave said curtly.

"I wasn't talkin' to you," Sullivan said, swinging a dark glare at Dave.

"You are now."

Anger glittered in Sullivan's eyes as he assessed Dave. "You ever do any boxin'?"

"Some. In college."

"Oh, in college." Sullivan snickered. Raising his voice, he said, "Hear that, folks? The man said he's boxed some in college." Bonner and his men laughed loudly. "And where might that be, College Boy?"

"M.I.T."

"Well, whatta you know? Me and College Boy here wuz neighbors. My home's in Boston."

"It's a big city," Dave said.

The indifference in Dave's voice was intended to discourage any further conversation, but Sullivan ignored it. "You think you're good enough to stay three rounds with me?"

The beer garden had quieted, all present listening intently.

"I'm not the least bit curious to find out," Dave replied, a heavy dose of sarcasm in his voice.

"'Fraid, College Boy?"

Cynthia had listened to the loudmouth bully long enough. Still awed by Dave's victory with the sledge and bell, she was convinced he would have no problem with the brash young man.

"No, he's not afraid, blabbermouth. Matter of fact, he can probably take you with one hand tied behind his back."

"It's time to go, Cynthia," Dave said, seeing where the conversation was going. The scene had already attracted a crowd as it was, many of his own crew among them.

"Tell you what, Mr. Sullivan. You double that fifty dollars and he'll do it," Cynthia said.

Sullivan's companion spoke up at once. "It's a deal, lady."

"I'm gonna enjoy knocking the block off this guy," Sullivan boasted.

Whispers of a grudge fight began to circulate among the crowd.

"Hey, hold up there. I said I'm not interested," Dave protested.

Sullivan began flapping his arms and clucking like a chicken, producing another outburst of laughter from Bonner's men.

"You won't have a problem with him. Look how easily you hit that bell," Cynthia assured Dave.

"Cynthia, hitting a bell and *being hit* are two different things. The bell doesn't hit back."

She put a hand on his arm and looked up at him with utter confidence. "I know you can do it, Dave."

His men picked up the chant. "Yeah, you can do it, boss."

Common sense told him to get out while the getting was good. He glanced at Sean; the foreman looked grim and solemn. Lydia had a glow of excitement in her eyes.

Then he made the mistake of looking at Cynthia again.

"Will you do it, Dave?"

Gazing into the adoration in her sapphire eyes, Dave realized exactly how helpless Adam must have felt when he reached for the apple.

"All right. It's a deal."

In the background he heard Sullivan's guttural laugh. "I'll see you later, College Boy."

Sullivan's threat was immediately followed by the drone of his companion's voice. "The bout begins at eight o'clock, Marquis of Queensberry rules. Tickets a dollar each and twenty-five cents for children; babies in laps admitted free. Get your tickets now while they last."

Dave heard it all but paid it no mind. His gaze remained locked with Cynthia's—savoring his first taste of the Forbidden Fruit.

Chapter 10

Most of Cynthia's students, who had become a tight-knit sorority, were sitting on the ground near the inflated hot air balloon that resembled a giant red-and-gold mushroom protruding from the earth.

For a dollar, one could buy a ticket to ascend straight up in the balloon, attached to the ground by two guidelines, and view the terrain much like a sailor high in a crow's nest scanning the sea.

"Boy, it sure must be scary up there," little Catherine Mary Dennehy exclaimed, hugging her knees to her chin.

"Bet it's more fun than climbin' a tree," Maggie replied.

The moment she saw the balloon, Cynthia couldn't contain her excitement. Tugging on Dave's arm like a child, she pleaded to take the ride.

"Not me," Lydia announced quickly. "I don't like heights."

"I've a mind to keep me feet on the ground as well," Sean added.

Cynthia looked hopefully at Dave. "Let's take the children."

"Cynthia, there's more than a dozen of them."

"You can rule out Catherine Mary; she won't go. She's more cautious than the others."

"I don't think it's a wise idea. Besides, we all won't fit."

"Let's ask the operator how many of us can go up at one time."

Since his revelation in the beer garden, Dave was finding it very difficult to refuse Cynthia's requests. He walked over to a booth where the balloon operator was deep in conversation with a frizzy-haired blonde.

Overcome with curiosity, Cynthia climbed into the gondola and saw it was a large wicker basket only six feet in diameter, with gas tanks, a burner, and several pipes leading to the inflated balloon. She bent over and picked up a pair of binoculars lying on the floor of the gondola.

"Hey, what are you doing there?" the operator shouted.

Startled, Cynthia dropped the glasses and jerked up. Then she saw he wasn't yelling at her but at several boys playing with the guidelines. Just as he shouted, the mischievous lads released one of the guidelines and dashed away.

Pandemonium broke forth as instantly and effortlessly as the snap of the other guideline.

"Help!" Cynthia screamed when the balloon started to rise.

"Miz Cynthia! Miz Cynthia!" the girls cried, springing to their feet. Shouting and jumping up and down, they scrambled about in panic, accompanied by the frenzied barking of their dogs.

Sean and Lydia ran to answer Cynthia's distress call, overtaken by Dave and the operator dashing past them in their race to reach the ascending balloon.

Leaping high, Dave managed to grab one of the trailing lines. For several seconds, as he dangled in midair, it appeared as if his weight would pull down the balloon. Then, like a sail in the wind, the silken fabric was caught by the breeze and the balloon began to drift away, setting up another series of frenzied screams from below.

With her heart in her throat, Cynthia watched Dave slowly climbing the rope. Her own danger was forgotten, her concern for him increasing as the balloon continued to rise. What if he lost his grip or the line snapped? She looked around helplessly for something to aid him. Spying a rolled-up rope, she tied one end to the railing and dropped the coil over the side.

Hand over hand, Dave had worked his way up the line, his arm and shoulders muscles now aching. After all, he wasn't a circus performer, he was a simple engineer. Pausing to draw in some much-needed breath, he glanced down and gulped—the ground was a good forty or fifty feet below. There was no place to go but up!

Suddenly, a heavy coil of rope hit him in the head, and his legs and one of his hands slipped off the line. For what seemed an eternity, he dangled in the air, finally grabbing the line and curling his legs around it. Glancing up, he saw Cynthia leaning over the railing about twenty feet above his head.

"Oh, Dave, I'm so sorry," she cried out.

He was too breathless to shout at her, but his anger gave him a much-needed surge of energy. Dave continued to shinny up the rope until he finally reached the gondola, where Cynthia's outstretched arms waited to pull him over the top.

For a few moments, he lay with his eyes closed on the floor of the gondola, dragging air into his burning lungs.

"Oh, thank God. Thank God you're okay," Cynthia chanted, kneeling over him.

Dave opened his eyes and looked up into the sapphire eyes that just a short time ago had given him a glimpse of Eden—and knew with certainty that

God had just given him the boot out of Paradise.

It had been a short but sweet stay.

He sat up and started laughing.

"Dave, are you okay?" she asked, confused by his bizarre behavior.

"I am now," he said, referring to his return to reality. "Unfortunately, now I'm up here in a hot air balloon with an impetuous, harebrained female."

"That's not fair—this isn't my fault! All I did was step into the gondola to see what it looked like."

"Lady, you go through life inviting trouble."

She threw up her hands in exasperation. "Am I the one who shinnied up a rope in midair, Kincaid?"

"Yeah, I do that all the time, I suppose. And if I hadn't, what would you have done?"

"About the same thing I'm doing now—wonder how I'll get down. I don't suppose you've ever flown one of these before?"

"Yeah, sure! It's my hobby," he teased. He got up to take a look at the controls. "I'm an engineer, remember? This probably works on the same principle as a steam locomotive."

"Not quite; there's no tracks up here," she said, peering over the side. "I wonder what's in these bags hanging off the sides."

"I imagine sand, for ballast."

"Ballast! We've got plenty of that with you here."

"A little stability in your life would be a welcome change, lady."

"Why? Because I enjoy life? You're such a spoilsport, Kincaid. I bet you've been a dog in the manger your whole life."

"And you're full of enough hot air to keep this balloon afloat forever."

"I'm not going to allow your nastiness to spoil

this ride. It's quite lovely up here, wouldn't you say?"

"Enjoy it while you can, because as soon as I figure out how this damn thing operates, I'm setting it down. Gotta get back for the big event, remember? I'd hate to renege on that fight you talked me into."

A gentle breeze ruffled Cynthia's hair as the balloon floated above the flat plain of desert shrub and cacti. "Oh, this is divine," she said, gazing in wonderment at the distant rolling hills that stretched to the horizon. "It's too lovely to describe. Can't you feel it, Dave?"

"Feel what?"

"The freedom of flight—of detaching oneself from all earthly concerns. Oh, I love it!"

He smiled, finding it hard to sustain any anger in the face of her zest for life. She brought enthusiasm to anything she did.

"I have to give you credit, Cyn. You manage to find pleasure in everything. I'm just hoping we'll get out of this in one piece."

"I know you'll figure out a way, Dave," she said with unabashed trust, then returned to studying the terrain.

Dammit, she was doing it to him again! Dangling a hint of Paradise in front of him. Not this time, lady. Not this time.

"Oh, look at all the people chasing us."

Dave glanced briefly over the side at the dozens of wagons and riders racing across the desert, than returned to analyzing the various valves.

Leaning over the rim, she shouted "Hello!" and waved.

"If you fall over the top of this basket, you're on your own," he warned, engrossed in the balloon's mechanism.

Cynthia retrieved the binoculars and peered

through them. She focused on one of the wagons bouncing over the desert below. "That's Sean Rafferty driving that wagon. And look, Lydia's with him." She sighed with affection. "And all my darlings are in the back of the wagon."

"Don't suppose they left the dogs behind," Dave grumbled, tracing the course of one of the pipes.

"No, the dogs are running alongside it."

He came over to her and she handed him the glasses. After a quick glance, he turned to look in the opposite direction. "Oh, my God!" Shoving the glasses at her, he hurried back to the burner.

"What is it?" Peering through the glasses, she saw the reason for his concern—they were headed directly toward a copse of cottonwood.

"I don't think we're high enough to clear those trees," he shouted, turning one of the valves on the burner. Flames immediately spurted from the burner's gas jets. "We need more altitude fast. We've got to get rid of the sandbags."

"Can't you just turn this around?" she said, as they frantically unhooked the bags and let them fall to earth.

"Lady, I can control the altitude, but the wind controls the direction. Let's hope that air heats up in a hurry."

"How fast are we traveling?"

"My guess is anywhere between three to five knots." His eyes remained focused on an altimeter mounted on the controls. After a couple of minutes he exclaimed, "We're beginning to rise!"

Cynthia glanced anxiously at the towering outlines of the trees looming in front of them. "I think it's too late." She turned to him hopelessly. "We're not going to clear them."

Dave grabbed her and pulled her down, covering her with his body. The basket careened violently when outstretched branches swiped at the gondola as it skimmed over the treetops. Finally, the basket settled into a gentle sway.

Dave raised his head. "You okay?"

With the danger past, Cynthia became conscious of the pressure of his body on hers—an excitement heightened by their near escape. She felt drugged by the male closeness of him, the heat of his body coursing down the length of her. Her heartbeat escalated, her breath coming in a ragged rhythm that sounded like drumbeats to her ears.

For an instant their gazes locked in a message of shared urgency, then his head descended slowly, and she parted her lips.

The kiss was slow—persuasive—sending spirals of exquisite sensation rippling through her. She responded uninhibitedly to the thrill of his kiss.

He had fought this moment from the first time he'd seen her. His need to punish, to humiliate her, had been a pathetic attempt to deny the real truth—his need to hold her, feel her in his arms, and taste the pure woman of her. He kissed her lingeringly, savoring every moment. Lord, how he wanted to sink into the luscious curves of her body.

Raising his head, he gazed into her eyes and recognized his own need in her beseeching stare. Driven by an all consuming need for another kiss, he traced the soft fullness of her mouth with his tongue, then slipped it past her parted lips to explore the sweet chamber of her mouth.

He knew within seconds they both would be out of control, and there'd be no stopping. Reluctantly, he forced himself to pull away.

"This is insane, you know. I think we'd better get back down to earth." Grinning, he added, "I meant that literally." He stood up and pulled Cynthia to her feet.

"Yeah," she said with a sheepish smile. "It's getting pretty warm up here."

"Must be the altitude," he said lightly, trying to ease the tension. "The higher you go, the thinner the air."

"Well, I'd say we were pretty high, then, because I'm sure having trouble breathing." She turned her back to him and walked over to the basket's rim. "So how are you going to get us back to earth, Kincaid?"

He turned off the burner to stop the flow of gas, then opened the relief valve and pulled on the depletion cord, expelling the hot air.

The hiss of the escaping air invaded the stillness as the balloon began to descend. Several times Dave opened and closed the relief valve and cord to control the speed of their descent.

"I can't offer any guarantees, Cyn. You'd better sit down and brace yourself against the side of the basket."

He continued adjusting the valves as they neared the earth, and right before they touched down, he closed all the valves and sat down beside her.

They glided to the ground and landed with a bump. Within minutes, the wagons and riders raced up to them.

Relieved to see that his balloon had not been damaged, the operator didn't charge them for the ride.

By the time they got back to the carnival, it was almost time for the boxing bout. The seats were sold out, and the standing-room crowd jammed the aisles. Most of the spectators were the crew from the railroad, supporting Dave; but the Boston boxer had begun to build a reputation by touring the country, doing exhibition bouts, on his climb toward the world's heavyweight championship.

Wearing purple tights and high boxing shoes, Sullivan looked to be a bear of a man. He stood a little under six feet and weighed almost two hundred pounds, with a broad chest and thickset arms.

Dave had removed his shirt and shoes. Despite their similar weights, he was several inches taller than Sullivan.

The bout was to be fought under Queensberry rules, but Sullivan had chosen not to wear gloves. Dave used his hands too often to suffer bloody knuckles, so he wore the pair of driver's gloves offered to him.

"'Fraid you'll bloody those little pinkies of yours, College Boy?" Sullivan taunted when they were called to the center of the ring for their instructions.

"Each round will last three minutes," the referee announced. "If a man's too bloodied to see, I call the match."

"Oh, my!" Lydia whispered. "I'm not certain I want to see this."

"Dave won't have a problem; you'll see," Cynthia assured her, but her bravado had taken a deep plunge. Surely, there wouldn't be any bloodshed!

"Shake hands, and at the sound of the bell come out fighting," the referee declared.

"Good luck, College Boy; you're gonna need it," Sullivan said. Grasping Dave in a handshake, Sullivan squeezed hard in an effort to break the hand. Then he smirked and went back to his corner.

Dave sat down, shaking his hand to restore the circulation.

"What's wrong with your hand?" Sean asked.

"That bastard tried to break it."

"Watch yourself, Dave. I''m thinkin' our friend Mr. Sullivan's not the fairest of fighters."

"That bigmouth needs his block knocked off," Dave mumbled.

"Don't let the lad rile you, son. That's what he's hopin' for."

Dave moved out cautiously as Sullivan rushed toward him like a bull and threw two punches to his chest. Dave felt as if he'd been hit with a hammer.

Sullivan threw a right cross to Dave's jaw, feinted with his left, and slammed another punch into Dave's midsection. The breath wheezed out of him and, gasping, he reeled back against the ropes. Sullivan closed in on him, but Dave warded him off with a one-two punch, then sidestepped out of Sullivan's reach, managing to keep far enough away to avoid the full force of the boxer's blows. But the continual jabs to his face broke the skin and he began to bleed.

When the bell clanged, it was as welcome to Cynthia as it was to Dave. She felt numb with guilt, not having expected Dave would have to take such a beating. She stole a glance at Lydia. Appalled by the whole event, the woman had been silent beside her throughout the round.

After splashing a wet sponge over Dave's head and face, Sean wiped him off. "Yer doin' well, lad," he said, sprinkling styptic powder on Dave's face cuts. "Just don't let him get in too close. If he drives you against the ropes or into a corner, he'll try to cut ya to ribbons. Give 'em the old one-two punch again."

"Cynthia, what's 'the old one-two punch'?" Lydia asked.

"According to a boxer I once knew, he said that you jab your opponent with your left hand and then follow it immediately with a straight right punch to the chin."

"Oh, dear!" Lydia exclaimed.

"I guess the important thing is to throw the right punch before he can lower his head, so that the chin's still at a vulnerable angle, unprotected. Of course, that right punch has to be right on target; that's why speed, timing, and marksmanship are so essential."

"I guess the chin must be a boxer's Achilles' heel," Lydia reflected. "It would appear they can suffer horrendous blows to their heads and bodies—but not to their chins." She shook her head. "Such a brutal sport. What a pathetic skill to try and prove to anyone."

Cynthia agreed—it was brutal. And Dave hadn't wanted to get involved. She was the one who'd encouraged him to accept Sullivan's challenge.

As soon as the next round began, Sullivan rushed at Dave and attempted to deliver the double body punches again. This time Dave expected it. Fending off the impact of the first blow with his shoulder, he blocked aside the second blow with his arm, feinted, and came back with a left jab to Sullivan's nose.

It was a sweet moment—but a short-lived victory. Sullivan came back with a right to the body. It was the hardest punch Dave had ever received. Had he taken it on the chin, he figured it would have knocked him out.

Shaking off the effects of the punch, Dave knew if he tried to slug it out with the man, Sullivan would come out an easy winner. Drawing on the skills he'd learned from his college boxing, Dave began to use more footwork, fending and dodging to avoid the blows, and causing Sullivan to throw missed punches. But the more he missed, the more aggressive the boxer became, and several of the punches found their mark.

As the round neared a finish, Dave landed an uppercut on the chin that sent Sullivan staggering, and while the dazed fighter was still tottering from the blow, Dave delivered a left jab and right cross to the boxer's face. He drew blood; Sullivan was bleeding from the nose.

This time when the bell sounded, *both* men returned bloodied to their corners.

The betting now was wilder than before: Dave's supporters were convinced he would finish the fight; Sullivan's aficionados, Bonner's men among them, were now certain that their boy would deliver a knockout.

"Sean, stop the fight," Cynthia cried frantically, no longer able to watch the cruel pounding Dave was enduring. "He can't take any more of this."

"I think yer right. We'll throw in the towel."

"No, I'm seeing this to the end," Dave said through swollen lips. "I can last another three minutes."

"Dave, it's not worth the money," Cynthia said, on the verge of tears.

"It's never been about money! No matter what, I'm in to the end."

At the start of the final round, Sullivan came out confidently, knowing he had to see that Dave did not finish the round. He landed a hard left on Dave's face, and the right cheek swelled immediately. Dave returned the blow with a left jab, but Sullivan ducked and the blow landed on his forehead instead. Pain shot up Dave's arm and a shiver rippled his spine—he knew he had broken a finger. Trying to avoid using his left hand, Dave backed away, hoping just to run out the clock.

Sullivan must have seen the shock on Dave's face, and intent on ending the fight, he pursued Dave relentlessly, setting up a flurry of punishing punches that Dave fought valiantly—but feebly. His arms felt heavy, and he was so numb he could barely raise them to put up a guard.

Despite the shouting crowd, Dave's words echoed in Cynthia's ears, and it all became clear to her: Sullivan could pound him to the mat, and she knew Dave would still get up and take the next blow. Winning was not the important issue to him—the issue was pride. Not a pride born of vanity or arrogance, but the pride of self-respect and dignity. In the face of his courage, she stood up and cheered.

"You can do it, Dave! You can do it!"

Cynthia's rallying cry penetrated Dave's pain-clouded mind. With a quick glance, he saw her standing on her feet, cheering him on to victory. And he knew that, whatever the outcome, in her eyes he had won the fight.

Drawing on his last reserves, Dave no longer cared if he broke every bone in his hand. He put everything he had into the punch, landing a right cross squarely on Sullivan's jaw, and the boxer stumbled back into the ropes just as the bell rang.

The spectators went wild; not a man or woman remained seated as the tent resounded with their cheers, whistles, and applause.

In his excitement, Sean grabbed Lydia and hugged her. Cynthia was weeping—tears of heartache and tears of pride.

Amazement at Dave's endurance showed on Sullivan's face as they met in the center of the ring and shook hands.

"You're a good man, College Boy," Sullivan said, this time with respect. "No hard feelings."

"No hard feelings, Sullivan."

Dave had never known such pain. His right eye was almost swollen shut, his hands were numb, and his face and chest were cut and bleeding, but he felt good; he had stayed on his feet.

"And, Sullivan," he said just before they parted, "you pack a hell of a punch. You're gonna make it—one day you'll be the world's heavyweight champion."

Sullivan grinned and winked. "You can bank on it, College Boy."

Chapter 11

Fortunately there was a doctor in town, and as soon as Dave's injuries were examined, Sean and Lydia helped Cynthia get him back to camp.

Over Dave's objections, Cynthia insisted he stay in her car, where the bed was larger and more comfortable than the bunk in the caboose. After removing Dave's boots and pants, Sean put him to bed. Convinced she could handle it from there, Cynthia shooed them out the door.

The doctor had given Dave a heavy dose of laudanum to ease his pain, and throughout the night, following the doctor's instructions, Cynthia covered Dave's face with hot towels.

She nursed him as he slept, changing the hot towels on his face and soaking his hands in hot water. Toward morning he awoke, restless and aching. After removing the towels from his face, Cynthia sat down on the edge of the bed and gave him another dose of the medication.

He was stretched out flat on his back, his arms extended to the sides with each bruised and swollen hand soaking in a basin of hot water. His face was swollen, one blackened eye was swollen shut, and his chest was covered with bruises.

"I hope you don't feel as bad as you look," she said gravely.

"That was the longest nine minutes of my life. Did they shoot the horse that kicked and trampled me?"

"I'm so sorry, Dave. I never dreamed you'd have to take a beating. The man was a dirty fighter."

"No, he wasn't," Dave denied quickly. "Sure, he was a loudmouth and braggart, but once the fight started, his punches were clean. He packs one hell of a wallop."

"Then I guess I have no one to blame but myself. If I'd kept my mouth shut in that beer garden, this never would have happened."

"Stop blaming yourself, Cyn. I still could have said no."

"And you would have, if it weren't for me."

She reached out and tenderly brushed back some strands of hair that were plastered to his forehead.

"At least your finger's the only broken bone." She lightly ran her finger down the bridge of his nose. "The nose survived."

Dave attempted unsuccessfully to open his eye, then gave up trying and closed his other one. "Oh, that was broken a long time ago when I boxed in college."

"M.I.T."

"Yeah.

"When was that?"

"Class of '76."

"Really! Beth and I were at Wellesley at that time. Did you ever attend any of the cotillions there?"

"Hell, no! Only those future Harvard lawyers were invited to those fancy affairs; invitations weren't sent to a poor boob like me working my way through a technical school."

"You wouldn't have come even if you had received one."

He chuckled. "Guess you know me better than I think."

"Well, I can assure you that you didn't miss anything—those dances were boring. In fact, the whole experience was boring. I took it for two years, then I left and went to Europe. You know the rest of the story."

"Yeah," he said grimly.

This was no time to get him riled over what he considered her tainted past. She quickly changed the subject. "What got you interested in railroads?"

"They fascinated me from the time I was a kid—and you could always get a job if you didn't mind hard work. I was always a big guy, so I lied about my age and got my first job at sixteen with the Union Pacific working on the transcontinental railroad. God, I'll never forget that day at Promontory Point when it was finished. Saved up my money and went back east in '72 to M.I.T. Then, after I graduated in '76, I started to work for the Chief. Guess you know the rest of that story."

"Well, that story's still unfinished, isn't it?"

"Tell you how it'll end if I have anything to say about it—there'll be a railroad connecting Denver and Dallas, just as the Chief dreamed there'd be."

"So, you've worked on railroads your whole life."

"At least half of it; dreamed of them the other half. I've been everything: a transit man, chainman, surveyor, spiker, gauger, bridge monkey. Done it all."

"Do you intend to stay married to the railroad? Don't you want a wife, children?" She thought about the picture on the table next to his bed.

"Of course. Someday when this railroad's completed. I've been thinking seriously about a wife, but I won't subject one to a part-time husband. Until I can devote the time and attention to her that she deserves, I won't consider marriage."

"That's a noble sentiment, Dave, but life doesn't always work to one's convenience. As the poet Robert Burns claimed, the best-laid plans can often go astray. There's no accounting for when or how love will strike you—or, for that matter, with whom you'll fall in love. That's what makes love so mysterious." Smiling, she said, "Well, I better get out of here and let you get back to sleep." Leaning forward, she gently kissed him, then lightly traced his swollen lips with her tongue. Carried away by an overwhelming need to comfort him, she sought out his bruises with feathery touches of her lips and tongue, returning often to his lips.

"God, Cyn," he groaned.

"Am I hurting you?" she whispered softly.

"No, you're not hurting me. It feels good—Lord, how it feels good. I'm beginning to forget all about my other aches and pains."

"It's probably the laudanum," she teased lightly. Shifting, she lowered her head and began to apply light kisses to his bruised chest.

"You drive a man wild, Cyn. I swore to myself you wouldn't win with me, but I lost that bout, too. I can't fight you any longer."

"Why did you try, Dave? We're both adults; we're attracted to each other. Why fight it so hard?"

"I guess for the same reason I stayed in the ring with Sullivan. Pride—"

"Stubbornness."

"Resentment at being taken for a fool."

"Why would you think I take you for a fool? I think you're wonderful. You're the most exciting man I've ever known." She ran a string of kisses down his chest. "And the smartest . . . the bravest . . . and the strongest," she whispered between kisses.

"I'm not strong enough to take much more of what you're doing to me. As soon as I'm well, Miz

Delightfully Sinful, you and I have some . . . unfinished . . . business . . ."

Suddenly his tensed body relaxed. She raised her head and saw that the laudanum had taken effect—he had fallen asleep.

Cynthia rose. Tenderly, she lifted his hands out of the basins and patted them dry, then gently kissed each bruised knuckle.

As she carried the basins to the bathroom, the lovely face of the girl in the photograph dominated her thoughts.

I'm sorry, honey, but I love him. You're there and I'm here—and all's fair in love and war. Besides, you had your chance. Why aren't you here with him? If he were my man, I could never stay away from him.

Returning to the bedroom, she wrapped his face again in hot towels, placed another light kiss on his lips and on the tip of his nose, then, exhausted, she slumped down on a chair. She maintained her vigil throughout the night, changing the water and towels whenever they cooled.

The next morning, Lydia had just dropped by to check on Dave's condition when Sean and Maggie appeared at the door.

Once Cynthia assured Sean that Dave had passed a peaceful night, he said, "Wud ya be troubled if we leave then? Me granddaughter has a mind to be returnin' to the carnival."

"Of course not."

"Cynthia, if you'd like to go with them, I would be glad to stay with Mr. Kincaid."

"No, Lydia. I think I've seen all of the carnival I care to. You go along with Sean and Maggie."

"Oh, dear, no. That would be very presumptuous of me. I haven't been invited."

Sean doffed his hat. "Beggin' yer pardon, Miz

Lydia. If you've a mind to, Maggie and me wud be pleased to have ya."

Lydia blushed with pleasure. "I wouldn't be averse to having another piece of that roast chicken."

"I'm going to have another ice cream, Miz Lydia," Maggie expounded excitedly. "Did you try one of the chocolate ones?"

"Oh, yes, it was good, too," Lydia agreed. "I think I shall have another one myself."

Smiling, Cynthia stood at the door and watched them walk away. Would Sean and Lydia ever admit their feelings toward each other? Oh, well, she thought, closing the door, she had her own romantic problems to worry about without trying to solve those of someone else. *Physician, heal thyself.*

Feeling the full misery and stiffness from the boxing match, Dave awoke later that morning irritable and short-tempered. He was aching and wanted to be left alone, insisting upon returning to his own quarters.

"I made a French gumbo I'm sure you would like," Cynthia offered. "It's nothing much more than rice and okra."

"I don't want anything to eat."

"How about a cup of coffee or tea?"

"I don't want anything to drink."

"Are you always this irritable in the morning? How about soaking in a nice hot bath, at least, before you leave? It will do you good."

"No, I just want to . . . well, maybe a hot bath would help."

"Fine, I thought you would like it. I've already heated the water. I'll draw the bath for you." When she returned a few minutes later, he was on his feet. "Let me help you?"

"I don't need any help," he said, staggering to the bathroom.

"Sure you don't want something to eat?"

He closed the bathroom door without responding.

After fifteen minutes, she tapped on the door and entered, carrying a cup. Dave sat in the tub with his head resting on his bent knees. "Here, since you won't eat anything, at least drink this."

"I said I didn't want anything to drink."

"This will do you good," she insisted.

"What is it?"

"Just your castor oil, sonny." That was enough to get him to raise his head. "Actually, it's a hot toddy; nothing more than brandy, a little sugar, and some hot water."

"All right," he said, reaching for it.

"Is the bath helping you?"

"Yeah, it feels good. I'm trying to think of a way to soak my head, instead."

"I always suspected you were uncertain which end is up, Kincaid."

"Don't think I've forgotten last night. Obviously you're a devout student of the Marquis de Sade."

Astounded, she exclaimed, "That pervert! Why would you say a thing like that?"

"Don't pull that innocent act on me, Miz Sin. As soon as I'm back on my feet, we'll settle that issue, too. Now get out of here."

"Ah, about last night—is that a threat or a promise, Kincaid?" she asked, pausing on her way out.

"Take it any way you choose, lady." He held his grin until she closed the door.

A short time later, wrapped only in a towel, Dave emerged from the bathroom and returned to the bedroom. He managed to pull on his jeans and plop his Stetson on his head. Then, after gathering up his boots and the rest of his clothing, he thanked her and left.

Cynthia came out on the observation deck, folded her arms across her chest, and watched him cross to his quarters.

"Hey, Kincaid," she yelled.

He stopped and turned around. "What?"

"The next time you leave my car, will you at least put *all* your clothes back on? You're compromising my reputation."

"The next time I leave your car, I'll be wearing more than you will be." This time he grinned broadly, grimaced from the pain, then continued on his way.

"Watch out, Miss Whatever-Your-Name-Is. All's fair in love and war." Smiling with satisfaction, Cynthia reentered the car. After emptying the tub, she put on her nightgown and finally went to bed, exhausted from her night-long vigil. The sheets still felt warm from the heat of his body—or was it just her imagination? Closing her eyes, she cuddled the pillow his head had lain on to her cheek and went to sleep.

With the holiday weekend behind them, the crew was back on the job bright and early Monday morning, and Tent Town returned to a normal routine.

Most of the swelling of Dave's injuries had gone down, and the cuts and abrasions had closed. His black eye looked as ugly as the bruises on his face and body, but at least he was now able to open the eye. Even his hands were healing; the swelling in the knuckles was gone, though his fingers were still too stiff to hold a pencil.

Leaning against a tree, he stood flexing them to work out some of that stiffness, as he indulged in a pastime he found himself resorting to frequently—watching Cynthia. At the moment she was at the riverbank. Surrounded by her cadre of pupils in white shifts, she was preparing to begin the swimming lesson for the day.

Dressed for a morning at the beach, Cynthia looked as enticing as ever in a black-and-white ruffled bathing costume, Dave observed, though nothing could compare to the way she looked in the tight jeans she loved to roam around in. His passion overruled his reason. He wanted her as much as she did him, and as soon as he healed, the outcome was inevitable. Since the day of the carnival, that truth was in their eyes each time they looked at each other. And the wait had become more painful than his wounds.

Suddenly, hearing a cry for help, Cynthia spun around and looked at the river. He followed the direction of her gaze and saw the crisis.

Catherine Mary Dennehy had wandered away from the group and ventured too far into the water. Caught by the swift current, screaming and thrashing helplessly, the youngster was being swept away.

Dave raced down the hill toward the river as Cynthia jumped into the water, swimming swiftly toward the drowning girl.

However, someone else had already rallied to her cry for help. Awakened by Catherine Mary's cry, Snoozer had leapt into the water, and now, several yards ahead of Cynthia, was paddling toward his beloved mistress.

The dog reached the child, grabbed her shift in his jaws, and began tugging her toward the riverbank. When Cynthia reached them, Catherine Mary was unconscious. Since Snoozer would not release his grip on the girl's shift, Cynthia managed to keep the youngster's head above water as Snoozer tugged the unconscious girl to the bank.

Several of the girls had run back to Tent Town,

screaming that Catherine Mary had drowned. By the time Dave scooped the youngster out of the water, a mob of apron-shrouded women were running toward them. Despite his aching hands, he flipped Catherine Mary onto her stomach and began to push the water out of her lungs. Snoozer licked at the little girl's face, ministering to his beloved mistress the only way he knew how.

A pall hung over the hushed circle of spectators as Dave worked over the girl. Holding a clenched fist to her lips and clutching a rosary between the fingers of the other hand, Patty Dennehy stood pale and silent, the poor woman's stricken look locked on the ashen face of her daughter. Finally, when the first spasms of coughs began and Catherine Mary opened her eyes, the quiet woman crossed herself and knelt down. Gathering her child to her breast, she rocked the crying child in her arms.

"Girls, gather up your clothes and go home. They'll be no more school today," Cynthia said.

Surprised, Dave looked at her. Cynthia's announcement had been delivered in a lifeless monotone. She looked stunned, and he was tempted to follow her when, without so much as a backward glance, she walked to her car.

Cynthia remained behind closed doors the rest of the day. In the evening, concerned about her unusual behavior, Dave tapped on her door.

Her appearance shocked him. She looked pale and drawn, her eyes swollen from weeping.

"What do you want, Dave?"

"I'd like to come in and talk to you."

"Not tonight. I'm in no mood to talk."

"Are you ill, Cynthia? Is there something I can do for you?"

"No. Please, I'd just like to be left alone." She closed the door.

Dumbfounded, he stood for a few seconds, then

walked slowly back to his car. The hair bristled on his neck as he felt a sense of foreboding. There was trouble ahead—big trouble.

He went to bed that evening with fear gnawing at his stomach.

A chorus of "Good morning, Miz Cynthia" greeted her as Cynthia walked into the tent to face the heartrending task ahead.

Unable to avoid it, she swung a guilty glance to the spot where Catherine Mary always sat. The five-year-old waited eagerly, looking none the worse considering her near brush with death the previous day. Cynthia took another few seconds to glance around at the other girls, their young faces aglow with trust and eagerness.

"How come you ain't wearing your swimming costume, Miz Cynthia?" Polly Callahan asked. "Ain't we gonna have a swimming lesson this morning?"

Swallowing the lump in her throat, Cynthia drew a deep breath and braced herself for what she had to say. "No, I'm afraid not. I have something to tell you this morning, girls. School will be cancelled for a while. I'm leaving . . . going back to Denver."

Disappointment replaced their previous anticipation.

"How long will you be gone, Miz Cynthia?" Maggie asked.

Cynthia gulped hard, forcing back her tears. "I don't know. . . . I'm not certain if I will return."

For a few seconds there was a stunned silence, then the tent began to fill with the sounds of sobbing.

"Are you mad 'cause I almost drowned?" Catherine Mary asked. "Is that why you're goin' away?" Tears streaked the youngster's cheeks, and she hung her head. "I'm sorry, Miz Cynthia."

"Oh no, dear, I'm not mad at you." Her heart felt near to bursting. "You mustn't ever blame yourself, sweetheart."

"Well, what did we do to make you want to go away?" Katie McGuire asked.

"Girls, believe me, none of you have done anything wrong. It's me—I'm to blame. But I promise you I'll find someone to replace me."

"We don't want anyone else," Shannon cried. "We only want you."

Shannon's outcry set up an even louder and steadier wail from the others.

Cynthia's misery was so acute it felt like a knife thrust in her chest. "This is your chance to prove to everyone what you've learned. I know you won't disappoint me. I've tried to teach you not to depend on others, to think for yourselves. To be free spirits and seek your own method of happiness. There will be other disappointments you will have to face, but if your spirit is free, you'll be able to accept them as part of what life has to offer."

"I don't want to be free. I want you to stay, instead," Maggie sobbed. "Please, Miz Cynthia. Please don't go."

The other girls joined the urgent plea.

Hot tears burned Cynthia's eyes and throat. No longer able to withhold them, she said, "I'm sorry. I must go." Her voice broke as she cried, "Goodbye. I love all of you."

Dave's foreboding became a reality when he saw Dan Harrington couple Cynthia's private car to the rear of the supply train.

"What's going on, Dan?"

The young fireman looked at him, puzzled. "Orders from Miz MacKenzie, Dave. Didn't you know?"

Dave hopped up on the observation platform of

the car, rapped on the door, and entered. Cynthia spun around in surprise when he barged in.

"You mind telling me what's going on here?" he demanded.

"I've decided to return to Denver for a while."

"Oh . . . just like that."

Quick anger rose within him—anger with himself, as much as with her. He had suspected something like this would happen from the beginning. Why had he ever let down his guard?

She walked over and gazed sightlessly out of the window. "I've thought it over carefully, Dave. Yesterday . . . yesterday, when Catherine Mary almost died because of my negligence, I thought of what you said about the ramifications of my actions. You were right—good intentions can often backfire and shoot you in the head. All I wanted to do was help the girls; instead, I almost got one killed. And look at you—almost beaten senseless because of me. Whatever I've done in the past, I never hurt anyone but myself. That luck appears to have run out. I have to get away and try to decide if I do more harm than good."

"So you were just going to slink away without an explanation—not even a good-bye," he said bitterly. His eyes blazed with contempt as hot anger burned away rationality. "It doesn't matter about me; I should have had enough sense to know better. But right this minute, there are twelve little girls over in that tent waiting for school to begin."

"I've just spoken to them and told them I was leaving," she said in anguish.

"I warned you that they would be the ones hurt when you got bored with playing teacher," he accused. "That once the novelty wore off, you'd run out on them—the same way you ran out on your father. And that poor sucker in Europe who loved you."

"That's not true!"

"It *is* true, Miss MacKenzie." He spun on his heel and slammed out the door.

Cynthia chased after him. Ignoring the people who could not fail to hear them arguing, she called out to him. "Wait, Dave. I just need some time to think this all out. How I feel about everything—about us."

He turned his angry gaze on her. "There is no *us*, lady. There never has been—and never will be. So go. Get out of here. You've had your laughs at the expense of poor slobs like us. Go back to your dukes and counts. Just stay away from here. I don't want to see your deceitful face in Tent Town again. And warn Elizabeth that if you show up here, I'll leave."

Consumed with rage, he turned toward his quarters—and stopped short as he became aware of the shocked expressions of those who had witnessed his outburst, and of the loud sobbing from the twelve little girls staring horrified at him. Cursing, he stomped into the caboose and slammed the door.

He sat down at his desk, cradling his head in his hands. When he heard the locomotive pulling out, Dave went to the window in time to see the tail end of the private car. In a symbolic gesture, the fancy car rocked back and forth on the track as if waving farewell.

Dave walked over and plopped down on his bunk. His body ached, his head ached, his eye ached, his hands ached—and his heart ached.

"Damn you, Cynthia MacKenzie. Damn you to hell!"

Chapter 12

How he could have fallen asleep was beyond Dave's imagination, but when he woke up, it was almost noon. He'd lost half the day! Grabbing his hat, he rushed out the door and ran smack into trouble—in the shape of twelve girls and three dogs sitting in the dirt outside his office.

" 'Bout time you woke up," Maggie, their chosen spokeswoman, said belligerently. The other girls just stared at him as if he were an ax murderer.

"Uncle Dave, why did you send Miz Cynthia away?"

Her chin puckered and the last word came out in a sob—which set the other eleven girls to crying.

"Maggie, I did not send her away. Miss MacKenzie made that choice herself."

"You're lying!" Katie lashed out at him. "We all heard you tell . . . you tell . . . her to go away and don't come . . . bac-c-c-k." Crying, she took off in the direction of the tents. Several more of the weeping girls followed after her.

The mournful whimpering of the remaining girls developed into a full-scale wail, made more shrill when the dogs added their howls to the lamentation.

Dave looked around with a nervous glance and saw a number of people standing nearby listening.

"The man should be ashamed of himself," one of the women said, glaring and shaking her head in disgust.

"Girls, please quiet down. Crying won't accomplish anything. You're going to make yourselves ill."

As if on cue, Polly Callahan bent over and regurgitated, splattering one of his boots in the process.

"You've made my sister sick, you mean man," her twin sister accused. "I'm gonna tell our papa." Slipping an arm around Polly's shoulder, Peggy led her away.

"I hate you, Mr. Kincaid," Catherine Mary shouted through her tears.

The pathetic sight of the sobbing five-year-old, running with outstretched arms across the clearing, flinging them around her mother's legs, and proceeding to bawl at the top of her lungs, was an image Dave would carry in his memory for a long time. The only redeeming aspect was that her dog left with her.

"I'm sorry, girls, but I have to leave." Shaking off the two remaining dogs sniffing at his soiled boot, Dave hurried back inside to the sanctuary of his humble, but private, quarters.

What had he ever done to deserve this!

He cleaned off his boot, then glanced out the window. Maggie and several of the girls were still camped on his doorstep. In no mood for any further confrontation with them, he sat down and attacked one of the projects on his desk.

Off and on throughout the afternoon, he checked and saw that the girls had been reinforced. *Ridiculous!* Dave told himself. Imprisoned by an army of young girls—and three dogs! He bent to his work again.

At dusk, smiling with satisfaction, he put the completed project aside. His forced internment had actually worked for the good; without anyone knocking on his door all afternoon, he'd gotten through a major project uninterrupted: a calculation and sketch of the needed elevation and angle of degrees to keep a speeding train from jumping track on a sharp curve ten miles ahead. First thing in the morning, he'd get a road crew started on it.

Venturing a glance out the window, he saw that his jailers were gone—but he doubted he'd heard the last from them. *How about* P *as in persistent pests, Miz Cynthia?* Disgusted, Dave threw down the towel he'd been using. *Dammit, forget her, Kincaid! She's out of your hair—out of your life.*

He received a few nods when he ate supper, but no one sat down and ate with him—the word had obviously spread among the single men, too. People had short memories, he reflected as he walked back to his quarters after the quick, lonely meal. Only a short time ago, there had been a hue and cry to send Cynthia away—now he was a scourge because they believed he had done so. Well, it would calm down in a day or two, the way all the controversy concerning Cynthia had done.

Spl-a-a-t.

He felt something hit his back. What the—? He hadn't heard any gunshot or felt any pain. Another missile whizzed past him, and he dove to the ground and tried to locate his attacker, but it was too dark to see. Then he fell under a barrage of fire as the flying objects slammed into the ground around him, one hitting his arm. Grabbing for his wounded arm, he came back with a handful of mud.

Mud! He'd been leveled by a couple of young kids throwing mud balls! What next?

Madder than hell, he stood up, believing it to be the mischievous work of the girls. In a patch of moonlight, though, he caught sight of a couple of boys scampering away. Shaking his fist, he shouted, "I'll get you for this, you little hoodlums!"

Several people came out of their tents and stared at him inquisitively. He glanced around at their stunned faces: Sean Rafferty, Lydia O'Leary, Tim McGuire, the Dennehys.

"Is something wrong, boss?" Sean asked.

Realizing how ridiculous he must look standing with a clenched fist and shouting into the darkness, Dave dropped his arm.

"Can't you people control your children?" He walked away in a huff.

Dave spent a restless night thinking about Cynthia. He woke up in a sweat from a dream in which he held her in his arms and told her he loved her. Why in hell would he dream anything like that? Love had never been an issue between them—only raw sexual desire. A need men and women had known since Eden.

He sat up. Dammit, he was doing it again! Forget Eden. Eden had nothing to do with the situation. What he felt for Miz Sin had more to do with hell than with Paradise.

"Oh, Lord, here they come again!" Dave moaned when he stepped outside the next morning and saw the lynch mob of mothers headed his way. The same women who had complained about Cynthia before now sang her praises and demanded he get her back.

"Our babies are cryin' themselves to sleep," Rosie McGuire declared.

"And it's not right our girls are being denied an education," Mary Callahan added.

"That was the decision you and your husbands originally made, and it didn't seem to bother you before," Dave argued.

Margaret O'Neill spoke up. "The men made that

decision, not us. What my Shannon has learned from Miz Cynthia, bless the darlin' woman's heart, is that we women have rights, too."

"Yeah, not just men," the others shouted in agreement.

"You men have had your way long enough. We want a change here," Patty Dennehy declared.

"Ladies, ladies," Dave said, trying to restore order, "your objections should be discussed with your husbands, not me. As for your girls' educations, Miss MacKenzie has assured me she will pursue hiring another teacher. Now if you ladies will excuse me, I have a railroad to build."

"Well, Mr. High-and-Mighty Railroad Builder, either you apologize to Miz Cynthia and get her back here or that railroad yer so spent on buildin' is gonna be built by some very unhappy men. We'll see to that," Rosie McGuire said confidently. "Let's go, ladies."

Good God! Now he was being blackmailed!

The rest of the day, the situation with Cynthia was shoved to the back of his mind as he got the road crew started on the problem ahead.

By the time he got back he'd missed supper, and after unsaddling his horse, he returned to his quarters under another volley of mud balls.

And on his way to breakfast the next morning, seeing Catherine Mary Dennehy, he said, "Good morning, Catherine Mary. How are you feeling this morning?"

The five-year-old stuck out her tongue and walked away.

Snoozer growled, then followed.

Dave knew it was inevitable that he'd be approached by Sean Rafferty. The visit came the following evening, after Dave had endured another day of grunts from the men, cold shoulders from the women, stuck-out tongues from the girls, snickering from the boys, and growls from the dogs. It even appeared he would have to start locking his door, because he had to track down his clean underdrawers and found them frozen in the ice shed.

"You gotta do what you must to get the woman back, lad," Sean told him. "The men said their women will not let it rest. Me own Maggie cries herself to sleep each night, and the others said the same is true of their girls. Even the lads are in a dither."

"Don't mention those hoodlums. I know they're responsible for my frozen underwear, as well as those mud balls. As for the women, I told them Miss MacKenzie said she'd find a replacement."

"Yer missin' the point, lad! They all want the woman herself."

"That's impossible. She's the one who wanted to leave."

"Then for the sake of the railroad, Dave, you've got to get her back."

"As long as everyone is making demands, Sean, you tell your men and their families that I've had all the mischief I intend to tolerate from their children."

Obviously Dave had made his point clear, because when he returned that evening, he was able to unsaddle his horse and walk back to his quarters unmolested.

Just as he prepared to enter, though, a single mud ball splattered on the side of the caboose, missing him by several feet. He peered out at the darkness. Somewhere out there was still a rogue avenger—with a bad aim.

Not more than an hour later, Sean Rafferty, accompanied by Lydia O'Leary, paid him a visit. This second appearance by Lydia, following so closely on the heels of her previous one, could only mean she wasn't making a social call. He shouldn't have been surprised; by now, she was about the only person in camp who hadn't expressed an opinion—one way or another.

"I can only assume you came regarding Miss MacKenzie, Lydia," he said after she was seated. "I hope you aren't offended if I address you by your given name."

"Of course not, Mr. Kin—"

"Dave," he corrected.

She smiled demurely. "Please do, Dave. And you are right; we are here regarding this school situation."

"We've been discussin' the matter," Sean interjected.

"I'm sure you have. Who isn't?"

"You tell him our idea, Lydia."

Dave noticed that Sean's free usage of Lydia's first name appeared to draw a loving smile from her. Perhaps the couple had finally gotten around to discussing more than the school situation, he reflected. *And about time, too!*

"Well," Lydia began, "it appears there is no immediate solution to the problem, unless you're . . ." She hesitated and cast a hesitant glance at Sean.

"What Lydia is tryin' to say, Dave, is that maybe you cud go to Denver, tell Miz MacKenzie you're sorry, and ask her to come back."

"What?" Appalled, Dave jumped to his feet. "You must be joking!"

"Mr. . . .ah, Dave, I'm sure dear Cynthia would keep an open mind if you approach her."

"Lydia, despite the consensus of opinion around here, *dear Cynthia* claims she left because she'd been shaken up by the Dennehy girl's near tragedy. I personally have my own opinion: that she was bored and used the incident as an excuse to leave."

"I don't agree with you," Lydia replied, a forceful

position for someone with her timidity.

"Whatever her reason, Dave me boy, there were many who heard you tell her not to be comin' back."

"So that makes me the villain!"

Sean's eyes twinkled with humor. "Come on, lad, we've known each other these many years, and I'm thinkin' y'ud not be averse to havin' the lady back."

"The *lady* was a problem from the moment she stepped off the train."

Sean winked at him. "And I'm thinkin' it's not the kind of trouble you much minded, lad."

"Sean and I have discussed the classroom problem," Lydia said, "and we think we've worked out a temporary solution. I have never liked the idea of the young ladies being denied an education. What if we combine the boys and girls into two general age groups? The older group can go to school in the mornings and the younger group in the afternoon. That should make the boys quite happy because they'll have to spend less time in school. As for the girls . . ." She sighed deeply. "I'm afraid I'll be a poor substitute for dear Cynthia, but at least the girls will be attending school. With your approval, of course," she faltered.

"Lydia, I think it's an excellent idea, but it sounds like twice the work for you."

"The new arrangement will add two more hours a day to my working schedule, but it should only be a temporary arrangement until you can convince Cynthia to return."

Sean smiled slyly. "And if Lydia be willin' to do her part, I'm thinkin' you should be willin' to do yours."

Dave struggled with the idea of eating crow—literally crawling to Cynthia and begging her to come back. It would be a bitter pill to swallow.

"Come on, lad, wud you really be mindin' it that

much? I'm thinkin' no matter what you say, you take pleasure in havin' the lass around."

"I'm not agreeing to anything right now. Let me think about it tonight. In the meantime, Lydia, feel free to put your plan in motion. I'll see you get whatever financial assistance you need."

"That's me boy," Sean said, slapping Dave on the back.

When the supply train headed back to Denver the following afternoon, Dave was on it.

Chapter 13

"Why is she going away to school?" Cynthia asked Beth as she watched Angie ride off with Giff. "She loves ranch life."

Beth smiled and put down her teacup. "Birds don't fly too far from the nest. We tried it, didn't we?"

Pain flickered in Cynthia's eyes. "Yes, we did. I tried to teach the girls the importance of testing their wings, but I can't say I'm a good example. It turned out pretty disastrous for me."

"That doesn't sound like you, Thia. You've always been so positive about everything."

"Well, look how I botched up my life: running off to Europe the way I did; my affair with Roberto."

"You loved him, didn't you?"

"I thought I did at the time." She smiled at Beth. "Neither you nor Angie have ever criticized me for what I did. Having a sister involved in a scandalous affair must have been shocking and embarrassing to the two of you."

"Thia, we love you. And we know you're a good person. You can try and fool others, but you never fooled us."

"What about Daddy? He was hurt by it. Dave makes a point of reminding me of that."

"I think Daddy felt he had driven you to it. He

loved you; you know that." Beth reached across the table and squeezed Cynthia's hand. "Thia, you're just feeling guilty about that little girl's accident. But whatever happened to her could have happened with or without you. None of us control another person's destiny."

"I always believed that before. I guess it was the shock of Catherine Mary's near drowning, following so closely after Dave's injuries. And don't try to tell me I wasn't responsible for the beating he took."

"It's not really the near tragedy with the young girl that's bothering you, is it?" Beth said, her probing gaze fixed on Cynthia.

"No, I guess not. I was shocked at first . . . and overreacted to it. Deep down, I *am* fatalistic." She forced a weak smile. "I don't try to play God with people's lives no matter what David Kincaid thinks."

"This is really all about Dave, isn't it? What happened between you two?"

"Oh, Beth, I've made such a mess of everything. He never had a high opinion of me to begin with, and I was going to show him—bring him to his knees—but he was wise to me from the start. He accused me of being just a spoiled rich girl out for a good time."

"Surely if you sat down now and explained to him how you really feel—"

"It wouldn't do any good, Beth. In the beginning I deliberately teased and taunted him, adding to his earlier impression of me. Now he loathes me even more for running out on the girls who trusted me."

"Well, just go back and prove him wrong, Thia."

Cynthia glanced woefully at her. "I can't go back, Beth. He told me to tell you he'll leave if I do."

Beth gasped, her eyes round with shock. "Oh, he can't mean that. He's dedicated to completing that railroad."

"He means it, all right. And Dave's stubborn enough to carry out the threat." Cynthia gave a short, derisive snort. "I have no one to blame but myself. Everything I've done has backfired. I'm in love with him, but he's more convinced than ever that he was right about me . . . and I have no way of proving that I'm sincere."

Cynthia rose and walked to the window. "I guess you'd call it retribution, Beth." For a long moment she stared out of the window, then turned back with anguish. "Oh, Lord, Beth, I miss him so much. It's only been five days and I feel as if it's been centuries."

Beth walked over and put a hand on her arm. "Why don't you go back to him, honey? Tell him how you feel—what you've just told me."

"I don't think it would do much good. He despises me."

"Forgive me for prying, Thia, but have the two of you been intimate?"

"No, through no fault of mine." Cynthia offered a hollow laugh. "But I was wearing him down. His injuries prevented it, or I'm sure we would have been by now."

Grasping her by both arms, Beth looked straight into Cynthia's eyes. "Then if you love him and want him, why did you run away? Go back and fight for him, Thia. The supply train's coming back today. We'll have them hitch up the car."

"Do you really think I should?"

"It's not like you to give up without a fight. Come on, I'll help you pack."

"Oh, Beth, I love you!" Laughing, the two girls hugged and kissed.

Suddenly Beth stepped away. "Oh, darn! We forgot about Angie. I promised her she could take the car when she leaves tomorrow for St. Louis. It'll be another week before it gets back here."

Cynthia's spirits felt buoyed. "I've waited this long; I can wait for another week. If I didn't need the car to live in down there, it wouldn't matter. I'll use the time to formulate a new strategy with Dave."

"Forget the strategy, Thia darling, and just let nature take its course. Remember, he's probably sweating it out the same as you are." Slipping her arm through Cynthia's, Beth added. "Oh, dear, what am I going to do with both of you gone? And Daddy, too. This house will be so lonely."

"You're going to have to find yourself a companion, Beth. Preferably one who is tall, dark, and handsome. Good luck in slipping him past Middy."

Giggling, the two women left the room.

Later that day, when Cynthia saw Angie and Pete Gifford ride in, she decided to get some fresh air. Grabbing her coat, she went outside. Pete Gifford came out just as she neared the stable. "Hi, Giff. What's Angie doing?"

"She's in there," he said, with a disgusted jerk of his head in the direction of the stable. "Saying good-bye to her horse. Don't make sense why she's leaving in the first place." He walked away, kicking at the dust.

For a moment Cynthia watched him, wondering what had upset him so much. Apparently she wasn't the only unhappy person on the Roundhouse.

Slipping into the stable, she saw Angie with her arms around the neck of her dun stallion, nestling her cheek against the horse's mane.

"I'll miss you, Calico. Giff will see that you get a workout every day, and he promised me he'd slip you an apple now and then." Angie turned and saw Cynthia. "I hate good-byes."

"Especially when you have to kiss a horse. I thought little princesses kissed frogs."

"I wish I could be as strong as you are, Thia. You don't let anything get you down."

"That's what you think. Look, Pumpkin, school will fly by. You'll be home in a few weeks for Christmas." She slipped her arm around Angie's waist as they walked back to the house.

"Promise me, no matter what, you'll be here when I come back."

"I promise, Pumpkin. Come on, let's finish your packing."

"You won't need all that heavy clothing," Cynthia said as she watched Angie jam another sweater into the trunk. "St. Louis isn't as cold as Colorado. Besides, if you take along too much, you'll only have to lug it all back when you chuck art school and decide ranching is the life for you."

"Cynthia MacKenzie, stop putting those kinds of ideas in her head," Beth declared, coming into the room.

"I think our little sister's going to bolt for home when she catches her first glance of one of those nude male models."

Angie spun around. "Nude models!"

"Of course." Beth winked at Cynthia. "How else can you understand the symmetry of the male body unless you see it unclothed?"

"I . . . I don't want to draw humans—particularly naked ones! I thought I'd like to sketch animals . . . or maybe sunsets and the like."

"You'll still have to dabble in sketching some models."

Angie looked on the verge of tears. "Well, can't they at least be females?"

"Beth, look, our little sister is breaking into a cold sweat."

"I am not," Angie declared. "Furthermore, I think the two of you are hoodwinking me. Nude male models, indeed!" She threw a pillow at Cynthia.

Cynthia caught it and immediately used it to swat Angie on the rear as her sister dived for the other pillow on the bed. Laughing, Angie lifted up her skirt, revealing a pair of lacy knee-length drawers, and hopped across the mattress, while Cynthia raced around the end of the bed to meet her on the other side. Like two duelists, the sisters parried with pillows, exchanging swats until Beth came chasing back in with her own pillow. Then it became a free-for-all.

Laughing and screaming, the girls chased one another into the hallway, dodging one another's blows. Then Cynthia's pillow broke at the seam, and a cloud of feathers burst into the air.

"Now we've got you," Angie yelled.

"Not fair," Cynthia screamed as Beth and Angie combined in an attack on her. She ran laughing down the hallway with Beth and Angie in hot pursuit. "You're both going to be sorry when I get my hands on another pillow," she threatened.

Under the fierce trouncing, the other pillows burst apart, and the air became so thick with floating feathers that the sisters could barely see.

Cynthia groped for the bannister, then stopped abruptly. With feathers raining down on her like huge snowflakes, she stared in astonishment at the figure below.

Hat in hand, David Kincaid stared up at her.

"Dave!" Beth exclaimed, stepping past Cynthia. "What a pleasant surprise. We weren't expecting you." Smoothing out her hair and her dignity, she walked majestically down the stairway, accompanied by a stream of floating feathers above her head.

"Hello, Elizabeth," Dave said, his stare still fixed on Cynthia. "Angeleen," he added.

"Hello, David. Nice to see you," Angie said

brightly. "If you'll excuse me, I'll start cleaning up this mess."

"You're darn right, you will," Middy declared, arms akimbo. "You three girls are too old for such nonsense."

"Tut, tut, Middy! No harm done," Beth said. "You get started, Angie, while I fetch the broom."

"And don't be expectin' any help from me. I've got me hands full with dinner."

"Oh, did we lose another cook, Middy?" Beth inquired.

"Useless, she was, too," Middy declared.

"I hope you'll stay for dinner, David." Slipping her arm through Middy's, Beth led the woman away.

Angie ducked back into her room, leaving Cynthia and David still staring at each other. Finally, Cynthia broke the silence.

"I'm glad to see you. You look good, Dave."

He started to climb the stairs.

"I mean, you look a lot better than the last time I saw you. That is . . . I mean . . . your bruises."

Reaching the top of the stairway, he grabbed her hand, hauled her down to the room he always used at the end of the hallway, then, kicking the door shut, he pulled her into his arms.

Her body trembled when he crushed her to him and his mouth descended. The feel of him, the smell of him, the strength of him, were a heady aphrodisiac, as potent and thrilling as the touch of his lips. Her senses reeled under the powerful combination and she melted into him and kissed him back, savoring every second of the divine sensation until their breath was exhausted.

Raising his head, he brushed a gentle kiss across her brow. "Oh, God, Cyn, I thought I could be free of you . . . of wanting you. But I can't."

He lightly kissed her closed eyes, the tip of her nose, and finally her mouth, the tender persuasion sending currents of desire through her.

"These have been the five longest days of my life," she whispered, their breaths mingling through their parted lips. The urgency of their kisses increased, and only Elizabeth's voice in the hallway brought them back to the reality of their surroundings.

"Come back, Cyn. Everybody wants you back as much as I do."

"I wanted to come back, but I was afraid you'd leave if I did."

"You know I didn't mean what I said. I wanted to hurt you, the way you hurt me when you said you were leaving."

"There's been a lot of hurt between us, Dave."

"Nothing that a kiss won't remedy," he said, reclaiming her lips. "I have to go back tomorrow," he whispered between kisses. "Will you come with me?"

"I can't tomorrow. Angie's leaving for school and taking the car. But I'll come as soon as I can. It shouldn't be longer than a week."

"A week!"

"A week, Kincaid. I'm sorry." She rose on her toes to press another light kiss on his lips.

As they heard Beth calling Cynthia's name, she reluctantly stepped out of his arms and crossed to the door. Glancing back at him, she saw that he looked devastated. "I have to help my sisters clean up the mess before dinner. But I'll see you later." She winked.

"She didn't! Not Catherine Mary!" Cynthia exclaimed.

Throughout dinner, Dave had kept them amused relating the incidents of the last few days while he was under siege.

"Yes, she did. Your sweet little Catherine Mary

stuck her tongue out at me. As did most of your *little darlings*. I hope you didn't teach them that in one of your school lessons, Miz Cynthia?"

"She wouldn't have to," Beth remarked. "Comes naturally, Dave."

"When I was young, I used to do it all the time to Giff," Angie said.

"Don't remind me," Giff replied, grinning. "You were a brat!"

"Well, until this happened to me, I never realized how vicious little girls can be if you cross them."

Beth smiled. "From what you told us, it appears the boys were no angels, either."

"Nor their parents," Cynthia added.

"That's for sure," Dave agreed. "Sean Rafferty and Lydia O'Leary were the only two who showed any common sense."

"You oughta take up ranching, Dave," Giff said. "Every time people start closing in on me, I just mount up and ride off. A lonely life does have its advantages."

"Believe me, Giff, I was tempted to."

"That kind of talk is ruining my meal," Beth said. "I can't imagine what we would do without either of you." She rose. "On that note, do you have time to drive Angie to the depot tomorrow morning, Giff? I'd rather do my blubbering in the privacy of my own room."

"Sure," he said. "Think I'll head back to my place now, too."

"Then I'll see you all at breakfast. Good night," Beth said. "Oh, Dave, can I see you in the study? I've got some figures to go over."

Cynthia looked at Angie. "Well, Pumpkin, that just leaves you and me. Come on, we'd better finish up your packing. Morning will come around before we know it."

* * *

Deciding to call it a night, Dave put aside the papers he'd been studying. He was about to turn off the bed lamp when the bedroom door opened and Cynthia slipped through it, closing the door behind her.

At the sight of her, he fought for control. Her long dark hair, brushed to shining luxuriance, flowed across the smooth alabaster of her shoulders, and the gossamer transparency of a black nightgown clung to the lush fullness of her breasts, hugging her slim hips.

Hot lust surged through him with every beat of his thudding heart; his knotted groin was hard and on fire as she moved slowly toward him with feline grace.

"Do you want it off?"

"The gown or the lamp?" he asked, forcing the words past a throat that had been burned dry.

"The lamp," she said breathlessly.

The prolonged anticipation had become painful; he ached to see the beauty of her naked body as much as he needed to touch it—to taste it. "Lamp on—gown off."

Cynthia pulled in a deep breath, trying to slow her hammering heart and pulse. The smoldering passion in his darkened eyes was like a magnet, holding her gaze and intensifying her desire for him. She could feel his tension; his anticipation sent shivers of excitement through her—and a giddy sense of power.

Unhesitantly, she pulled the nightgown over her head. Dave quickly shed his drawers and lay back. Climbing into the bed, she stretched out on top of him. Desire spiraled through her from the contact.

Dave reached up and buried his fingers in the silken richness of her hair. "I was afraid to hope you would come." His voice was thick with a huskiness that sent a shiver down her spine.

"I'd never be able to bear another whole week wondering how this moment would be," she murmured.

His warm hands splayed over the sensitive nerves of her spine and cupped her rounded derriere, drawing her body closer to his. Lowering her head, she shut her eyes just as his mouth closed over her parted lips with a fierce possessiveness, flooding her with arousal.

The pressure of his mouth increased, and his tongue lightly traced the inner moistness of her mouth. Then, with a throaty groan, he rolled over, the pressure of the kiss thrusting them deeper into the downy mattress.

Reveling in the aggressive power of the body trapping her, Cynthia slipped her arms around his neck, raking her fingers through the crisp thickness of his hair.

When breathlessness forced their mouths apart, he lifted his head and she smiled into the warm mahogany of his eyes. Cupping his cheek, she caressed it, her fingertips tingling from the friction of his dark whiskers.

"Why did we fight this so hard?" she asked in a voice made sensuous by passion.

He raised her hand to his mouth and pressed a kiss into her palm; then his tongue traced the delicate curve of her jaw to the sensitive hollow of her ear. "Because I'm a damn fool," he said in a husky whisper, his breath ruffling her hair.

For several seconds, he teased her ear in a titillating probe with his tongue, then he reclaimed her lips in a tender kiss that quickly became demanding. By the time he pulled away, her breath was coming in ragged gasps, her eyes almost black with passion.

Shifting his gaze to her breasts, he lowered his head, his tongue tantalizing the nubs to their fullest.

As his moist mouth toyed with the turgid peaks, he skimmed his roughened hands—exquisitely abrasive against her soft flesh—along the sides of her body, from breasts to thighs. Her whole being flooded with desire. In a fiery response, she arched reflexively under him as the heat within her raged out of control.

With hands and mouths, they explored each other, arousing and discovering the pleasure points and ways to bring the greatest enjoyment to each other. With every movement, every kiss, every touch, their ardor mounted, until control became too tenuous to maintain.

He entered her, sucking in a breath when she tightened around him and matched his rhythm.

"God, Cyn!" he groaned.

"Dave! Oh, Dave!" Her sigh became an ecstatic cry of rapture when their bodies shuddered in a tumultuous, fulfilling release, and he captured her cries with a passionate kiss.

Her chest ached from the intense throbbing of her heart until the erratic breaths gradually returned to a steady rhythm. Only then did she become aware of David's arm around her shoulders and her head resting against his chest. Raising her head, she stared down into the warmth of his eyes.

The look of deep satisfaction they exchanged said more than words ever could.

Her breasts tingled against his hair-roughened chest when he pulled her down and hugged her tightly for a few seconds; then, rolling over, his powerful body pinned her again to the bed. For a long moment, he studied her face intently, then he leaned down and gently kissed her swollen lips. Lying back once more, he cradled her head against his chest. Warm and satiated, she had never known such a feeling of satisfaction, of contentment—of completeness. She snuggled closer to his long body.

He had not told her he loved her, but she knew with certainty that, too, would come. Smiling, she closed her eyes.

Neither knew which was the first to fall asleep.

Chapter 14

"I'll wire you as soon as the car gets back here," Cynthia said as she and Dave said good-bye the following day. "Then I'll be on the next supply train out of here."

"Sounds like a lifetime away," he murmured.

"It's just as well I'm staying. Beth has really been depressed since Angie left this morning. I hope my being here will help her get past it."

"Yeah, you're right. But you can bet I'll be doing a lot of thinking about last night."

Sliding her arms around his neck, she smiled into the intoxicating warm draw of his brown eyes. "So, you liked last night, Kincaid."

"Yeah, I liked it." His hands circled her waist, pulling her closer. "You know damn well I liked it, Miz Sin," he murmured in a half growl as his head descended.

His mouth claimed hers forcibly, devouring the softness of her lips with masterful heated sweeps of his probing tongue that set the pit of her stomach into a mad whirl. Her body ached for his touch.

He raised his head, and she could tell by his grin that he knew the kiss had aroused her. "A week's beginning to seem like a long time away now, isn't it?"

"You bastard, Kin-cad," she said lovingly, returning his grin. "Don't try to make me think you won't be counting the days either."

His next kiss was long and tender, with such an underlying intimacy to it that she couldn't believe he failed to recognize the depth of his feelings for her. Whether he admitted it or not, she was convinced he loved her.

Reluctantly, Dave released her. "I gotta go. I'll be thinking of you."

"I know you will," she called out, unable to resist the gibe. "And give my regards to everyone at Tent Town. I'll be thinking of all of you." The wind whipped at his dark hair as he looked back and waved his Stetson. "Especially you, David Kincaid," she whispered.

In the days that followed, she spent her time accumulating additional supplies to take with her—and spent the nights thinking about Dave. It had been five days since his departure. Five days of missing him every moment.

But the nights were the worst—restless and hard to bear, she reflected, as she gazed out her window at the starry sky. Below a clock chimed the midnight hour, and sighing, she hugged herself to ward off the fall chill—there were still many hours to go before dawn.

Her sweeping glance fell on a light shining from the stable. Curious as to who could be in there at that time of night, she went down to investigate, stopping long enough to pull on a long mantle over her robe.

Pete Gifford was in the corral riding Angie's stallion.

"Giff, what are you doing this time of night?"

"Just giving Calico a little workout."

Climbing down, he led the animal into the stable, and Cynthia followed.

"I promised Angie I'd see that her horse gets a daily workout," he said as he unsaddled the horse. "Didn't get back until dark."

"One day wouldn't have made any difference, Giff," she said kindly.

"Yeah, I reckon not, but I'll be just as busy tomorrow. We've started rounding up the herd and moving it over to the south range for the winter."

"I'll work him out tomorrow for you, Giff."

"I thought you didn't like horses."

"Oh, I've got nothing against them personally. I'm just not fond of ranch life the way Angie is."

"Yeah, she's got a real feel for it. Don't make sense why she'd want to go off to some art school." He scooped up a handful of straw and began rubbing down the horse. "I can tell Calico misses her, too."

"Probably almost as much as you do," Cynthia said.

"I just worry, thinking of her off there in St. Louis by herself. You know she's never been farther away from home than Denver."

"You read the wire from her. She's fine and she's settled in at school. She'll be okay, Giff."

"Yeah, I reckon so."

"Have you ever told her how you feel about her?" Cynthia asked gently.

He looked at her, surprised. "What do you mean?"

"Hey, Giff, I'm Thia, remember? When have we ever lied to each other?"

"Never could fool you, could I?"

"Why don't you tell her?"

"And make a damn fool of myself? She'd never be interested in an old run-down cowpoke like me."

"Giff, there's only ten years' difference in your ages."

"Well, she kinda looks at me as her big brother.

It'd just make her uncomfortable if I told her how I really felt about her."

"Men are so stupid when it comes to the opposite sex. Did it ever occur to you that she might be thinking the same thing about you? You're as bad as Dave. He's convinced I'm just a spoiled rich girl looking for a good time."

Giff came out of the stall. "You ever tell *him* differently?" he asked, grinning.

"I've tried to, but he's convinced himself otherwise." She hesitated, then asked softly, "Giff, could you love a woman who's done what I've done?"

"Whatta you figure you've done that's so bad?"

"You know, run off to Europe. My relationship with Roberto. Dave figures that I'm . . . well, that I'm loose."

"Reckon I'm gonna have to take him behind the barn and beat the hell out of him," he said, slipping an arm around her shoulders. "Just like I did to the guys who called you names when you were younger."

She looped her arm around his waist and they began to walk back to the house. "I'm afraid that won't work. This is one battle I've got to fight for myself, Giff."

"Sounds like you're pretty stuck on Kincaid, Thia."

She stopped and looked up into his bronzed face. "I'm in love with him, Giff. But you didn't answer my question. Could a man love a woman who's done what I've done?"

Gentleness softened the lines of his rugged features. "You're a good woman, Thia. Any man would be as proud as a passel of peacocks to know you loved him. And Kincaid's a damn lucky guy." He lowered his head and kissed her cheek. "Night. Dawn'll be here before we know it."

"Good night, Giff." She watched him walk away

with his familiar loping stride, his broad shoulders slightly slumped in weariness. She had known this man her whole life and loved him dearly. Funny how fate had led both of them down a road of unrequited love.

Open your eyes, Angie, and see the happiness waiting for you right on your own doorstep.

Her thoughts turned to Dave. *And you, David Kincaid, just need a little more convincing.* Shrugging off her gloom, she entered the house.

In the morning a messenger brought them the word Cynthia had been waiting for: the MacKenzie private car had returned to Denver, and she could leave for end of track the next day. By tomorrow evening, she would be back with Dave!

Honoring her promise to Giff, Cynthia saddled Calico and took a ride around the Roundhouse, knowing that when she returned for Christmas the ground would probably be waist-deep in snow. The splendor of the golden aspens was breathtaking, and she realized that she had always taken the beauty of her home for granted. Had falling in love given her a keener appreciation of the beautiful things in life? Smiling, she goaded Calico to a gallop and raced across the countryside.

As she rode back into the homestead, a young woman stepped out of a carriage. Cynthia dismounted as the woman approached her.

"Excuse me, are you Elizabeth MacKenzie?" Blond and petite, the young woman appeared to be even younger than Angie—and looked vaguely familiar to Cynthia.

"No, I'm her sister, Cynthia MacKenzie. Perhaps I can help you."

"I'm anxious to reach David Kincaid."

The woman's words faded as Cynthia realized why the woman looked familiar—she was the one in the framed photograph on Dave's bedside.

And the girl looked the epitome of innocence: even lovelier than the photograph, with hair the color of corn silk and eyes as soft and blue as a summer sky. She had the kind of innocence that medieval knights once jousted to protect and nineteenth-century railroad engineers would strive . . . to marry.

In a daze, Cynthia said, "Come with me. I'll take you to Elizabeth. I'm sure she can answer any questions you may have."

"Thank you, Miss MacKenzie. And may I express my sympathy over the death of your father. My brother often mentioned him in his letters; David thought very—"

"Dave is your brother!" A cry of relief burst from Cynthia's lips.

"Yes," the young girl said, looking somewhat puzzled by Cynthia's behavior. "I'm Sally Kincaid, David's sister."

"Well, it's a pleasure to meet you, Sally," she said buoyantly. "I didn't realize David had a sister. He never . . ."

"He never mentioned me," she said, her blue eyes twinkling with mirth. "Oh, that doesn't surprise me."

"Well, you know how reticent David is about his personal life," Cynthia added, trying to cover up her blunder. "He never spoke of any of his family."

Still ecstatic, Cynthia wasn't sure her feet were on the ground. She tucked her arm through Sally's. "So you're David's sister. Well, you're just going to have to tell me all about yourself." Smiling broadly, she led the girl into the house.

That night at dinner, Cynthia and Beth listened intently as Sally related some of the details of her past.

"I was four and David was sixteen when our parents, our brother, Matthew, and our sister, Rachel, died in the fire that destroyed our house. If David hadn't carried me out, I'd have died, too. When he tried to go back in to help the others, the house was burning so badly that the firemen held him back."

"Oh, you poor dear," Beth said. "How tragic."

"Dave and I went to live with our mama's sister. But Dave left; that's when he started working for the railroad. Aunt Rachel died three years later. She left us enough to keep me in boarding school for a year, and Dave's been paying my tuition since. I'm grateful to him, but I'm not going back."

"Were you unhappy at boarding school, Sally?" Cynthia asked.

"No, it's a nice school; and Miss Spencer, the director, is real congenial. When I reached sixteen, she even permitted me to help teach a class of the younger girls. I liked that very much."

"Then why did you leave, Sally?" Beth asked.

"I've been there for ten years, and I think it's time I start a new life and pay my own way. I've been a burden long enough. I feel guilty taking David's money."

"Dear, I'm sure he's glad to do it," Beth said. She exchanged a worried glance with Cynthia, then asked, "What are your plans, Sally?"

"I'm going to find a job and start paying him back."

"Sally, Dave would never take your money," Cynthia said gently.

Sally folded her hands in her lap and tears started to slide down her cheeks. "I just want to see him . . . spend some time with him. Just get to know him. It's been ten years. I only got to see him at Christmas and a couple of times when he was in college, because he always had to work so hard just to keep us going."

Sympathetic tears glistened in Cynthia's eyes. "Dave's in New Mexico right now. And I have an excellent idea, Sally—I'm leaving for end of track tomorrow morning, and you can come with me! I've started a school for the young daughters of the crew. How would you like to be their teacher? That way, you could be near Dave, as well as earn a living. There's a salary that goes with the job, isn't there, Beth?"

"Yes, of course, but, Cynthia, perhaps it would be wiser to discuss this arrangement with Dave first," Beth cautioned. "He may prefer Sally remain in school herself."

"I won't go back," Sally declared. "No matter what Dave says. Oh, I think your idea is wonderful, Cynthia!"

"Then we'll do it. I imagine you're tired after your long trip from Massachusetts. As soon as we finish dinner, I suggest you go upstairs, get a good night's rest, and we'll leave first thing in the morning."

"I can't thank both of you enough," Sally exclaimed. "You've been so good to me."

"Honey," Cynthia said confidently, her thoughts turning to her plan of getting a marriage proposal from Dave, "just think of us as your family."

As soon as Sally went upstairs to her room, Beth pulled Cynthia into the library and closed the door. "Thia, you aren't certain if Dave will agree to these plans you're making. I think you should have talked to him first about them."

"Oh, nonsense. Why should he have any objections?"

"I don't know, but it seems to me that you're interfering in his personal life. I love you dearly, Thia, but if this sets off a powder keg with him, remember, Dave's in charge of building this railroad. He's got the final say on everything. I will not override his authority."

But now, with the elimination of any possible rival for Dave's affections, Cynthia floated on a cloud of blissful confidence. Hugging Beth, she murmured, "Trust me, darlin'. I can handle Dave Kincaid."

The next morning, standing on the observation platform of the private car, Cynthia and Sally waved good-bye to Beth and Pete as the train pulled away from MacKenzie Junction, headed for end of track.

Get ready for a surprise. What in hell had she meant? Dave pondered, going over the wire Cynthia had sent him. She was so unpredictable, it scared the daylights out of him to think what it could be. Well, he'd find out soon enough—the supply train was puffing into camp at this very moment.

He shrugged off his negative thoughts. Her unpredictability was one of the qualities that made her so captivating, he told himself—that and the most desirable, responsive body he had ever known!

Dave leaped up on the deck of her car before the train stopped and opened the door eagerly. Cynthia stood a short distance away, looking as beautiful as ever. For the brief span of a drawn breath, it crossed his mind how good it felt to open a door and find her waiting for him. "Hi, honey! Have I missed you!" He opened his arms.

Cynthia grinned broadly. "Hi. I've missed you, too."

When she made no move in his direction, he shifted his glance and saw the reason for her hesitation. She was not alone.

Dave froze on the spot. A shock of astonishment shot from his brain to his toes as he recognized the woman smiling mischievously at him. "Sally! Is it really you, Sally?"

"Oh, David!" she squealed joyously and broke for him, racing into his arms. After they hugged and kissed, he stepped back, the initial shock worn off. "It's good to see you, Sally, but what are you doing here? You should be in school."

Cynthia had watched the reunion in silence, and on that note, she slipped outside. It was best Sally did her explaining in private to him.

Her heart seemed to leap to her throat when she saw her little class all waiting up ahead at the side of the track. She waved gaily. As soon as the train came to a full stop, Cynthia stepped down into the cluster of girls, who welcomed her with hugs and kisses.

By the time they finished, Dave and Sally had joined them. After he introduced Sally to the girls, he came over to Cynthia. With a firm grip on her arm, he excused them for a moment, saying he wished to speak to her privately.

As the girls led Sally to their school, Dave literally forced Cynthia back on the train and closed the door.

"I hope you have a good explanation for bringing Sally to Tent Town."

Cynthia's first reaction was that Beth had guessed correctly—he was upset. "Didn't Sally tell you that she doesn't want to return to boarding school?"

"Yeah, she told me," he said with rancor.

"Well, under the circumstances, since we are looking to hire a teacher, I thought it would be a good idea to offer Sally the job."

"You did, did you? Cynthia, I do the hiring of everyone related to this project: gaugers, cooks . . . and schoolteachers. Did you consult me?"

"Oh, good heavens, Dave, is that what's bothering you? You're angry because I've stepped on your toes by going over your head?"

"Apparently you still haven't grasped the importance of maintaining a smooth-running operation around here. I would have thought you might have learned from the mistakes you made before."

Cynthia had initially tolerated his anger to allow him to get the shock out of his system, but he was beginning to become irritating.

"Why do you feel there will be a problem, other than the one you're creating right now, Kincaid?"

"There are a lot of single men in this crew, and Sally is a young, single girl. I just don't want her . . . well . . ." He started to rub the back of his neck in the gesture she had grown to recognize when he was hedging.

"You don't what, Kincaid?"

"Well, did you stop to think where she'll stay? There's certainly no room in my quarters."

Cynthia had to admit to herself she hadn't even given that a thought. "She can stay here in my car, or we can bring in a tent for her."

"If I wanted my sister living in a tent the rest of her life, I'd have brought her with me," he lashed out angrily, "and not spent every cent I earned keeping her in that boarding school back east."

"You can't be certain she'll remain with the railroad the rest of her life, Dave. Maybe she'll settle down in one of the small towns we come to."

"You know damn well that if she stays, inside a year she'll be married to one of the crew with her belly swollen with his baby!"

"It didn't happen to Lydia, did it?"

"Oh, come on, Cynthia. Lydia was a forty-year-old spinster when she joined us. Sally's seventeen. When these men get a look at that blond hair and those big blue eyes of hers, what do you think's gonna happen? They'll be at each other's throats."

"So, it's not really Sally you're concerned about, it's maintaining harmony among your crew."

His temper had cooled, and he grinned at her. "You ever try to keep a hundred Irishmen from getting into fights with each other, especially after they've all had a couple of beers?"

"No, I've got my hands full with just you."

"And I'm only part Irish," he said, advancing on her.

"What's the other part?"

"Lover. I'm a lover, not a fighter." He slipped his arms around her waist and pulled her to him.

Cynthia started laughing. "I can't believe you said that."

"I guess I'll just have to back it up with action." He kissed her hungrily, reigniting their passion for each other.

"I mean, it's so unlike you," she said breathlessly, sliding her arms around his neck. "You're always so serious. Mr. Business-First-and-No-Time-for-Pleasure Kincaid."

"You're corrupting me," he said, kissing the tip of her nose, then he began to lightly tug at her lips, sending shivers down her spine.

"I'm corrupting you! If my memory is correct, there were some things you did to me that I sure didn't teach you."

"Yeah, but you liked it, didn't you?" he said in an intimate voice, their lips so close they were breathing as one.

"I loved it," she whispered as his mouth closed over hers.

When he finally released her mouth, her legs were trembling and she leaned into him, for support as much as from desire.

"This isn't quite the reunion I had planned." Slipping his hand into her bodice, he whispered, "I need you, Miz Sin." She sighed when his warm palm cupped her breast. "Oh, Lord, do I need you. I've thought about nothing else for the past week."

She closed her eyes and threw back her head, giving him free access to her neck. He trailed heated kisses down the slender column. She had no idea when he unbuttoned her bodice and shoved up her chemise, but suddenly his moist mouth closed around one of her nipples.

"Oh, my God," she moaned when the exquisite sensation filled her being. She knew they had to stop now before their escalating passion made them mindless. "Dave, Sally could come in here any minute."

She couldn't have produced quicker results had she poured ice water over him. Raising his head, he stepped back. His hands were shaking as he rebuttoned her blouse.

"Tonight, Dave. Come to me tonight," she whispered.

"'Fraid I can't do that, Miz Sin. Looks like you'll be sharing your bed with my sister."

He walked out, leaving her staring in frustration at the closed door.

Chapter 15

"A man is a fool to get mixed up with women," Dave grumbled as he headed for his office. "Women are too impetuous; they don't stop to reason out the long-range aspects of a situation, but settle for immediate solutions." He loved his crew, but it was a hard life for their families, and he was not going to submit his sister to that life. He only had Sally's interests at heart. Why couldn't Cyn understand that? Why did they have to argue about it?

He spun around at the sound of thundering hooves and saw eight horsemen galloping into camp. They looked threatening, and Dave realized how vulnerable the camp was to any kind of attack. With the crew away on the job, he and the four cooks were the only remaining males in a camp full of women and children.

The leader of the riders was Will Bonner, the rancher he'd seen the day of the carnival. Now, with his steel-gray eyes glaring down at Dave, Bonner asked gruffly, "You the ramrod of this goddamn operation?"

"I'm in charge here, if that's what you mean," Dave replied.

"I'm Will Bonner." His tone carried the implication that the name should mean something to Dave.

It did. Dave had already received a letter from Elizabeth and anticipated the rancher would make an appearance. "How do you do, Mr. Bonner. I'm Dave Kincaid," he said, extending his arm to shake hands.

Bonner ignored Dave's outstretched hand. "You're on my spread, Kincaid."

"No, sir, the government had an easement on this particular stretch of land. They assigned it to the Rocky Mountain Central Railroad."

"I don't give a good goddamn what the government did. This is a part of the Lazy B—has been for the past twenty years. Now get all this equipment and your people out of here."

"I can assure you, Mr. Bonner, we have a legal right to be here. If you'll come into my office, I'll show you that we cross this end of your spread."

"I ain't interested in lookin' at any of your damn maps. There's a water hole 'bout a quarter mile from here—and your damn railroad's between that water and my cattle."

"That's regrettable, sir, but the railroad now owns the easement."

"Well, if I was you, railroad man, I'd find me a new route, 'cause I ain't gonna try and stop my cattle from gettin' to that water."

"Unfortunately, sir, there's nothing we can do to change it," Dave said.

"Don't say you ain't been warned, Kincaid." Bonner wheeled his horse, and he and his men rode off as quickly as they had appeared.

Shaking his head, Dave entered his office. He knew he hadn't heard the last from Will Bonner. But first things first: he had to convince Sally to go willingly back to school without alienating her. At the moment she was very angry with him. If he just sent her back, he was afraid she'd run off somewhere—and Lord knew what might happen to her.

He'd give her time to cool off, then he would try to discuss it calmly with her.

In the past, whenever she had a problem, Sally had always taken a walk. Somehow the exercise and isolating herself from others had always helped her to reach a solution. But today, after her argument with David, she wasn't having much success.

As she trudged through the countryside, Sally was so angry she just wanted to get as far away from David as she could. Why was he being so unreasonable? He had had a chance to make his own choices when he was even younger than she. Didn't she have a right to make hers?

Well, if he wouldn't let her stay with him, she would find some other place—but she was not going back to boarding school, no matter how much he insisted. She couldn't stop him from sending her back to Denver, but he couldn't force her to go back to Massachusetts.

She loved David and was grateful to him for the sacrifices he had made in the past for her, but her mind was made up. She was old enough to be out of school. David was just too stubborn to see that.

Cynthia understood how she felt—why couldn't her own brother? Funny how the one person she had depended upon for ten years now turned out to be her greatest adversary. But perhaps Cynthia was right; maybe Dave just needed a little bit of time to adjust to the idea.

Climbing a summit, she sat down on a rock. Momentarily shoving her problems to the back of her head, she took time to enjoy the view. This was a beautiful country—vast and serene. More barren than anything she had seen in Massachusetts, but awesome in its very starkness.

The railroad slithered across the countryside like a mammoth silver snake, and the distant crew and the people moving about Tent Town appeared like huge ants to her. Farther to the west she saw a cattle herd quietly grazing on a patch of grass. The distant sights seemed like paintings.

Sally rose to her feet. The serenity of the scene had dissolved her previous anger, so she began the long walk back. In a short time the hot sun began to take a toll; she felt tired and thirsty, and now wished she had not walked so far.

She was surprised, a short time later, when two men rode up to her. Neither one of the cowboys appeared to be much older than she was.

"Well, where'd you come from?" one asked.

"How do you do," Sally replied in her politest boarding school manners. "I'm with the railroad."

"Hear that, Ben?" he said. "The li'l lady here is one of 'em railroad trash."

The unexpected slur took her by surprise. "I beg your pardon?"

"Whatta ya doin' on the Lazy B, lady?" Ben asked.

"The Lazy B?" she asked, perplexed.

"This here's Bonner land. 'Pears like yer trespassin'."

"Oh, I'm sorry. I didn't realize that."

"Hear that, Charlie?" Ben said. "The li'l gal here jest didn't realize that." He inched his horse closer, pinning her between the two horses. "How'd we to know if y'all been up to no good?" he asked, smirking.

"I can assure you gentlemen I have done no harm. I merely took a walk."

The snorting horses and their pungent odor were quickly becoming overpowering to her. "Please, I'd like to leave."

"You was mighty anxious to come here in the first place," Charlie said. "Now ya want to leave. Sounds downright unneighborly of you, li'l lady."

"Yeah, how 'bout the three of us sittin' down and passin' some time together?" Ben said. He winked at Charlie. "Kinda have ourselves some pleasure, Blondie."

Despite her innocence, the cowboys' intent was clear. When Ben started to dismount, she shoved his horse, broke free, and started to run.

Within seconds, the mounted cowboys caught up with her and began playing cat and mouse, letting her loose, then trapping her again as she yelled at them to stop.

"What's going on here?"

Sally glanced hopefully at the man who had just ridden up. He didn't look much older than the other two men. Would he help her or join her harassers?

"Charlie and me was jest funnin' with her, Clay," Ben said. "We'd never of hurt her."

"You two are supposed to be rounding up stock, not tormenting ladies. Think you both better get back to the herd—now."

"Sure thing, Clay," Charlie said, goading his horse to a gallop. Ben followed in his dust.

"Thank you," Sally said. She walked over to a shaded area and sat down to catch her breath. Her rescuer followed, dismounted, and unhooked a canteen from his saddle.

"Are you okay, miss?" Unscrewing the top, he handed the canteen to her.

She smiled gratefully and took a deep swallow of the water, then gave the canteen back to him. "Thank you again. I was really thirsty."

The cowboy plopped down beside her. "Don't pay Charlie and Ben no mind. Believe me, they'd never have hurt you. They're just a little wild, that's all."

She looked askance at him. "Well, they certainly scared me."

He took off his hat to reveal a shock of blond hair,

so light some of the bleached strands appeared almost white in the sunlight.

"I'm Clay Bonner. My father owns this spread."

"Oh, so that's why they listened to you. I'm Sally Kincaid. My brother is the engineer in charge of building the railroad."

He grinned, his teeth gleaming whitely against his deeply bronzed face. " 'Fraid the railroad's not the most popular subject around the Lazy B. How'd you stray so far from it?"

"I went for a walk. I never thought that this might be private property."

"I don't recommend you go off like this alone, Miss Kincaid. It can be dangerous."

"I found that out for myself."

"No, I mean there's snakes, wolves, wildcats, and bears out here. No telling what you might come upon."

"Not to mention wild cowboys," she said, laughing.

"They're the tamest of the lot."

"I'll take your advice, Mr. Bonner, since I'm new to these parts. Actually, I just arrived here today."

"Where from?" he asked.

"Massachusetts." She stood up. "I guess I better get back; my brother's probably started to organize a search party."

"I'll give you a ride." He mounted, then reached down a hand to her. "Just climb on behind me."

"I've never been on a horse before," she said nervously.

"Nothing to worry about." He swung her up behind him. "Just slip your arms around my waist and hold on. Crow won't do anything I don't tell him to do."

"Crow? What an odd name for a horse."

"I named him that because he's so black."

"And how do you tell him to do what you

want?" She began to relax as they moved along.

"With my knees or the reins. Crow's real smart, though. He don't need too much instruction."

"Is it true that you cowboys talk to your horses?"

"Sure it is. Gets pretty lonely riding the range. Your horse is your only companion—and your best friend. Don't you city folk talk to your dogs and cats?"

"Yes, I guess we do . . . although I've never had a pet."

"No pet! Sally Kincaid, you've led a powerful sorry life," he said with a rueful grin.

"That's what I've been trying to tell my brother."

She smiled, knowing Clay couldn't see her. This was the first time she had ever been so intimate with a man—actually sitting against him and holding him around the waist. She liked it. It was an exciting feeling and made her feel very feminine.

They rode in silence until they neared the railroad. Aware of David's protective attitude, Sally had Clay stop in a copse of trees.

"I'll get off here." He dismounted and swung her to the ground. "Thank you for the ride, Mr. Bonner."

"Mr. Bonner's my father—just call me Clay."

"Thank you, Clay." She started to walk away.

"Hey, Blue Eyes." She looked back at him. "If you've a mind to take another walk, I can meet you here tomorrow."

"If my brother has his way, I might not be here tomorrow."

"Well, I'll be here just in case."

When she looked back, he had climbed onto his horse and was watching her. She waved, and he waved back, then rode off on his big black stallion.

That night Cynthia insisted the three of them sit down together and try to resolve the problem, so

Dave agreed to join them for dinner in Cynthia's private car.

The chicken she prepared in a cream sauce was a welcome change from Dave's accustomed heavy meal of beef and beans, but the relations between him and Sally remained strained throughout the meal until he told her she could at least remain in Tent Town until they reached an agreement on her future.

Sally's spirits heightened considerably, and when they finished their meal, the two women went off to work out a schedule with Lydia, leaving Dave to the dishes.

By the time the last pot was dried and put away, Cynthia and Sally had not returned, so he went back to his own car and began to go over the plat of the Lazy B boundaries once again.

Technically, the water hole was on the easement owned by the railroad, but since it had been government land previously, the Lazy B had used the hole for twenty years. He could see Bonner's problem: water holes were essential to a ranch's existence in this part of the country. Dave was sure a compromise could be worked out if he and Bonner kept cool heads.

He went to bed with the problems of cattle and water holes still on his mind, but soon thoughts of Cynthia invaded his senses and any considerations for thirsting cattle were forgotten in his struggle with his own thirsts.

In the morning, the rail train with the crew chugged back into Tent Town only a short while after it had left, and Sean Rafferty hopped off.

"The track we laid yesterday's been ripped up, boss."

"What are you talking about?" Dave asked.

"Rail's been pulled up and bent, and the ties are busted up. It ain't a pretty sight."

"How much?"

"'Pears to be 'bout an eighth of a mile of track."

"That's fifty rails! Damn! It's Bonner. I should have figured he'd pull something like this. I bet he's behind the missing rail, too. Last night I went over the plat of his land. That rail started showing up missing about the time we approached the Canadian, and Bonner's spread begins on this side of the river. I bet those missing rails are on the bottom of that river."

"Then I'm thinkin' we shud be payin' Mr. Bonner a visit," Sean said ominously.

"No, he's got a lot of men riding for him, and they're all armed. I don't want any of the crew shot up—or killed. I'll ride back into town and talk to the local sheriff. Let the law handle this."

"So what do you want us to do, boss?"

"Nothing to do except lay new rail, Sean. We'll have to post guards at night on the site. In the meantime, I'll take the handcar."

"You want company?"

"No. I need you to get the men going—and cooled down. Sean, don't let them get their Irish up."

"It took a lot of their sweat to lay that rail."

"I know that, but I don't want to see any of them hurt. I'm depending on you, Sean."

When Cynthia awoke and heard about the latest trouble she hurried over to Dave's office, but he had already departed. As she started to leave, she glanced at the stack of paperwork on his desk. With all the problems he had to deal with, she saw no reason why he should be bogged under by paperwork. Cynthia sat down and began to go through it. An hour later, she had it separated into several piles: one relating to engineering, one to past deliveries that she knew had to be entered in a daily expense log, and another consisting of correspondence that needed to be filed. Putting aside the engineering pile, she attacked the filing.

After a frustrating day of waiting for the sheriff to return to town, it was almost midnight when Dave returned to camp. Surprised to see a light burning in his quarters, he approached the caboose cautiously, not knowing what to expect.

Opening the door, the first thing he saw was Cynthia, her head slumped on his desk. He entered and moved to where she sat, relieved to discover she was only sleeping.

Gazing down at her, he felt a poignant wave of tenderness that obliterated all of the day's frustrations. When had his feelings for her become more than just a physical craving? When had he fallen in love with her? He believed it was that night on the trestle when she had looked up at him and declared they would make the ride together. That moment had scrambled his mind; had changed an image of her that he had carried from the moment he had first heard her name mentioned two years before. It had been easy to hate her then; now, as much as he wanted to for the sake of his own sanity, it had become impossible.

Was he being disloyal to his memory of her father? Was that why he was feeling guilty for daring to love her? Or was it his own fears? He had dared her—challenged her—to try to break him, to bring him to his knees. How she would laugh if he admitted she had won.

Yeah, Miz Sin—my precious Miz Sin—you've won. She had brought the smile to his face as she once vowed to, but did not realize her face had brought a smile to his heart. She had taught him to laugh at himself, and she had taught him how to have fun.

He never realized before how easy it was, until she had shown him how.

He gently slipped the pencil out from between her fingers. Curling her arm around his neck, he slid one arm under her knees and the other to her back and lifted her gently into his arms.

Cynthia opened her eyes. "What are you doing, Dave?" she asked drowsily.

"I'm going to take you back to your car, Cyn."

"I'm not through yet."

"You're through for tonight," he said.

Cynthia slipped her other arm around his neck and rested her cheek against his. When she felt the irregular rhythm of his breath against her face, she pulled away and looked at him. Her heart lurched—his steady gaze, riveted on her face, blazed with undisguised desire.

She couldn't deny how his passion excited her. "Put me down, Dave." His fixed stare never wavered. "Dave, please put me—" The final word was smothered by his lips.

The kiss was hard, drugging. Exploratory, demanding—and so exciting she felt shivers of desire racing through her, curling into a knot in the pit of her stomach. When breathlessness forced them apart, she buried her head against his throat.

"Oh, God, this isn't a game anymore, is it?"

"No, the game's over, Miz Sin . . . my irresistible Miz Sin."

Her feet touched the floor an instant before he reclaimed her lips, and the heady sensation of his mouth and tongue set her head spinning, her legs trembling. She leaned into him, matching her body to the hard curves of his.

"I've wanted to do this from the moment you came back," he whispered, and traced a trail of hot, moist kisses down her neck.

"And I'd be lying if I didn't admit I wanted you to."

She didn't attempt to stop him when he slid the gown off her shoulders and down her arms, but before she could free them, his tongue caressed her breasts, swelling the sensitive peaks to hardened nubs.

Chills of arousal raced up and down her spine. Closing her eyes, she reveled in the thrilling sensation. She wanted more—so much more. The wait was becoming unbearable.

"Take it off me, Dave," she whispered, her hands trapped by her own gown. He yanked the sleeves past her hands, popping the buttons on the cuffs. The gown slid away, freeing her arms. Shoving her petticoat and drawers off her hips, he lifted her into his arms and carried her to his bunk. After quickly disposing of her shoes and hose, he gazed at her in a slow and seductive appraisal.

"Lord, Cyn, you're beautiful."

Trembling with anticipation, she watched with wanton pleasure while he shed his clothes, then she reached up to embrace him as he lowered himself to her, his long body covering and caressing her. Under a torrent of drugging kisses, his mouth teased and explored with light whispering kisses, then deep, hot probes of his tongue sliding past her parted lips.

His warm palms and fingers sought and found the pleasure points of her soft curves until she could no longer control her cries of delight or moans of ecstasy, the urgency of her passion matching his with lusty uninhibitedness.

Giving and taking, their escalating passions lifted them higher and higher until they soared on wings of sensation to an explosive burst of shuddering ecstasy, greater than either of them had ever known.

Chapter 16

Sally thought Cynthia would never leave. For the past five days, as soon as school was over, Cynthia had been going to David's car and helping him with paperwork. Today she hadn't gone, and Sally was afraid Clay would think she wasn't coming. Dare she tell Cynthia she was meeting Clay Bonner? Could she trust her friend not to tell David? Finally, with every second becoming more critical, Sally asked, "Aren't you going to help David today?"

"Not today, honey. Lydia said there's something she wants to discuss with me, so I'm waiting for her."

"Well, that sounds very private. I'll leave so you two can be alone."

"That's not necessary, Sally. I'm sure Lydia wouldn't care if you remain."

"I really don't mind." Sally grabbed her shawl and hurried away.

Forcing herself not to run, Sally headed for the trees. Would Clay still be waiting? He probably thought she wasn't coming. For the past five days they had met every day. Although their meetings were brief, she looked forward to them. What if Cynthia did tell David? After all, she was one of the railroad owners, and would never believe that Clay had nothing to do with whomever was vandalizing the railroad track.

Entering the trees, she saw that Clay had just mounted up, preparing to leave.

"Clay!"

He turned and smiled. "I was afraid you weren't coming."

He reached down and took her hand, swinging her up behind him. She slipped her arms around his waist and they rode off.

As soon as Lydia arrived Cynthia offered her a glass of lemonade, then they sat down and went over the teaching schedules.

"The students are very fond of Sally," Lydia said with a bright smile. "I think everything is working out delightfully. In your brief absence, I had suggested to Mr. Kincaid that we mix the boys and girls and divide the classes by ages. I don't think that's necessary now. What do you think, Cynthia?"

"Sally is so young, I feel the girls are enough for her to handle for now. Since my return, I've only been working with them a few hours a day, giving me more time to help Dave out with his paperwork. The girls all like Sally and appear content with the arrangement."

"Do you think Mr. . . . ah, Dave, will permit Sally to remain?"

Cynthia laughed lightly. "I don't think he'd let her go until she agrees to return to school. She more or less has him where she wants him. Everything is running so smoothly with the children, and the important thing is that they are *all* getting an education."

Lydia nodded, but Cynthia could see that the woman looked uncomfortable. "Is there something bothering you that you haven't told me, Lydia?"

"Well, it's nothing to do with the children; it's a personal issue."

"What did I do now?" Cynthia joked.

Flustered, Lydia said quickly, "Oh no, dear, it's nothing you've done. It's me." She blushed profusely. "This is very embarrassing to me, but I feel I can trust you not to break a confidence, Cynthia."

"Of course you can. What is it, Lydia?"

"Well, I know you'll think me foolish, but for some time I have had strong feelings for Mr. Rafferty."

"Why would I think that's foolish, Lydia? Sean is a very nice man."

"And a very handsome figure of a man," Lydia added.

"Yes, I would say he is."

"And I am not very comely, so I . . . oh, Cynthia," Lydia said, her defenses crumbling, "you're so knowledgeable in everything. I was hoping you could tell me what I can do to appear more appealing to him."

"But you *are* appealing to him, Lydia. He appears more comfortable with you than any other woman in the camp."

"I mean physically appealing to him. Let's face it, Cynthia, I haven't one redeeming feature. And truthfully, I accepted this about myself years ago; but since I've met Sean, I have developed a deep affection for him, and I'm asking you to tell me how I can make myself appear more attractive."

"Well, Lydia, I'd say the major obstacle has already been overcome—he's comfortable with you. Despite what you may think, that is a very important element between a man and a woman. The next thing is to make certain that he's not so comfortable that he forgets you're a woman." Cynthia winked at her. "There are subtle ways of reminding him. Certain gestures, perfume, occasionally changing your hairstyle. A new gown. There are a dozen little things a woman can do to make a man aware of her."

Cynthia stepped back and took a long look at Lydia. The woman was thin, but not to the point of boniness. A change in wardrobe would solve that. "I notice most of the clothes you wear are gray or black, Lydia. How about adding a little color near your face?"

Hurrying into her bedroom, Cynthia came back with a red silk scarf. She tucked it around Lydia's neck and into the front of her bodice. "There, that helps to bring out some color in your cheeks. Now let's think of what we can do about your hair. There's nothing like a new hairstyle to catch a man's attention."

Cynthia began pulling the pins out of Lydia's hair. "This is too severe looking," she said, releasing the bun Lydia wore on the nape of her neck. Besides, pulling her hair back so tightly emphasized the length of Lydia's nose.

"Now I'll heat the curling iron and we'll add a few curls around your face. You know, Lydia, you have high cheekbones, which is a great advantage—the wrinkles don't show as much when you grow older." After brushing Lydia's hair for several minutes, Cynthia exclaimed, "Why, you have a lovely wave to your hair. Shame on you for rolling it up in a bun and hiding it."

"It's really not proper for a woman my age to wear it long, Cynthia."

"I know, but your hair is lovely. I'm sweeping it up to the top of your head and making a loose knot."

By the time Cynthia finished, she had added a hanging curl on each side of Lydia's face. "There, it looks much better and gives your face a softer look. See for yourself." Cynthia handed Lydia the mirror.

"Oh my, it does, doesn't it!" Lydia said, pleased.

"Now, what do you think is your most unbecoming feature?" Cynthia asked.

Lydia took another look in the mirror. "I have a very long nose."

"Then the thing to do is distract attention from your nose." Cynthia took her kohl stick and lightly darkened Lydia's lashes and brows. "This will draw people to your eyes, and your nose will no longer be a problem."

Upon viewing herself in the mirror, Lydia exclaimed, "Oh, I like that!"

Taking Lydia by the hand, Cynthia drew her into the bedroom, where she could see the complete results in a full-length mirror.

"My, I look so different! I can't believe it's me."

"But it is you, dear. Now all you have to do is be your usual sweet self. That, along with your lovely smile, will have Sean Rafferty begging you to marry him."

"I can't wait until he sees me," Lydia exclaimed. "Do you think he'll like the change?"

"How could he not like it?" Cynthia said confidently.

"But what if he doesn't?" Lydia asked, beginning to have doubts. "I'd die of embarrassment."

"Lydia, how long have you had these strong feelings for Sean?"

"Almost two years."

"Two years! And there's been no progress in the relationship?" Cynthia asked, astonished. Lydia shook her head. "Not even a casual kiss?"

"No," Lydia replied, hanging her head.

"I can see the time has come for me to take matters into my own hands," Cynthia declared firmly.

"What are you going to do?" Lydia asked nervously.

"Just trust me. At seven o'clock Sean will be coming to dinner, so make enough for two," Cynthia said.

Lydia was astounded. "Cynthia, how do you know that? Sean has never eaten dinner with me."

"You mean in two years you've never invited him to dinner? Well, he'll be there tonight—I'll see to that."

"Oh my, then I better get back," Lydia said, atwitter. She rushed back to her tent.

The next thing Cynthia did was find Maggie and invite her to dinner. Having set the stage, Cynthia made a point of being in the area when the crew returned several hours later. She greeted Sean as soon as he climbed off the work train.

"Sean, if you don't mind, Maggie will be having dinner with me tonight."

"That's most kind of you, Miz Cynthia," he said. "And a pleasant change for the lass."

"Lydia said you're welcome to have dinner with her, so she's expecting you at seven o'clock." Cynthia hurried off before the astonished man could refuse.

"I've done everything short of cooking the meal for you, Lydia. It's up to you now," Cynthia mumbled to herself. She had her own romance to worry about. As he had done since Sally's arrival, Dave would be joining them for dinner. What should she wear? Smiling, she headed to her car.

Before returning to her tent, Lydia stopped at the general store. Not only would she show Sean her new image, he would also see she was a very respectable cook—a skill she had perfected at the orphanage.

After a furious scurrying for several hours, she had everything ready as it neared seven o'clock. Since there was very little breeze that evening,

Lydia tied back the tent flaps and set her table near the entrance.

Although Dave had offered her the greater stability of a railroad car when he hired her, Lydia had preferred the two-room tent that gave her a lounging and cooking area as well as a separate bedroom. Although the tent might appear primitive to one accustomed to the walls of a house, Lydia loved her tent home. Raised in an orphanage, where she had shared a room with others, she cherished the privacy she could achieve by merely closing and tying shut the flaps.

She also had grown to love the families around her. Respected and revered by them because of her position as the teacher, Lydia held a special status in the mobile community. It was the only distinction she had ever received, and despite her natural shyness, she enjoyed this small measure of importance.

Lydia basted the chicken roasting in the oven of her small stove and checked the potatoes and carrots braising in a covered pan. Satisfied that everything was ready, she lit the candles on the table.

Her heart began to palpitate when Sean called to her from outside. Removing her apron, she nervously tucked a few strands of hair in place. Then, recalling Cynthia's advice, she smiled as she went to greet him.

From his appearance, it was obvious he had visited the bathhouse. His face was clean shaven and he smelled of bay rum; his shock of white hair was wet and slicked back. With mouth agape, Sean stared at her for a long moment, his eyes round with surprise.

"What have ya done to yerself, woman?"

Lydia felt her newfound self-assurance begin to dwindle. "What . . . what do you mean?"

"You look different, Lydia."

Her hands fluttered to her head. "Oh, you must

mean my hair. I thought I'd try a different style. Don't you like it?"

"'Tis very lovely, but I'm thinkin' it always was."

"Really, Sean? You never said so," she said, her confidence restored.

"It wasn't my place to," he said. "And I'm thankin' ya for the dinner invitation. 'Twas most kind of you, Lydia."

"Well, I saw no sense in your eating alone when I had this whole chicken. Sit down, Sean. Dinner is ready."

Once they were seated, he grinned widely. " 'Tis been a long time since I've had the pleasure of dinin' with a beautiful woman."

"Mr. Sean Rafferty, we've been friends too long for any need of that Irish blarney."

Sean frowned. " 'Tisn't blarney, Lydia O'Leary. I've not shared a dinner with another woman since my Katie passed away."

"I meant it's not necessary to flatter me, Sean. I don't expect it."

"I'd not be sayin' it were it not the truth, Lydia Mary."

Lydia glanced at him and smiled. "Eat your dinner, Mr. Rafferty, before it gets cold."

They finished the rest of the meal in silence—and awkwardness.

"Yer a fine cook, Lydia," he said after finishing his second piece of apple cobbler, still warm from the oven. Rising to his feet, he said, "I best be leavin' now before me Maggie returns."

"Of course," she said in a voice heavy with disappointment. Laying aside her napkin, she stood up. "I'm happy you came, Sean."

"And I'm happy you asked me."

The moment was so awkward, Lydia didn't know what to say or do. She had hoped that by some miracle, her transformation would have swept him off his feet and produced a declaration of undying love and affection. But in truth, other than an ambiguous reference to her hair, he had not made any further mention of her changed appearance. Cynthia was wrong—he obviously disliked it.

Adding to her misery was a feeling of guilt for scheming to get him to propose. He was a fine, decent man and did not deserve such deceit. Other than keeping her real feelings for him a secret, she had always been open and honest with him. Brushing aside a tear, she turned away.

"Are ya cryin', Lydia?"

Drawing a deep breath, Lydia forced a smile and turned back to him. His brow was furrowed and his anxious look revealed his concern. "I'm ashamed of myself, Sean."

"Ashamed? Why wud ya be ashamed, Lydia?"

"Because tonight was all planned to . . . to entrap you." She could feel the heated blush sweeping through her. "I hoped by changing my appearance, you'd find me attractive. But I guess it's true that you can't make a silk purse out of a sow's ear. At least in my case," she said self-derisively.

"And why wud ya ever want to make yerself more attractive to me?"

"Because I hoped you'd ask . . ." Too embarrassed to continue the confession, she whirled away.

Sean grasped her shoulders and forced her to face him, but she couldn't look him in the eye.

"Tell me, what was it ya were hopin', Lydia?"

Drawing a shuddering breath, Lydia lifted her gaze to meet the confusion in his eyes. Gathering up all her courage, she blurted, "I was hoping you'd ask me to marry you. I know it was a ridiculous dream."

"Ridiculous! Are ya daft, woman? Did ya not know 'tis me dream, too? But I'm an old man—too old for the likes of ya. I've not the right to ask ya to be me wife, for I've nothin' to offer. All I'm knowin' is railroadin', and I have me Maggie to raise as well. But how cud ya not know I luv ya, Lydia Mary O'Leary?"

Lydia couldn't believe her ears. She felt as if she were fantasizing the whole thing. "Did you say you loved me?"

"And how cud I not luv ya, with yer sweet ways?"

"Sean, I'm am unattractive spinster—"

"Hush, woman. I'll not listen to that talk, for 'tis nonsense." His rough finger wiped away the dark kohl streaking her face. "Did ya not know yuv always been beautiful to me, just the way ya were?"

"I thought you would like this change."

His loving gaze swept her face. "Aye, lass. I'm thinkin' yer more beautiful than ever, Lydia Mary. And now the young lads will see it too—and I'll soon be losin' ya."

Her heart felt as if it were swelling to near bursting, to the point where she could barely breathe to speak. "Oh, my dearest. I could never love anyone but you."

Tears trickled from beneath her closed eyelids when he lowered his head and covered her mouth with his own.

Chapter 17

The following morning Cynthia breezed into Dave's office. Seeing him sitting behind his desk, she plopped down on his lap, put her arms around his neck, and kissed him.

"Good morning to you, too," he said.

"Isn't it wonderful! Love is in the air today," she exclaimed.

He lifted her off his lap and set her on the edge of his desk. "I'd say that kind of air is hovering around you *every* day, Miz Sin, but as much as I'd like to take you up on the offer, unfortunately, I've got work to do."

"This is Saturday—your day off, remember? I know for a fact your employer does not expect you to work every day. Apparently you haven't heard the good news."

He looked up with a hopeful glance. "Sally's agreed to go back to school?"

"Good try, Kincaid, but that's not it."

"Oh, too bad." He returned his attention to the map in front of him.

"You aren't the least bit curious?"

He rolled up the map and put it aside. "All right. I can see there's no getting rid of you until you tell me. So get it out, Cyn."

She sat back down on his lap. "Lydia and Sean are getting married."

"What!"

"He asked her last night."

"Well, I'll be damned! That *is* good news. I'm happy for both of them."

She slipped her arms around his neck. "Don't you think it would be nice to make it a double wedding?"

"Why? Your count show up again?"

"You don't fool me for a minute, Kincaid. How long are you going to keep playing hard to get?"

He slid his hands up her sides until they came to rest on her breasts. "Until you get bored with the game, Miz Sin."

The remark caused a quick stab of pain. Managing to keep her tone light, she said, "I thought that the night we made love, we agreed it wasn't a game anymore."

He shifted her deftly and she ended up lying back, her head cradled on his arm. "It will always be a game with you, Cyn. I'd be a fool to think otherwise." His mouth covered hers, flooding her body with the exciting, delicious sensation that his kisses evoked.

Through the fabric of her gown, she could feel the heat from his hand cupping her breast, and she yearned for his touch on her flesh. As if reading her mind, he released the buttons and slid his hand into her bodice. The divine warmth of his palm closed around a breast and his thumb toyed the nub to hardness. A moan slipped past her lips when he lowered his head to her breast and drew the nipple into his mouth.

"Nothing has ever excited me like the touch of your hands and mouth," she said breathlessly. "Oh, Lord, how I want you, Dave," she whispered as he continued the exquisite torture. "I have no pride . . .

no shame where you're concerned. I've never wanted anything or anyone as much as I want you."

He raised his head. "And how long will that last, Miz Sin?"

She opened her eyes. Despite the skepticism in his voice, she could see that his desire was as great as her own.

"Why won't you allow yourself to trust me, Dave?"

He rebuttoned her blouse. "I guess you can't teach an old dog new tricks, Cyn."

"Not old, Kincaid, just stubborn." She stood up. "I promised Lydia I'd go to town with her and Sean. We're shopping for her wedding gown. Why don't you come with us?"

"I might as well. Thanks to you, there'll be no keeping my mind on my work now."

"Oh, so you admit you're weakening, Kincaid."

"Physically?" He shrugged. "Of course! I'm only human. But just because my scalp's dangling from your coup stick doesn't mean you've won the mental battle."

She smiled confidently. "Oh, but we both know I will, don't we? And that's what has you running scared."

"Anybody ever warn you about a double-edged sword, Miz Sin?"

Truer words were never spoken, she thought, already bloodied by their duel of wills. Arching a brow, she again tossed down the gauntlet. "Well, as a wise poet once professed, 'To the victor belongs the spoils.' "

Instead of a wagon, they chose the handcar to ride the forty miles to town, with Dave and Sean doing the pumping.

"I don't understand why Sally didn't come,"

Dave said. "Seems strange she'd turn down a chance to go to town."

Cynthia had thought the same thing when Sally decided not to join them. "She told me she wasn't feeling well and thought she'd just rest and read a book today."

"If I'd a knowed she wasn't coming, I'd a stayed in camp, too," Maggie said.

"And worked on your verb tenses," Cynthia teased.

"Why wouldn't you want to go to town, Maggie?" Lydia asked. "After all, you need a new dress for the wedding."

"Do not. It's not my wedding," Maggie said belligerently. "'Sides, this handcar ain't suitable for ridin'."

"Mind your manners, lass," Sean said with a warning frown at his granddaughter.

"Maybe we would have been wiser to take a wagon," Cynthia agreed, shifting to get more comfortable. "Five people on a handcar is a bit crowded. I think Sally had the right idea."

"This is faster," Dave assured them.

"Bet it ain't faster than a team of horses," Maggie said skeptically.

"Maybe not at a full gallop, Maggie, but you can't race a team for forty miles."

"Besides, dear, why tire a good team of horses, when we have the sweat of the brows of Uncle Dave and your grandfather," Cynthia added, tongue in cheek.

"Just for that, Miss MacKenzie, you and Lydia can pump on the way back," Dave declared.

Lydia giggled and Maggie chortled. Sean just shook his head in amusement.

Once in town, the two men went their way when the women entered a dress shop advertising the latest in Paris fashions.

After trying on a ruffled wedding gown and veil, Lydia shook her head. "I don't feel comfortable in this. Perhaps I'd be wiser just to find a plain gown."

Cynthia agreed—the frilly gown had looked unbecoming on Lydia. They found a more suitable white faille gown with pale blue gauze drapery.

Maggie's spirits rose when they turned to shopping for her dress. The clerk had her try on a white organza dress with a tiered ruffled skirt, but Maggie took one look at herself and stuck out her tongue.

"I agree, dear," Cynthia said. "Too flouncy!"

Next the clerk brought Maggie out in a green taffeta dress with a high, rose-colored lace collar, long sleeves, and matching cuffs that buttoned at her wrists. Cynthia and Lydia burst out laughing when Maggie turned around with her eyes crossed.

"The gown is very elegant, Maggie, and would be perfect if you were the bride's grandmother."

"These are two of our most popular patterns," the clerk said indignantly. "We have one remaining dress in her size, but it's considerably less formal." Grabbing Maggie by the hand, she pulled the reluctant girl back into the dressing room.

Maggie soon reappeared in a blue cotton gown with capped sleeves and a white collar edged with a thin ruffle of lace. A white satin sash was tied in a large bow at the back of her waist. The simple gown was perfect for the young girl's looks and personality.

"Oh, Maggie, you look lovely," Cynthia said. "Don't you think so, Lydia?"

Lydia nodded, dabbing at her eyes with a handkerchief.

"Do you like the gown, Maggie?" Cynthia asked.

Maggie's blue eyes were round with enthusiasm. "Oh, I love it. I never had a gown so pretty, Miz Cynthia."

"Are you sure you'd rather not have the white

gown or the green one?" Cynthia teased.

"Oh, no! This is the one I want," Maggie declared. "Please, may I keep this one?" She turned and looked at herself again in the mirror. "Do I really look lovely, Miz Cynthia?"

"So lovely it hurts my eyes to look at you."

Maggie turned back grinning. "Wait 'til Grandpa sees me." She ran over and threw her arms around Cynthia's waist. "Oh, thank you for the dress. I love you, Miz Cynthia."

"And I love you, darling, but thank your grandfather and Lydia—they're the ones paying for it."

"Thank you, Miz Lydia," Maggie said politely, but failed to offer Lydia a hug.

After buying a few more necessary accessories, they rejoined the men.

"There's no priest in this town, Lydia," Sean said glumly. "It wud not be proper to get married without a holy father blessin' the union."

"Maybe there's one in the next town," Dave suggested.

"If not, Sean, you can always get married by a judge and have a priest bless the marriage later," Cynthia suggested.

"No, there'll be no weddin' without a priest," Sean declared. "We'll just have to wait until we find one."

Lydia's disappointment was evident, and as soon as the engaged couple and Maggie went off to select a wedding ring, Cynthia grabbed Dave's hand.

"Where are we going?" he asked.

"To the telegraph office. I've got an idea. I met a priest from this region when I was in Rome. I'm going to wire him and see if he'd be available."

"Why send a wire now?" Dave asked. "You can do that from camp."

"I don't want to raise Lydia's hopes until I'm certain."

Smiling, Cynthia left the telegraph office a short time later and hurried over to the barbershop, where Dave had just finished getting a haircut.

"I've got them the priest. He'll be here in two weeks," she told him.

"Hope you ain't expectin' me to cut your hair, lady," the barber said with hostility. "This shop ain't for females. I don't cut women's hair."

Glancing disapprovingly at some ragged edges still remaining on Dave's head, Cynthia gave the barber a disgusted look. "And from what I see of that cut you just gave him, I'd say you don't cut men's hair either."

Dave grabbed her hand and pulled her out the door. "Cynthia, must you always have the last word?" he declared once they were outside.

"Well, he asked for it," she said. "The man would make a better butcher than barber. I'll trim your hair when we get back to camp."

"No, you will not. Like I said this morning, you've already got my scalp as a trophy. I don't need mothering. Stay with what you do best."

"What's that?" she asked playfully, slipping her arm through his.

"You know damn well what it is, Miz Sin."

Cynthia glanced at the nearby hotel. "Shame we're not spending the night in town, because you sure sound like you need some of that *what I do best*, Kincaid."

"Hussy," he accused.

"Horny," she retaliated.

Laughing, they sought out their friends.

Relieved not to have to worry about Cynthia or David discovering her absence, Sally felt free and exhilarated as she sped to keep her tryst with Clay. She found him waiting astride Crow. Smiling, she ran to him. He grinned and swung her up behind him. Sally curled her arms around his waist, and they rode off.

Were she preparing for her own wedding, Cynthia could not have worked harder in the two weeks that followed. As an added surprise, she swore Sally and the girls to absolute secrecy and they spent the afternoons learning a Celtic reel to perform at the wedding.

As if blessed from above, the day dawned bright and sunny, with white fluffy clouds and a blue sky as a complement. Dave, assisted by several of the women, was relegated to decorating the huge tent erected for the occasion; the four railroad cooks prepared the food and wedding cake; while the musicians—an accordion player, a mouth organist, and a fiddler—tuned up their instruments.

Cynthia and Sally dressed, then hurried over to assist the bride and her seven-year-old attendant. All was in readiness, awaiting the arrival of the priest.

As it neared the noon hour, Sean began pacing back and forth like a caged animal. "Are ya sur ya got the day right, Miz Cynthia?"

"Positive. Relax, Sean; he'll be here."

A series of surprised murmurs passed among the assembled crowd when a huge carriage, accompanied by six outriders, rolled into camp.

"Faith and begorra!" Sean mumbled when he saw the crest painted on the door of the carriage.

The hundred people in attendance appeared to breathe as one when two priests alit from the carriage and reached up to assist an older man. Cynthia stepped forward to greet him. Grasping her hand, the new arrival broke into a broad smile.

"My dear Cynthia, what a pleasure to see you again."

"Your Excellency, I can't thank you enough for

taking time from your busy schedule to do us this favor."

"My dear, I'm delighted to do so. Now, where is the happy couple?"

Dave had to give the spellbound Sean a nudge. He took Lydia's hand and the awestruck couple stepped forward.

"Sean and Lydia," Cynthia said, "I'd like you to meet the Most Reverend Joseph Fleming, Archbishop of New Mexico."

Archbishop Fleming held a private consultation with the bridal couple, then the wedding mass uniting Sean and Lydia as husband and wife was performed with as much pomp as the surroundings provided.

After a wedding toast for the future happiness of the couple, Cynthia again expressed her thanks to the archbishop as she bid him farewell.

"My prayers were with you when I read of your father's passing. I thought of the many times you spoke of him. You were so troubled. Tell me, my dear, did you make your peace with him?"

When Cynthia nodded, Archbishop Fleming said, "Then I must ask, are you now at peace with yourself?"

"I think I am for the first time, Your Excellency."

"Then it does not surprise me that you broke your engagement to Count Fellini."

"I realized before my father died that I didn't love Roberto, Your Excellency."

He patted her hand. "I suspected as much. You did the wise thing, my dear. Roberto could never have brought you the happiness you deserve." His eyes suddenly gleamed with amusement. "But I've noticed a certain sparkle in your eyes when you look at young Mr. Kincaid over there," he said, glancing to where Dave stood leaning against a tree a short distance away.

"You always were too observant, Papa Joe."

He threw back his head in laughter, almost losing the tall red hat on his head. "Papa Joe! I haven't heard that since Rome; and only you would dare. I didn't think you could keep up the formality of calling me 'Your Excellency.' What a refreshing delight you are, my dear Cyn." He leaned over and whispered in her ear. "And Papa Joe will feel insulted if he's not asked to perform the rites when you wed that young engineer." He squeezed her hand. "May the Lord bless you and keep you, my dear child."

"Good-bye, you precious old dear," she whispered, tears glistening in her eyes.

As she watched the carriage depart, Cynthia was surprised when Sean Rafferty approached her alone.

"Miz Cynthia, I want to thank ya for what yuv done. Because of ya, this is the finest day of me life. There's ne'er been a person who's done what ya did for Lydia and me today. We've had our differences in the past, and I ain't sayin' I agree with all ya done, but yer a good woman, Cynthia MacKenzie, because yu've a pure heart. Lydia and meself are proud to be callin' ya our friend. And there'll ne'er be a livin' soul that will speak bad of ya in me presence." He began to back away awkwardly. "Well, I've said me piece and I'll be gettin' back to me bride."

"Thank you, Sean, and I know you and Lydia will be very happy."

Cynthia walked over to Dave, who had remained leaning against the tree. "Are you going to hold up that tree all day or are you going to ask me to dance?"

He straightened up. "I don't dance. You know, if I didn't see it for myself, I wouldn't believe it."

"Believe what?"

"How you manage to get every man you meet eating out of your hand. I see you picked up another champion to defend your honor, Miz Sin."

She batted her eyelashes outrageously. "Whatever are you talking about, Mr. Kincaid?"

"Sean Rafferty. The list keeps growing: an Italian count, a ranch foreman, my crew boss . . . even an archbishop. Neither age nor background are barriers to you. How many others are there, Miz Sin?"

She slipped her arm through his. "Ah . . . I don't think I heard railroad engineer mentioned in that list?"

"And you won't. I must be the only man alive who's got you figured out."

"No, Kincaid, you're wrong. You're the only one who *hasn't* figured me out. In your eyes, good is good and bad is bad—never the twain shall meet. But they do, Dave. There's a little of both qualities in all of us. Believe it or not, even in you, Sir Lancelot!"

Drawn to the sound of the music, she skipped ahead of him and was immediately claimed for a dance by one of the men.

After an hour Cynthia decided the time had come for the girls to perform the surprise they had prepared for the occasion. However, at the last moment Maggie refused to participate, so Sally filled in for her. After a few instructions to the accordion player, Cynthia called for everyone's attention.

"Ladies and gentlemen, in honor of the occasion, the ladies of Miss Sally's and Miss Cynthia's class have prepared a special performance. It is my pleasure to present Tent Town's own Celtic dancers!"

Lining up in two rows opposite each other, with their arms held down at their sides, heels pointed in, feet turned out as instructed, the girls began the reel.

Clapping to the music, Cynthia counted out the movements: "Step, shuffle, hop, stamp; step, shuffle, hop, stamp."

In pleasure and encouragement, the enthralled crowd clapped along to the music and jumped to their feet with cheers and applause when the dance ended.

Then the girls got their fathers from the audience for partners, and the dance began again. Soon some of the women, familiar with the steps, joined them. In no time, the floor was filled with dancers.

Seeing Maggie watching from the fringe of the crowd, Cynthia went over to her. "What's wrong, Maggie? You should be dancing with your grandfather. Aren't you feeling well?"

"Don't want to dance. 'Sides, Grandpa's got Lydia to dance with now."

"Oh, honey, just because your grandfather married doesn't mean you're not as important as always to him." She hugged the little girl. "Your grandfather has enough love in him to include you and Lydia both, honey." Before she could continue the conversation any further, Cynthia was claimed for a dance.

Day passed into evening, and as the hour grew late, one by one the celebrants began returning to their quarters. Exhausted, Cynthia decided to call it a night as well.

"It was a nice wedding, wasn't it?" she said as Dave walked her back to her car.

"You helped to make it one, Cyn." He slipped an arm around her shoulder. "You're an amazing woman, Cynthia MacKenzie."

They reached her car and stepped up onto the observation platform. Turning to him, she said, "Even though you don't approve of my wicked, wicked ways?"

"I've been thinking all evening about what you said earlier, and you were right. I've been guilty of painting people either all good or all bad. Until now, I saw no reason for thinking differently."

She leaned back against the wall. "And what made you change all of a sudden?"

"You." He cupped her cheek, sliding his hand into the thickness of her hair. "You're a paradox, Miz Sin," he said tenderly. "I'm always struggling between wanting to shake you or kiss you."

"Dave, I won't make any apologies for who or what I am. I may regret some of my past, but I'm not ashamed of it. And since this could probably lead to an argument between us, I'll say good night, because I refuse to spoil what's been a lovely day."

"I guess I've done a miserable job of what I wanted to say, Cyn. Everything you said is true: I did look at life with a closed mind, but thanks to you, I see now that people aren't always what they appear to be—that everything in life isn't all black or white."

He pulled her closer. "I've never met anyone with your capacity for bringing happiness to others—even a closed-minded bastard like me. You've taught me how to laugh, Cyn. To have fun. And the one undeniable truth is that I want to be with you. It's time I stop denying the present because of suspicions of the past and fears of the future. So I don't want to end this perfect day by arguing either. I want to end it by making love to you, Cyn. By you making love to me."

He kissed her long and hungrily. When their lips parted, he pulled her closer and whispered. "Mindless, earth-shattering love."

Slipping her arms around his neck, she asked, "The kind of lovemaking with bells ringing? Roman candles exploding?"

"The carnal, lusty, sweaty, all-out, no-holds-barred kind of lovemaking, Miz Sin."

"Ah, Kincaid—did I mention that Sally is spending the night with Maggie in Lydia's tent?"

"She's what! Then why the hell are we standing out here just thinking about it?" he growled. Sweeping her up into his arms, he carried her inside.

Chapter 18

Cynthia had just finished dressing the next morning when Sally came rushing in breathlessly. "Have you seen Maggie?"

"No. Why?"

"She ran away about fifteen minutes ago. I hoped she had come here."

"Did you tell Sean?"

"He and Dave have already ridden off somewhere. I guess some more track was ripped up last night."

"Well, couldn't you have stopped her, Sally?" Cynthia said worriedly.

"I wasn't dressed. By the time I got my clothes on, there was no sign of her. I even checked the school tent just in case she went there."

"Did she take anything with her?"

"Yes, she had a small bundle of clothes tied in a red-and-black bandanna."

"What was she wearing?"

"That old blue dress of hers."

"I'll start looking for her. You better send one of the men to tell Sean and Dave."

Seeing no sign of Maggie near the river, Cynthia headed for the trees, repeatedly calling out the little girl's name. When there was no response, Cynthia followed her instinct and figured the girl must have headed for the nearest town. She climbed on the handcar and headed toward Childs. In a short time, she caught a glimpse of blue ahead and started to pump faster to catch up with the youngster. As she drew nearer, she could make out Maggie walking along the track.

Then Maggie turned and caught sight of her. She dashed away from the track, running west. Breathless, Cynthia stopped the handcar, jumped off, and pursued Maggie; but now, without a track to follow, she had no way of knowing if the girl veered off again to the north. Climbing a rise, she caught a flash of blue in a nearby stand of trees.

She ran on, and upon reaching the woods, she called out, "Maggie! Maggie, where are you?"

Cynthia entered the trees, hoping to catch another glimpse of the girl. She looked around hopelessly, with no idea which direction to follow. Praying for guidance, she started out, and a short time later was elated to see a small black-and-red bundle of clothing lying on the ground.

"Maggie!" she shouted. She knew the child had to be nearby or she'd never have abandoned her clothes. Exhausted, Cynthia slumped down against a tree. As she looked around, she caught sight of a patch of blue beneath the trunk of a fallen tree not more than ten yards away.

"Thank God," she murmured in relief. "Maggie, I see you under that tree," she called to her. "Come on out. And if you start running again, when I catch up with you I'm going to put you over my knee and paddle you."

Maggie's head popped up. "My grandpa will be real mad if you do."

Cynthia opened her arms. "Come over here, sweetheart."

The youngster scrambled out of the debris and ran into Cynthia's outstretched arms. For a long moment Cynthia hugged her to her breast. Finally, she drew away and looked Maggie in the eye.

"Where were you going, young lady?"

"Away," Maggie said, hanging her head.

"Why, sweetheart?"

"'Cause I don't wanta stay in Tent Town no more. Grandpa ain't got room for me, 'cause he married Miz Lydia."

"Maggie honey, of course your grandfather has room for you."

"Then why'd I have to sleep in Miz Lydia's tent last night?" she lashed out angrily. "Why couldn't I sleep in Grandpa's tent like I always done before?"

"Well . . . that was because it was your grandfather's and Lydia's wedding night."

"Shucks, that weren't no secret; I knowed that, didn't I? So why'd he send me away?"

"Well, you see, honey," Cynthia said, trying to choose her words carefully, "on their wedding night a man and woman need to be alone."

"What for?"

"Well, to ah . . . get to know each other."

Maggie looked confused. "They knowed each other for two years!"

"I mean to become acquainted as a husband and wife."

"You talkin' 'bout kissin' and that kind of stuff that men and women do?"

Heaving a sigh of relief, Cynthia nodded. "Exactly. But it can be a very awkward time, especially for someone as shy as Lydia. That's why it's easier if the couple is alone for the first night or two."

"I seen you and Uncle Dave kissin', and you two ain't married."

"Well, Dave and I are practicing for when we do marry," Cynthia said quickly. "Then it won't be so awkward for us."

"I saw Miz Sally kissin' in the trees, too."

"Sally!" Cynthia was appalled. Dave's predictions were coming true—and he would hit the ceiling when he found out about it. "Who was the man, Maggie?" Cynthia asked. The little girl knew every man in the crew.

"Don't know him. He rides a big black horse," she said, unconcerned.

This news was even more horrifying to Cynthia. The man had to be a cowboy, probably one of the riders who worked for Bonner. When Dave found out, Sally was as good as halfway back to Denver already.

"S'pose when you and Uncle Dave get married, you won't want me around either . . . same as Grandpa and Lydia."

Preoccupied with this newest developing problem, Cynthia said, "I'm sorry, honey. What did you say?"

"I s'pose you and Uncle Dave won't want me around either when you get married."

Hugging Maggie, Cynthia couldn't help chuckling. "Sweetheart, your Uncle Dave's going to be so upset with me that by the time I can convince him to marry me, you'll be old enough to understand what this conversation was all about."

She kissed Maggie on the check and stood up. "Come on, youngster, we better get going. We have a long way ahead of us."

Grinning, Maggie looked up at her. "I'm glad you found me. I love you, Miz Cynthia."

Cynthia felt a rush of emotion swell her breast. "Oh, honey, I love you, too."

She stiffened upon hearing a low, ferocious growl. Turning toward the sound, she saw that a shaggy dog had come out of the trees less than a hundred feet away. Cynthia stared in horror as the crouched animal bared its yellowed fangs, its eyes gleaming with feral madness. White foam dripped from the dog's mouth as it continued to snarl, a low, terrifying growl that made the hair prickle on the nape of Cynthia's neck. She knew it was only a matter of seconds before the rabid dog would make an aggressive move at them. She looked around for a weapon, but the only sharp stick lay closer to the animal than it was to them.

"Maggie, you're a good tree climber, so I'm going to lift you up and I want you to grab the branch above our heads. Then get up that tree fast; I'll be right behind you. You must do it quickly, honey," she warned, "because we don't have much time. Do you understand?" When the terrified girl nodded, Cynthia said, "Let's go!"

The instant she hoisted Maggie, the dog charged. Maggie grabbed the branch and started to climb; then Cynthia leaped up and managed to grasp the limb just as the dog sprang at her. Missing her swinging legs, the crazed animal caught a hunk of her skirt betweeen its teeth and tried to pull her down. In a frenzy, the animal tugged and yanked until Cynthia felt her grasp begin to slip. Then mercifully the material gave way, and the dog fell back with a patch of her skirt between its fangs.

Swinging her legs over the limb, Cynthia managed to straddle it. Then, after taking several deep breaths, she climbed up to where Maggie sat huddled.

"You did very well, honey," Cynthia said to the trembling child. "I'm so proud of you."

Below on the ground, the snarling dog ripped apart Maggie's tiny bundle of clothing, then began to scrape and leap at the trunk of the tree in an effort to reach them.

"Are we safe up here?" Maggie asked, barely able to speak.

"Yes, honey. A dog can't climb a tree. We're fortunate it isn't a cat."

"Yeah, but a cat's not so scary cause it's small and not so big and strong like that dog."

"Maggie dear, in this case the size of the animal doesn't matter. The tiniest bite or scratch can infect you."

"Why is it tryin' to kill us?"

"The poor thing has rabies. It's crazed and doesn't even know what it's doing."

"What's all that white stuff on its face?"

"That's one of the symptoms of the disease, honey. The throat muscles become paralyzed; then the dog can't swallow and all of its saliva foams up. From the amount of foam on its face and mouth, my guess is that the dog's been infected for some time. The other muscles in its body have probably started to become paralyzed, too, because a dog that size could easily have leaped higher and pulled me down. That makes me think the animal's probably very close to dying."

The little girl's compassion overrode her fear. "Oh, the poor doggie. I wish we could help it."

"Nobody could get near it now, honey; the disease is too advanced. That's why the dog is so aggressive and tried to attack us. The only way anyone can help now is to shoot it to put it out of its misery."

"Too bad we don't have a gun," Maggie said sadly.

"Well, it looks like we're going to have to stay up here until the dog dies or goes away."

However, they soon discovered the dog had no intention of going away.

They passed the time by working on Maggie's language skills. Toward sunset, Cynthia noticed that the dog was lying on its side.

"You think it's dead, Miz Cynthia?" Maggie asked sorrowfully.

"It could be sleeping, but I don't know if an animal sleeps when it has rabies."

"We could throw something at it and see if it moves."

"Maggie, that's a great idea." Cynthia broke off a small limb and dropped it on the dog. The animal didn't flinch a muscle. "What do you think?"

"Maybe it's pretendin', hopin' we'll come down."

"I think the dog's dead; but I'm not taking any chances. We'll stay up here. It'll soon be dark, and I don't think we can find our way back to the track in the dark."

"You mean we're lost?"

"Without the sun, I don't even know what direction to head in. So it looks like we're going to be a couple of night owls, honey."

"What if we go to sleep and fall out of the tree?"

"Maggie, I am neither going to fall asleep nor fall out of this tree. If you want to sleep, I'll hold you."

"What if another animal comes and climbs the tree?"

"Very unlikely, my dear."

"What if we get cold?"

"Well, that is more likely. If I knew for certain the dog is dead, we could get down and build a fire. I'm sure folks are out searching for us, and maybe someone would spot our fire." She broke off another branch and threw it at the dog. Once again, the animal didn't move a muscle.

"Miz Cynthia, we ain't got no matches, so we couldn't start a fire anyway."

"Yes we can. It's not easy, but it can be done. The cavemen and the Indians didn't have matches, Maggie. You create a spark with friction—like striking two stones together. Once, when we were very young, my sisters and I got lost on our ranch. When they found us, the first thing my daddy taught us was how to start a fire without matches, in case it ever happened again."

"Wow! That sure is somethin'. Did you ever get lost again?"

"Yeah," she said, nuzzling the youngster. "Right now. Maggie, I'm going to climb down, and no matter what happens, I want you to stay up here until I tell you to come down. Promise?"

"Don't go, Miz Cynthia. I'm afraid somethin' will happen to you."

"Nothing's going to happen to me. But I have to leave you alone while I find a couple of stones and gather up enough wood. But I'll be back, honey. I promise."

"Will you keep yelling, so I'll knowed where you're at?"

"Maggie Rafferty, *know* is one of the words we practiced today."

"So I'll know where you're at," Maggie corrected.

"Yep. And you yell out every now and then, so I can find my way back. Okay?"

"Okay."

Cynthia kissed her, then climbed down. She didn't go near the dog, but it appeared dead from the rigid position it was lying in.

"Miz Cynthia, should I start yelling now?" Maggie called out.

Cynthia glanced up at Maggie, peering down at her through the branches. "I haven't left yet."

Cynthia could get plenty of firewood from the fallen tree, but finding two stones was going to be a bigger problem. She dared not stray out of shouting range, and it was getting darker by the minute. Finally, after gathering a half dozen that looked suitable, she hurried back to the fallen tree. Fortunately the dead tree limbs had long dried out, so they snapped easily, but it took Cynthia at least another fifteen minutes to strike enough sparks to ignite the twigs. Once she had a good fire started, she fed in several of the larger pieces of wood.

"You can come down now, Maggie," she called, returning to the tree.

As happy as Maggie felt to set her feet on the ground, the sight of the dog saddened her. "Maybe we should bury it, Miz Cynthia."

"We have nothing to dig with, and I don't think we should touch it with our hands."

"I feel sorry for it just laying there, even if you said it's better off now."

"I'm sure there's a dog heaven it's gone to, honey. Now, let's go over to the fire and you try and get some sleep. You've had a long day, Maggie."

With plenty of accessible wood, Cynthia kept the fire built up as high as she could in the hope of attracting attention.

She and Maggie sang songs to keep up their spirits and take their minds off their empty stomachs.

"Just a glass of water would be a welcome relief," Cynthia said.

"Too bad that dog tore up my clothes, 'cause I had a big piece of wedding cake in them," Maggie said. She was lying on her back with her head on Cynthia's lap.

"Well, the next time you run away from home, remember to take water. You can go a long time without food, but not without water."

"Boy, you sure know just 'bout everything," Maggie said. "How'd you get so smart, Miz Cynthia?"

"Oh, honey, I've just always been curious about people and things. And I've done some traveling, which is an education in itself."

"You think I could ever be as smart as you?"

"Certainly, sweetheart," Cynthia said, stroking the child's cheek. "Smarter, if you want to be. Of course, that means you can't keep running away, and you'd have to stay in school and learn all you can."

"I won't run away again, Miz Cynthia. I promise."

"Everyone's entitled to one run-away. I ran away, too, didn't I?"

"But you came back. That's all . . . that matters . . ." Her voice trailed off as she drifted into sleep.

Cynthia sat thinking about the events of the past couple of days. Funny how everyone thought yesterday was such an idyllic day, and nobody gave a mind to what a miserable day it had been for a little seven-year-old who believed she was losing the one person she had remaining in the world.

With a tender smile, Cynthia looked down at the sleeping child and brushed back the hair that had fallen in Maggie's face.

Cynthia awoke with a start. She had no idea how long she had slept, but the fire had burned down to low flames. She gently shifted Maggie out of her lap and got up to put more wood on the fire.

Then she saw two amber lights glowing in the dark, too small to be anything but the eyes of an animal. Her heart seemed to leap to her throat when she recognized the low growl. Barely able to walk, the dog was moving toward the fire. This had to be a nightmare. The animal had died! She was certain it had been dead!

Picking up a heavy stick to use as a weapon, she yelled to Maggie to wake up. The two glaring eyes were getting closer, and the growl louder. Since they were on the other side of the fire from the animal, Cynthia was uncertain if the dog even saw them.

Maggie opened her eyes and, upon hearing the

growl, bolted to her feet screaming. The dog attempted to run, but the paralysis slowed its speed.

"Hurry and climb another tree, Maggie!"

Screaming, Maggie was too petrified to move.

The crazed dog reached the fire. Driven beyond reason, it also was beyond caution, and it leaped through the flames to get to them. Suddenly a shot rang out, and the dog fell to the ground.

Maggie continued screaming at the top of her voice, and Cynthia felt near to doing the same. Only the need to calm the hysterical child helped her to hold on to her control. She gathered Maggie in her arms and was rocking her back and forth when a man riding a black stallion and carrying a rifle rode up to the fire. Sally Kincaid was with him. Cynthia stared in a daze at the two people who had just invaded her nightmare.

Dismounting and rushing over to them, Sally knelt down and wrapped her arms around them. "Are you both okay?"

Cynthia could only nod. Maggie was sobbing and hiccoughing. Her little body trembled so hard that Cynthia feared the child was having a seizure.

The man came over and knelt down. "Ma'am, maybe a drink of water will help the little girl?" he said kindly.

"Thank you." She took the canteen he offered and held it up to Maggie's mouth. "Here, sweetheart, take a few sips of this water." Glancing up at the young man, she asked, "Do you have a blanket?"

"Yes, ma'am. I'll go get it."

She managed to get some water into the girl, and when the man returned they wrapped Maggie up and Cynthia held her on her lap. She turned away from the dead dog, unable to look at it without feeling ill.

Gradually, her own tremors ceased and her

breathing returned to normal. "I can't thank you enough, sir."

"Cynthia, this is Clay Bonner," Sally said. "His father owns this ranch."

"Oh yes, I've heard the name. Again, I can't thank you enough, Mr. Bonner. That was a remarkable shot. Maggie and I owe our lives to you—the dog had rabies."

"Yeah, it's been prowling around these parts for the past week. Killed some of our cattle, too. It didn't scratch you or anything, did it?"

"No, but it had us trapped up in a tree most of the day. I thought it was dead. That's why I thought it was safe to come down and build a fire in the hopes someone would see it."

"Folks have been looking for you most of the day. As soon as we saw your fire, we rode over here. I'm sure glad we got here in time."

"Not half as glad as we are, Mr. Bonner."

Maggie had quieted. Glancing down at her, Cynthia saw that the child had cried herself to sleep. "Poor darling, this all has been a nightmare for her."

"Sounds like we're about to have another visitor," Clay said. He had no sooner finished speaking when Dave rode up to the fire. Dismounting, he hurried over to them.

"Are you all right, Cyn?" She nodded. "Maggie?"

"Maggie's fine, Dave. She's just scared."

"Thank God! When I found the handcar, I knew I was in the right area. Then when I saw the fire and heard the gunshot, I didn't know what to expect. What happened here?"

"A mad dog had us trapped, David. Mr. Bonner came along and shot him," Sally said.

Cynthia gasped aloud. Sally was deliberately giving Dave the impression she had been with her and

Maggie the whole time. The girl was just making matters worse with such a lie.

Sally looked at her, pleading with her eyes. Disgusted, Cynthia turned away. She was being forced into a situation she wanted nothing to do with. Sally's relationship with Clay Bonner was an issue that had to be settled between Sally and her brother.

"Well, Mr. Bonner, I'm grateful for what you've done," Dave said.

"Dave, can we go now?" Cynthia asked before any more lies could be said.

"It's a long ride back to the tracks, ma'am. If you climb on behind Mr. Kincaid, Miss Sally can ride with me and I'll hold the child." He began throwing dirt on the fire to snuff it out.

"Appreciate your help, Bonner," Dave said.

As soon as the fire was extinguished, they rode back to the tracks. "I'll be glad to help you back to your camp, sir," Clay said.

"That won't be necessary, Bonner. You've done enough already. Thanks again for your help." After shaking hands with the cowboy, Dave tied his horse to the handcar, started to pump, and they rolled away.

Looking back, Cynthia saw the dark outline of the rider and horse standing still beside the track.

It was almost midnight when they reached camp. Dave handed Maggie to a tearful Sean, with Lydia at his side.

Sally said she'd spend the night in Lydia's tent and said good-night.

Dave walked Cynthia to her car. "You need any help, Cyn?"

"No, I just want to go to bed."

He kissed her lightly on the forehead. "I understand. Good night."

Too exhausted to even grab a bite to eat, Cynthia pulled off her clothes and climbed into bed.

Chapter 19

With morning came the confrontation with Sally that Cynthia was not looking forward to. At seventeen, the young girl had begun to choose a path of lies and deception. A clandestine relationship with the rancher's son could only lead to more trouble than Sally already had.

Before school began, Cynthia sought her out.

Whether out of guilt or resentment, Sally took the offensive as soon as the two of them were behind the closed door of Cynthia's car. "I suppose you want to talk about last night."

"Apparently it involves a lot more than last night, Sally. How long have you been meeting this rancher?"

"From the first day I arrived," Sally lashed out defiantly. "Clay and I are in love."

"Sally, I have no right to lecture anyone on the choices they make in their lives, but sneaking off in the bushes to meet a man is not a healthy beginning for any relationship."

"We wouldn't have to if it weren't for Dave. He's so pigheaded that Clay and I are forced to meet secretly. Dave's not my father and you're not my mother, so I wish the both of you would stop treating me like a child. I can take care of myself. I'm a woman just like you, Cynthia. And no matter what you think, Clay and I aren't doing anything wrong. We like being together, and he's been teaching me how to ride so I won't be afraid of horses. He said a rancher's wife can't be squeamish around them."

"A rancher's wife!" Cynthia couldn't help scoffing. "Are you saying that in the short time you've known each other, Clay Bonner has asked you to marry him?"

Sally lifted her head proudly. "Yes, he has, and I told him I would."

"Oh, Sally dear, you're being naive. Men say things like that to get what they want from a woman. He's handsome and a rich man's son—his father owns practically the whole county. Clay Bonner probably has all the single girls in the county chasing after him."

"What are you suggesting—that because he's rich and I'm poor I'm not good enough for him? Is that what all you rich people think about people like me?"

"No, I'm not implying you aren't good enough, Sally. I'm trying to point out he's a very eligible bachelor—possibly even betrothed already to another woman. And it's not necessary for a man in his position to sneak off and meet a girl unless he's just—" Cynthia stopped. "Sally dear," she said calmly, "has Clay told his father about his intentions to wed you?"

"How could he? We have to keep our relationship a secret because of this stupid fight between David and Clay's father."

Cynthia felt a rise of resentment at Sally's disloyalty to her brother. "I agree it's a stupid fight, Sally, but Dave is not the one responsible. Will Bonner has been destroying our track. That's against the law, and if he continues, somebody is bound to get hurt. As a matter of fact, Juliet, has it occurred to you that your Romeo is probably one of the night riders who's carrying out that destruction?"

"If you knew Clay, you wouldn't say that. He's honest and decent."

Cynthia lost her temper. Sally was quick to condemn the brother who had looked out for her welfare for the last ten years, but would not hear a word of condemnation against some rich man's son who was probably teaching the naive girl a lot more than how to ride a horse.

"Oh, forgive me," Cynthia declared, "I must have missed this honest and decent young man recanting that bold-faced lie you told your brother last night."

"Well, I'm surprised you didn't tell Dave, Cynthia, since you feel so strongly about it all."

"I believe everyone should face up to their own actions. I don't like lies, Sally. And I don't think Dave deserves to be lied to by the sister he trusts. Furthermore, I don't appreciate being made a party to that lie and deceit."

"And obviously you also don't appreciate the fact that Clay Bonner saved your life."

"That's not true. I'm grateful to him, and that's the only reason I didn't say anything last night. I think Dave should hear the real truth from you, not me. If anyone is lacking appreciation, it's you, Sally. It's about time you recognize your obligations—particularly to Dave, considering how he has recognized his toward you through the years."

Sally broke into tears. "I thought you were different—that you understood why I wanted to live my own life and not go back to that dreary boarding school. But you don't, Cynthia. You sound just like Dave." She rushed out sobbing.

Cynthia walked over and peered deeply at her image in a mirror. As she hashed over her conversation with Sally, Cynthia realized she *had* sounded more like Dave than she did the woman she'd been several months ago. What had become of the old Cynthia—that carefree young woman who lived each day to the fullest, doing what she wanted, when she wanted? The woman who had never worried whether or not a few girls needed a schoolroom or whether a young woman lied to her brother about a clandestine relationship? *That* woman would never have risked her life to try to fulfill another person's dream—even if that dream had been her father's.

And for damn sure, that self-assured, independent woman would have thumbed her nose at any man who continually reminded her that his only interest in her was sexual.

And he accused her of corrupting him! Ha! she reflected in amazement, *she* was the one who'd changed! Without realizing it, she had burdened herself with a sense of righteousness, duty, obligation.

Just like Dave!

Cynthia thought it was best she try to smooth over her quarrel with Sally. After all, she, above anyone, should have been more understanding of the mistakes a young woman often makes when falling in love for the first time. Her intolerance of Sally's relationship with Clay had been pure hypocrisy, considering she had been no less guilty when she fell in love with Roberto.

However, Cynthia did resent the girl's ingratitude toward Dave. Sally had to learn to face the consequences of her own actions without looking for someone else to blame. But to Sally's credit, she wasn't running off to Europe or the like, as Cynthia had done herself. She had agreed to remain in Tent Town.

Lydia had offered Sally the tent she'd lived in before her marriage to Sean, so when school ended that day, Cynthia went to Sally's tent to apologize for her unkind comments about Clay Bonner. The effort was well met, because Sally then promised to tell Dave the truth at the proper time.

As Cynthia left the tent, she heard sobbing and realized it was coming from Sean's tent. Maggie had not been in school that day, but Cynthia felt that was to be expected, considering the traumatic events of the previous day.

"Hello," she called out, and entered the tent. On a cot in the corner, Maggie lay sobbing, curled up with her legs and arms drawn to her chest. Hurrying over to her, Cynthia gathered the weeping child in her arms and rocked her as she had done the previous night at the fire.

"What is it, sweetheart? Did you have a nightmare?"

"No," Maggie managed to blurt out between sobs.

"Honey, calm down. Breathe slowly and let yourself relax."

After a few more seconds Maggie stopped crying, a shuddering sob still escaping now and then. When the child was finally composed, Cynthia said gently, "Why don't you tell me why you're crying, sweetheart?"

With tears streaking her cheeks, Maggie looked up pitifully at her. "Miz Cynthia, can I come and live with you?"

"Maggie, you don't still believe your grandfather doesn't want you, do you?"

"I knowed . . . I mean, I know he don't want me. He scolded me real bad this mornin' for runnin' off yesterday. He never scolded me so bad before. He don't . . . love me no more." She started to cry again. "I wish my daddy was here."

"Oh, Maggie," Cynthia said, choking back her tears. "Don't ever think your grandfather doesn't love you. You are the dearest thing on earth to him, and he worships you, Maggie. If he scolded, it was because he was scared that something might have happened to you. If he didn't love you, sweetheart, he wouldn't have cared, now would he?"

Cynthia hugged the girl tighter. "You want to know something, Maggie? My father used to scold me when I did something reckless, where I could have been seriously injured—or even possibly killed."

"Like running away?" Maggie said, sniffling.

"That's right, dear. And whenever he yelled at me, I thought he didn't love me. But I was wrong; my father yelled for just the opposite reason: he loved me so much that he was frightened something bad would happen to me—the way it happened to my mother."

"You mean gettin' killed?"

"Yes. It's very hard for a child to understand. I know I didn't, until my father was dying. Don't make the same mistake I did, Maggie. I know you're too young to really understand what I'm trying to say, but never doubt your grandfather's love, and never deny yourself the pleasure of that relationship. To be loved by someone you love is the greatest happiness there is."

"Will Miz Lydia love me sometime, too?" Maggie asked.

A gentle voice answered, "She loves you already, dear child."

They turned their heads and saw Lydia standing in the entrance. She walked over to the cot, and the two women's gazes locked in understanding. Rising to her feet, Cynthia stepped away, and Lydia sat down, gathering Maggie in her arms.

Cynthia moved to the entrance. The time and need had arisen for her to step aside and let Lydia fill the role so necessary in Maggie's life. She slipped quietly out of the tent.

Early in the morning after the search for Maggie, Dave made a quick trip to Denver to discuss with Charles Rayburn and Elizabeth what legal course they could take with Will Bonner. Without the co-operation of the local law enforcement, and without legal proof that Bonner was actually behind the vandalism, they were not on solid ground; so they decided their only option was to contact a federal marshal to investigate the situation.

Upon arriving back in Tent Town late the following afternoon, Dave was greeted by Sean, carrying a beaming Maggie on his shoulders.

"Well, young lady, you sure look better than the last time I saw you," Dave said to her. "You playing hooky from school?"

"Miz Sally said there's no school today," Sean said.

"Bet she's meetin' that fella again," Maggie spoke up.

"What fellow, Maggie?" Dave asked.

"The one she's been kissin'. You know, the one what shot the dog."

Shocked, Dave exclaimed, "Bonner! Maggie, when did you see Sally kiss Clay Bonner?"

"Oh, she kissed him lots of times, Uncle Dave."

"But I thought they met the night you were lost."

"No, I seen 'em kissin' afore that, when I was up in my tree testin' my wings."

"Maggie, was Sally with you and Miss Cynthia the night you were lost?"

"Not at first. She come with Mr. Bonner when he shot the dog. He's a real nice man."

Dave's jaw clenched. "Sean, I'll go over this Will Bonner situation with you later. In the meantime, we brought in some new rail. Will you see that it's unloaded? The day's shot already, but we can get the crew moving first thing in the morning."

"Sure, boss." Sean hesitated. "Ah, lad, if ya be lookin' for yer sister, she's moved into Lydia's old tent."

"Thanks, Sean."

Dave headed for the tent. He'd get to the bottom of whatever was going on between Clay Bonner and his sister. And it appeared that not only Sally was deceiving him, but Cynthia was also a party to the deception.

Dave found his sister in her tent. "Sally, I want to talk to you."

"Then be sure it's talking, David, and not shouting," Sally said.

"I just found out you've been sneaking off and meeting Bonner's son."

"Well, she didn't waste any time telling you, did she?"

"Is it true, Sally?"

"Yes. So what?"

"How long has that been going on?"

"From the first day I got here, and I intend to continue seeing Clay whether you like it or not."

"Well, I don't like it and it's not to continue. My God, Sally, don't you have any loyalty? Bonner's son is undoubtedly one of the men who's ripping up our track!"

"Clay has nothing to do with that. I asked him," she said hotly.

"For heaven's sake, Sally, he's Bonner's son. Do you think he'd admit it?"

"You don't know if Mr. Bonner is even responsible. You just assume he's doing it because of the argument over that water hole. Clay told me all about it."

"And you'd rather believe him."

"I love him, David."

"Love? You're seventeen years old. What in hell do you know about love?"

"That's what I mean—you think you know everything and the rest of us are stupid. Well, I love Clay Bonner and I'm going to marry him!"

"Over my dead body! I forbid you to see him again. Do you understand?"

Sally looked at him, astonished. "No, you're the one who doesn't understand, David. You aren't my legal guardian. You can't tell me what I can or can't do."

"Is that the advice your friend Bonner is feeding you?"

"No. I'm old enough to make my own decisions—and choices."

"And you're saying you're *choosing* Clay Bonner."

"I won't take your orders, so you leave me no other choice, David. I don't understand why it has to *be* a choice. You can order me out of this camp, but if you do, I swear you'll never see me again. And somehow, Clay and I will continue to see each other, because we're in love. Neither you, his father, nor anyone else can keep us apart."

"Your mind seems to be pretty well made up. I wish to God I knew as much at seventeen as you think you do," he said, throwing his hands up in frustration. He was trying to keep her from making a big mistake, but arguing with her was an exercise in futility. She'd find out the hard way. "Why in hell should I care how you live your life?" he stormed. "Thanks for relieving me of the burden."

Chapter 20

Infuriated enough to take on anyone, Dave sought out Cynthia. He stalked to her car and banged on the door. Wearing a white robe, she opened the door, took one look at his angry scowl, and walked away, leaving him standing in the doorway.

After sitting down on the round sofa, she leaned back and crossed her arms across her chest. "Okay, let's get it over with."

Dave had already stepped in and closed the door. "How long have you known that Sally's been sneaking off and meeting Clay Bonner?"

"I found out the day Maggie ran away."

"Why didn't you tell me? Why did you let me believe that lie she told me?"

"I thought it would be better if she were the one to tell you the truth. I'm glad she finally did."

"She didn't tell me—Maggie did."

"Well, Sally promised me she'd tell you at the proper time. Give her the benefit of the doubt."

"Apparently, despite my objections, she intends to continue seeing Bonner."

"What do you expect? She says she's in love with him. Put yourself in her place, Dave; she's been cooped up in a girls' boarding school for ten years and then she meets this handsome young man. And let's give the devil his due; Clay Bonner *is* a handsome young man, rich, and he rides around on a big black horse." She sighed. "I think he would turn any seventeen-year-old girl's head and heart. Ah, to be that young again."

"I'm glad you can treat this so lightly, Cyn, but I sure as hell can't see anything humorous about it. And don't try and tell me it's because I don't know how to have fun. What if that was your sister Angie in Sally's place? Would you find it so amusing then?"

"Oh, Dave, I don't think it's amusing. When I first heard it, I was as upset as you are. Sally and I even had words over it."

"Well, thank you for that much," he said sarcastically. "Then why the change of heart?"

"Because, obviously, you're not going to get anywhere by demanding Sally not see this man. The more you do, the more you'll drive her right into Clay Bonner's arms. She claims he loves her; I have my personal opinion on that score—but she will have to find that out for herself."

"Sally's too young to know what love is all about."

"Apparently age doesn't have that much to do with it, Kincaid, because you're a darn sight older and *you* haven't figured out what love's all about yet."

"Shall we keep my love life out of this conversation?" he said.

"I'm only implying that had you ever allowed yourself to fall in love, you'd be more understanding and tolerant of Sally's situation."

"You don't believe for a moment Bonner's in love with her, do you?"

"No, I don't; but I could be wrong, Dave, and so could you. You're too protective of her. She has to have enough freedom to learn from her own experiences."

"So tell her to climb a tree to test her wings, Teacher."

Cynthia smiled. "I think she's figured out a different way. Let's hope she knows her limitations."

"That's exactly my concern. Sally doesn't understand what she's doing. She's going to be hurt."

Cynthia got up and went over to him. Sliding her arms around his waist, she gently said, "And that's what's really bothering you, isn't it? You're trying to spare her that hurt, but you can't. The time has come to let her make her own choices and decisions. Sally appears to be a pretty levelheaded young woman."

"Sure she is!" he scoffed, pulling her closer. "She's barely out of the schoolroom door and she's got herself mixed up with some range Romeo."

Cynthia's eyes sparkled with amusement. "And to think you thought *R* was for reading, 'riting, and 'rithmetic."

"It's not funny, Cyn," he said, nuzzling the fragrant silkiness of her dark hair.

"No, I imagine Sally's in for a little heartache; but it's a lesson she has to learn for herself. You've got to cut her some slack, Dave, or she'll only rebel more." Stepping back, she looked up at him again. "Speaking of rebelling, Kincaid, it's been a long time since you've kissed me."

Sliding his hands down her back, he began to stroke the hollows of her spine. "You're a temptress, Miz Sin. How do you expect me to keep my mind on the issue at hand when you're in my arms?"

"When I'm in your arms, I *am* the issue at hand," she said, unbuttoning his shirt.

"Or the issue *in* hand." Slipping his hand into the front of her robe, his warm palm cupped her breast.

"Guess what else has popped into my mind?" he asked, and nibbled a trail of kisses down the column of her neck.

"What?" she whispered in a voice heavy with expectancy as she felt the exquisite fire of arousal ignite within her. She stroked the wall of his chest, her fingertips tingling from the feel of his bare flesh.

"Gosh, you smell great," he murmured, his breath tantalizing her ear.

"I just took a bath and was going to eat a light meal, then go to bed with a good book."

"How about forgetting the meal and book?" Shoving the robe off her shoulders, he laved the swell of her cleavage. "I'm thinking about carrying you into that bedroom and laying you down on that big bed." Her nightgown followed her robe to the floor as he closed his mouth around one of her nipples.

"Then what?" she asked breathlessly, sliding her hands down to his belt.

"Then I'm going to sink myself into that soft, luscious body of yours," he whispered in a husky growl.

"Action speaks louder than words, Kincaid," she challenged. Her fingers trembled as she released the buckle.

His mouth crushed hers and he drove his tongue into the warm, moist recess of her mouth the way he soon would drive his organ into the velvet sheath of her sex and feel her tighten around him. Sweeping her up in his arms, he carried her into the bedroom, laying her down gently on the bed.

Within seconds, he had shed his clothes and joined her.

Later, Dave lay staring pensively up at the ceiling.

"You're thinking about Sally again, aren't you?" she said.

"No, I was remembering the first time I was in this bed."

She shifted and leaned across his chest. "You mean the night of the prizefight."

"Yeah. Matter of fact . . ." Before she could anticipate his intention, he grabbed her arms and flipped her onto her back. Pinning her hands down on each side of her head, he straddled her.

"What are you doing?" she asked, startled by his sudden, aggressive move.

"An experiment. So—you do recall that night. And you can visualize me lying here on my back, too stiff and sore to even move."

"Yes, bloody and pathetic creature that you were," she teased.

He released one of her hands just long enough to snatch a scarf from the bed table and fling it over her eyes. "Well, turnabout is fair play, Miz Sin. As I said, this is an experiment. I want you to use that very active imagination of yours and imagine you're lying here naked."

"Not unlike what I'm doing now."

"That's right, only you're aching and bruised and deliberating on how dying is beginning to hold a special appeal to you. Can you do that?"

"I'll try. At least it's comforting to know you aren't contemplating slapping me around for the sake of science. Go on with your experiment, Dr. Kincaid."

"Now, as you're lying here, imagine I'm not holding you down, but that your arms are stretched to the sides of you with your hands—so damned swollen you can't close them—soaking in basins of hot water. Would you prefer I tie your hands to the bedposts so you can better experience the feeling?"

"No, I've got the picture," she replied lightheartedly.

"And, of course, the scarf on your face is really a towel. And it's wet and hot."

"Uh-huh. Very wet. Very hot."

"But it still feels good, doesn't it?"

"Yeah, kind of helps to relieve the pain."

"Now the painkiller is starting to kick in, and your aches and pains are beginning to diminish slightly. You're slipping into a euphoria where everything is starting to feel warm and fuzzy. No aches. No pains."

"Right. Warm and fuzzy. No aches . . . no pains."

"Even the thought of dying has lost its appeal, and you're thinking you just might take another shot at living." He leaned over and whispered in her ear. "Can you imagine all that, my seductive little Miz Sin?"

Lulled by the mesmerizing huskiness of his voice, Cynthia relaxed and closed her eyes, allowing her mind to slip into the tranquil stage he was describing. "Uh-huh. Feels real good."

"Tell me how you're feeling right now, honey."

"Oh, just like you said . . . all relaxed and warm inside, with that fuzzy, drowsy feeling you have just before you fall asleep. Matter of fact, Dr. Kincaid, I think you're gonna lose me," she murmured as she began to drift off.

"I don't think so, Miz Sin." Removing the scarf, he began to cover her face with kisses so light they felt like feather strokes.

Half asleep, she smiled. "Ummm, I like that. Feels so good, Doctor."

He ran his tongue along the bridge of her nose, then kissed the tip of it before moving to her mouth. She parted her lips reflexively when he traced the fullness of her lips with light angel kisses. "Oh, yes. Nice, Dr. Kincaid. So nice."

Suddenly, she popped her eyes open, jolted to

wakefulness by the feel of his flickering tongue on the peaks of her breasts.

"Oh, no! That's not fair! I didn't do that to you. I only kissed your chest."

"This is your chest, Miz Sin. And, thankfully, it's shaped deliciously more appealingly than mine." He ran his tongue along the cleavage. "And so much smoother, tastier," he said. Closing his mouth over a nipple, he began sucking and tugging at it.

Tremors of arousal licked at her loins as he savored her breasts. She bore the exquisite pain as long as she could, then started to squirm.

"What's wrong, Miz Sin, aren't you sleepy anymore? Something disturb your euphoria? Beginning to feel all those previous sensations again—all those aches and pains? Only now, a new one's been added, hasn't it—a fire in your loins."

"I wasn't trying to arouse you that night. Good grief, Dave, that was the farthest thing from my mind. I felt compassion . . . guilt. I wanted to comfort you."

"You comforted me all right! Once again, Miz Sin, your good intentions went awry. I was aroused, baby, and stayed that way until that night in Denver."

He pressed kisses down her stomach, stopping just above the source of the flames firing her body. She writhed beneath him, trying to pull free, but his hold on her arms held, and she fell back, abandoning herself to the exquisite sensation swirling within her.

She lost all awareness of when he released her hands, when she curled her arms around his neck, when they rolled entwined: kissing, touching, feeling, savoring—loving.

Drowning in the hot tide of passion, she became mindless to everything except the thrill of his hands and mouth, the strength of his arms—and the sublime ecstasy of him filling her.

When Cynthia awoke the next morning, Dave was still sleeping soundly beside her. Knowing he had overslept already, she was tempted to wake him, but decided to prepare him a quick breakfast first. Slipping out of bed, she retrieved her gown and robe from the other room and had just donned them when a heavy knock sounded on the door. Giving the robe's belt a tighter tug, she opened the door.

Sean Rafferty doffed his hat. "Sorry to bother you, Miz Cynthia. I've been lookin' for Dave. He's not in his quarters, so I thought maybe—"

"He's sleeping, Sean." She had the composure not to blush. "I'll get him."

"No, let him sleep. Train's gettin' ready to pull out anyway, so I'll be goin'. Will ya tell him I've a problem at end of track and I'd like him to ride out later?"

"I'll tell him, Sean."

"Thank ya, ma'am. Sorry to ha'e disturbed ya," he said, backing away.

After brewing the coffee, she carried a cup in to Dave and put it down on the bed table. Sitting on the side of the bed, she stared at the sleeping man, her heart swelling with emotion. Lord, how she loved him! It was a mystery how or when this feeling had grown so potent within her. For certain, she had never felt this strongly for Roberto.

She studied his sleeping countenance. Asleep, he looked like a young boy, slumber relaxing the serious frown he usually wore. Her life seemed so frivolous and shallow in comparison to the hard life he had led. She wished so badly she could bring happiness and contentment into his life. How was it possible for a woman to want to mother and make love to the same man? Unable to resist the temptation, she reached out and brushed back the rumpled hair that had tumbled onto his forehead.

Dave opened his eyes, catching the emotion in her eyes and face. For a long moment they gazed in silence into each other's eyes, then he reached up, cupped her nape, and drew her head down. His kiss was long and incredibly tender.

"Good morning," she said when they separated. "I've brought you a cup of coffee."

He bunched up the pillow behind him and sat up. "This is a first for me," he said, taking the cup from her.

"What? Staying in bed after the sun comes up?" she teased.

"No, having a woman bring me coffee in bed." He grinned and sipped the hot brew.

"Really! What did the women you've known usually bring you in the morning?"

"Wouldn't know. I never stayed around till morning."

"Haven't you ever been in love, Dave?"

"Nope." The sheet slipped down as he leaned over to put the cup back down on the table. Fascinated, she watched the muscles bunch across his shoulders and then expand when he set the cup aside. His body was so beautiful, she never tired of looking at it.

Lying back, he patted the bed beside him. "Hey, Miz Sin, why don't you take off that robe and get back in here?"

"Hey, Kincaid, you better get out of that bed. Sean Rafferty was here earlier and he said there's a problem at end of track. He wants you to ride out there."

"To hell with it. I'm tired of chasing problems. Come on, Cyn, get back in bed." He grabbed her hand. "We'll spend the rest of the day and night here, thinking of delectable things to do to each other."

She smiled tolerantly. "The thought's very appealing."

"So-o-o-o, what's stopping you?"

"You'd hate me in the morning for encouraging you to do it."

"Isn't it a little late for you to be developing a conscience?"

"And too late for you to pretend you don't have one. Dave, you take life too seriously to ignore your responsibilities."

"And I'm tired of it. For over ten years, I've put responsibilities above all else in my life. It's time I had fun like everyone else."

"It can only be fun if there are no reservations. I think you'd have some. You can't change a lifetime's habits overnight."

"Dammit, Cyn, who's talking about changing my lifestyle! I'm talking one day—not a lifetime! Forget I asked." He bolted out of bed and pulled on his drawers and jeans.

"I hope you'll stay for breakfast."

"Oh, can't do. Duty calls—remember?"

Utterly confused, she said, "I don't understand why you're so angry with me."

"What's the matter—not in the mood this morning, Miz Sin? Still playing games, huh? Well, I don't like to be led on at your convenience."

Stunned, she stared at him. How could he think that after what they had shared? The accusation was a knife driven into her heart.

"Is that what you think, Dave? All right, fine—let's do it." She pulled off her robe. "Come on, we'll get back into bed and indulge in the rawest, steamiest, no-holds-barred sex we're capable of. Fornicate until we're brainless, Kincaid, if that's all you want. After all, just as you said: this is all just a game with us. We're both only out for a good time." Tears streamed down her cheeks as she pulled the nightgown over her head. "You've sure got me figured out, Kincaid. I don't give a damn about anything or anybody except myself—Cynthia MacKenzie, the biggest pleasure seeker in the world."

She climbed into bed. "Come on, Kincaid," she cried, on the verge of hysteria. "What are you waiting for? Can't you see *Miz Sin* is ready and willing? Oh, that's spelled with an *S* of course—as in sensualist slut!" She hiccoughed on a sob.

"Oh, God, Cyn, I'm sorry."

Dave sat down on the bed and gathered her into his arms. "I didn't mean it the way it sounded, honey. I'm so sorry, Cyn." He hugged and kissed her in an attempt to comfort her. "You were right about my responsibility to my job. I resented you for reminding me of it, that's all. I didn't mean to hurt you. I didn't mean one damn word I said."

"No one has to remind you of your responsibilities, Dave. I never should have tried."

Wiping away her tears, he cupped her cheeks in his hands, his eyes filled with contrition. "Lord, Cyn, don't ever call yourself those names again. That's not how I think of you at all. I've been so wrong, right from the beginning. You're the best thing that's ever happened to me."

"You bet I am," she said with a trembling smile. "I don't know what got into me to cause that outburst. I'm usually not so sensitive." He kissed her lightly. "Dave," she said, looking deep into his eyes, "I'm not playing any game. I stopped that a long time ago. I thought you understood that."

"I do. I think we both started out challenging each other, and the situation got away from us. We've been acting like a couple of kids—hurting each other just to get even. I'm grateful to you, Cyn. Grateful for the joy you've brought into my life."

He lightly traced her lips with his finger. "Remember when you did this to me and warned me you'd teach me how to laugh? Well, you have. I laugh now. . . . I smile just thinking about you, Miz Sin." He grimaced in disgust. "Dammit! There I go again! I didn't know the name bothered you, honey. It's just been my way of teasing you."

"I know that, Dave. I really don't mind it. It's kind of a special thing between us."

He hugged her, holding on desperately. "I don't want you to leave me, Cyn."

"I'm not going anywhere, Dave. As long as you want, I'll stay. I don't think I could leave you if I wanted to."

He stood up and reached for her hand, pulling her to her feet. "How about that breakfast you mentioned? I'm so damn late now, a few more minutes won't make any difference." Picking up her nightgown, he handed it to her. "And please put on some clothes. There's a limit to my control." He pulled her into his arms and kissed her.

"So I've noticed," she said with a grin.

They were eating breakfast when Sally knocked and entered. Seeing Dave, she hesitated. "Oh, excuse me. Am I interrupting something?"

"Yeah, breakfast." Dave shoved back his chair and stood up. "I was just leaving anyway." Bending down, he kissed Cynthia on the cheek. "See you later." He grinned, looking into her eyes. "You sure I'm forgiven?"

"I'll be here when you get back," she said, laughing.

"So long, Sally," Dave said on his way out.

"My, you two looked very cozy," Sally remarked when Dave left.

"Would you like some breakfast?" Cynthia asked, ignoring the snide remark.

"No, it's quite late. I've eaten already."

Cynthia took a deep breath to try to keep a hold on her patience. "What do you want, Sally?"

"Considering your relationship with David, I should have known you wouldn't keep your promise to me."

"What are you talking about?"

"You just couldn't wait to tell him about Clay, could you? After promising me that you'd let me tell him in due time."

Cynthia had had enough quarreling and accusations to last her a lifetime. She didn't appreciate Sally's bursting in and adding some more. Gritting her teeth, she said in a patient voice, "I am not the one who told Dave about you and Clay."

"Then how did he find out?" Sally accused.

"Have you forgotten about Maggie? Remember, she knew you hadn't been there when that dog attacked us. Apparently she innocently blurted out the truth to Dave. I hope you didn't expect a seven-year-old child to be a party to deceiving your brother."

The look on Sally's face was exasperating.

"Is there some reason why you're smirking, Sally?"

"Don't you think it's rather hypocritical that you and David lecture me on my behavior, considering the whole camp knows what's going on between the two of you?"

"Dave and I are both old enough to face up to the consequences of our actions, Sally. Whereas you and your friend Mr. Bonner are hiding behind the excuse of inexperienced youth."

"Clay and I don't have to make excuses."

"I hope so. I hope when the time comes to admit your mistakes, you'll have your brother's integrity. How dare you criticize him?"

"Oh, here comes the lecture again about what I owe David."

"No, that's not even the issue anymore. What bothers me is your self-indulgence. Dave has faced the demands of responsibility his whole life; don't you think he's entitled to some fun, too?"

"Yes, of course."

"Fine. Now that we understand one another, if you'll excuse me, I'd like to get dressed."

"You're angry with me, aren't you, Cynthia?"

"No, I'm not angry, Sally. I just wish that since you want to be treated like an adult, you'd start acting like one. You use your youth as an excuse when it works to your convenience, and you deny your youth when it's inconvenient. It's got to be one or the other, Sally, if you expect anyone to take you seriously."

Cynthia was too good-natured to hold out against the confused young girl. She walked over and hugged Sally. "Hey, honey, why don't you show us all what an adult you are by going and making your peace with your brother?"

Sally started to cry. "I don't want to fight with Dave, Cynthia. I love him."

"I know you do; and he loves you. But you're both beginning to say things that hurt one another. Dave's got an explosive temper, honey, but he's also got a fair mind under that temper. I'm sure if you sit down and talk it out, the two of you can reach an understanding."

"I'll try, Cynthia."

"That's a beginning," Cynthia said.

Chapter 21

There was no sign of David in his office, so Sally returned to her tent prior to the beginning of school. When Cynthia arrived later that afternoon to take over the class, Sally headed for the trees and her rendezvous with Clay.

They rode out to their favorite spot, where he had been teaching her to ride Crow.

"Clay, let's forget the riding lesson today. I have to talk to you."

"I kinda thought you had something on your mind, Sally. You've been quiet the whole trip. I bet I'm not gonna like what you have to say."

"My brother found out about us and has forbidden me to see you."

"Because of the trouble between the railroad and my dad."

Sally nodded. "He says you're probably one of those night riders who have been tearing up the track."

"I swear, I'm not, Sally."

"I believe you, Clay, but I can't convince my brother or Cynthia. I'm going to try talking to David again when I get back."

"Maybe I should talk to your brother, Sally. It's not fair that we have to suffer because of their fight."

"Isn't it your fight, too, Clay? You're part of the ranch."

"Yes, but I've had words already with my dad on this issue. I think we should try to work out a compromise with the railroad: after all, they're on legal grounds, we aren't. Dad's just so used to riding roughshod over everybody, he can't accept that."

Pulling her into his arms, he kissed her deeply. Then he eased her gently to the ground and pressed quick kisses on her face and eyes. "I'm scared this fight'll come between us. I love you, Blue Eyes."

"Cynthia says you're only saying that to get your way with me. She said you can have any girl in the county because you're rich and good-looking."

"I don't want any other gal but you, Sally Kincaid," he murmured between kisses. "I fell in love the moment I saw those blond curls and big blue eyes." He slipped his hand under her bodice and fondled her breast. "I'm crazy about you, sweetheart. Let me make love to you."

"We mustn't, Clay," she whispered. "It's not proper. That's just what they've accused us of doing." But the sensation his warm palm was creating felt so good she didn't want him to stop.

"It's proper if we love each other, Sally. You do love me, don't you?"

"Oh, yes. I love you, Clay."

He reclaimed her mouth and slipped his tongue between her lips. She was breathless when he released her. "Then let me make love to you. I've wanted to from the first time I saw you. I can't hold out any longer, sweetheart." He pulled the bodice over her head. "There's nothing wrong with what we're doing; you're gonna be my wife."

He took the nipple of her bare breast into his mouth, and she gasped with pleasure from the exciting jolts that coursed through her. "Just trust me, sweetheart," he whispered. "If you love me, you'll trust me."

Closing her eyes, she offered no resistance when he slid her skirt off her hips. "Oh, yes, I love you, Clay. I trust you," she sighed when he did the same to her drawers.

As soon as she finished school, Cynthia hurried to Dave's with great expectations and found him hard at work behind his desk. "Well, what happened between you and Sally?"

"What do you mean? I haven't seen Sally since I left you this morning."

Cynthia was disappointed. "I was so sure she was sincere about sitting down and talking to you."

"About what?"

"About this situation with Clay Bonner, of course."

"What more is there to say? She made herself pretty clear on that subject, and I thought I did the same."

"Dave, you've got to keep an open mind or there'll never be a solution to this problem."

"Cyn, Sally made herself pretty clear. She'll do whatever she wants to do, whether I like it or not."

"I think you're right about that. But the two of you can't go on being angry with each other. You must reach some kind of an understanding."

"We're sure at an impasse right now."

Cynthia sat down on the edge of his desk. "What was the big problem Sean had this morning? More ripped-up track?"

"Missing track again—rails and ties. If we don't get some help from the law on this, that damn Bonner's gonna bankrupt the Rocky Mountain Central. It's very costly to keep replacing rail and labor."

"I thought you had guards posted at end of track."

"I did. The extra rail was between us and them. Bonner and his men slipped in between. I suppose they dumped them in the river."

"Seems like a lot of work just to harass you," she said.

"Honey, this is beyond harassment. This is out-and-out vandalism. And it's costing us a great deal of money and labor that we can't afford. Rayburn wants to hire some gunslingers, but that's the last thing I want to do. I'm going to try speaking to Bonner again."

"And what's Beth's position?"

"She doesn't want any bloodshed either. But we can't let this go on."

Cynthia shifted over to his lap and looped her arms around his neck, feeling the delicious slide of his hands up her sides. "Do you want to come to dinner tonight?"

"I don't know. I'm pretty busy. I might need some coaxing."

She trailed kisses along his jaw, then claimed his lips in a long, lingering kiss. "Is that enough coaxing?" she asked when the kiss was over.

"Hmmm, what's for dessert?"

"Me," she said.

"It's a date, Miz Sin."

"Then I guess I better get out of here."

"Yeah," he said, kissing her again. When they parted breathlessly, he said, "Or I might have to end up eating my dessert before the meal."

Reluctantly, she rose from his lap. "Dinner's at seven. And be on time, Kincaid."

Cynthia hastened back to her car. She had a little over three hours to accomplish everything she wanted to get done. Checking the freezer compartment, she decided the fish that Pete Gifford had caught and filleted for her on her last trip to Denver would be perfect for dinner. Setting them out to thaw, she checked the ingredients in her pantry, prepared a vanilla soufflé for baking, and made a fast trip to the general store for more eggs and milk. To Cynthia's delight, she was able to purchase some mushrooms Mrs. Collins had just gathered.

For the following two hours she worked nonstop preparing the meal and setting the table for an intimate, candlelight dinner, finishing with almost forty-five minutes to spare.

Cynthia used the time to take a leisurely bath, then donned a lacy, black fitted dressing gown that buttoned down the front. Smiling wickedly, she viewed herself in the mirror. "Kincaid, this is going to be a night to remember."

Hearing his knock, she paused long enough to light the candles, then she opened the door.

Dave took a long look at her in the gown clinging to every curve of her body. "Wow! Miz Sin, I hope I'm up for this!"

Smiling seductively, she took his hand and drew him into the room. "I'll make sure you are, Kincaid."

As soon as she closed and locked the door, he pulled her into his arms and trailed a string of kisses down the column of her neck. "Why don't we forget dinner and just cut to the chase?"

"Not again tonight! I've just spent over two hours preparing it."

Slipping out of his arms, she took his hand and pulled him into the kitchen. "Sit down and pour the wine while I serve the food."

Throughout the meal, they chatted comfortably, avoiding any mention of Sally to mar the mood.

"Dinner was delicious, Cyn," Dave said after finishing his second helping of the soufflé.

Cynthia was pleased at how well the meal had

turned out: the fillets had been baked to just the perfect texture, and the Madeira she'd added to the cream sauce had given it a zesty flavor; the rice and mushrooms had tasted savory and delectable; and the soufflé had melted in the mouth.

"Where'd you learn to cook like this?" he asked.

"Believe it or not, I took a cooking course in France."

He arched a brow. "I admit, it's not what I visualized you doing when visiting Paris."

"I suppose it does sound bizarre. I've always liked to cook, even as a child. Middy used to teach me her recipes. Roberto was very upset. He said the whole thing was ridiculous, because it would never be necessary for me to cook. He didn't understand that it was something I really enjoy doing. Anyway, he got tired of Paris and announced we would be leaving." She smiled. "Whether it was him telling me what I had to do, or the thought of cooks preparing my meals for the rest of my life—whichever, I told him I was staying. That's when I broke my engagement to him."

"Seems a flimsy reason to break an engagement."

"It was, but I'd been looking for an excuse and I found one." She thought of the many times Dave had issued her an order or ultimatum, and she had always forgiven him. "A person in love wouldn't use such a feeble excuse for breaking an engagement, would they, Dave?"

"I'm the wrong person to ask, Cyn."

A long pause followed his statement as they stared at each other, until finally he said, "You're a paradox, Cynthia MacKenzie. You're the most carefree woman I've ever known, yet the most accomplished at whatever you set your mind to doing."

"Well, you may not be too happy with what I've got in mind right now."

"I bet you want me to help with the dishes."

"Heavens no! I'm not going to spoil this evening with the thought of dishes."

"So, nothing to do with the kitchen. Bedroom?" She shook her head. "Bathroom? I don't think both of us will fit in that tub."

"Wrong again, Kincaid."

"All right, if you think so. We can give it a try."

"No, wrong again about the bathroom, not the tub. That's not it," she said, laughing.

"Okay, I give up. What do you have in mind?"

"You, Kincaid, are going to learn how to dance."

"Oh, no!" he groaned.

"How can you refuse after I just cooked you that delicious meal?"

"You're resorting to bribery and blackmail. Have you no conscience, woman?"

"All's fair in love and war. Besides, it gives you the excuse to hold me," she said with a wicked smile.

"I thought I didn't need one."

"All right, it gives me the excuse for getting you to hold me," she added devilishly.

"You don't need one either," he shot back.

"Come on. Did you ever think you might enjoy it?" She took his hand and led him into the lounge.

"I hope you don't think you're going to get me to hop around doing that Irish dancing."

"No, just the opposite. A Celtic dance is just not you. When I look at you I think of something more slow, seductive—like an adagio, for instance."

"What's an adagio?"

"It's danced very slowly and has some difficult maneuvers involving balance, lifting, and such—"

"Ah, come on, Cyn, I'm not an acrobat," he said, disgusted.

"You don't have to be. Now, turn to me so we face each other, then you put your arm around my waist and pull me to you. Then we'll just sway back and forth." Grudgingly, he reached for her.

"Bravo!" she exclaimed when he executed the move perfectly. "That wasn't hard, was it?"

"If you keep up that rubbing against me, it soon will be, Miz Sin," he teased. "You should have warned me about the hidden advantages of this dance. Just how long do you figure we can stand here doing this?"

"Now bend me back, and lean over me as if you were going to kiss me."

"How in hell do you expect me to do that without falling on my face?"

"You wouldn't be concerned about falling, Kincaid, if you were really trying to kiss me."

"Why don't I do that?" he said.

"Because I don't want any distractions. We're dancing, remember?"

"This whole thing is ridiculous," he said, bending her back.

"Sometimes you have to forget appearances and just have fun."

"This is not fun. Matter of fact, you're beginning to feel heavy."

Wide-eyed, she fluttered her lashes outrageously. "Why how could I feel heavy to a big, strong, steel-drivin' man like you?" He straightened, pulling her up against him, mere inches separating their mouths. "Improvising, Kincaid?"

"No, just keeping my back from locking, Miz Sin."

"Admit it, this isn't so bad, is it?"

"I guess not. But if you breathe one word of this to anyone, I'll never forgive you," he warned.

"You see, you can have fun if you just give in sometimes and do what others want to do."

"Like take a ride in a hot air balloon," he said, swinging her out again.

"Good example."

He pulled her to him again. "Or even being willing to stand here and dance an adagio." This time he bent her back so far, they were only a few feet from the floor.

"Now you've got the idea."

"Yeah, but it's a waste of time, because I'll never have a reason to do this again."

"Why does there always have to be a reason? For a change, just do it for the pleasure of doing something entirely out of the ordinary. Now grasp me around the waist and lift me, then slowly lower me back down."

"By 'out of the ordinary,' do you mean like going three rounds in the ring with the probable next heavyweight champion of the world?"

"Yes. Now you're really getting my point," she murmured when he slowly slid her down along the length of him.

"No, Miz Sin, you're missing mine. *I have done* those things, and, might I add, for your pleasure, not mine." He dipped her back and leaned over her. Lowering his head, he closed his mouth around the peak of a breast, a stiff outline under the clinging gown. Suddenly surprised, he raised his head, then slid a hand along her spine and cupped a cheek of her rounded derriere.

"Cyn, are you wearing anything under this gown?"

Her wicked gleam tied his groin in a knot. "Of course—French perfume."

Dave burst out laughing. Off balance, he was unable to stay on his feet, and they tumbled to the floor and lay laughing like two mischievous children.

Cynthia lay flat on her back, and he stretched out, leaning over her. She slipped her arms around his neck and he kissed her lightly.

"You are absolutely incorrigible, Miz Sin." Gazing tenderly into her eyes, he said, "And I never suspected how much laughter has been missing from my life until you came into it, Cyn."

Then he lowered his mouth to claim her lips.

Chapter 22

The saloon keeper stared across the bar at the three men loitering at one of the tables, then glanced at the wall clock and shook his head.

Bet I don't make another two bits off the lot of 'em, he thought resentfully. They were silly drunk, even though they'd ordered only one round of whiskey over an hour ago. *Must be the kind what just can't hold their liquor, to get skunk drunk on just one shot.*

On the other hand, maybe the tightfisted sidewinders had brought their own bottle with them! Well, he wasn't gonna start an argument. That could be dangerous.

Standing up to stretch, he was caught in midyawn by the sound of an all-too-familiar and unpleasant shout coming from the top of the back stairs.

"Mordecai McGilligan!" He hurried to the bottom stair, expecting the inevitable tirade. "It's the wee hours of the mornin' and I want you up here, *now!* Do you hear me?"

"Yes, Merribelle, I'm comin'," he called up dutifully.

Sighing, he looked back at the men. Short and slimly built, he did not relish trying to persuade the men to leave. 'Sides, they were all packin' iron, and that could mean trouble. But then, facing Merribelle would not exactly be the best part of the evening, either.

Reluctantly he crossed the room, pulled down the window shade, and eyed the trio.

"Hey, Billy Bob," the tall, youngest man in the group said, "this sure ain't no fun. Shucks, we shoulda gone with Curly and Stew up to the madam's. I bet they're still at it." He punched Billy Bob in the shoulder.

"Oh, yeah? Well now, Jeb boy, you don't know the first thing about it. I bet . . ." Billy paused, then, weaving on the rickety chair, he began searching his pockets. Finally he found a lonesome coin and slammed it down on the bar. "There! I bet you one . . ." Leaning forward, he squinted at the coin. "I bet you one plug nickel that by now Stew is sittin' in the kitchen stuffin' his belly and playin' poker with the madam's bouncer. And as for Curly, I bet ole Curly never got to lay even one hand on saggy ole Sheila."

"Zat so? How'd you come to figure that?" Jeb asked, casting a bleary eye on his unsteady companion.

"Yeah, how'd you come to figure that?" the third man in the trio said.

"Awh, come on, Hank. You knowed ole Curly as well as I do. He was just too drunk to diddle any ole cow, much less Sheila."

With a knowing smirk, Hank nudged Jeb. "Shucks, pluggin' don't take no effort. 'Sides, a man's never too drunk to shoot a wad." He projected his chaw of tobacco toward the spittoon.

They watched the sloppy cud splatter on the floor. "Reckon we can call that one for the sweeper," Hank said sheepishly, wiping his mouth on his sleeve.

When Jeb chuckled, Hank looked at him sternly. "Jeb boy, for someone always tryin' to prove hisself a man, you gotta stop that giggling. 'Taint manly."

Jeb stood up to answer the challenge. "Zat so? Well, let's you and me just mosey up to that henhouse right now and I'll show you a manly trick or two."

"Nothin' doin', kid. Don't reckon them lovely ladies cotton to greenhorns like you. 'Sides, this man knows they ain't worth the price they're askin'."

"You wouldn't be sayin' that if you had some money."

"Never mind that," Billy Bob interrupted. "Let's stick to business here. Now, I'm bettin' you, Jeb boy, that even if'n ole Curly made it up 'em stairs, he most likely forgot why he was there. And even if he did remember, he was just too drunk to steer straight."

Jeb giggled and Hank jabbed the youngster's ribs.

"We're about closed for the night, boys," Mordecai said patiently as he walked over to them.

"Zat so!" Bewildered, Jeb looked around the room. "Looks to me like the party ain't started yet."

"Hey! What about them up there?" Billy Bob asked, pointing up behind the bar. "I'm not leavin' 'til they do."

Hank glanced up at the luscious paintings on the wall and turned a steely eye on Mordecai. "He's right! Soon as 'em two naked ladies leave, we'll be followin' 'em right out the door. And you can bet on it."

Smiling, but unamused, Mordecai tried again. "All right, boys, but it's gettin' a little late, so you best be thinkin' about . . ." His voice trailed off as he noticed Billy Bob slowly sinking forward until his head clunked down on the table.

Jeb stared wide-eyed at his loudly snoring companion. "Gee, look at that, Hank. Now what are we gonna do?"

"Don't rightly know. 'Pears Billy Bob's already made camp for the night."

"No, you don't. Not here," Mordecai declared boldly, but when he saw Hank's menacing look, he backed off and said in a high cracking voice, "I'll . . . I'll go get a bucket of water. That'll make him feel better."

"Water!" Jeb said incredulously. "You fixin' to kill him? He's already had too much to drink!"

Suddenly, distracted by stomping on the saloon porch, the men watched the swinging doors burst open with such force they hit the wall. All except Billy Bob turned their attention to the two late arrivals.

" 'Bout time you showed up, Stew," Hank said.

"How'd you fellas make out?" Jeb asked.

"Won a few, lost a few. But them calico cats wuz sure good."

"What about you, Curly?"

Curly staggered forward, then fell flat on his back when he failed to notice a chair in his path. Standing up, Jeb shook his head. "How come Billy Bob always wins the bet?"

"'Cause he's good at sniffin' out a man's nature, kid. Next time, better make sure you can cover your bet. Guess you got lucky this time, seein' as how the boss ain't noticin' much at the moment."

Conceding his loss, Jeb retrieved the slug and stuck it into Billy Bob's shirt pocket.

Mordecai picked up the tattered Stetson that had rolled to his feet and looked at the prone body. "Here's your hat, Curly," he said, but much to his amazement, the burly man sat bolt upright and peered at him through bloodshot eyes.

"Say, that's pretty good, stranger. How'd you know my name?" he asked, running his hand over his bald pate. A shaggy mass of golden curls hugged his ears and straggled down the back of his neck.

Shrugging innocently, Mordecai hooked his thumbs on his suspenders. But his confidence quickly disappeared when he heard an ominous clatter coming down the stairs.

"Oops! Look out, boys. Better get goin' while you still can," Mordecai advised as he hastily retreated and ducked down, pretending to be looking for something on the bottom shelf.

Blissfully unaware of the warning, Billy Bob—amid wheezes, snorts, and whistles—snored on while his pals could only gape at the bulky apparition that entered the room.

Garbed in a tattered sheepskin jacket, far too small to cover the voluminous flannel nightgown she wore, Merribelle McGilligan clopped across the floor in a pair of muddy, oversized boots. Entwined in her hair, strips of torn rags, flopping in all directions, crowned a face obliterated by a layer of stark white paste.

"Mordecai McGilligan!" the hefty she-devil shouted, waving a shotgun in one hand and a rolling pin in the other. "Where are you hiding *now?*"

When no answer was forthcoming, she wound up the arm with the rolling pin and smashed it down on the nearest table, sending a whiskey bottle and several glasses hopping up into the air and crashing to the floor.

"All right, you drunken varmints, this here saloon's closed. Get out!" she hollered as she pulled the trigger on the rifle, blasting a shot into the rafters.

"'Tis a banshee herself come to get us," Curly wailed. Crawling with all his might, he headed toward the swinging doors right behind the stumbling feet and hustling backsides of his cohorts.

A split second later, Curly yowled and doubled

up in pain when a swift and heavy kick got him where it hurt the most. Quickly turning around, Jeb grabbed Curly by the ankles and dragged him out the door.

"And don't you never come back! You hear me?" she shrieked after them.

Haughtily adjusting her rag-bedecked curls, Merribelle plunked the rifle on her shoulder and clopped over to pick up her rolling pin.

"Okay, Mighty McGilligan, now that them varmints are taken care of, you can come out here and clean up this mess," she ordered. "And drag out that other bum while you're at it," she declared. "I swear, them stupid buzzards are even more pathetic than you," she added, making her way up the back stairs.

Having watched the ruckus through a knothole, Mordecai rose to peek over the top of the bar. He glanced around the strangely silent room, then cast an eye at the sleeping drunk. Before he could move, Hank and Stew streaked through the swinging doors. In an unhesitating swoop, one clutched Billy Bob by the armpits, the other grabbed his ankles, and the two swiftly hefted the deadweight out the door.

Blowing air through his lips, Mordecai gazed after them, and for a fleeting moment wished he could tag along. *On the other hand, that could be dangerous,* he thought wistfully, glancing back at the stairs.

The following morning, Billy Bob awoke to a persistent buzzing sound. He slapped his ear, but the marauding insect continued to buzz around his head. Finally he sat up, then immediately clutched his throbbing head.

"Oh, she-e-e-t!" he moaned.

"C'mon, boss. Have some coffee. You'll feel better

with a little grub in ya," Jeb said, handing him a tin cup and plate.

"What in hell is this?" Billy Bob said, looking at a hard clump on the plate.

"Oh, that! Stew stuffed his pockets afore he left the madam's last night. It's a biscuit, I think. Try dunkin' it, boss. 'Taint any worse than Curly's usual grub. But don't tell him I sa—"

Suddenly Billy Bob grabbed for his pistol, as he saw someone emerge from the bushes twenty yards away. Jeb turned around quickly, then chuckled.

"That's just ole Curly comin' from a squat."

" 'Course it is. I can *see* that!" Billy Bob postured.

Truth was, he knew he couldn't have recognized the face of his own brother at that distance. "I just get quick triggered when I'm in a strange place." He gulped some coffee and looked around the makeshift camp. "Just where are we, and how did I get here?"

"Don't rightly know where we are," Hank said. "We just beat it out of town and rode 'til you fell off your horse."

"Yeah, even though you wuz tied to it." Jeb giggled, whereupon Hank shoved his elbow into the youngster's ribs.

Billy Bob scowled, trying to remember anything from the previous night.

"I wanna know where do we go from here?" Stew mumbled, shoveling beans into his mouth.

"Yeah, Billy Bob. Where *are* we goin'?" Jeb complained. "You're supposed to be doin' all the thinkin' 'round here, and it looks to me like we're nowheres."

"I don't care where we're goin', just so long as we got some money to spend when we get there," Curly added.

"You figure out how we're gonna get some money, Billy Bob?" Hank asked.

"Now, boys, don't go gettin' yerselves all fired up over nothin'. Of course, we're gonna get some money. What's more, we're gonna do it today," Billy Bob answered with bravado.

"How we gonna do it?" Hank pressed.

"I ain't tellin' you nothin' 'bout it 'til we get there," Billy Bob snapped as he struggled to think. "You just break up this here camp and get on your horses. The Walden Gang is once again about to ride and plunder. Yes, siree, this very day!"

"Yippee!" Jeb enthused until Hank gave him a shove.

Mounting their horses, they followed at a respectful distance as their fearless leader gallantly led the charge—even though he had no destination in mind. After a long ride, the gang approached the crest of a hill. Reining up, Billy Bob dismounted and all followed suit.

Skeptically, Hank looked up toward the crest. "You thinking there's gold dust in the pasture on the other side, Billy Bob?"

Ignoring him, Billy Bob strolled to the top of the hill with the other men in tow and sat down in front of a large rock. Hank, muttering to himself, lagged behind.

Billy Bob was tired. He knew the boys were getting restless, and Hank was downright nasty. He'd have to come up with some idea pretty soon or he'd have a gawldang mutiny on his hands.

Munching on a piece of jerky and gazing off into the distance, Stew spied something and nudged Jeb. "Look over there," he said, pointing north. "See anything?"

Jeb shielded his eyes and looked across the valley. "Yeah, 'pears to be a train."

Billy Bob got up, squinted against the sun, and pretended to study the scene.

"I'll be dadblamed!" Curly said. "What's a railroad be doin' out here?"

Billy Bob couldn't see a thing out there, but Curly's words gave him all he needed to know. He tightly closed one eye, widely opened the other, and began twirling one end of his mustache—scheming for all he was worth.

"Zat why you brought us here, boss?" Jeb asked.

"Hell no!" Hank grumbled. "He's as lost as the rest of us."

"The hell you say!" Billy Bob denied. "Knowed what I wuz doin' the whole time. We're gonna hold up that train. Let's ride, boys."

With pistols blazing, the gang rode up to the train. O'Hara brought the locomotive to a screeching stop.

"Hands up there and come out. Don't try anything dumb or you'll end up buzzard bait," Billy Bob ordered.

Raising their hands over their heads, O'Hara and Harrington climbed out of the cab.

"What are you holdin' us up for?" O'Hara asked. "We ain't carryin' nothing' but rails and ties."

"What about the passengers?" Jeb asked.

"Passengers?" O'Hara and Harrington exchanged baffled expressions. "What passengers?" O'Hara asked, looking down the long row of flatcars piled up with rail.

"You carryin' any payroll?" Hank asked,

"We don't carry payroll, mister. We just haul supplies back and forth."

Billy Bob scoffed. "You don't think we're gonna believe that, do ya?"

"Well, look for yerself," O'Hara declared.

"That's what we're gonna do," Billy Bob said. "You two sit yerselves down over there while we do."

After a lengthy inspection, they produced nothing of value except forty-two cents from O'Hara and twenty-eight cents from Dan Harrington.

"How long you fellas been outlaws?" O'Hara asked as the gang prepared to ride off.

"Why ya askin'?" Hank said.

"Seems to me yud be a lot better off if ya took to an honest day's work."

"You ain't one to talk, when there ain't even six bits between the two of you," Hank said.

"Where's this train headin'?" Billy Bob asked.

"To a tent town. We're laying track between Denver and Dallas."

"Zat so?" Jeb said. "Who owns this railroad?"

O'Hara pointed to the name on the side of the car. "The Rocky Mountain Central."

"We kin see that," Billy Bob replied. "You thinkin' we cain't read? Who *owns* the railroad?"

"Name's MacKenzie."

Billy Bob's head jerked up and his right eye started to twitch. "You say MacKenzie? They from Texas?"

"Naw. Denver. Lived there thirty or forty years."

"I *hate* the name MacKenzie. MacKenzies killed my brothers."

"It's a common name," O'Hara said to the agitated Billy Bob.

"Yeah, but they're all related somehow. Get yerselves back on that train, and you tell your MacKenzie boss for me that he ain't heard the last from the Walden gang."

Pat O'Hara and Dan Harrington related the whole account to Dave as soon as they pulled into Tent Town.

"Davey, me boy, I ain't ever seen the likes of it," Pat said. "What were the damn fools thinkin'? Must of figured we wuz haulin' gold dust, not rails and ties."

"They were just downright stupid," Dan Harrington interjected. "The dumbest gang of fellas I've ever met."

"Well, let's not mention the incident to the women. I'm sure the outlaws are long gone, so there's no sense in getting the womenfolk worried. Obviously they were harmless, or they wouldn't have let the two of you off so lightly."

"Whatta ya mean?" Pat declared. "Cleaned me and Danny out, didn't they?"

Dave laughed. "Yeah, a whole seventy cents. That alone should have made them mad enough to shoot the two of you." He jumped down from the train cab. "Remember—don't alarm the women."

Chapter 23

The next morning, through his spy glasses, Billy Bob watched the hardworking railroad crew at the end of track. A toothy grin stretched his chubby jowls to his ears. "I got a plan, boys."

Because Billy Bob had ridden with the notorious Charlie Walden gang, the responsibility of leadership fell on his shoulders. In truth, he had been afraid of his brother Charlie; Charlie was teched in the head—he enjoyed inflicting pain and killing people. Billy Bob had no heart for such actions. When they raided a ranch, he'd hide in the bushes sobbing until it was all over. Once in Texas, he'd even helped an old Mexican, carrying a young Anglo boy, escape from the carnage. Billy Bob knew his brother would have been furious if he'd known.

He'd actually been relieved when he was arrested in Stockton for shooting a gambler. Even though his brother Beau had killed the man, Billy Bob took the blame to get out from under Charlie's domination.

And because he had ridden with the famous gang, and had served time for killing a man, his personal prestige had grown, which was why men were willing to make him their leader and follow him.

Billy Bob enjoyed the importance that gave him.

"Hope you ain't got any idea 'bout attackin' that railroad."

"The hell you say, Hank, and shut up, 'cause that *is* what we're gonna do," Billy Bob barked.

"What for?" Hank hollered back.

"To settle the score, of course. We're gonna get them MacKenzies for everything they've got."

"MacKenzies? Why are you still fuzzing about them? Your brain must be rotting out, Billy Bob! 'Sides, that mob down there would nail us to the track. And they ain't got no money with 'em anyway—or did you forget?" Hank spat tobacco juice.

"Yeah, your beef with them MacKenzies don't mean shet to us, Billy Bob," Curly interjected. "We tried robbin' their freight. Wasn't nothing in it and we got nothin' for all our trouble."

"Shut up and get on your horses. We're riding north," Billy Bob commanded, already mounted.

Jeb climbed on his horse and looked back at the train site. "Why are we goin' north?" he whispered to Stew.

"Beats me." Stew shrugged, shelled a peanut, and popped it into his mouth. "Best not to ask no questions when you ride with the Waldens, kid."

They'd ridden a good ten miles when Curly yelled, "Hey, boss, what's that over there?"

Billy Bob raised his arms, signaling a stop. "Where are you looking?"

"Over yonder, 'bout a mile or so down that track. Looks like a couple railroad cars and maybe tents or somethin'."

"Oh, yeah!" Billy Bob said with certainty—even though he was not at all certain. "That's Tent Town; just what we're looking for. Dismount, boys."

The gang gathered around as Billy Bob revealed his plan.

"So you think that's where they keep their money?" Jeb finally questioned.

"Where else? Like I told ya, they have to stash money to pay the crew. And then the women hide it, or maybe it ends up at the saloon. It's gotta be somewheres."

"Makes sense to me," Stew said as he took out some more peanuts.

"Now, I reckon it won't do for us to ride in together like a pack of wolves, so . . . Jeb and Stew, you're gonna ride double with Curly and Hank, and leave your horses by this tree. You can walk into town when we get close. We'll all meet back here afore dark."

"Good idea, boss!" Jeb said eagerly. "But couldn't we jest as well ride double and lead our horses behind us? That way—"

Hank gave him such a shove Jeb landed on his backside.

"Hey, why'd you do that for, Hank?"

Exasperated, Billy Bob looked down at Jeb and shook his head.

"Curly and I will hitch up at the saloon; Hank, you hitch up further down the road. Now remember, boys, we spread out when we get there and try to look innocent. Act like we don't know each other. Talk nice and friendly-like, and don't make no threatenin' moves. Matter of fact, let's hide our guns in our saddlebags. We don't want 'em to think we're gunslingers. They'll be hoodwinked into thinkin' we can't possibly do 'em no harm."

"Wait a minute," Hank said, wiping tobacco juice off his mouth. "You could be right about the money, but I ain't leavin' my gun holed up in no saddlebags. What if somethin' goes wrong—or there's some men in there?"

"Shet, Hank, like I told you, there's only a passel of women and kids in there. The men are all workin' up the track. 'Sides, we ain't plannin' no shoot-out, so, if'n we don't show no guns, there ain't gonna be no shoot-out. See?"

Hank nodded. "So we just con 'em with sweet talk, look around, and pick up what we can find. Then we leave without anyone being the wiser."

"That's it! We'll be long gone afore anything turns up missin'."

Hank thought for a moment, then nodding approval, he zinged his cud against the rock.

The gang mounted and turned toward their destination, walking their horses slowly. Jeb and Stew quietly joined Curly in a tone-deaf rendition of "My Darlin' Clementine," while Billy Bob and Hank traded bawdy stories—all trying their darnedest to look innocent.

Far to the west beyond the town, snowcapped mountains lined the horizon as the noonday sun shone brightly on the haphazard community of Tent Town. After the crew had departed early that morning, the women had immediately set about their household chores. Several women piled their baskets of washing on a horse-drawn cart and walked alongside as Patty Dennehy led the horse to the river. After the washing was done, they hung their clothes on ropes attached to wooden poles staked between the tents.

"You all finished hanging up your clothes, Mary?" Patty asked.

"Just about," Mary Callahan answered. "You girls get out from underfoot," she told her daughters, who were chasing each other under the clotheslines. The twins spied Catherine Mary playing with Snoozer and ran over to her.

"Let go! Come on, let go, Snoozer," Catherine Mary said, pulling on the stick clenched in the dog's mouth. Peggy and Polly quickly lined up behind Catherine Mary, but even so, Snoozer won the tug-of-war and ran off into the open field with the three giggling girls chasing him.

"Peggy! Polly!" Mary called. "You better get back to help Miz Cynthia." Laughing, the twins turned back in response to their mother's call.

"Mind you now, Catherine Mary, don't be teasin' that bonnie Snoozer," Patty called out. "Oh! The water's about boilin'," she said, glancing at the pot on the fire pit.

Patty invited Mary in for tea, and the friends chatted about the surprise the women were planning for the men that evening. It would be a very special dinner the ladies were preparing.

"Will ya be makin' your meat dish with the baked spaghetti crust, Mary?" Patty asked.

Mary nodded, pleased to be asked. "Won't it be grand?"

"Can't wait to see Sean's face," Patty said.

"Sure and I never wud have thought up this shindig meself."

"Leave it to Miz Cynthia to get it right," Patty said. "Things sure have brightened up considerable since she came."

"Say, Patty, how old do you think Sean is today?"

"I don't know, but I'll be bettin' he's ne'er had a birthday party like this before, and—"

She was interrupted by Snoozer's loud barking as he came racing into the tent. Before she could move, she found the dog's huge front paws in her lap and his wet tongue licking at her chin.

"Get you down, Snoozer, you're all wet," she said, trying to push the bulky, wiggling dog away as Catherine Mary came running in.

"Mama! Mama!" she said excitedly.

"For land's sake, me child, yuv got this fool mutt all lathered up. Get him out of here."

"But Mama, Mama, me and Snoozer saw some big men on big horses come riding out there . . ."

Catherine Mary pointed, biting her lower lip.

Patty looked askance. "Uh-huh, and might I be supposin' they'd be wearin' a suit of armor, carryin' shields, and big plumes a bobbin' on their helmets? Saints preserve us, Catherine Mary, you up and told me that story nary a week ago. Get ya goin' now, lass. Go help Miz Cynthia. She told you younguns to be comin' right back after lunch," Patty said, shooing dog and daughter out the door.

"We did too see them big men, didn't we, Snoozer?" Catherine Mary said as she ran alongside her beloved companion toward the school tent, where Cynthia and her girls were drawing pictures and making decorations.

Lydia Rafferty had taken the boys for a nature study and picnic down at the river to get them out of the way. However, Tommy O'Neill and Dennis McGuire had been left behind to work with the girls as punishment for slinging mud balls the previous day.

"Miz Cynthia! Miz Cynthia," Catherine Mary cried breathlessly.

"Move, Snoozer," Cynthia said, pushing the dog out of the way.

"But Miz Cynthia—"

"What is it, honey?" Cynthia said pleasantly. "Remember, we have a lot of work to get finished in time for the party. Have you sat down and made your drawing depicting Mr. Rafferty's life yet?"

Catherine Mary sighed in frustration and sat down obediently. She busily scribbled green grass at the bottom of her sheet of paper. The top had a lavender sky with a big orange sun on one half, and multicolored, polka-dotted rain coming down on the other.

"Oh, my! This is so lovely," Cynthia exclaimed when the little girl presented it to her.

The afternoon went quickly, with Cynthia darting

from one area of activity to the other, watching the girls finish their drawings and crepe paper decorations, while Tommy and Dennis hung them in the big tent at Cynthia's direction.

In the ovens of the kitchen car the women baked cakes, breads, potatoes, and several casseroles. The aroma of a roasting pig outside, where Sally Kincaid and Rosie McGuire had kept a watchful eye since early morning, was making everybody hungry.

"Everything looks so nice," Cynthia said, making a final inspection of the huge tent. She smiled when she spied Maggie's stick figure drawing of a small, curly-headed boy standing behind a huge sunflower that dwarfed a large boxcar on the other side of him.

"Beggin' your pardon, ma'am," a voice from behind said. She turned around and saw two strangers standing in the doorway. "I be William Robert Walden," the stocky man said, doffing his hat. "And this here is—"

"Curly Francis Ringo at your service, ma'am," the second man said with a nod of his bald head.

"We wuz jest ridin' around the range this mornin' and saw your spread," Billy Bob said, "so we moseyed in to see how the tracks wuz comin'. Spent the day meetin' some mighty fine folks here."

"Glad to welcome you, gentlemen. I'm Cynthia MacKenzie."

Billy Bob's eyes bugged out and his mouth locked into a toothy grin. "MacKenzie, you say?"

"And we were just preparing—"

"Yeah, we heard about your big doings," a strange voice said.

Cynthia looked out and saw three more strangers in the doorway.

"Sure smells good. Yes, siree. Hello, ma'am. I'm Stewart Leon Potts, but you can call me Stew."

Puzzled, Cynthia looked at the next man.

"I'm Jeb Bloomer," the young man said, adding pleasantly, "Don't worry, ma'am, we ain't gunslingers, and we ain't here to do no one no harm." An elbow in the ribs made him gasp, "No, siree!"

Billy Bob cleared his throat nervously and said to the latest arrival, "Say there, it ain't polite to shove a stranger, stranger."

Ignoring him, the third man bowed. "Henry Withers, ma'am."

"Do you men work on the Bonner spread?" she asked.

"No, ma'am. We just heard that this here outfit might need some extra hands."

"Oh, I don't know about that," Cynthia said hesitantly.

"Mind if we just hang around 'til the boss gets back?"

"Well, I suppose it can't do any . . . harm," she said, feeling extremely suspicious.

"Maybe we can make ourselves useful," Billy Bob said.

"By doing what, boss . . . er, stranger?" Jeb asked.

"By watching the pig roast," Billy Bob said, stepping onto Jeb's foot.

As she watched them walking jovially toward the pig pit, Cynthia noticed something curious: while not one toted a gun, they were all wearing fully loaded gun belts.

Resolving to keep an eye on them, Cynthia hurried to the kitchen car. "How is everything doing in here? The men will be home in less than an hour."

"Everything is fine, Cynthia. The spaghetti is about done boilin'," Mary said. "Just have to put 'em in the pie tins, bake 'em a few minutes, and add the stew."

"Okay, let's get the cakes to the tent, and—"

"Miz Cynthia," Katie McGuire said, running up to them, "Mama wants to know if she should start slicing the pig."

"Tell her yes, dear, and we'll keep the pieces warm in the oven."

Katie took the platter and had just started to run out the door when Cynthia stopped her and asked, "Are those strangers still out there?"

"Strangers? I didn't see any strangers."

"Really?" Cynthia asked, surprised as Katie shook her head.

"Well, okay, honey. Go back and help your mama."

After Katie left, Cynthia went out the door and looked around outside. Shaking off her puzzlement, she headed toward her private car to freshen up and change clothes.

"Miz Cynthia!"

Looking around, she saw Maggie and Catherine Mary running behind, her accompanied by Snoozer.

"Can we come with you?"

"Why yes, Maggie. Matter of fact, I need you to take some boxes back to the party."

"Boxes? What's in them?"

"Oh, they're not heavy. But don't let Snoozer get too good a sniff," she teased.

"Them boxes got chocolates?" Maggie asked eagerly.

"And candy corn?" Catherine Mary inquired.

"I'm not giving away any secrets," Cynthia said. Laughing, she opened the door of her car, the girls and dog at her heels.

Startled by an unexpected sound, she stopped so suddenly that Maggie bumped into her, and Catherine Mary bumped into Maggie, ending up on the floor.

"Shhh. Quiet!" Cynthia whispered to the giggling girls.

Snoozer, however, would not be shushed. Barking loudly, he bounded over Catherine Mary and suddenly stopped and growled. Then he made a flying leap at the window, sinking his teeth into the drapes and some phantom quarry.

A wailing yowl and cries for help sent Cynthia and the girls scrambling to yank at the dog, but all became enmeshed in yards of red velvet as the drapery rod gave way. Falling to the floor in a heap, the struggling bodies flailed and thrashed against the heavy drape until Cynthia found a corner of the fabric with one groping hand and a fistful of hair with the other.

"Let go!" a voice hollered. "I give up! Let go!"

Immediately releasing her grasp, she scrambled to her knees, flinging aside the end of the drape as the girls managed to free themselves while dragging Snoozer off the hapless intruder.

"You!" she said aghast, looking into the face of Stewart Leon Potts. "What are you doing in here?"

"Ah . . . I beg your pardon, ma'am," he stammered. "I was just lookin' for . . . for my buddy Jeb. Oh, Jeb, are you in here?" he called out.

"What!" she said incredulously. "Whatever would he—"

"Snoozer! Snoozer!" the girls called out in a losing battle as the yapping dog broke loose. Instantly Stew ran for the door, tumbled out of the car, and fled with Snoozer in pursuit.

"Well, what do you make of that?" Cynthia said, amazed.

Her major concern was that there wasn't a man in camp, since the four cooks had not returned from taking the crew their lunch. She decided to alert the other women; unarmed though they might be, the strangers were up to no good. "You girls stay here and keep this door locked. I'll be right back."

The girls watched from the window as Cynthia

headed toward the kitchen car, but they saw no sign of Mr. Potts or Snoozer.

"I hope old Snoozer got 'em right in the seat of his pants," Catherine Mary said with a defiant pout.

"Why do you say that, Catherine Mary?" Maggie asked.

"Because when Mr. Snoozer don't like somebody, they ain't worth liking—that's why."

The girls stood quietly looking out the window for a few moments when a clicking sound came from somewhere behind them. They looked at each other fearfully and quickly turned around. With mouths agape, they saw the door of the water closet start to open slowly.

"Who's there?" the girls cried out in chorus, and the door slammed shut.

Maggie nudged Catherine Mary, gesturing toward the gun rack, and the girls cautiously tiptoed over to it. Standing on a chair, Maggie reached for a rifle while Catherine Mary kept an eye out for any further door movement.

"All right, whoever you are, come out of there with your hands up," Maggie said in the deepest voice she could muster. "We've got a gun and we're gonna blow a hole in that door."

At first there was silence, then a man's voice answered, "Don't shoot. I'm a comin'."

The door opened a crack, then a head popped out, followed by a body with two trembling hands in the air.

"Well, I'll be dadblamed! What are you little girls doin' with that big gun?" the intruder said.

"Never mind that. What are you doin' in Miz Cynthia's privy?" Maggie asked.

"Who me? I . . . wuz jest . . ." he mumbled with a silly grin. "You know what people do in privies."

Catherine Mary giggled, then the man giggled, relaxing his arms.

"Keep 'em up, mister," Maggie warned, waving the gun.

"Watch out there, little girl," he said, raising his hands again.

"A girl ain't little when she's holdin' a shotgun, mister."

"Zat so? I mean, you're right. 'Sides, I ain't meanin' you no harm, so why don't you jest lower that barrel and we'll talk it over friendly-like."

"Turn around and put your hands behind your back, Mr. . . . Mr.—"

"Bloomer, little lady. Jeb Bloomer. Now if—" She took aim, and he turned on his heel.

The girls tied his hands with the drapery cords and shoved him back into the water closet. Then they pushed one of the large lounge chairs in front of the door and, with Maggie toting the rifle on her shoulder, they ran from the car.

"Maggie, Catherine Mary, wait up," Rosie McGuire called out as she and Katie came running from the fire pit. "What're ya doin' with that rifle, girl?"

Talking all at once, the girls began to excitedly relate their adventure when Sally caught up to them, a piece of pork still in her hand.

"Say, what's going on around here?" Sally asked. "First I saw Snoozer chasing some man, then Cynthia running—"

"Come on, we've got to tell Miz Cynthia," Maggie said, racing toward the kitchen, the other four females close behind.

Seeing the stream of women come running across the yard, Cynthia hurried out of the kitchen car. "Maggie Rafferty! What—"

"Oh, Miz Cynthia. We tied him up and he's in your privy this very minute," Maggie said breathlessly while everyone tried talking at the same time.

"Tied who up?" Cynthia asked.

"A stranger, Miz Cynthia," Catherine Mary said.

"He didn't do you no harm?" Rosie McGuire asked.

"No, he never had a chance," Maggie said proudly.

"And you didn't find out what these men were doing here?" Sally asked.

Now convinced they were up to foul play, Cynthia wondered where the other four men were this very minute.

She didn't have to wonder long when she saw Billy Bob and Curly come walking from the tent area. "Hold on there," she shouted as the women walked toward them. "I want to know straight out what you men are doing here."

By this time, several of the women and children had left their chores to see what the fuss was about.

"Why, we're just making friends and looking for a job, ma'am," Billy Bob said, doffing his hat. Seeing the rifle, Curly reached for his gun—which wasn't there.

"You forget something, Mr. Ringo?" Cynthia asked, taking the rifle from Maggie and waving it at the men. "Now you just get yourselves up in that car until I find out what this is all about," she ordered as the women started nudging the men forward. Just then, Margaret O'Neill came running across the yard.

"Miz Cynthia! Miz Cynthia, come quick. There's a man in my tent."

It was enough of a distraction for Billy Bob and Curly to bolt away.

"To arms! To arms!" Cynthia shouted at the top of her voice. Those within earshot stopped and looked around, startled. Heads poked out of the windows of the kitchen car. "Stop them!" Cynthia cried.

Billy Bob and Curly ran alongside the windows

of the car with the women inside yelling after them.

"Shoot, Miz Cynthia. Shoot," Maggie urged, but Cynthia pushed the rifle back to Maggie. "I can't. It's not loaded."

Up ahead, Tommy O'Neill and Dennis McGuire saw the pack of women pursuing the two men. Tommy made a flying tackle at Billy Bob, catching his ankle while Dennis hurled his bag of marbles. Bouncing off Curly's head, the marbles spewed in all directions. Curly stumbled into a clothesline, was flung backwards, and ended on his backside.

Wrestling on the ground with Tommy, Billy Bob pulled his ankle free, got up to run, and skidded on the marbles. Falling backwards, he landed on Curly. The two quickly sat up, but too late to crawl from the line of fire.

"Look out below," Patty Dennehy called out, dumping out two huge strainers balanced on the window ledge.

"Ah, shet!" Billy Bob hollered, as he and Curly found themselves awash in a torrent of slithering wet spaghetti that plopped on their heads, sliding down their faces and into their shirts.

"Watch your noodles," Mary Callahan giggled, taking aim and emptying a bucket of warm, juicy homemade jelly from the window onto their heads. Laughing and clapping, the women gathered around as the men struggled to regain their footing in the gooey, slippery, marble-infested mess.

Cynthia came running up, and standing with arms akimbo, she shook her head. "My, oh my! You sure had me fooled. Here I was thinking you fellas were up to no good, and all the while you were just looking for something to eat."

"'Pears we got more than we . . . I mean, yep, I guess that's what we wuz doing, all right," Curly said, pulling jellied spaghetti off his face as he struggled to his feet.

"Well, to tell you the truth, ma'am," Billy Bob sputtered as Curly gave him a hand up, "we wuz more hankerin' for some of that pork."

Cynthia snorted in disbelief. "Just why were you running away from us?" she demanded.

The two men looked at each other, stupefied, then shrugged. "'Cause you wuz chasin' us," Billy Bob said. "Like I told you, ma'am, we just rode in here real friendly-like to—"

"And where are your horses now?" Cynthia asked.

"Hitched up by the saloon. 'Ceptin' the saloon ain't open."

"It doesn't open until later, when the crew returns. And where are the other three men you came with?"

"Other three men?" Billy Bob asked innocently.

A large screeching howl answered part of the question. Stumbling from the school tent, Hank tried to protect himself from the bevy of shuttlecocks bombarding his head and face. Falling to the ground, he fell under the blows of a half dozen girls wielding badminton racquets. One was smashed over his head and now hung around his neck as he managed to crawl away under a barrage of firm blows to his posterior. As soon as he was free, he ran out of town.

"Now listen here," Cynthia said, losing her patience with Billy Bob and Curly. "Five of you showed up here a short time ago. Then we caught two snooping in my private car and the others skulking around the tents. So you—"

"Oh, th-them!" Billy Bob stuttered. "We just met them strangers right here today."

"And to tell you the truth, them hombres didn't seem on the up-and-up to me either," Curly said. "No siree, ma'am. We've got nothin' to do with them."

Not believing a word of it, Cynthia said, "Well, you're on your way out. Come on, girls. Come on, Tommy and Dennis." Taking the rifle from Maggie, she said, "We're going to escort you no-goods to your horses, and you better ride away from here as fast and as far as you can."

Having no other choice, Billy Bob and Curly, surrounded by twelve girls, two boys, Patty Dennehy, Mary Callahan, Margaret O'Neill, Sally, and Cynthia, trudged toward the saloon, leaving a trail of spaghetti in their wake.

"Hold up there," Billy Bob said as they approached their horses. "We've got some grub in our saddlebags. You mind if we eat a biscuit or two afore we ride off?"

Without waiting for an answer, Billy Bob turned toward his horse, but Polly and Peggy, jumping ahead of him, ran to the horse and stood between him and the saddlebags, their arms folded across their chests.

"Good going, girls," Cynthia said, poking the rifle in Billy Bob's back. "Go ahead, Polly, let's see what goodies we'll find in there. Help her out, Peggy."

It didn't take long for the girls to search the bags, flinging various items to the ground. When they reached the bottom, each girl came out with a pistol in hand.

"Look out, little girl," Billy Bob said, shielding his face. When nothing happened, Billy Bob peeked between his fingers, dropped his hands, and sheepishly turned to Cynthia.

"Plumb forgot about them old things. I mean, you know, a man's gotta carry a gun in these parts just for killin' snakes and such."

"Uh-huh, I see. Well, we'll just have to hold on to them in case we run into any snakes and such,"

Cynthia said, prodding him with the rifle toward his horse.

Laughing and cheering, the girls watched Billy Bob and Curly ride off while vainly dodging stones from the boys' slingshots.

Once they were out of reach, Billy Bob reined up and wheeled his horse. Shaking his fist, he shouted, "You ain't seen the last of Billy Bob Walden. I'll be back to give you MacKenzies your just desserts!" Then he and curly rode off.

"Good job, men," Cynthia said, patting the boys on their shoulders.

"Don't forget, we got one tied up in your privy, Miz Cynthia."

"That's right. Let's go and get rid of him, too. We want them all out of here."

"Yeah, Miz Cynthia. We can't let anything spoil Grandpa's birthday party," Maggie said.

"You bet not," Cynthia said, taking her hand.

As soon as they released the quaking Jeb Bloomer, he went running out of town without a backward glance. "I think we've seen the last of him," Cynthia said with satisfaction. "Now we'll split up in threes and search this whole tent area for the last one. Tell everyone you see to pass the word, and they'll help, too. We'll meet back here in fifteen minutes."

The children ran off in all directions, but when they returned, no one had caught sight of the man. "Let's get back to the car," Cynthia said.

Just then Snoozer trotted up to them. Seeing a piece of fabric clenched between the dog's teeth. Cynthia grinned. "I think we can abandon our search, ladies. It appears that Snoozer did our work for us. I'm sure Mr. Stewart Leon Potts is already miles from here."

* * *

All evidence of the afternoon's struggle had been cleaned away by the time the crew returned that evening from end of track.

"Hey, what's going on here?" Sean Rafferty asked as he smelled the roasting pig.

"Surprise, Grandpa!" Maggie said, running up to him.

All the women and children began to sing a raucous chorus of "Happy Birthday," with the deep voices of the crew joining in.

Cynthia pulled David aside and told him about the afternoon's adventure.

"So the Walden gang has struck again," he said, laughing. "It's a funny story, now that I know you're all okay. That's the same bunch that tried to raid our freight train, but you gals sure outwitted them. I'm very proud of all of you. They must have been the five riders we passed coming back. The one in front shook his fist at us. We thought they rode for Bonner."

"You don't think they'll come back, do you?"

"I doubt that. With Billy Bob on the run, I bet they've all disappeared by now. I heard the Walden gang used to be a murderous bunch, but they're all dead now, except for that half-wit Billy Bob and his stumbling fools." He kissed her lightly and said, "Hard to believe a handful of women and children could run off five armed outlaws without even firing a shot."

"Never underestimate the resourcefulness of a woman, Kincaid." Cynthia's mouth was curved in a smug smile.

"I'd be as big a fool as Billy Bob if I did. Although actually, I probably am," he said, tucking her arm in his. "At least *he* got away, Miz Sin."

Later that night, a mile past the river, Hank sat by a tree eating beans. The sound of music and laughter from the Tent Town carried to him on the night air, sounding like the celebrants were having a grand old time partying.

Reaching into his pocket, he pulled out the total of his grand heist for the day—a half-eaten plug of tobacco—and bit off a chaw. He could have gotten more if that damn fool woman hadn't caught him in her tent and chased him into the other tent with those crazed little monsters and their clubs.

Stew bent over the fire to fill his plate with beans.

"What happened to your pants?" Billy Bob asked, seeing a huge patch missing across Stew's buttocks.

"Oh, that damn dog got his teeth into 'em afore I could reach my horse," Stew said, rubbing his rear end. "I think the critter was part wolf."

"Well, we sure showed them a thing or two, didn't we, boys?" Billy Bob said.

Hank snorted. "How'd you figure that, boss? We didn't get anything."

"Sure we did," Billy Bob said.

"What exactly?" Hank asked hopefully, eyeing their saddlebags.

"Well . . ." Billy Bob hesitated, looking at Curly for support. "We got lots of satisfaction."

"Yes, siree!" Curly said agreeably.

"We messed up that party they had planned real good," Billy Bob said, folding his arms across his chest. "Bet they had to cook all new pots of spaghetti. Yep," he said with a toothy smile of satisfaction, "ain't a MacKenzie alive who ever got the best of Billy Bob Walden."

"Zat so?" Jeb said, and started giggling.

Hank poked him in the ribs.

Chapter 24

"Look, Dave, since I'm one of the owners of the railroad, maybe Bonner will talk to me," Cynthia said at breakfast the next morning, trying to convince him to take her with him when he rode out to the Bonner ranch house.

"I don't think so, Cyn; it may not be safe. Who knows what he might do? I don't trust the man."

"If he intended to harm anyone physically, he'd have done so by now. Furthermore, if that's a concern, why are you riding there alone? You'd be his logical target. I don't think Mr. Bonner will resort to violence. I'll pack us a lunch, and we can picnic on the way back."

"Picnic! Cyn, who's got time for picnics? Is this another one of your how-to-have-fun theories?"

"Did you enjoy the dance lesson the other night, Kincaid?" she asked with a gleam in her eyes.

His dark-eyed gaze swept her face. "Yeah, I enjoyed the other night, Miz Sin. Especially what followed the lesson. I liked it a lot. I'm even lucky to have survived it."

"Well, then, maybe my fun theories have some merit. After all, there's more than one way to have a good time. A nice ride together, a calm talk with Bonner, then a relaxing picnic lunch. Doesn't that sound like it could be great fun?"

Dave shook his head. "You amaze me, Cyn. If you ever met Bonner, you'd know there's no such thing as a calm talk with him. The man is a keg of dynamite with a lit fuse."

"He sounds a lot like the David Kincaid I know and love," she teased. "Besides, I've never met a man I couldn't talk to. Don't underestimate my feminine skills."

"Miz Sin, after the other night, there's no way I'd *ever* underestimate your feminine . . . skills. All right, I'll go and saddle us up a couple of mounts."

She jumped up from the table, rushed over, and kissed him. "I'll be ready in fifteen minutes."

He looked around at the soiled breakfast dishes stacked in the sink. "What about all these dirty dishes?"

"Dave, that's what I've been trying to explain to you—you've got to learn to be flexible. The dirty dishes will be here when I get back. If I stop now to wash them—*you won't be.*"

True to her word, Cynthia had changed into a riding skirt and packed a lunch by the time Dave returned with the horses.

"Sean sent me a message back from end of track. At least there was no damage to the track last night," he said, adjusting the stirrups for her. "Wonder what Bonner's cooking up for us now?"

"Think positively, Dave. Maybe he'll listen to us."

On their way out, Dave stopped to give Pat O'Hara a letter to deliver to Elizabeth. "Paddy, I mentioned it in my letter, but when you get back to Denver today, remind Miss MacKenzie that the sooner she gets a U.S. marshal down here, the sooner the vandalism will stop."

"I'll do that, Davey me lad." O'Hara flashed his wide grin at Cynthia. "Top o' the marning, darlin'."

"Good morning, Paddy. Tell my sister that I love

her and miss her, and give her a kiss for me."

"It'll be me pleasure, darlin'."

"Better yet, maybe you should do it, Dan," she said to the fireman. "You're younger and handsomer than this old codger. Only wash the coal dust off your face before you do. 'Bye, boys."

O'Hara gave two blasts of the whistle in reply as she waved and rode off with Dave.

"Is there any man you can't wrap around your finger?" he asked as they cut through the trees.

"Just you, Kincaid."

He looked at her askance. "I'm serious, Cyn."

"I think you're probably getting closer to understanding me than any man I've ever met."

He started to chuckle. "I don't think there's a man alive who could ever understand you, Miz Sin. I know I'm closer than I was before, but I'd be a wizard if I completely figured you out."

"Don't flatter yourself, Kincaid. I only said you're getting *closer* to understanding me. I'd hate to think there's nothing mysterious about me. While I, on the other hand, have you figured out down to the bone."

"Yeah, that's what worries me. Now that you've chewed me up, I'm wondering when you're gonna spit me out."

"If that's what's worrying you, Dave, you don't understand me as much as I thought you did."

They had not gone more than five miles when the sky darkened.

"I think we're in for a storm," Dave said, glancing skyward. "You might have to forget that picnic you've got planned."

Cynthia looked up at the fast-moving black clouds overhead. A rumble of thunder and a flash of lightning in the distant sky supported Dave's words.

"Maybe we should turn back. I don't imagine Bonner would offer us shelter."

Large raindrops began to splatter the ground, and they halted under a tree. Within minutes the storm struck with all its ferocity: rain falling in a torrent, and the sky—as black as night—lit only by flashes of brilliant lightning. Suddenly a lightning bolt streaked out of the sky, shearing the top off a nearby tree. There was a simultaneous boom of thunder, causing Cynthia's horse to rear up in fright. She quickly brought the terrified animal back under control.

Dave scanned the terrain for safer cover in the next glittering flash of lightning. "It looks like there's some rocks ahead, and I think I caught sight of a gap on the face of that wall." Another incandescent flash lit the sky, and this time an opening was clearly outlined in the rocky crag.

Prodding their horses to a gallop, they reached the opening of what appeared to be a cave. Dave waved Cynthia in and, grabbing the reins of the two horses, followed with them.

Drenched and shivering, Cynthia waited as her vision adjusted to the dark cave, grateful to be out of the force of the storm. Gradually she was able to discern that the cave wasn't much more than fifteen feet wide, but it appeared to be very deep.

"Dave, is this a cave or a mine?" she asked.

"Looks like a cave to me. We'll be able to tell as soon as we get a fire going."

"I hope this place isn't occupied. Lord only knows what might have come in to get out of the storm."

"I think the horses would have let us know," he said.

"Not if they're just as glad to get under cover as we are," she said.

"I'm heading back to those trees to try and find some wood."

"There's no sense in going out in this storm, Dave." She hugged her arms across her chest to try to stay warm.

"We have to get out of these wet clothes or we'll get sick. I should be able to find enough dry wood to take the chill out of here anyway."

"Be careful, Dave," she said.

As soon as he left, Cynthia started to look around the area near the door. To her relief, she found several pieces of wood and some scattered leaves that had blown into the cave, enough to get a fire started. After finding a couple of stones to strike a spark, she formed a small pile of dry leaves.

Cynthia was shivering so intensely, she could hardly rub the stones together. When she succeeded in striking a spark, it glowed for several seconds, then faded. Her teeth had begun to chatter and her hands felt like ice as she continued to struggle to get a fire started.

"D-d-damn!" Finally, when she was just about to give up, a spark caught the leaves. Putting aside the stones, she began to feed some more leaves to the tiny flame just as Dave returned.

Dripping wet, he dumped an armful of wood next to her. With a quick snort, which might have been a sneeze, the horse shook itself off, spattering raindrops in all directions. Horrified, Cynthia watched as several drops rained down on the fire, extinguishing the meager flame.

Sighing, she picked up the stones and started all over again.

"Here, try these," Dave said, tossing her a box of matches.

"M-matches! Wh-where did you ge-get m-matches?"

"From my saddlebags."

"Wh-why d-didn't you t-tell me you had m-matches?"

Trying not to laugh, Dave said, "How was I to know you were going to try and play Hawkeye?"

She glared at him. "Light the d-damn f-fire, Kin-Kincaid."

When he knelt down and put a match to the leaves, his shoulders were shaking, and she knew it wasn't because he was shivering. Within minutes she began to feel the welcome warmth from the fire, and her own shivering lessened.

"Okay, Cyn, get your clothes off," Dave ordered. "We'll spread them out by the fire and dry them off."

She stripped down to her chemise, hose, and pantaloons; Dave stripped to his drawers. "Our best bet would be to cuddle together," he suggested.

"Under any other circumstances, I wouldn't hesitate to cuddle with you, Kincaid, but I have no desire to press up against a pair of cold, wet drawers—even if they're yours."

"What if I remove them?"

She arched a brow. "That's beginning to have some appeal."

He flashed the devilish grin that she always found irresistible. "Cuddling up next to a pair of wet ruffled pantaloons doesn't exactly hold too much appeal to me, either."

"I see," she said, trying not to smile. "Well, what if I removed my underclothing?"

He shrugged. "I suppose it would make it more tolerable."

"More tolerable!"

His grin widened. "More tolerable."

"For you or for me, Kincaid?"

Cynthia slipped one of the straps off her shoulder, and with a coquettish smile, she did the same to the other. Her breasts shimmied as she shook the straps down her arms and off her hands. The thin fabric, made transparent from wetness, continued to cling to the curve of her bosom. She lowered the garment to the dusky pink aureoles of her breasts. "Maybe I should keep this on."

"If I were you, I'd take it off," he insisted.

She arched a delicate brow. "You've usually done so, Kincaid. How about giving me a hand?"

"You're doing just fine on your own, Miz Sin," he said. Sitting down, he folded his arms across his chest.

"You're really enjoying this, aren't you?"

"Thanks to your teaching me how to find pleasure in simple things."

"You ought to know by now there's nothing simple about me, Kincaid," she purred sweetly. She slowly pulled the chemise over her head. "What next?"

"I'd say the hose. Yes, definitely the hose. Who likes to feel wet feet touching them?"

Cynthia smiled sweetly. "You're so right, darling. How could I not have thought of that?"

Walking over to him, she raised her leg. Through the sodden hose, she felt the heat of his warm palm as he grasped her leg and peeled the stocking off it. Then he raised her other leg and did the same. When she lowered it, he grasped each leg and ran his hands up them from ankle to knee. The provocative caress flooded her body with a tantalizing warmth.

Stepping back, Cynthia slid her hands to the band of her drawers. "Here comes the good part, Kincaid."

She slowly inched the pantaloons past her hips, swaying sinuously until the wet garment dropped to the ground and she stood naked before him.

Dave's last vestige of control plunged along with the pantaloons.

Bolting to his feet, he pulled her into his arms. "Lord, Cyn, how can you make even shedding wet underclothes seductive?" He kissed her passionately.

"Haven't you forgotten something?" she murmured, amused. "Only one of us is naked."

Moving swiftly, he shed his drawers, then drew her into his arms. Their naked bodies molded together in search of warmth as his mouth sought hers. When he lowered her to the ground, his probing tongue sent waves of warmth through her. He covered her like a blanket and she slipped her arms around his neck, drawing him nearer. Her shivers became those of arousal as their bodies were consumed by flames of passion.

In the warm afterglow of their lovemaking, they fell asleep, cuddled together.

Cynthia awoke later and gently nudged Dave awake. "Dave, the fire's going out."

She felt his manhood stir as he pulled her closer. "Then we'll just have to light it again, sweetheart," he murmured sleepily.

"I'm referring to the fire heating this cave," she giggled.

Her words jolted him awake, and he shot up. "Oh, damn! I forgot about that."

Dave quickly got to his feet and within minutes had a hot blaze going again. "We're getting low on wood."

"Luckily, it sounds like the storm's passed over," she said, pulling on her underclothes. They were still slightly damp, but tolerable. She left her skirt and blouse to continue drying.

Dave's jeans were still quite damp, so he settled for just his drawers. They both donned their stockings and boots, then laughed at their appearance.

Walking to the entrance of the cave, Dave peeked outside. "It's still raining, but you're right, the worst of the storm's passed over. I think we're better off sitting it out for a while longer."

Cynthia sat down. "The fire sure feels good. I hope our clothes finish drying before the fire dies out."

"Unless it stops raining, they'll only get wet again when we go out."

"Well then, I hope our clothes dry *and* it stops raining before we run out of wood."

Dave came over and sat down beside her. "You're really a good sport, Cyn. You take everything in stride."

"Thank you, sir."

"Now me, I'm just the opposite; I don't like adversity. Everything has to turn out the way I anticipated or charted. Must be the engineer in me."

"They say that opposites attract, Kincaid. What are you planning on doing when the railroad is completed?"

"I haven't thought about it. I'll just have to face that when the time comes. This project has dominated by life for over two years, so I haven't really thought about the future."

"You once said that when you had the time, you'd think about settling down and starting a family."

"Yeah, I'd like to do that. But that can't be for a while, either. I've still got a lot of railroad to finish right now."

She hugged her knees to her chin. "Don't you ever think of how nice it would be to have a child of your own?" she asked, unaware of the wistfulness that had crept into her voice.

"Do you, Cyn?"

"Sometimes." Then she shook her head and stretched out her legs. "Then I remember what a terrible mother I'd make."

"I've watched you with the kids. You'd make a great mother, Cyn."

She glanced at him in surprise and saw that he was staring at her intently. "You must be the only one who thinks so."

"You have a lot of love in you, Cyn."

"It takes more than just love to be a good parent, Dave. To give discipline, you have to be disciplined yourself. I don't think I fit that description."

"So what are the plans for your future?"

"Me? Remember, this is the gal who's already broken one engagement. I don't make any long-range plans anymore. I'd only end up disappointing myself." She brushed off her hands and stood up. "I'm getting hungry. And remember, I had the foresight to bring along a picnic lunch," she said smugly.

Walking over to her horse, she dug the food, wrapped in a red-and-white checkered tablecloth, out of her saddlebags.

"You are the most amazing woman I've ever met," Dave remarked when she began to lay out beef sandwiches, pieces of fruit, and hard-boiled eggs.

"This is the best I could do in the fifteen minutes I had to get ready."

They consumed the food ravenously, and in a short time not a bite remained. Sated, Dave swung his glance to the rear of the cave. "I think I'll take a look around."

"I'll come with you," she quickly replied.

Using a piece of wood as a torch, hand in hand they began to explore the darkened cave that remained in shadows. They had not gone more than a few yards into the dark bowel of the cave when they stopped and stared in shock.

Dave let out a long, low whistle. "Well, Miz Sin, what have we got here?"

Both stared in astonishment at the haphazard piles of railroad ties and rails.

Chapter 25

Pushing the locomotive to full throttle, Pat O'Hara sang out at the top of his voice, "Oh, me darlin', oh, me darlin', oh, me darlin' Clementine." Having waited out the storm and Dave's return as long as he could, he was trying to make up for lost time. "You are lost and gone—" He cut off the words of the song and peered forward. "What the dev'l!" he exclaimed. "Hold on, Dan'l," he shouted, slamming on the air brakes.

In a squealing, earsplitting clamor, the locomotive hit a missing stretch of track, the train's momentum causing it to continue to slide forward. Dragging the empty flatcars behind it, the huge locomotive reached the next rail. Miraculously, the wheels grabbed the rail and the engine managed to remain upright as it came to a halt.

Rocking violently, the attached flatcars teetered precariously without turning over. However, the last car, whipped from side to side, slammed into the stalled car in front of it, catapulting it almost perpendicular. The coupling snapped and the car toppled off the track, rolled over once, and came to a stop in a cloud of dust swirling above it like an erupting volcano.

Pat and Dan jumped down from the cab and ran back to the wreckage. With hands on hips, Pat stood shaking his head as he surveyed the damage.

"We best be gettin' back to Tent Town for help," he said.

"I'll go, Pat. You stay with Clementine," Dan volunteered.

Suddenly Pat stiffened. "Hush, lad. Did ya hear that?"

"Hear what?"

"I'm thinkin' I heard groaning," he said. "Me ears must be playin' tricks on me."

The men exchanged startled glances when a moan sounded again. Hurrying to the other side of the wreckage, they stopped and stared in alarm.

"Holy Mother of God!" Pat murmured, and crossed himself.

The bodies of a man and woman lay on the ground. Kneeling down, Pat turned over the woman. "Why, 'tis Miz Sally," he said, shocked. "She must have been on the train." At that moment, she groaned. "Dan'l, get the canteen and kit from the cab. And bring the blankets, too."

The fireman raced back to the locomotive and returned quickly with the items, among them a box containing a few basic medical supplies.

"The lass isn't bleeding, and there's no break in her arms or legs," Pat said.

"What about the man?" Dan asked.

"There's a bad gash on his forehead, and I'm thinkin' that his left arm and leg are broken. But he's breathin'. The doc's in Tent Town today; we need help, Dan'l."

"I'll get goin' now. We can't be more than ten miles from there. With any luck at all, I'll be back in less than an hour."

"Hurry, lad," Pat said.

Dan took off on a run.

While he waited, Pat covered Sally, then bandaged the unconscious man's bleeding head. He covered him securely but did not attempt to do anything with his broken arm and leg.

The minutes passed like hours to Paddy, and he sighed in relief when he heard the distant whistle of the approaching labor train.

Dan Harrington, accompanied by the camp doctor, Sean Rafferty, and a dozen men, jumped off the train when it stopped nearby.

"Get movin', lads," Sean shouted. "Some of you men get these rails and ties unloaded, while we uncouple 'em cars and move 'em off the track. Then we'll lay that missin' rail."

The men set to work at once, and Sean walked over to O'Hara. "How's the lass?" he asked worriedly.

"Doc said she's comin' around," Pat said. "Do you recognize the lad, Sean?"

Sean went over and stared at the face of the unconscious man. "No. I've not seen him before. What were they doin' on the train?"

Pat shrugged. "I didna know they were on it."

"All right, I've done what I can here," the doctor said. "Let's get these people on board and back to camp."

The railroad crew quickly replaced the missing track and attached the flatcars, and after loading up their tools, they climbed on board. O'Hara began to slowly back down the track to return to Tent Town.

Dave and Cynthia had forsaken their visit to Bonner, and by the time they got back to Tent Town, the doctor had set Clay's arm and leg and stitched the gash on his forehead. Sally had been fortunate enough to sustain only a minor concussion, but both of the young people were confined to beds in the infirmary, where the doctor could keep a watchful eye on them.

After hearing the details from O'Hara and Sean,

and relieved to see that his sister had not been seriously hurt, Dave sought a further explanation.

"Sally, what were you and Clay Bonner doing on that train?"

Clay spoke up at once. "Sir, don't blame Sally; it was my idea."

"I'm not interested in hearing what you have to say, Bonner," Dave declared, "considering your father is to blame for the accident."

"But Clay isn't, David," Sally said. "This proves it."

"It's true, sir," Clay said. "If I'd known about that missing rail, do you think I'd have risked Sally's or my own life?"

Cynthia put a restraining hand on Dave's arm. "That makes sense, Dave," she said softly.

"I suppose that's true," Dave said in a calmer tone, "but that doesn't change the fact that your father is behind it. And this time, he's gone too far—he committed a blatant act of destruction that could easily have killed my engineer and fireman."

"I don't believe my father would commit such an act, sir. I know he's opposed to the railroad cutting across our range, but he'd never harm anyone intentionally."

"You mean his own son," Dave fired back.

"No, sir, I mean *anyone.* He may be hotheaded and downright mulish at times, but he doesn't risk people's lives."

"Considering we found piles of our missing rails and ties on your ranch, Bonner, I don't view him quite the way you do." Dave turned back to Sally. "Just what were you doing on that train?"

Sally glanced apprehensively at Clay. "We were going to Denver to get married."

"You were what!"

"Dave," Cynthia warned.

"Sir, I'd appreciate it if you wouldn't shout at her," Clay said.

"Yes, Dave," the doctor interjected. "These two people are my patients, and if you are going to shout at them, I must insist that you leave."

Dave drew a deep breath. "All right. I'm sorry. It won't happen again."

Cynthia walked over and clasped Sally's hand. "Why were you running off to get married without telling us, dear?"

"Pretty obvious, ma'am," Clay said. "You can see Mr. Kincaid's reaction. My father's would have been just as bad. Sally and I love each other and we knew neither side would consent to our marrying, so we decided not to let this stupid quarrel between the railroad and my father interfere with our happiness." Clay looked at Dave. "I love your sister very much, sir. I know you think we're too young, but my mother was a year younger than Sally when she married my father, and he was only nineteen at the time."

Dave walked over to the entrance and stood staring out for a long moment. "And what if your father refuses to accept her?"

"Sir, my father isn't the ogre you think him to be."

"Even though he might have killed two of my men, as well as you and Sally?"

"If he's responsible, I'm sure he thought no one would be harmed. One thing I know for certain is that he loves me. If Sally's my wife, he'll accept her."

"And if Clay's my husband, I hope you'll accept him," Sally pleaded. "I love him, David."

"Yeah, honey, I'll accept him. I only want your happiness." He bent down and kissed her cheek, then straightening up, he said, "Bonner, it—"

"Please call me Clay, sir. I'll soon be your brother-in-law, because no matter what, as soon as Sally and I are able, we're going to get married."

"I won't try to stop you, Clay, but you've got to realize that your father has to stand accountable to the law and the railroad for what he's done."

"And just what might that be, railroad man?"

They all swung their attention to the entrance, filled by the sizable bulk of Will Bonner. Ignoring the others, the rancher walked over to Clay's bed. He blanched when he saw his son's arm and leg in casts, and the bandage wrapped around his head. Grasping Clay's hand between his own, Bonner asked, "How do you feel, son?"

"I'll be fine, Dad," Clay said. "The doctor here has fixed me up real good."

There was a glint of moisture in the big man's eyes when he turned to the doctor. "Is he gonna be okay?"

"I see no reason why he shouldn't be, once he heals."

Bonner nodded. "I'm beholdin' to you, Doc. Now tell me, what were you doin' on that train, Clay?"

"Dad, I want you to meet Sally Kincaid. We're going to get married."

"You're what!" Bonner roared.

"Mr. Bonner," the doctor quickly said, "we've already traveled that route. I must ask all of you to leave now."

"I ain't leavin' here 'til I get to the bottom of this," Bonner declared. "Why was my son on that train?"

"Mr. Bonner," Cynthia said in an effort to ward off a scene, "we'll go outside and I'll explain it all to you."

"Who the hell are you, lady?" he declared.

"I'm the woman who's going to try and get you out of the serious trouble you're in. Let's go, Mr. Bonner."

The rancher took a final look at Clay. "You rest,

son. I'll be back with a wagon to haul you home."

Outside, a half dozen Bonner riders were clustered together waiting. "How's Clay, boss?" one of them asked.

"He's got a busted arm and leg, but the doc said he'll mend."

As the cowboys murmured their relief, Bonner glared at Cynthia. "Who's this gal that's got her claws sunk in my son? Some of that railroad trash?"

"Mr. Bonner, you have a big mouth," Cynthia said. "Why don't you just calm down and listen? Sally and Clay were eloping. Unbeknownst to anyone, they sneaked onto the train."

"And due to your malicious actions, both of them might have been killed, as well as the locomotive engineer and fireman," Dave said angrily. "Furthermore, Bonner, *that gal* is my sister. You refer to her as trash again and that army of yours is going to have to pick you up from the dust."

"Don't threaten me, railroad man. I don't scare easy."

"Oh, for heaven's sake!" Cynthia exclaimed. "Will you two please stop rattling your swords at each other? You both sound like children. We have a serious problem here. Let's try to sit down and resolve it."

"Bonner's the one with the serious problem," Dave said. "That sheriff he's got in his pocket won't get him out of this. I'm calling in a U.S. marshal."

"Dave, please let me handle this for a moment," she said. "Mr. Bonner, I'm Cynthia MacKenzie, one of the owners of the Rocky Mountain Central. How about joining me in my car, where we can relax and discuss this further?"

"Cynthia, I hope you don't think I'm going to let this bastard get away with almost killing my sister and two of my men."

"I ain't responsible for that," Bonner said. "A

couple of my men did that on their own. When I heard about it, I sent them packin'. My riders were always told no one was to get hurt. I rode over here to warn you, but got held up by the storm."

"That alibi sounds very convenient, Bonner," Dave said.

The rancher glared at him. "You sayin' I'm lyin'? Nobody calls Will Bonner a liar."

"I'd say it's one of the kinder names they probably call you."

Exasperated, Cynthia declared, "Will both of you remember that you have to think of Sally and Clay, too? They're in love, and whether the two of you want to accept it or not, they're going to get married. If you don't sit down and try to clear up your misunderstandings, you'll drive them away and may never see them again. Is that what you want? Now, please—shall we go sit down . . . gentlemen?"

As soon as they entered her car, Bonner looked around contemptuously. "This looks like a fancy whorehouse."

Gritting her teeth, Cynthia managed to smile. "I wouldn't know; I've never frequented one, Mr. Bonner. Please sit down and I'll get us some wine."

Bonner plopped down in one of the chairs, and Dave took a seat on the opposite wall. When she returned, the two men were sitting there looking as if they weren't even aware of each other's presence.

"Now," Cynthia said, after handing each of them a glass, "the first thing you both need to accept is that Clay and Sally will marry, so it's a settled issue that no longer has to be discussed. I have one thing to say, which is that you're both very lucky men. If I were you, Dave, I couldn't imagine my sister marrying a finer young man than Clay; and as for you, Mr. Bonner, you couldn't hope for a sweeter or more loving wife for your son than Sally Kincaid. Congratulations, gentlemen, on your good fortune."

Both men appeared speechless, and Cynthia continued. "Let's get down to the real crux of the problem—that water hole. Dave, why don't you tell Mr. Bonner your idea on how to resolve the situation?"

"After what he pulled today, I don't think I want to resolve it."

"I'm sayin' this for the last time," Bonner declared. "I had nothin' to do with that wreck. My word is gold, railroad man."

Dave looked at him measuringly for a moment. "All right. What I had considered previously was this, Bonner. You don't want our track to interfere with your cattle getting to that water hole, right? What if we both requested to have the easement changed to run on the other side of the hole? We'll reroute the track; that way it won't cut between your grazing cattle and the water hole."

"You figure the government would do that?" Bonner asked.

"Why not? What difference should it make to them, as long as it's agreeable to both of us? The Rocky Mountain Central will pick up the cost of the extra rail—but I'm telling you, Bonner, guilty or not, you're paying for those cars damaged today."

"Seein' as how I almost lost my son, I reckon I should make amends for my earlier actions, too. It's been my men who's been tearin' up that track as fast as you can lay it."

"You aren't telling me anything I don't know, Bonner. I found the cave where you've been dumping the rails."

Bonner let out a hearty laugh. "Reckon you're holdin' all the cards, railroad man."

"Name's Kincaid, Bonner. Dave Kincaid."

"Well, Mr. Kincaid, seein' as how we're soon gonna be kin, let's make one thing clear: my son's a rancher. Don't go gettin' any ideas about teachin' him how to drive steel on that railroad yer buildin'."

Dave put out his hand. "We've got a deal, Bonner."

The two men shook hands, then Bonner said to Cynthia, "Now how about another glass of that wine, little lady? Figure some kind of a toast's in order here."

"You know, Mr. Bonner, I think you're right," she said.

The following day, Dave and Will Bonner made a trip to Denver. With Elizabeth and Charles Rayburn's help, the necessary papers for a change of easement were filed with a federal judge, who assured them there would be no problem getting them approved by Washington.

On the return trip to Tent Town, Dave and Bonner said little to each other. But for the first time since they'd met, a grudging respect had formed between them.

That evening, the good news about the end to the feud was cause for celebration among the railroaders and cowboys. The saloon tent was opened for the occasion, and since the following day was Saturday, the men's day off, the celebrating went on long into the night.

Sitting at a table in the corner of the packed saloon tent, Cynthia and Dave shared a table with Will Bonner. With the tension between the two factions over, camaraderie now flowed between them as freely as the whiskey.

Cynthia shook her head in amusement as she listened to what had to have been at least the fiftieth toast to the coming nuptials of Sally and Clay, even though the future bride and groom were not there to hear them. Clay was in the infirmary, a dozen pictures of get-well wishes from Miss Sally's class pinned to its walls. His prospective bride was sitting at his bedside, reading to him.

Inevitably, tension or not, a game of arm wrestling developed between a cowboy and a rail driver standing at the bar. A crowd of spectators instantly gathered to cheer them on.

The two men were equally matched: one muscle-hardened by years of pounding spikes, the other conditioned by years of roping and throwing steers.

The duel of strength went on for over five minutes, the men's powerful muscles and taut cords bulging under the strain of their effort. Finally, in a forceful burst of strength, the railroader succeeded in slamming his opponent's arm to the bar. Raising his arm in victory, the winner inadvertently hit a lantern with his elbow and it fell. Smashing against the bar, the lantern knocked over a bottle of whiskey. Instantly a line of flame followed the stream of whiskey flowing down the bar. People started to scramble in all directions, dropping and spilling their own drinks in their effort to escape. Fueled by the spilled drinks, the flames spread on the ground. Pandemonium prevailed as the crowd tried to get out of the crowded tent.

Dave put an arm around Cynthia's shoulders, and by the time he managed to get them outside one of the tent's sides was burning.

"Sean, get a bucket brigade formed," Dave shouted. "We've got to get that fire out before the whole camp goes up in flames." Will Bonner had also begun issuing orders, forming another line leading from the water and rain barrels.

A strong night breeze was whipping the flames. Fortunately, the wind was blowing them in the opposite direction from the tents, but directly in its path were the parked railroad cars, the school tent, and the infirmary.

"Don't go near that fire, honey," Dave warned, then rushed to move the cars.

The frightened cries of awakened children mingled with the shouts of the men and women in long lines passing buckets of water to each other.

Seeing Lydia among the spectators, Cynthia ran over to her. "This is too dangerous for the children. Let's clear everyone out of this tent area just in case the wind shifts."

Lydia nodded, and she and several of the women began to pass the word. Those not in a bucket line started moving away, toting whatever cherished items they could carry.

In the meantime, the scent of the smoke had reached the livestock. The terrorized whinnying and restless stomping of the horses and mules added to the din. Bonner's cowhands rushed over and began roping and moving the stock farther upwind.

Pat O'Hara and Dan Harrington had already fired up Clementine, and some of the men were scrambling to hook up Lydia's schoolroom and the huge dining and dormitory cars. Once they were attached, O'Hara started to pull out toward the turnaround. Only Dave's caboose, Cynthia's car, and a half dozen flatcars remained.

Sparks and small pieces of burning debris were flying through the air as Dave drove the work train back toward the remaining cars. By the time the flatcars were coupled, the old wood on Dave's caboose—which stood between the train and Cynthia's car—had ignited.

"Shove the caboose off the track or we'll lose the other car, too," Dave shouted to the men dodging the sparks.

Seeing the impending danger to her car, Cynthia dashed into it, trying to decide what she should attempt to save. She ran into the bedroom and looked around helplessly. Hurrying to the dresser, she pulled out the drawers and her glance fell on the acorn thimble case her father had left to her. Without hesitation, she grabbed it and the letter he had written her. Were the car to burn, these were the only items that were irreplaceable.

She felt a sudden jolt and realized they were coupling the car to the train. Rushing out on the deck, she managed to jump off just as the car started to move.

Dave cleared the turnaround, then jumped out of the cab. "Sean," he shouted to the foreman, "take over and ease the train up the track until you're sure it's out of the path of the fire."

The man nodded and took over the controls.

Running back to Cynthia, Dave grabbed her by the arm. "Didn't I tell you to stay out of danger?"

Before she could answer, they heard frantic cries for help. Cynthia was horrified to see that the flames had leaped to the infirmary, and the tent was on fire. The shouts were coming from Sally.

Cynthia chased after Dave, who had bolted to Sally's aid.

"Help us, Dave," Sally cried frantically. "Clay's in there."

Cynthia fought to restrain Sally as Dave ran into the burning tent. The air was thick with smoke, and the crackle of flames was terrifying. In the corner, the doctor was struggling to help Clay out of the bed. Between them, Dave and the doctor managed to carry Clay outside to a spot out of harm's way, then both men hurried off to offer their assistance where needed.

Breathless, Cynthia and Sally sank down on the ground beside Clay and watched as the fires were brought under control. The caboose was half burned, but the inside was salvageable. However, the saloon, the school tent, and the infirmary burned to the ground.

Dawn was cracking the horizon by the time the trains backed into camp again and the men returned wearily to their quarters. Bonner and his crew stretched out outside on blankets around Clay, who had been moved to a cot. Too dirty and exhausted to consider climbing into Cynthia's bed, Dave laid down on the lounge floor of her car. Cynthia curled up beside him, and they slept.

Chapter 26

In the bright light of day, the burned-out end of the camp looked desolate to Cynthia as she stepped onto the observation platform of her car.

Dave already had a crew moving the charred debris out of the tents. Bonner and his men were preparing to pull out, having loaded Clay into a wagon to take him back to the ranch house. Since the school tent had been destroyed, Sally was accompanying them.

Cynthia walked over to the cluster of girls sitting on the ground, staring woefully at the blackened area that had once been their schoolroom. Snoozer was stretched across Catherine Mary's lap, looking equally forlorn.

"Hey, what are all the sad faces about?" Cynthia asked cheerfully.

"We ain't got no school anymore, Miz Cynthia," Maggie said, on the verge of tears.

"All our books and crayons and stuff are all burned up," Katie McGuire lamented.

"Ladies, everything lost can be replaced. The important thing is that no one was injured or killed in the fire."

"That's what Uncle Dave told us," Maggie said sadly, sounding unconvinced.

"Besides," Cynthia added, "in a few more days

school would have been closed for Christmas vacation, remember? By the time that's over, we'll have everything back to normal. So you see, it's not as bad as you think. When I'm in Denver, I'll be certain to replace everything we lost."

"Badminton racquets, too, Miz Cynthia?" Peggy Callahan asked.

"Yes, dear, badminton racquets, too," Cynthia assured her. "Now, I don't want to see any more long faces. Enjoy your early vacation."

"How long will you be gone, Miz Cynthia?" Katie asked.

"Just for a couple of weeks. I'm going home to spend the holidays with my sisters."

"I bet Mr. Kincaid will sure miss you," Catherine Mary said. The other girls started to giggle.

"You think so?" Cynthia asked, grinning back at her.

"He sure will," the youngster said emphatically.

Cynthia winked at her. "I sure hope so, Miss Catherine Mary Dennehy. Now off with you, ladies. I've got work to do."

She smiled as she watched them skip away laughing, their desolation forgotten. Her smile dissolved when she glanced at the half-burned caboose. Sighing, she walked over to it.

Dave was sitting behind the desk going through papers. "How much did you lose?" she asked.

"Surprisingly enough, very little," he said. "The files are still intact, and none of the diagrams or prints are ruined."

"It sure stinks in here, though," she said.

"After a couple of days of airing the place out, it should be okay. Structurally, the car is still usable."

"You aren't planning on sleeping in here, are you?"

"No, there's some empty cots in the dormitory

car. I can bunk there but still use this as my office until I find a replacement."

"Dave, I can leave you my car and go back to Denver on the supply train."

"That's not necessary, Cyn. This will work fine." Glancing out the open door, he frowned and stood up. "Now who is that coming? He's not one of that Walden gang, is he?"

Cynthia turned to see a horseman ambling over to the car. "No, I've never seen him before."

The man's casual slouch was that of one long accustomed to being in a saddle. Rawboned, he appeared not to have an extra ounce of fat on his tall, lean body.

They stepped outside and he reined up. "Howdy, folks. I'm told I can find Dave Kincaid here."

"I'm Kincaid," Dave said.

As the man dismounted, Cynthia saw the badge gleaming on his vest. He shook Dave's hand. "Name's Jess Tankard; I'm the U.S. marshal in these parts." Nodding at Cynthia, he brought a finger to the brim of his hat. "Ma'am. Looks like you folks had a bit of trouble here."

"Yeah, a couple of our tents burned down last night, Marshal."

"I understand you're havin' some problems with a local rancher named Will Bonner."

"Bonner had nothing to do with it; the fire was an accident," Dave said. "Matter of fact, Marshal, the problem between Bonner and the railroad has been resolved."

"Sure glad to hear that, Mr. Kincaid. Hope there wasn't any bloodshed."

"No bloodshed. We solved it peaceably."

"Well then, reckon you don't need me. I'll leave you folks to buildin' your railroad."

"Actually, Marshal Tankard, we did have an unusual incident a few days ago," Dave said. "Five men, calling themselves the Billy Bob Walden gang, held up our supply train and later harassed the camp when all the men were gone."

"Not them again!" the marshal groaned. "I've had a dozen reports on that gang, but armed robbery of a train is about the worst thing they've done. How much did they get?"

Dave grinned. "Seventy cents."

Tankard chuckled and shook his head. "They sure are their own worst enemies. You say they harassed the camp?"

"Yes," Cynthia said. "All the men were gone and there were only women and children here."

The marshal frowned. "They didn't harm any of the ladies, did they?"

"Oh, goodness no! Matter of fact, it was the other way around. They were so inept it was more amusing than threatening. We ran them off ourselves using marbles, cooked spaghetti, and jelly."

"I ain't even gonna ask what you mean by that, ma'am. I'm just glad to hear they didn't hurt anyone. Reckon one of these days I'm gonna have to track 'em down and lock 'em up for their own good—before somebody puts a bullet into one of 'em. Heard tell, though, Billy Bob Walden had a bad hombre for a brother. Name was Charlie. He was a cold-blooded killer—even women and children."

"What happened to Charlie?" Dave asked.

"Him and his gang went to the well once too often. Took on three brothers down in Texas named MacKenzie. Charlie died, along with most of his gang. Fortunately for Billy Bob, he was sitting in a penitentiary at the time."

"Did you say MacKenzie?" Cynthia exclaimed. "That's my name, too. And I have three cousins who live in Texas: Luke, Flint, and Cleve."

Tankard thought for a moment. "Well, whatta you know! If I recall right, Miz MacKenzie, one of the brothers was an ex-sheriff named Luke. Sure is a small world, ain't it?"

"I'm beginning to find that out, Marshal Tankard," Cynthia said. "And this railroad we're building here is going to make it smaller."

"Well, since you've no call for my services, I'll be ridin' on."

"Can we offer you something to eat or drink before you go?" Dave asked.

Tankard climbed onto his horse. "No, thanks. I best head out; got a long ride ahead of me. And I'll keep my eyes open for that gang, folks, but they've probably moved on by now." He tipped his hat. "Pleasure meetin' you, and good luck buildin' that railroad. Maybe someday I'll have a chance to take a ride on it."

"There'll be a seat waiting for you, Marshal," Cynthia called out to him as the lawman waved good-bye.

It did not take long for Tent Town to fall back into a normal routine. By the end of the week, no one even spoke of the fire anymore.

Every moment of Dave's time had to be spent at end of track making certain the track was properly rerouted on the revised easement skirting the water hole. By the time he came back in the evening, he was tired and would sit long into the night working out the next day's specifications.

Now, facing the prospect of leaving for Denver on the following day, Cynthia was determined to spend as much time as she could with Dave on this last remaining day.

"Like it or not, David Kincaid, you are going to have lunch with me today," she declared aloud. Humming, she set to work preparing them a picnic lunch.

When Cynthia finished, she saddled one of the

horses and waited until she saw the cooks leave for end of track with the lunch for the crew. Then she followed at a suitable distance, to time her arrival for when the men would break for their lunch.

A loud blast from the train announced the noon hour just as she reached the site. The activity halted and the noise quieted to a low drone of voices as the crew lined up for their meal and midday break.

All, she observed, except Dave, who was bent over a clinometer telescope measuring the slope of the ground surface.

Cynthia rode up to him. "Hi!"

He glanced up in surprise. "Cyn! What are you doing here?"

"I thought we could have a picnic."

"A picnic! Cyn, this is a bad time. I've got to delineate these measurements to keep the graders moving."

"You have to eat, don't you?"

"I'll grab a bite on the run."

"Since I'm leaving tomorrow, I thought it would be nice to have lunch together. After all, I rode all the way out here, David Kincaid. The least you could do is indulge me this one time."

Dave shrugged in defeat. "Okay, Cyn. Just let me finish up this one graph."

Cynthia smiled broadly. "I'll set up the lunch."

Spying a grassy spot under a tree somewhat remote from the men lounging around, she rode over and dismounted. She couldn't have hoped for a nicer day for a picnic; despite the season, bright sunshine and a westerly breeze made the day summerlike. Humming, Cynthia set to unpacking the basket, and by the time David joined her she had the luncheon spread out on a tablecloth.

"Sit down and I'll pour the wine." She quickly filled two Waterford crystal wineglasses. "I propose a toast." Raising her glass in the air, Cynthia said,

"Here's to separations. I hope you'll be unbearably miserable in the two weeks we are apart, and you go to bed every night thinking about what you're missing." She clinked her glass against his.

Grinning, he asked, "Why, is that what you'll be doing, Miz Sin?" He cut off a small piece of cheese and reached out to hand it to her.

When Cynthia leaned over and took it with her teeth, many of the men emitted loud whistles and hoots. Dave glanced around uneasily. "Cyn, behave yourself. There's a hundred pairs of eyes watching every move we're making."

"Ignore them, Kincaid."

"How can I? That's my crew. What do you think they're thinking when they see us drinking wine and you eating out of my hand?"

"Probably how uncomfortable you look doing it," she replied.

"Well, I am uncomfortable."

"Because, as usual, you won't relax and enjoy yourself. I thought you had learned how, but I can see you're still worrying about impressions, Kincaid. Most men, if they were in your position right now, would be thinking of nothing other than enjoying the delicious food, the fine wine, and the company of the beautiful woman—even if I have to be the one to say it—sitting opposite."

"Under different circumstances I would be, Cyn. I'm just embarrassed with my whole crew watching. They're washing down the usual beef and beans with a cup of black coffee, watching me sitting here dining on cold salmon, liver paté, whatever the hell you call that black stuff—"

"Caviar," she said.

"—crackers, and sipping wine out of a crystal glass. So don't try and tell me what they're thinking, because I know damn well what that is."

"I didn't mean to embarrass you, Dave. I thought you'd enjoy the change."

"Ah, Cyn, I don't want to sound ungrateful, honey. I know you went to a lot of trouble and effort, riding all the way out here and all. This just isn't the time or place."

"But this is the only time and place offered us, Dave. In the past few days, we've barely seen each other. Now we'll be separated for another two weeks."

"I don't like it any more than you do, but it's just been unavoidable. Having to change the route has thrown a monkey wrench into everything just at the time you're leaving. We'll make up for it over the holidays."

Just then two blasts from the labor train ended the midday break. The men got up to resume their work.

"Cyn, I'm sorry, but I've got to get back."

"Yeah, duty calls," she said with a forced lightness. "Go build your railroad, Kincaid."

Desolately, she watched him walk away, then she packed up and rode back to Tent Town.

Cynthia looked up in surprise when Dave entered his office that evening. Glancing at the clock, she saw that it was only seven o'clock. "I didn't expect you back so early." The last several nights, he hadn't gotten back to camp until long after nightfall.

"Since you're leaving tomorrow, I thought I'd come back earlier tonight."

"I was hoping I could finish what I'm doing before you got back."

"What are you doing?"

"I've divided this mess you had on your desk into piles. This pile on the right needs your immediate attention, and these other two piles need filing. I can probably do the filing in the morning before I leave." As she spoke, she continued with the task she had begun. "Are you hungry?"

"Yeah, real hungry."

She glanced up at him. "Why don't you go over to my car and get something to eat while I finish up here? It shouldn't take me more than another half an hour."

"I can't wait another half hour," Dave said. He swept one of the piles off the desk.

"What are you doing?" she cried out, horrified. "I've just spent hours separating all that!" Racing around the desk, she tried to stop him, but he sent the remaining papers sailing to the floor, too. "What's gotten into you, Dave?"

"I said I was hungry."

"And I told you to go to my car and get something to eat."

"What I'm hungry for is right here, Miz Sin." Before she could guess his intent, he picked her up.

"Dave, what are you doing?" she said, shocked when he put her down on the desk. Leaning over her, he gently pushed her back until she lay flat. "Tell me, Miz Sin, did you ever make love on a desk?"

She laughed nervously. "No, and I imagine you haven't either. I wish I knew what's gotten into you."

"Wrong, Teacher. The question should be, what am I about to get into? Answer: you, my seductive Miz Sin."

Parting her legs, he slid his hand under her skirt, skimming her thighs and hips. His mere touch sent a delightful shiver of expectation racing up her spine. "Dave, this is insanity," she said, her breath quickening as he pulled off her underpants. "What if someone comes in?"

"You've got to learn how to relax, Miz Sin, and stop worrying about impressions."

"So, this is about today," she said in breathless gasps as his hand continue to explore the flesh under her skirt.

"What about today?" he asked, pulling off her shoes and hose. "You mean just because you wanted to picnic when I was trying to work? Well, guess what, honey—now I'm ready to picnic, and you're it."

Raising one of her legs, he bent his head and ran his tongue across the sensitive skin behind her knee, then traced a string of nibbles up the soft flesh of her inner thigh.

"Oh, dear God!" she moaned when he hooked her legs over his shoulders.

Raising his head, his eyes sought hers. For an infinitesimal moment they held, then he lowered his head and took her.

Her senses flooded with a spine-tingling sensation that sent shocks of sensual delight throughout her body. The feeling continued to build with heat and excitement, driving her to a delicate line of madness. Writhing in rapture, she groaned his name incessantly until, in an exquisite release, her body imploded in waves of divine tremors.

When her trembling ceased and she was able to draw an even breath, she felt his lips brushing her temple, then move to her lips. He kissed her deeply. To her pleasure, she felt the rise of passion again.

"Dave, I can't get enough of you," she whispered feverishly when he pulled away to shed his clothing. Returning, he released the buttons on her bodice and impatiently ripped her chemise down the front. The weight of his body pressed her more firmly against the hard wooden desk, but she was only aware of the arousing friction of his chest hair against the peaks of her breasts.

This time they made love in a slow exploration

with hands and lips, until, bound together, they reached that moment of shared bliss.

Afterward, when Dave hadn't stirred for several minutes, Cynthia asked, "You aren't planning on spending the night on this desk, are you, Kincaid? If you are, you can shift to the bottom and give me the upper bunk."

He lifted his head. "Is that how you show your gratitude? What do you have to say about making love on a desk?"

"I say, next time you're on the bottom, Kincaid. You're getting heavier and this desk is feeling harder by the minute."

He got to his feet and then pulled her up. "You're an ungrateful wench, Miz Sin. Don't try and tell me you didn't like it," he said, pulling his pants on.

"Well, it was a little risqué, which did give it a certain element of excitement, but I'd say the pleasure wasn't all mine—you weren't exactly a spectator, Kincaid." She finished dressing, then grinned at him. "Actually, I loved it. You're just as effective on a desk as you are behind one."

Slipping her arms around his neck, she smiled up seductively. "How about coming over to my car and I'll show you how effective I can be in a bed?"

He kissed her quickly; then, groping among the scattered papers on the floor, he grabbed their shoes and stockings. "You're on, Miz Sin."

Hand in hand, they raced to her car.

Chapter 27

When they awoke in the morning, they made love again. After Dave got up and left, Cynthia lay in bed thinking of how much she loved him. Now that the actual day of leaving Tent Town had arrived, she regretted her promise to Beth to come home two weeks before the holiday. Although Dave intended to join the family for the week between Christmas and New Year's, the two-week separation from him now seemed an overwhelming length of time. But Christmas was always her favorite holiday, and this would be the first one she and Dave would spend together. That expectation buoyed her spirits considerably and she climbed out of bed.

Cynthia had just finished dressing when Sally tapped on the door. "I'll be leaving soon, and I came to say good-bye and wish you a Merry Christmas," she said.

Flushed with excitement, Sally was leaving to spend the coming holidays at the Bonner ranch. Despite his condition, Clay had even weathered the ride in a buckboard to come and get her.

"The same to you, dear," Cynthia said as they hugged and kissed.

"Oh, Cynthia, I'm so excited. The doctor just told Clay his leg cast can come off in another month, so we've decided to get married at the end of January.

You'll be back in time for the wedding, won't you?"

"I wouldn't miss it. I'm returning right after the New Year."

"I'm so happy, Cynthia, and I'm so grateful to you. You've done so much for me. If it weren't for you, Clay and I would probably have never met."

"Nonsense, love. Don't you believe in Fate? The two of you were destined to meet somehow."

"Oh, I have to go. Mr. Bonner and Clay are waiting." She hugged Cynthia again. "Give Beth my Christmas greetings. I love you."

"Be sure and give Clay and his father mine," Cynthia called out as Sally dashed away.

As soon as she closed the door, Cynthia returned to her bedroom and began to pack. In six hours the train would be pulling out. Glancing out the window, she saw Sally saying good-bye to Sean and Lydia Rafferty. Cynthia watched as Sally climbed up onto the seat of the buckboard next to Clay. Smiling, he slipped his good arm around her. The young couple were so in love that she couldn't help but feel a pang of envy, looking at them.

It was strange, she reflected, how differently love could strike people. With Sean and Lydia, it had grown from an association of respect and admiration, whereas the younger couple had known that glorious burst of instant love when two people look into each other's eyes and recognize their lifelong soul mate.

She had never known either kind of love. Roberto saw in her a pretty bauble he could have fun with, and Dave saw her as a great sex partner. Love, respect, finding a soul mate—those considerations had never entered into either relationship. One didn't *love* a Cynthia MacKenzie—she was just a good-time gal who didn't need to be loved to have a good time with a man. And now, because she was deeply in love with Dave, she was feeling sorry for herself.

Tears started to trickle down her cheeks and, disgusted, she brushed them aside. "It's called 'paying the piper,' Miz Sin."

But she couldn't help taking another lingering look outside at the two couples whose love had been strong enough for them to make a lifelong commitment to each other.

She turned away to resume her packing. Slowly, she reached in and picked up the acorn-shaped thimble case.

What are you saying to me, Daddy? What message are you sending me?

Beside it lay the letter he had written. Did the answer to the puzzle lie there? For a moment she thought of opening the letter; then, recalling his instructions, she decided against doing so, knowing that the day would come when she'd have a greater need for his words of comfort and wisdom.

Glancing out the window, she clutched the thimble tightly in her hand when she saw that Dave had joined the group. He kissed Sally, then shook hands with Clay and Will Bonner. The buckboard rolled off, and after exchanging a few words with the Raffertys, Dave hopped up onto her car's platform, rapped, and opened the door.

"Cyn, you in here?" he called out.

Hastily, she put the thimble back in the drawer. "I'm in the bedroom, Dave."

He came striding into the room. "What are you up to?"

"Packing my clothes. No sense in leaving any of them in the car after I get back home."

"Sounds like you're losing a schoolteacher, Cyn. Clay and Sally are planning their wedding for the end of January. That's about when I figure we'll finish the track around that water hole and be moving out of Bonner's range."

"I know," Cynthia said. "Sally told me when we said good-bye earlier. I'm happy for them, aren't you?"

"Yeah. Clay seems like a nice enough fellow. They both just seem so young to me."

"They're in love, and they both are pretty level-headed. Sometimes age doesn't necessarily reflect wisdom—we're sure prime examples of that, Dave." Fearing that her feelings would show, Cynthia turned away.

"What do you mean?" he asked.

"Maybe what I should have said was, considering how we conduct our lives, we can hardly be critical of other people's honest emotions."

He walked over and turned her to face him. "Honest emotions? What are you trying to say, Cyn?"

"Oh, I don't know," she said, shaking her head helplessly. Having backed herself into a corner, she now felt a sense of desperation. "I guess I mean that if anyone is childish, it's us. A relationship based on sex alone has got to begin to run thin after a while."

"I see." He dropped his hands and walked over to the window. After a long pause, he said, "If I understand you correctly, you're telling me that you're getting bored with our relationship. You ready to call it off, Cyn?"

Feeling as if the breath was being squeezed out of her, she closed her eyes. "Is that what you want, Dave?"

"I'm not the one calling the shots, Cyn. I'm just along for the ride. I knew we'd reach this moment some time be—"

"Why?" she flared. "Why were you so certain? Do you believe *Miz Sin* isn't capable of loving, or is it that she's not worthy of being loved?"

"No, of course not. I meant our eyes were open when we started this affair. You made yourself clear from the beginning—you were out for a good time."

"And you were just as *clear*—I was a cheap little floozie not worthy of your love."

Dave looked astounded. "I never said that. We both knew what we were doing."

"Did we? Or were you just trying to get even because you loathed me, Dave?"

"If anyone tried to get even, I'd say it was you, Cyn. That's why you followed me here, wasn't it?"

"Maybe it was. And why do you suppose I stayed around?"

"Probably because we couldn't keep our hands off each other."

Appalled, she turned and looked at him. "For God's sake, Dave, are you that naive?"

"All right, I admit I was wrong about your feeling for the girls. I can see you genuinely care for them."

Near to screaming, she questioned, "And that's it? There's no other reason for my remaining?"

"What other reason could there be?"

Her control snapped and she shouted, "Because I'm in love with you, you blind fool!"

For a long moment he stared at her, their gazes locked. The air was so charged with tension that she felt it would suffocate her. Then he walked over and, grasping her by the shoulders, he said, "Did I hear you right?"

She tried to shrug loose, but his hold on her remained firm. "Don't you have a railroad to build or some other work to do?" she snapped, unable to look him in the eyes.

"I'll leave when you answer me. Did I hear you right? Did you say you love me?"

"What difference does it make?"

"Cyn, please. Look at me and answer my question. You didn't say you *loved* me; you said you *love* me."

"All right! I said it! So have your laugh, but do your gloating elsewhere."

"Love me as in present tense—not past tense—right, Teacher?"

"Yes! Yes! Yes!" she cried out. "I love you. How many times must I say it?"

"The rest of my life, Cyn," he whispered.

He pulled her into his arms, his mouth closing over hers, devouring its softness in a long, lingering kiss that left her trembling by the time he freed her mouth. His lips brushed her temple as he murmured, "Do you have any idea how I've wanted to hear those words from you? How I believed I never would? Oh, God, I love you, Cyn. I must have loved you from the first time I kissed you, but I fought it, refusing to admit it to myself because I figured I was letting myself in for a lot of heartache. I kept telling myself to keep emotions out of it—to just enjoy our relationship while it lasted, because then you'd leave me. But I couldn't help myself—I fell in love with you. I've forgotten every noble sentiment about love and marriage that I ever held. I've still got a railroad to finish, so I don't have the time to devote to a wife, much less a family; but Lord, Cyn, it would be comforting to know that when I come home at night you'd be there waiting for me—that somehow we'd salvage a few hours to be together. I know it's selfish, unfair of me. It's everything I condemned, everything I vowed never to be guilty of—but I want to marry you, Cyn. I want you to be my wife. To be near me always." Cupping her cheeks in his hands, he gazed into the sapphire depths of her eyes as she smiled up at him. "I don't think I could start a day without seeing that smile."

As the warm glow of his love washed through

her, Cynthia felt an unequivocal joy she'd never known before.

"Will you marry me, Cyn? I can't promise you Italian palazzi or even mansions in Denver, but do we need them to be happy? Please, Cyn, please say you'll marry me?" he pleaded. Then he reclaimed her lips.

When breathlessness parted them, she slipped her arms around his neck. "Yes! Yes! Dear God, yes, I'll marry you," she gasped.

She felt weightless as he lifted her in his arms and carried her over to the bed. Laying her down gently, he stood above her, his gaze of adoration locked with hers as he began to unbutton his shirt.

"Still want me to get to work, Miz Sin?"

Cynthia raised her arms, reaching impatiently for him. "Yes, with no delay. Your work's cut out for you, Kincaid—at least for the next six hours."

Later, as Cynthia lay in the curve of his arms, they spoke of their future.

"Let's get married right away, Cyn," Dave said. "Before you change your mind," he added with a warm chuckle.

"Not a chance. I'm not letting you get out of this, Kincaid. Why don't we marry when you come to Denver for Christmas?"

"Why not marry right now?"

"Because there isn't time, or anybody to marry us; plus the fact that my sisters would never forgive me."

He raised up and, leaning on his elbow, gazed down at her. "All right, Miz Sin, I can wait for two weeks."

Reaching out, he began to trace the curve of her jaw. "Besides, it will give you time to make certain that this is what you want. That it's not just the sex."

Cynthia wove the fingers of a hand through his dark hair. "I've known what I wanted for a long time, Dave. I fell in love with you before we even made love."

"I think I did the same with you. It had to have been that rainy night on the trestle."

Closing her eyes, she let a soft smile curve her lips. "There's so much I love about you, Mr. Kincaid: your fairness and logic when you're dealing with a problem; the way your smile carries to your eyes when you laugh; the sound of that laughter. I love your dedication to your job, to your responsibilities. And your integrity." She traced a finger across his brow. "I love that little frown when you're concentrating real hard on something; I love waking up and finding you next to me, feeling the warmth of you, watching you sleeping. And whether you love me or not, I know that I'm a better woman for having loved you."

"I thought we were going to keep this conversation in the present tense," he said, pressing a light kiss to her lips. "Tell me you love me, Cyn—not loved me. I can't hear it enough."

"I love you, David Kincaid. For all the reasons I've mentioned and a hundred others. And as for our lovemaking—that's the icing on the cake, because yes, I love that, too. Your nearness excites me, your touch, your lips on my lips, on my breasts, on my body. There are no words to describe how I feel when you enter me and our bodies are linked together. It's as if we become one being . . . one soul."

She looked up at him with the full measure of her love and adoration in her eyes. "And whether you marry me or not, I want to have your child, my darling."

"Cyn, I can't think of anything I want more."

Lowering his head, he covered her mouth in a deep kiss that reignited their passion. She closed her eyes in the throes of ecstasy as his mouth left hers to claim the taut peak of a breast.

And as their few remaining hours together slipped past, they loved one another, proclaiming that love by word and touch until it was time for her to leave.

With an occasional blast of the whistle, Pat O'Hara slowly inched the train along the track as the women and children shouted and waved good-bye to Cynthia.

Dave remained with her on the observation deck as long as possible, then kissed her good-bye and prepared to jump off.

"Two weeks, Miz Sin, then it'll be Mrs. Kincaid."

"You won't get cold feet, will you, Kincaid?"

"Nothing will keep me away, sweetheart." He kissed her once more hurriedly and then hopped off the deck.

O'Hara picked up speed, and Cynthia waved one last time. She stood on the deck watching, until she could no longer make out Dave's figure standing alone beside the track.

Chapter 28

Pete Gifford was waiting for Cynthia with the buckboard when the train pulled into MacKenzie Junction in Colorado. The distance between the two states made a big contrast in the temperature, as well. The cold wind sweeping down from Canada was a far cry from the warm Pacific breeze that had been warming New Mexico when she left. Cynthia gathered her coat around her to stay warm while Giff loaded her luggage on the wagon and O'Hara maneuvered the car into the roundhouse. Then he and Dan waved good-bye, and the train puffed away.

"Is Angie home yet?" she asked as they rode to the house.

"Due in tomorrow," Giff said.

"How does she like school?"

"Can't say. Beth said she doesn't write too often."

Surprised, Cynthia looked at him. "That doesn't sound like Angie. Doesn't she write to you?"

"She wrote me one letter to ask how her horse was doing."

"Did you answer it?"

"Of course," he said. "Didn't hear from her again. Out of sight, out of mind, I reckon."

"Giff, Angie will never guess how you feel about her unless you tell her."

"I told you it's best she doesn't know."

"Men can be so stupid when it comes to women," Cynthia declared. If she hadn't given Giff her word to respect his confidence, she'd tell Angie herself.

"Sounds like you and Kincaid must not be getting along," he said jokingly.

"We're getting along just fine, Giff." She would have liked to tell him of her wedding plans, but she was determined to keep them a surprise until Dave arrived.

They rode in a companionable silence the rest of the way.

Beth was waiting at the door. "Oh, it's so good to have you home," she gushed enthusiastically. "This place has been like a mausoleum with everyone gone."

They no sooner hugged and kissed than Middy rushed in with open arms. "I missed you, darlin'," she sniffled after Cynthia kissed her. Wiping her eyes on her apron, she sighed. "I best get back to the kitchen if we're to have dinner tonight."

"We've lost another cook," Cynthia said.

"Aye, and it's just as well," Middy sniffed. "Marching around here with her highfalutin ways—I've forgotten more about cookin' than she ever knew." Mumbling under her breath about the difficulty of getting good help, she returned to the kitchen.

"Well, how are things going at Tent Town?" Beth asked once Cynthia had shed her coat and they'd moved to the parlor.

"Just fine now that the Bonner situation is resolved. And believe it or not, Sally Kincaid is going to marry Bonner's son, Clay, at the end of January. They managed to fall in love despite the feud."

"Sounds like Romeo and Juliet will live happily ever after," Beth said jokingly. "Speaking of feuds, how are you and Dave doing?"

"Oh, he said that he was coming here for Christmas."

"Yes, he has been for the last couple of years. But that's not what I asked, dear sister. I want to know what's happening between you two."

"Well, maybe you should wait and ask Dave that question."

"You're being very evasive, Thia MacKenzie. What aren't you telling me?"

"I've got nothing to say."

"Since you're going to be so closemouthed about it, I guess I'll just have to wait for now. But don't think I won't ask Dave when he gets here."

"What about you, Beth? Did you take my advice and find yourself a tall, dark, and handsome fellow to keep you company?"

"Thia, I don't have time for romance. Maybe I can think about settling down and starting a family once the railroad is completed."

"Is this some kind of disease that strikes you dedicated railroad moguls? I remember hearing similar talk from Dave. I wish I understood the reason behind such dedication."

"You still don't believe in this project, do you?"

"I believe in it only to the extent of fulfilling Daddy's dream, Beth." She grasped her sister's hand. "But that was *his* dream, honey; you're entitled to your own life and dream. You can't spend the rest of your life living out his."

Beth looked at her earnestly. "You don't understand, Thia. I love what I'm doing; the railroad is my life, my dream."

"Well, you can snuggle up to a cold, steel four-four-zero locomotive if you wish, but I personally prefer about six feet three inches of warm-blooded flesh and muscle." Smiling, she hugged her sister. "How's the capital holding out?"

"Charles and I managed to squeeze a small grant

out of the government. Barring any unforeseen setbacks, we should have enough to reach Texas. Once we do that, we're home free; we'll be able to raise money easily."

Beth's eyes glowed with excitement when she spoke, and Cynthia realized that everything her sister had said was true: Beth's life was the railroad. All her interests and energies were devoted to it.

"I know Daddy would be very proud of you, Beth," Cynthia said. "You're the son he always wanted," she added with light laughter.

"Oh, Thia!" Beth gave Cynthia a playful shove.

The following day, as they waited for Angie to arrive, Cynthia and Elizabeth were as excited as young schoolgirls at their first cotillion. Peering out the window, Cynthia exclaimed finally, "They're here!"

Racing to the door, Beth flung it open and Angie burst through it like a ray of sunshine. For the next few minutes the girls hugged and kissed, all chattering at once.

"Where's my baby? Where's my baby?" Middy cried, rushing into the foyer. Angie ran into the housekeeper's arms, setting off another series of hugs and kisses, just as Giff came in with her luggage. He put it down and stood back, a wide grin on his face. It was the first time Cynthia had seen him smile since Angie left in the fall.

It wasn't long before they went upstairs and ended up on the bed in Angie's room, chatting and giggling as if they hadn't seen each other for years.

For a brief moment Cynthia allowed her mind to drift from the conversation. How often through the years had they sat in the same manner in the middle of Angie's bed, their legs crossed under them and their heads together? Despite the many rooms and cozy nooks in the house, this was the spot where they always gathered to share their secrets and laughter or shed their tears.

How little really changes in life, she thought. *People may come and go, but there are patterns in one's life that never change.*

Beth's voice invaded Cynthia's musings. "Well, if you aren't that fond of school, Angie, what would you like to do?"

"I think I'd like to come home and attend the music conservatory right in Denver."

"You sure it's not just homesickness, honey?" Beth asked. "We all went through it, and it does pass."

"I think it's the nude male models that are scaring you away," Cynthia teased.

"I haven't seen one nude male model, Thia MacKenzie," Angie declared.

"No wonder you want to leave the place," Cynthia said.

"Well, I haven't made up my mind yet." Angie suddenly jumped to her feet. "Oh, my! I've been home over half an hour and I haven't gone to see Calico." She began to pull off her clothes. "I've got to change."

"If you're planning on going riding, dress warm," Beth warned. "It's cold outside."

"Yes, Mother," Angie replied. "You know, I did manage to make my own decisions at school."

"Will you look at that, Beth? Our little Angie has grown up," Cynthia said, part in jest and part in seriousness. There did appear to be a greater maturity to Angie than before she went away.

Beth scoffed. "Nonsense, a couple of months can't make that much difference."

"Oh, you'd be surprised," Cynthia replied, reflecting on how the last couple of months had changed her.

In an attempt to play Cupid, Cynthia called out

as Angie dashed off, "Have Giff ride with you."

"I don't need any watchdog either," Angie yelled back.

Their gaiety carried over into the next week, and despite how much Cynthia missed Dave, she managed to keep herself busy shopping, wrapping gifts, and attending the round of holiday parties. Traditionally, the MacKenzie New Year's Eve Ball was the highlight of the season, and the girls had decided to carry on the tradition that had meant so much to their father. Secretly, Cynthia thought it would also be a great occasion to celebrate her wedding and introduce her husband to her friends.

At all the holiday parties, the MacKenzie sisters always generated the most interest among the bachelors. Cynthia found most of them quite dull in comparison to the devastating man in New Mexico with whom she was madly in love.

"This is the last of these boring affairs I'm attending," Cynthia grumbled to Beth and Angie as they entered the ballroom of the governor's mansion.

"Thia, why are you limping?" Beth asked.

"Because I'm wearing a pair of Angie's shoes."

"But her foot is a full size smaller than yours."

"I know; I'm telling everyone I hurt my ankle. I don't want to dance tonight, especially with Willard Hepplewhyte. He monopolizes my time and he has sweaty palms." She stared in repulsion at a stodgy young man headed in her direction. "Oh, Good Lord! Here he comes now."

Cynthia limped over to a chair and sat down, pursued by the determined young man.

"My dear Cynthia, you are limping. Have you injured yourself?"

"Yes, I have." Besides being overweight, he also had the palest complexion she had ever seen on a man. *He must run from one shady spot to another to stay that pale.*

"Does this mean I cannot claim a dance?"

"That's what it means, Willard," she said.

"I'm devastated."

"Exactly how I feel. But you mustn't allow it to spoil your evening, Willard. I'm sure you'll have no problem finding a partner among the many lovely young ladies."

"You won't be offended if I leave you?" he asked.

"Not at all. Go, Willard! By all means, go!"

Cynthia sighed with relief when he left her. After a short time, she got up and started to go over to the punch bowl. Remembering she was supposed to have a sprained ankle, she increased her limp.

Beth strolled over to her. Raising her fan to conceal her mouth, Beth said sotto voce, "That is the most overdone limp I have ever seen. Methinks you should be in a cast with such a painful injury."

"Now why didn't I think of that?" Cynthia said. "However, this *did* get rid of Willard Hepplewhyte, did it not?"

"Yes, and he immediately snatched Angie for a dance and filled in two more spaces on her dance card. She told me to warn you that she intends to kick you in the ankle so that you'll have much more cause to limp than just a pair of tight shoes."

"Tell her I'll make it up to her somehow." Seeing the approach of another young man, Cynthia put a hand on Beth's arm. "Do help me back to my chair, dear sister. It is so difficult for me to walk."

Another dance began just as Cynthia sat down, and Beth was claimed instantly for the waltz. As Cynthia watched the dancers, Angie waltzed past in the arms of Willard Hepplewhyte and threw her a scathing look.

Cynthia slipped off her shoes and began to massage her cramped feet.

"I'm told I give a fantastic foot rub."

Cynthia glanced up to discover Michael Carrington grinning down at her. Dressed in formal wear, he looked incredibly handsome.

"Caught in the act," she said.

He sat down in the chair beside her. "You don't really have a sprained ankle, do you?"

"Can you keep a secret, Mr. Carrington?"

"Keeping secrets and foot rubs are my specialties."

"You're right, I didn't sprain my ankle. I didn't feel like dancing tonight, so I wore a pair of Angie's shoes." She leaned over and whispered, "They're a size too small for me."

Carrington threw back his head in laughter. "I admire your ingenuity, Miss MacKenzie."

"Please call me Cynthia."

"If you'll call me Michael."

"So, what brings you to Denver, Michael?"

"I came here on business and decided to stay through the holidays."

"The holidays! My goodness, I would think you'd want to spend the holidays with your family."

"Actually, there's no one I need to hurry back to."

"No wife? No sweetheart?"

"No wife . . . and no sweetheart of importance, Cynthia."

"That's hard to believe. Handsome, rich as Croesus—what's your flaw, Michael Carrington?"

"Secret?"

"On my honor."

"Unrequited love."

"Sad," she said, shaking her head. "But forgive me if I find that hard to believe. As long as you're remaining in Denver, you must attend our New Year's Eve party, Michael."

"I'd be glad to if you're sure your sister won't object."

"Of course she won't."

Another dance had begun, and Cynthia saw that

Willard Hepplewhyte still had not relinquished Angie as a partner.

"Speaking of sisters, Michael, would you be interested in doing me a big favor? I want you to cut in on Angie's dance partner."

"I'll be glad to. Now will you do me a favor in return? Can you convince your sister Elizabeth to dance with me? She's turned me down three times already."

"I'm sure I can get her to agree."

With a determined stride, he headed for the dance floor.

Obviously the man is attracted to Beth, Cynthia thought. *She's a fool if she doesn't give him a chance.* Between Giff's feeling for Angie and Michael Carrington's obvious interest in Beth, her sisters sure were blind not to see what was right before their eyes.

Watching the dancers, Cynthia was pleased to see Angie waltzing in the arms of Michael Carrington. He circled his finger and thumb in an okay sign as they passed her. Cynthia couldn't help smiling, and began tapping her shoeless foot to the music.

Pete Gifford came over and sat down beside her. "How come you aren't dancing?"

Cynthia pointed to her bare foot. "Can't."

"What did you do to your foot?"

"Shoes are too tight."

Giff shook his head. "I swear I don't understand you women. Why'd you ever want to buy a pair of shoes too small for your feet? That's downright vain, Thia. Didn't think you were that way."

"I didn't buy them; Angie did."

"Well, that's still no cause for you to wear them."

"It's a long story, Pete Gifford, and quit lecturing me. You're beginning to sound like Daddy." She said it with a grin, more compliment than censure.

"And why aren't you dancing, handsome and eligible bachelor that you are?"

"I'm not much of a dancer. Too used to being on horseback."

"Do you remember the time we tried to teach you how to dance?"

Giff chuckled. "Yeah, I was taking Melissa Danforth to a ball the next night."

"It took us all night to teach you that you had a right foot and a left foot—not just two left feet. Beth and I were near to collapse, and Angie's fingers were actually swollen from playing the piano."

"Well, can't say I'm much better than I was then."

"You and Dave. He's just as clumsy. I tried teaching him to dance, and we ended up in a heap on the floor."

"Reckon some fellas have a knack for it," Giff said, his gaze following Angie and Michael Carrington as they waltzed by. "That Carrington sure looks as smooth as ice. 'Pears like Angie's enjoying it, too."

At that moment Beth came hurrying over to them, looking distressed. "Quick, Giff, dance with me. That Willard Hepplewhyte is pursuing me."

"You must keep the next waltz open for Michael Carrington," Cynthia said. "He did me a big favor and I promised you'd dance with him."

Beth was stunned. "How could you do that, Thia, without asking me first?"

"I was desperate, Beth," she said in a tragic voice. "Please, you'll do it, won't you? You wouldn't embarrass me after I've given him my word, would you?"

"Don't use those theatrics on me, Thia MacKenzie." Seeing Willard Hepplewhyte bearing down on her, Beth grabbed Giff's hand and yanked him to his feet. "Very well. I'll do it for you this time, Thia, but don't expect me to do it ever again," she warned, towing Giff to the dance floor.

Often in the next couple of days, as they baked cookies and decorated the house together, Cynthia was tempted to tell her sisters about her wedding plans, but she held on to her idea of surprising them. Excitement mounted with every day, and the house smelled of gingerbread baking in the oven or a spicy plum pudding bubbling on the stove.

Two days before Christmas, Angie and Giff went out and chopped down a Christmas tree. That night they sang carols as they strung popcorn and hung peppermint sticks on the tree's boughs. Pausing time and time again, one or the other of them stopped to reminisce over a favorite ornament.

"Oh, this was Daddy's favorite," Beth said, hanging a miniature bell on one of the limbs. She tapped it with a finger and the bell tinkled lightly.

"He loved Christmas so much," Angie said, her eyes misting. "It just won't be the same without him."

"Listen, girls," Cynthia said firmly. "We've held up so well, let's not break down now. You both know he'd never want to miss Christmas, so he's here in spirit, isn't he? And as long as we hold that spirit in our hearts, he'll always be able to celebrate it with us."

When Giff climbed up on a stool to place the star on the top of the tree, they stepped back to admire the result of their efforts.

"I think it's the loveliest tree we've ever had," Angie said.

"You say that every year, Angie," Giff teased.

"This year it's definitely true," she said. Glancing out a window she squealed with delight. "Look, it's started to snow."

Huge snowflakes were floating gently through

the air, covering the ground and sparkling in the moonlight like tiny crystals.

"Oh, Giff, let's all go for a sleigh ride," Angie said.

"Don't you think we should wait until there's a little more snow on the ground?" he asked, amused.

"I can hardly wait," Angie enthused. "Now we'll truly have a lovely Christmas."

The day before Christmas they woke to discover that the snowfall was no longer gentle but had turned into a winter storm. At least a foot of snow was on the ground, and a strong wind was whipping it into drifts as high as the windows.

Waiting for Dave to arrive, Cynthia was torn between anxiety and hope. Her common sense told her that Dave wouldn't arrive that day as planned, but she held out hope that the storm would stop and he could make it in on Christmas Day.

That hope died when Christmas dawned with another new snowfall. Any possibility of his arriving plummeted as the snow continued to fall.

She tried to be cheerful as they gathered around the tree and opened their gifts, but her disappointment over Dave's absence was devastating to her spirits. With false gaiety, she made it through the day, and spent a restless night remembering that they would have been celebrating her engagement tonight.

"At least it's stopped snowing and the sun is shining," Angie said the next morning at breakfast. "Maybe now we won't have to be prisoners in our own home."

"I wonder if they had this much snow in Denver," Beth said. "I wish I could get there and send a wire to Tent Town. Since Dave didn't show up for Christmas, obviously the freight train isn't running."

Finally, three days after Christmas, the snow had melted enough to be able to move around outside.

They had just sat down to dinner when Middy showed Charles Rayburn into the dining room.

"Charles, what a pleasant surprise," Beth said. "Sit down and join us for dinner. You're the first guest we've had in a week."

"I'm afraid I've come with bad news, Elizabeth."

With a sense of foreboding, Cynthia felt a tightening in her chest. Sensing what he was about to say, she sat motionless, waiting for him to speak.

"We've lost Clementine, Elizabeth. The train left Tent Town the day before Christmas and never arrived in Denver. It must have hit one of those bad canyons during the blizzard and gone over the side."

"Oh, dear God, no!" Beth gasped. "Maybe they turned back when they hit the storm," she said hopefully.

"No, we finally got a wire through to Tent Town. The train left on schedule. We pulled in another train from our other line, put a plow on the front, and started searching for the wreckage, but the storm covered over fifty miles and the blizzard caused massive drifts. Without knowing where they might have gone over, we might have to wait until the snow thaws in the spring."

Cynthia sat staring blankly.

"Who was on the train, Charles?" Beth asked.

"The engineer O'Hara, Harrington the fireman, and—"

"Dave Kincaid," Cynthia mumbled numbly, still staring blindly ahead.

Chapter 29

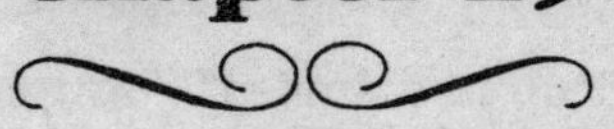

Cynthia moved in a daze, willing herself not to cry. She heard the talk around her but didn't participate in it—their constant speculation whether Dave was alive or dead was inconceivable to her. How could they even consider he might not be alive? For all they knew, the train had stalled in the blizzard and the men had sat out the storm with plenty of coal in the tender car to keep the engine operating as a source of heat.

Of course, that was it. It was all so clear, so simple. Dave was too intelligent to get himself killed. Why couldn't they see that for themselves? Tomorrow ole Clementine would come puffing up to MacKenzie Junction, O'Hara tooting the whistle, Dan Harrington grinning and waving, and Dave—Dave would jump off the train and take her in his arms.

The next day, Cynthia waited all morning for news, then finally in the afternoon she saddled up a mount and rode to the junction.

Pete Gifford found her there a few hours later, huddled on the floor of the private car. "Thia, what are you doing here?"

"Waiting for the train."

"Thia, it's freezing in here. Come on, let's get back to the house."

"I'm waiting for the train."

"It soon will be dark, Thia. There's no train coming in anymore today."

"I'm sure it'll come soon. The snow's probably delayed it."

"Probably."

She looked up and smiled. "You believe it, too, don't you, Giff? Beth and Angie don't, though. They think he's . . ." She got up and walked around the car. "This was the last place we made love. Where he asked me to marry him."

"Thia, have a good cry. Let it out, honey."

"Don't you know there isn't such a thing as a *good* cry, Giff?"

He came over and took her in his arms. "Just let it out, honey. We'll keep this all between you and me if you want, but let it out."

Cynthia finally began to cry, and within seconds was sobbing uncontrollably. Giff continued to hold her until her tears subsided, then he pulled a bandanna out of his pocket and made her blow her nose.

"Ready to go home?"

"I'm ready to go home," she replied.

New Year's Eve arrived, and with it the evening of the annual MacKenzie ball. Beth tapped on Cynthia's door, then opened it. "What's keeping you, Thia?" She drew up in surprise. "Why, you haven't even started to dress!"

"I'm not coming to the party."

"Aren't you feeling well, Thia?" Beth asked, concerned.

"I told you at the governor's ball that I was not attending any more of these boring affairs."

"But this is *our* ball, Thia."

"And it's the same people attending, making the same aimless talk. Besides, what difference does it make if I'm there or not? I missed it the last couple of years, didn't I?"

"Even more reason why you should be there with Angie and me. I don't understand, Thia. After we heard about the accident, we discussed it and agreed not to cancel the ball; yet now you're saying you have no intention of attending it."

"I never had any intention of attending it."

"Why? We're all grieving, honey," Beth pursued, "but we agreed to keep a stiff upper lip and carry on."

Pushed to her limit, Cynthia cried out, "I agreed because I believed Dave would be here . . . that we'd be celebrating our wedding by now."

Stunned, Beth stared at her. "Your wedding? Were you and David married, Thia?"

"No. We had planned to wed as soon as he arrived."

"Oh, dear God." Beth came over and put her arm around her sister. "Why didn't you tell us, Thia? Why did you keep all this extra heartache to yourself?"

"I wanted to surprise you with the wedding, and when we heard the news about the wreck, it seemed too melodramatic to blurt out that we planned to wed, with all of you believing Dave is dead. But I don't, Beth. I'd know if he were dead. I'd feel it—and what I know and feel for certain is that if anyone has the intelligence and strength to find a way to survive, Dave is that person."

"Oh, honey, I hope you're right. Now I understand why you don't wish to attend the ball. I'm sorry I made such an issue of it."

"Maybe I am wrong about that, Beth. Maybe by sitting up here in my room brooding tonight, I'm conceding Dave's dead, whether I admit it to myself or not. Maybe I should attend the party."

Clasping Cynthia's hands, Beth asked, "Are you

sure that is what you want to do? Under the circumstances, Thia, anyone would understand why you don't want to attend."

"Yes. The more I think about it, the more I'm convinced I should attend the ball." Trying to smile, Cynthia took her handkerchief and wiped away the tears streaking Beth's cheeks. "But regardless," Cynthia joked with a game smile, "I am not dancing with Willard Hepplewhyte."

"Would you like me to help you dress?"

Cynthia shook her head. "Get back to our guests, Beth. I promise I'll be along shortly."

As soon as Beth left, Cynthia listlessly went through the motions of dressing. By the time she finished, she regretted her hasty decision to attend the ball.

Even though she believed Dave was alive, how could she keep up a front of gaiety when there was the possibility he could be injured and need help?

Staring at her image in the mirror, she saw the toll the past days had taken on her—she looked pale and drawn. But what a greater price must have been paid by Dave.

Leaning forward, she took a closer look at herself. "You look even paler than Willard Hepplewhyte." She added a touch of color to her cheeks, then, unable to postpone the inevitable, Cynthia went to a drawer and pulled out a fresh handkerchief. The acorn case and letter caught her eye. Impulsively, she picked up the letter and tucked it into her bosom.

Beth met her at the foot of the stairway. "You look lovely, dear."

"I look terrible, Beth, but thank you for trying to be kind."

"We've got a full house, Thia. I guess after the storm, people couldn't wait to get out again."

"The very thing I was hoping to avoid, Beth. I

don't want to make small talk about the accident."

"Thia, I haven't made an announcement. Charles and Giff are the only ones who know about it, and I don't think either of them will mention it."

"Good, that will help to make the evening bearable."

Beth suddenly stared in distress at a new arrival who was now approaching. "What is Michael Carrington doing here? There's no doubt he's heard about the accident." She exploded in an angry outburst before he could even greet them. "Well, it doesn't take long for the vultures to start circling. Did you come here to gloat, Mr. Carrington?"

"Beth, I invited Michael to our ball on the night of the governor's ball," Cynthia said.

"Despite what you think to the contrary, Elizabeth, I do wish to express my sympathy. I liked David Kincaid. I know you've suffered a great personal loss, but the railroad industry is a loser, too. Kincaid had a brilliant future."

"That hasn't changed, Michael," Cynthia quickly interjected in a solemn voice. "He's only been missing a week. Why does everyone assume Dave is dead?"

Carrington looked at her with sympathy. "That's very true, Cynthia." There was little conviction in his voice.

"Well, Mr. Carrington, you may get your wish after all," Beth continued belligerently. "Or have you lost interest in buying the Rocky Mountain Central? There's no way we can finish the line without Dave Kincaid—he was the head and heart of the project. In addition to which, we've also lost Pat O'Hara and Dan Harrington, the train engineer and fireman. They were my best team. And besides the devastating loss of those three men, financially we can't afford to replace the engine and Lord knows how many freight cars. So you've got us right where you want us. Happy New Year, Mr. Carrington." Beth walked out of the room.

"I'm sorry, Cynthia," Carrington said. "Under the circumstances, it might be better if I leave."

"Nonsense, Michael. I don't understand Beth's animosity toward you, but we made a decision not to cancel this ball, so please join the others and enjoy yourself. I only ask that you don't mention the accident to the other guests. There's no sense in spoiling their pleasure for the evening."

"You were in love with Kincaid, weren't you?"

Startled by the direct question, she said, "Why do you ask?"

"I'd thought perhaps Elizabeth was in love with him, but I've since changed my mind. She's grieving his loss, but her anger is with me alone. It's not the same kind of anger often sparked by the loss of a loved one. But I sense, Cynthia, that you are grieving the loss of a loved one."

"You're very perceptive, Michael, but you're wrong about one thing—I don't believe Dave is dead."

"Or won't believe it, Cynthia," he said gently. "So, how are the feet holding up tonight?" he asked in a lighter vein.

She could tell he was hoping to cheer her up, and she smiled at him. He was really a nice person; why couldn't Beth see that?

"I'm wearing my own shoes tonight, but I'm afraid I still don't feel like dancing."

"Well, if you have a change of heart, Cynthia, I claim the first waltz."

After suffering the ball for three hours, unable to bear the celebrating any longer, Cynthia slipped into the study and closed the door. Tears streaked her cheeks as she walked over to look at her father's portrait, hanging above the fireplace.

"He's alive, Daddy. I won't stop believing that. But what if he's out there alone, hurt and cold? What if he needs my help, Daddy? I feel so helpless, so useless . . . so lost."

Withdrawing the letter from her bodice, she glanced up at the picture again. "I think it's time to open your letter, Daddy, because I need you now, to tell me I'm right in believing Dave's alive. Nobody else believes me; I can see it in their eyes."

Cynthia opened the letter and with a heavy heart began to read her father's message to her.

My Dearest Thia,

When I sat down to write you this letter, I asked myself what circumstances will cause you to open it. I narrowed it down to two possibilities: the day you find love, or the day that love is lost to you. I pray it will never be the latter. Perhaps by now you may have guessed the message the thimble carries—this tiny symbol of domesticity. That, my dear Thia, is the contentment you seek—to settle down and be loved and give your love. You believe that you are driven by boredom, my dear, when in truth, love and peace of mind are what you have sought so desperately and often with such recklessness. The end of that quest will bring an end to your restlessness. Trust me, my dear, love will prevail, and the day will come when you will find the man deserving of the love you have to give. I pray that this is that day.

Cynthia sighed. "You were right, Daddy," she told the portrait. "I did find that man. I found contentment and peace with him. I could never know another day of boredom with Dave at my side. But even though you speak of finding happiness, you say nothing of how lasting it will be. Did I find that contentment, only to have it quickly snatched from me? Yet you said love will prevail. I trust you, Daddy. That is the belief I must hang on to, must never doubt—the strength I must draw from. *Love will prevail.* And Dave will come back to me."

She stared blankly at the clock on the mantel as it began to chime. Midnight had arrived, and with it the start of a new year. The din of shouts and horns sounded from the other room, and when the orchestra struck up the strains of "Auld Lang Syne" the words of the sentimental ballad drifted to her ears—a symbolic reminder of the past, as the hope and promise of a new year filled the heart.

Cynthia closed her eyes to force back her tears. The new year could hold no hope and promise to her until Dave was found.

"I thought it was customary to kiss at midnight on the eve of a new year," a voice said softly behind her.

Unable to believe her ears, she spun around. Dave stood there smiling at her—his warm, tender smile that kissed her heart.

"Happy New Year, sweetheart."

"It's you! Oh, Dave, it's really you!" Joyous tears streaked her cheeks as she threw herself into his arms and kissed him.

"I knew you'd come back. I never stopped believing you were alive," she sobbed as he rained a dozen kisses on her cheeks and eyes. "I always believed it, no matter how dismal it looked."

Dave firmly reclaimed her lips. "I told you nothing would keep me away, sweetheart," he said when he freed her lips. Tightening his embrace, he murmured in her ear, "Oh, God, Cyn. There were times when only the image of your beautiful face kept me going."

"I can't even bear to think about what you went through out there in that storm."

"It all happened so fast. We didn't know we were riding into a blizzard. O'Hara had cut his speed to a snail's pace, which was probably why we didn't tip when we went over the side and slid down the slope. I guess the snow slowed the descent and padded the impact when we slammed into the trees and rolled over, but that was one hell of a sled ride. Dan and I were shaken up pretty badly, but poor Paddy got the worst of it—he ended up with both legs broken. We were able to put a couple of makeshift splints on him, but we didn't even know which direction to head in until the sun rose. We must have been about halfway down the slope, and the flatcars were scattered all over the place. We knew we had to get out of there in case the engine continued tumbling down the mountainside, so Dan and I took turns carrying Paddy. But the going was slow—the snow was deep and blowing so hard we couldn't see a foot ahead of us. Finally we reached the track, and the searchers picked us up today."

She looked at him worriedly. "Are you okay? Your toes? Your fingers?"

"All fine. Thank God I was wearing gloves. At night, we'd make a small shelter of packed snow just big enough to crawl into. It was good enough to keep the new snow off us while we slept, and we'd huddle together to stay warm."

"Are Paddy and Dan okay?"

"Yeah. They're in a hospital in Denver. Dan's got a couple of frozen toes, and Paddy's a tough old bird. The doctor in Denver doesn't see any reason why he won't be as good as new once he mends."

"Oh, good heavens! Here I am asking a dozen questions, when you must be exhausted. Are you hungry, Dave? Do you want anything?"

"I just want to hold you for a while, Cyn—then take a hot bath, shave, and make love to you. I told Elizabeth I'd tell her the whole story in the morning." He wrapped his arms around her and pulled her against him again. They clung to each other, words no longer necessary. Only the ticking of the clock and the music from the other room broke the silence.

After a long moment, he began to slowly move her to the rhythm of the music. It took her several minutes before the significance struck her.

"Dave, you're dancing!"

"Yeah."

"You told me you couldn't dance."

"Lydia and Maggie have been coaching me the past couple of weeks. I was determined to dance with my bride on our wedding day." He kissed her again. "I love you, Cyn."

"I love you, too, Dave. I love you so much." She glanced up at the portrait of her father. "You were right again, Daddy."

"What did you say?" Dave asked.

"Oh, just a little bit of fatherly advice Daddy gave me."

He hugged her to his side, then slid an arm around her shoulder as they left the study and went to the kitchen.

"Glory be to God! It's Mr. Dave," Middy exclaimed when she saw him.

Cynthia and Dave paused long enough for him to kiss Middy on the cheek, then they climbed the back stairs to the floor above.

Cynthia drew him a bath and he lay back, soaking in the warmth of the hot water while she bathed and shaved him.

Wrapped in a towel, he said, "My clothes, the gifts . . . we had to leave them all behind."

"They're not important, my love. We can find you something of Daddy's to wear in the morning. And your being here is all the gift I need."

Dave picked up his shirt and dug into the pocket.

"I did bring this with me," he said, holding up a small gold band for her finger. "Unless you've had second thoughts about marrying me."

"That's right, Kincaid," she said, striking a pose with her hands on her hips. "I've had second thoughts, third thoughts, fourth thoughts, and endless thoughts on that subject. I couldn't stop thinking about marrying you. That's why I refused to believe you were dead—I wasn't going to let you off the hook that easily." She turned the key in the lock. "No one is coming through that door tonight," she declared with a cocky toss of her head. "We'll welcome the new year in our own fashion."

Later, as Cynthia lay in his arms, she spoke of the depth of her love. "Tonight, when I kept telling myself you were still alive, there was a moment when I felt as if I'd known Paradise, only to have lost it."

Dave chuckled. "That's a coincidence—because you once had me seeing myself as Adam, tasting his first bite of the Forbidden Fruit."

"Are you suggesting I tempted you?"

"Totally."

She laughed. "If that's so, instead of Miz Sin, perhaps you should call me your *Original Sin,* Kincaid."

"Or Scintillating Sin . . . Sumptuous Sin . . . Seductive Sin?" he murmured between kisses to her eyes and the tip of her nose.

"I'd have expected you to think Sassy Sin would be more appropriate," she teased.

He raised up and gazed in adoration into her eyes. "You're all of them, Cyn, but don't you know, my love, that *S* can only stand for my *Sweet, Sweet Sin?*" he murmured, just before his mouth covered hers in their return to Paradise.

Epilogue

Cleve MacKenzie glanced up from the letter he was reading when his two brothers and his nephew Josh came into the room. "The Triple M will be getting some visitors soon."

"Who?" Luke asked.

"Seems our cousin Cynthia got married. She and her husband intend to stop here on the way to honeymooning in Dallas. She's anxious to meet all of you."

"Oh, Cleve, that's where we honeymooned," Adriana exclaimed. Her eyes were dewy when she looked at her husband, even though they had been married for nine years and she was pregnant with their fourth child.

"Is this one of those rich cousins of yours who's building that railroad, Dad?" Josh asked. Tall and broad-shouldered, the seventeen-year-old youth bore a striking resemblance to his handsome father.

"Reckon so, son, but I've never met her," Luke replied.

"Aha!" Honey suddenly exclaimed, turning over a card. "Za baby vill be a girl."

Adriana rose from the table and came over and sat down on the arm of Cleve's chair. "*Querido*, Madame Rosa just told me the baby's a girl."

"Good, we'll name it after her," Cleve said, slipping an arm around his wife's waist.

"Hmmm, Rosa MacKenzie. It does have a nice ring to it," Garnet said.

"I think he meant Honey Bear MacKenzie, Redhead," Flint said, winking at Cleve.

"Don't put any stock in whatever Madame Rosa said, Adee," Luke warned. "The woman is definitely a charlatan."

"I happen to be very accomplished at reading Tarot cards," Honey declared with mock indignation. "Didn't I predict how mad you were about me, Luke MacKenzie?"

"Was that mad *about* you or mad *at* you?" he asked.

Honey began to shuffle the cards. "All right, who's next?"

"How about me, Mama?" Josh said, sliding into the chair Adriana had just vacated.

Flint and Garnet's nine-year-old son sidled up to the table. "Auntie Honey, tell Josh if he's gonna marry that Rory Martin he's been sparkin'."

"Mind your manners, Andrew," Garnet censured. "That's no concern of yours."

"Yeah, blabbermouth, listen to your mother," Josh declared, faking a punch at his cousin.

Her blond curls bobbing, Kathleen MacKenzie declared vehemently, "My brother can have a girlfriend if he wants, Andy."

"That's right, Kitty." Picking up his seven-year-old sister, Josh set her on his lap. "Let's hear what Mama has to say about my future."

The other children had already picked up the chant, though, and began dancing around the table with shouts of "Josh has a girlfriend!"

"Okay, that's enough," Flint ordered. "No excuse why all you kids can't go outside and play."

"What else did Cousin Cynthia have to say?"

Luke asked once the six children chased outside.

Cleve resumed reading the letter. "This is interesting. She says the railroad was attacked by a gang led by a Billy Bob Walden."

"Walden?" Garnet murmured.

The three women exchanged meaningful glances. Even after nine years, the name still struck a chord of fear.

"Billy Bob Walden!" Luke broke into laughter.

"What's so funny?" Flint asked.

"If it's the same Billy Bob Walden I arrested, you'd know why I'm laughing."

"Is he related to Charlie Walden?" Adriana asked.

"Yeah, he's Charlie's brother, but that's where the resemblance ends. Billy Bob's harmless—a complete idiot! He's the most inept man I've ever met."

Garnet remained less optimistic than her brother-in-law. "What did you arrest him for, Luke?"

"Murder."

"Murder!" all three women exclaimed simultaneously.

"Murder sure don't sound harmless, Dad," Josh remarked.

"I was sheriff of Stockton at the time. Billy Bob and his brother Beau had been playing poker with some gambler. Beau accused the man of cheating, and you can guess what followed. Both of the brothers drew their Colts. I'm sure Beau actually killed him, because Billy Bob couldn't hit the broad side of a barn, but Billy Bob claimed he did. Turns out the gambler wasn't crooked—Beau was just a bad loser. That's why I had to arrest Billy Bob."

"What happened to Beau?" Adriana asked.

"When I tried to arrest Billy Bob, Beau tried to put a bullet in me. I had to shoot him. Then I took Billy Bob up to Sacramento and turned him over to the U.S. marshal. He was tried and sentenced to ten years in the penitentiary." Luke pulled Honey to his side. "And that, brothers and sisters, is how I chanced to meet Miz Honey Behr." After kissing her on the cheek, he walked over to the fireplace and began to fill his pipe.

"Well, if the man is as stupid as you say, how can he lead a gang?" Flint asked.

"They'd have to be dumber than he is, Uncle Flint," Josh remarked.

Cleve nodded. "Sounds like they must be. According to Cynthia, the gang held up a freight train carrying nothing but rails and ties. Then, when they later attacked the railroad town, apparently they were captured and run off by the women and children in camp."

When the men broke into laughter, Honey's blond head bobbed emphatically. "It doesn't take more than a few good women to capture any man—even you MacKenzies. Right, ladies?" Garnet and Adriana agreed with her instantly.

"You won't get any argument from me," Cleve said. "Especially if those women were anything like the she-wolves in this room." He exchanged an amused grin with his brothers. "Reckon we all know what a force that can be! A man's an out-and-out fool if he underestimates the power of women."

"Well, I hope that this Billy Bob is behind bars again," Adriana said.

"No, he got away. Cynthia wrote that when he rode off, he shouted he'd be back."

"She's got nothing to worry about," Luke said, packing tobacco into his pipe. "Knowing Billy Bob Walden, he'll be back all right—but to the same spot where he left them—and the poor fool won't be able to figure out where everybody disappeared to."

Their contagious laughter circled the room.

TEXAS STAR

ELAINE BARBIERI

Buck Star is a handsome cad with a love-'em-and-leave-'em attitude that broke more than one heart. But when he walks out on a beautiful New Orleans socialite, he sets into motion a chain of treachery and deceit that threatens to destroy the ranching empire he'd built and even the children he'd once hoped would inherit it. . . .

A mysterious message compells Caldwell Star to return to Lowell, Texas, after a nine-year absence. Back in Lowell, he meets a stubborn young widow who refuses his help, but needs it more than she can know. Her gentle touch and proud spirit give Cal strength to face the demons of the past, to reach out for a love that would heal his wounded soul.

- -

YANKEE EARL

SHIRL HENKE

Jason Beaumont, brash American privateer, is now Earl of Falconridge, and the Honorable Miss Rachel Fairchild could not be more horrified. Until she finds herself making the brute's acquaintance lying flat on her back in the mud, gazing up at a particularly fascinating portion of his anatomy. She grows still more flustered when the arrogant colonial proceeds to set London's tongues wagging with his daring exploits, and challenge her own cutting wit with his outrageous innuendoes. But most shocking of all is a surprise betrothal ball where she learns her own father has conspired to see her leg shackled, for better or worse, to the Yankee earl.